in position, being lead o
on as [illegible] they
wy takeover from the 17th i
line by the La-Bassé canal
ms, not a bit like a War.
this I walked, then notice
the entrance, communicatio
of few bullets, began to
ent, then coming across i
rs. Then began to Know that
ate a was were Battle of
a few months earlier.
an to build new stables
we collected bricks from
apart from Coal mines
stables, it would appear
manent, but the Germans
as in order help them to see
overed the stables with lovely
e had them finished, the bod
nished the [illegible] really
the clock [illegible] 18th
s, killing [illegible]

Dear Reader,

The book you are holding came about in a rather different way to most others. It was funded directly by readers through a new website: Unbound. Unbound is the creation of three writers. We started the company because we believed there had to be a better deal for both writers and readers. On the Unbound website, authors share the ideas for the books they want to write directly with readers. If enough of you support the book by pledging for it in advance, we produce a beautifully bound special subscribers' edition and distribute a regular edition and e-book wherever books are sold, in shops and online.

This new way of publishing is actually a very old idea (Samuel Johnson funded his dictionary this way). We're just using the internet to build each writer a network of patrons. Here, at the back of this book, you'll find the names of all the people who made it happen.

Publishing in this way means readers are no longer just passive consumers of the books they buy, and authors are free to write the books they really want. They get a much fairer return too – half the profits their books generate, rather than a tiny percentage of the cover price.

If you're not yet a subscriber, we hope that you'll want to join our publishing revolution and have your name listed in one of our books in the future. To get you started, here is a £5 discount on your first pledge. Just visit unbound.com, make your pledge and type WAG in the promo code box when you check out.

Thank you for your support,

Dan, Justin and John
Founders, Unbound

Friends of *Wag*

Louise Anderson
Peter and Hester Cherneff
Geraldine Cook
John Lahr & Connie Booth
Richard Littlejohn
Sally Noble
Anthony Pye-Jeary
Rob Raisin
Saskia Sidey
Edith Velmans
Loet Velmans

For the others who pledged, please see p.335

Paul Sidey

The Book of Wag

unbound
LONDON

This edition first published in 2016

Unbound
6th Floor, Mutual House, 70 Conduit Street, London W1S 2GF

www.unbound.co.uk

Text Design by Peter Ward

A CIP record for this book is available from the British Library

ISBN 978-1-78352-265-1 (trade hbk)
ISBN 978-1-78352-264-4 (ebook)
ISBN 978-1-78352-276-7 (limited edition)

Printed in Great Britain by Clays Ltd, St.Ives Plc

1 2 3 4 5 6 7 8 9

This book is dedicated to my beloved wife, Marianne.

Editor's note

In the two and a half years between his retirement and death, my husband Paul managed to write four and a half novels. But *The Book of Wag* was personal to him, and the one he most wished to see published. It is a hybrid of truth and fiction: inspired by his mother's sprawling south London family, the book is full of family anecdotes and memories; and the lives of the two narrators share certain elements with the real Uncle Wag (his mother's eldest half-brother) and with Paul himself.

But although many of the anecdotes are based on real memories and events, Paul used them to weave a fiction combining them with the stories he loved about the criminal gangs that ruled the streets of south London from the 1920s to the 1960s. Of course connecting these gangster elements to the family story was totally fictional. He made it clear to me that it was not his intention to suggest that anyone in his family had really had any connections with that underworld, or had ever lived on the wrong side of the law.

My thanks to all those who helped get this book published after Paul's death, in particular Caradoc King, Gillian Stern for her brilliant editing, all at Unbound, and everyone who pledged.

Marianne Velmans

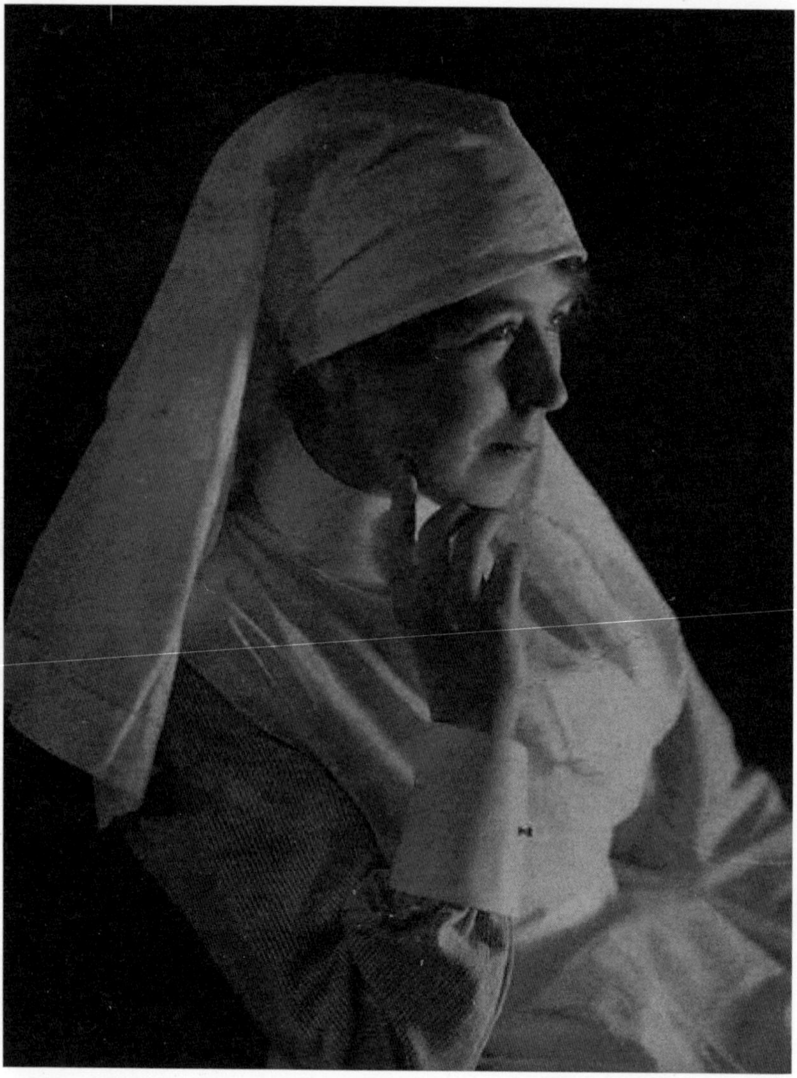

The following lines were inscribed in my Uncle Wag's dense, angular scrawl at the back of his cloth-bound memoirs.

I lost the sunshine and the roses
I lost the heavenly leaves of blue
I lost the beautiful rainbow
I lost the morning dew
I lost the Angel you gave me, summer the whole winter
    through
I lost the gladness that turned into sadness
When I lost you

I guess he must have composed the poem himself. Underneath is some indecipherable squiggle, and the doodle of a knight's helmet with the visor down above a shield decorated with two fleurs-de-lis and a diagonal stripe with three blobs.

The Book of Wag

CHAPTER I

Jack

Shall I tell you about the underwear or the ghost? I think, perhaps, I'll start with Aunt Ethel's silk and satin underwear. After Uncle Wag's death at the age of ninety-two from cancer of the pancreas, my mother Ivy was left the house in Surbiton and its contents, as well as a small fortune, some of it in neatly bound fifty pound notes in a shoebox under the stairs.

When we were clearing Wag's sister's bedroom – he had kept everything as it was since her death, also from cancer, twenty years earlier – my mother discovered pristine knickers, slips and bras, folded immaculately, exuding a slightly camphorated perfume, in the top drawer of Ethel's ornate Regency dressing table. Her monogrammed silver-backed hairbrushes, without a single grey hair entangled, stood side by side, next to some antique, silver-topped perfume bottles and sprays.

The gilded, three-part mirror was slightly foxed round the edges. My mother sat down in front of it and stared at a couple of sepia photographs in a battered black leather wallet: Wag is dapper in uniform, legs astride, peaked hat, puttees, a swagger stick under his left arm and a leather strip containing a series of pouches that stretches from left shoulder underneath his right arm, like a bullet-stuffed bandallero; Ethel is wearing a cloche hat, a long skirt, fox fur round her shoulders, hands concealed in a muff. Both snaps have been cut out very carefully and pasted on a piece of yellowing paper. Wag must have carried the wallet round with him through the Somme, until the gas got him.

Looking at my mother's reflection and at the pictures of

her half-sister and half-brother, there was only the slightest suspicion of a physical resemblance between the three of them.

Ivy Matilda, my mother, was the runt of the litter, the last and, perhaps, most beloved daughter of Beatrice Bourton, whose first husband had sired eleven children before he gave up the ghost. Beatrice then took up with my mother's father but didn't actually bother to get married to him. That was a family secret kept until comparatively recently. As far as I was concerned, the grandfathers in my family, on both sides, were just men in moustaches in old photographs.

Although I was present at times when my grandmother was still up and about, the image that remains in my head is of her propped up in bed during the afternoon, in a gloomy room with dark green velvet curtains. Ornate, dangly earrings dragged down her lobes. On the few occasions I visited her, she always pressed a silver half-crown into my hand and told me I had been a good boy. And I was more than aware that I hadn't been, that I wasn't a good boy. In that, I was to discover I had something in common with her oldest son . . .

I've kept a few of her things. Some kitsch Meissen candelabras, a clock and a fruit bowl. My wife doesn't like them. But they're staying.

I also have a tapestry that used to cover a crack in the Old Rectory where Grandmother breathed her last. It depicts a turbaned warrior spearing a lion, with decorative palm trees and a distant mosque. Isobel and I have no quarrel about that. It now hides a crack on our living room wall.

The cancer came quickly. Uncle Wag had seemed to be in robust health. He continued to do occasional speciality work as an engraver with James Purdey & Sons right up to the age of ninety. Then, suddenly, he was ill. Having never mentioned the war, he spoke of little else in those last days before he was taken to hospital, where he died the morning after I drove him in.

'I was cheeky to an officer,' he told me. 'This group of them came riding over to our position. We had been under heavy bombardment for a week. The enemy was in a good position on a ridge above us. "I wouldn't go up there, if I were you, sir," I said to a young captain with gleaming boots. "There's a war on, you know."' Wag shifted in his chair. 'They tied me to one of the wheels of the gun we were pulling. For two days.'

I keep the photo of my uncle and aunt in my study alongside a few other keepsakes – including a 50-yard reel of khaki linen thread, a standard issue to soldiers. Doesn't look as though Number 23281 W.C. Bourton of B Battery ever used it. I also have in my possession his *Soldier's Small Book*. The battered and blotched binding has come loose, and a critical page has been torn out, the page that ends with 'Effects of Wounds'.

It does confirm, though, that W.C. Bourton enlisted on 19 April 1915; that he lived in Brixton, south London; that he was an engraver by trade or calling, height five foot five inches, eyes brown, hair brown, complexion 'Fresh' . . .

Inside there is advice on everything from the Correct Method of Challenging and the Saluting of Officers to Field Cooking and How to Prevent Sore Feet.

In the house he shared with Ethel after the Second World War, he had a grandfather clock, which I admired when I was a boy. He always said he would leave it to me in his will and he did. It's a fine piece of work, made by Edward East, clockmaker to Charles I. Wag had found it in pieces in an auction house in Cheam, and reassembled it himself. Only the brass hinges on the walnut door that concealed the pendulum were not original. Wag made them and inscribed a message there: 'In the possession of William and Ethel Bourton, 1947'.

The clock kept perfect time until recently. Isobel isn't a woman who complains about things, but she found the loud tick intrusive. For me, the noise was reassuring. I wanted Wag to know that his presence was felt.

Something clogged in the winding mechanism. I had the fault fixed for an exorbitant nine hundred smackers. All was well for a while. Then one day the clock stopped again, and that is how I've left it.

CHAPTER 2

Wag

My name is not Wag. I was not the age I said I was when I enlisted. Height, hair colour and profession I did not bother to disguise. They could have been changed at any time. In the army, though, no one bothered what you looked like, as long as your kit was properly pressed, brass polished.

I cannot say I joined up out of patriotism, or because I liked fighting, although I was useful in a scrap. I joined up because I had to, because I was in a bit of trouble with some bad men over a job and I had to make myself scarce.

It is never fair to blame your parents, but I wonder if I didn't inherit the odd crooked gene. My father was done for embezzling and died in prison, and my mother – dear old, grand old Beatrice Bourton in all her heavy Victorian finery – wasn't strictly kosher herself. Of course, she would have drawn herself up to her full height, and sniffed at the very idea that she had ever been guilty of the slightest impropriety, but many was the time we had to slip away before the bailiffs came banging at the door.

It cannot have been easy to look after such an army of children even while our father was alive. The old house had to be sold. After that, we lived in rented accommodation, and kept on the move when times were hard, which was most of the time.

As a young man, I found ways of supplementing my paltry income as an apprentice engraver. We would have starved to death otherwise, especially later, living in that draughty old south London rectory, complete with tennis court and ghost. I didn't want the money for myself. All the family members who lived there had to pay what they could. As things worked out, I contributed more than the rest of them put together.

Not one of them was good at holding down a steady job – except for the straitlaced Ted who worked in a haberdasher in Croydon. They said he was a dreamer. I have no idea what he dreamed about. He never said much. He wore these thick glasses, too, which acted like a screen. It was almost impossible to look into his eyes.

Florence and Violet were showgirls. Both had ambitions to become serious stage actresses, but neither got beyond heavy make-up and a high kick. Both had a penchant for handsome, feckless men who drank too much.

Between them came Martin. It's funny how you can lose track of someone in a family. He and I, separated only by a couple of years, were never close. As a boy, he had his own bunch of friends and preferred to play with them. As an adult, he was civil enough, and performed some kind of fund-raising job with the Salvation Army. I never had any time for prayers, hymns, brass bands or good works. Martin and the family went their separate ways. He was the first to move out. That was a shame in one respect – he was good with money.

Aurelia was a spiritualist. She had a guide called Redwing and held séances in the rectory attic, where George the ghost had reputedly committed suicide. Sad men in shiny suits and moth-eaten women climbed upstairs to commune with the souls of their dearest departed, and dropped the odd crumpled note or handful of coins in an inverted black velvet hat Aurelia left on a chair by the door.

Rose came into the world before Aurelia. The spirit world – orthodox or barking – held no interest for her. She preferred a good time in the here and now, which didn't guarantee a steady income.

Then there was good old Jago. He was flush from time to time and generous too when he had some readies left over.

I haven't included the whole brood here – only the ones old enough to pay their way. It's not a very impressive list.

For a while, my mother Beatrice took in paying guests. How she must have hated that. They had to be theatricals. For some reason, that made the idea acceptable. For a few years, a collection of second-rate music-hall performers helped pay the rent, but the word must have got round that you had to keep a close watch on your valuables at Mrs Bourton's and that source of income dried up. For me too. Petty pilfering was how I made my start.

We weren't all dodgy or deluded. The youngest, my half-sister, little Ivy, was the apple of my eye from the time she could walk. No wonder she was Mother's favourite. And my sister Ethel was a shining angel. The most beautiful woman I ever knew, skin as white as the Meissen porcelain women on Beatrice's favourite candelabra, the one that stood on the grand piano she couldn't play. Ethel trained as a nurse, the most honourable of professions. All her life she tended to the sick, and refused to hear ill of anyone.

Out under the stars at Ypres, or in the midst of a bombardment on the Somme, I could think of Ethel and the horror of the present would melt away.

CHAPTER 3

Jack

The scent of money, it would seem, can waft enormous distances. From Brisbane, as soon as he heard the diagnosis was fatal, Wag's nephew Randal got on the first plane he could book out of Australia to be by his uncle's side.

Bold as brass, Martin's son set up camp in Wag's living room. I don't know why he thought, after maintaining radio silence for over ten years, that he would automatically inherit even a chunk of the estate. Randal exhibited a determination unusual in the Bourton family. He had made his own way after his father died, emigrated to Australia, returned to the mother country from time to time, and, to his credit, entertained Wag and Ethel when they took an adventurous holiday Down Under.

Back home, the only people who ever visited Wag were my mother, my father and me. Everyone else ignored him, including his last remaining sister Florence, as well as all the numerous nephews and nieces. Wag had no children of his own. He never married. He lived with his beloved Ethel, worshipped her until the day she died and beyond.

Randal was a tall streak of piss, unlike the rest of the elf-like Bourton clan. He had had some minor success as a long-distance runner, had been a pacemaker, so he claimed, for the great 1,500-metre gold medallist world record holder Herb Elliott. They trained together on sand dunes.

Randal didn't need to call on any of his legendary stamina for a long haul in the south-west London borough of Kingston.

My mother nursed Wag for as long as she could, but, when

he could no longer control his bowels, she couldn't cope. Before that day came, Wag had given Randal his marching orders. I see and hear Wag now, still vigorous the night before he died in his hospital bed, talking about this wretched nephew. 'He came for this . . .' Wag rubbed the forefinger of his right hand against his thumb. 'And I gave him that.' With a big grin, he jabbed a V-sign in the air.

Ivy had no idea how much money Wag had accumulated during his long life. 'Where did he find all that money and what on earth was he saving all that cash for?' my mother asked when she discovered the shoebox under the stairs. Her half-brother lived frugally. There was no Bentley in the garage, no yacht, as far as anyone knew, moored in Monte Carlo, no mistress in Mayfair.

When Wag and Ethel had moved to their three-bedroom redbrick terraced house, the 90-foot back garden looked out over cornfields. There was an abattoir about a mile away. It was another world. In fact, the house was bigger than it looked. As I was to discover, there was nothing obvious about Wag.

We found two volumes of a memoir in pale, cloth-bound A4 books. I knew of their existence, and had in fact been given a similar one by Wag as a wedding present, so I was prepared for his rambling scrawl in blue ink, not at all like the work of the man who had made that neat copperplate inscription on the hinges of his grandfather clock. It was a struggle to read more than a few lines at a time. The sentences were jam-packed together and Wag seemed to have no clue about paragraphs. He had created a wall of words. My mother took the books home to read, but, as far as I know, she never got around to it.

Apart from the grandfather clock, I've kept a few of Wag's other things – including an art nouveau Doulton jug, which commemorates the death of the Queen Empress Victoria in

1901. It was a present from his uncle. It's a shame I have no nephew, no one special to pass it on to. I have no brothers or sisters. Nor does Isobel. My wife and I are childless.

Mum and Dad retired to Goring-on-Sea and a cottage called the Dolphins. Yet no such mammals have ever been spotted in the cold and murky Channel waters of this pebbly bit of Sussex coast. A month or so after Wag's death, a letter reached my parents postmarked Brisbane, Australia, with 'The Dolphins' scored through on the envelope's address and substituted with 'The Sharks'.

Randal had trained in the law, but an apoplectic fury disturbed any attempt to restrain his prose.

> So much for family. I have nothing but the most profound contempt for the way you and Fred have wheedled your way into an old man's affections and caused him to neglect the rest of us. After the trip he and poor Aunt Ethel made out here a while ago now, the valuable time Julie and I spent and the efforts we made to ensure they were comfortable, at the very least, my wife and I would have expected the tiniest recognition of our hospitality. But what did we get? Sweet FA. Thanks a bunch, Ivy.
>
> Clearly, you are unable to locate in your hard heart the generous spirit of giving now you've got your greedy paws on my uncle's hard-earned money . . .

It went on like this for three pages. The handwriting became more and more of a scribble as he concluded: 'If anything bad can happen in the world, I hope you both get what you so richly deserve. As ye have sown, so shall ye reap.'

Randal only left his initials after that.

Ivy was a generous woman. She had expected nothing from her half-brother. But she certainly did not expect to be abused by her nephew. However, she did airmail him Wag's photograph album of the Australian trip, so he would have a memento of the valuable time he had spent with his uncle and aunt. Randal didn't acknowledge receipt.

Once upon a time, however rackety, the family of Beatrice Bourton stuck together, lived together, laughed together, mourned together. By the time Wag died, my mother was his only surviving sibling. His will left everything to Ivy Matilda Armitage. And, effectively, that was the end of that. The end of relative values.

CHAPTER 4

Wag

I would be the first to agree that my little memoir doesn't reveal much. I wrote it a long time after I came back from what has become known as the Great War, the war to end all wars. Why did I bother? Is it a record or a smokescreen or a puzzle, or all three? It amused me in some ways to cover my traces by leaving evidence of a quiet, simple fellow who resembled me very closely . . . I confessed nothing about my secret life or feelings. For those who care to look, however, there is some information concealed in the pages that could be of definite interest.

A note near the beginning of my book records a rare event. My father gave me a present. When I was six, on Coronation Day, 9 August 1902, he solemnly handed me a freshly minted penny with the face of the new King Edward upon it. 'So you remember your old dad,' he said. 'Who wished he had been a better person.' I wish he had been, too.

The Prince of Wales had problems with his old mum. He was forced to feed his hairy face and pursue young actresses while the stubborn Queen refused to abdicate. We were not royalists in our family. And we were not alone. On Coronation Day there was no bunting out in our street, no street parties. But from a top window of our house in Camberwell, with my sister Rose, I remember watching a strange procession. Maybe the revellers had got lost on their way from a nearby pub. The first group to pass our house was a merry band of chimney sweeps, each covered in leaves to resemble the Green Man of English legend. A fertility symbol, I believe. They were followed by some raucous Italians with a chained bear. As they meandered down Elmington Road, they mimed a fight, but with real, sharp knives. A long, red piece of cloth faked blood. A policeman was on hand to make sure there was no actual fighting in the streets. He was given no cause to blow his whistle. They were hardly trying to start a revolution.

My friend Nat Devlin claimed that his father was a revolutionary. He might as well have been a bicycle repairman as far as I was concerned. Apparently, Nat's dad was a mate of Lenin's. They discussed workers' rights and exchanged racing tips at a pub in Tooting.

I had never heard about the 'Kingdom of Socialism'. When I went with Nat Devlin to Tooting, it was to the Common to catch newts in the pond. But every now and again, Nat would point at a man in a bowler hat in the street and say, 'Look at that petty bourgeois.' I didn't know what he meant. But the spotting game was fun. 'They should all be put against a wall and shot,' was Nat's other favourite line. We both used to shout it. My mother would have disapproved.

In my family, politics were never mentioned. We belonged to the party of just jogging along. And at school I wasn't the most attentive of students. Ask me about Peel's Repeal of the Corn Laws, though, and I can give you an answer: 1846. The beginning of free trade. Perhaps there was a reason why that piece of information stayed in my head. Free trade came to mean that I could do more or less what I liked as long as I didn't get caught.

Basically, I was an ignorant bastard. Communism, the workers' revolution, were just words I picked up in snippets from my friend Nat, who parroted a few slogans from his dad.

Apart from the newts, I wouldn't say I was a child who had

interesting hobbies. I liked to kick a ball around with a few mates. And, on rainy days at the kitchen table, I could spend hours with a sharp pencil and tracing paper copying the outline of a building or a decorative motif.

Given my later experience in the army, it's curious that horses didn't interest me in the slightest when I was a lad. There was a knackers' yard not far from our house, near a place that made tennis balls. My sister Rose worked there for a while. The pay was thruppence a dozen for doing the stitching. You had to ignore the smell of blood from next door, and the regular whinnies of terror and pain. I wonder if that helped when I signed on as Gunner Bourton.

In Croydon (and I wrote this down so many years after the event), I was once allowed to sit up next to the driver of a horse-drawn bus, knees covered by a heavy piece of Melton cloth. I remember the crack of the whip, and the steam rising from the animals' backs on that cold winter's day. But I had never so much as got on a horse to ride until I found myself in uniform.

CHAPTER 5

Jack

I quoted that poem from Wag's memoir at the very beginning of this book. Was it a piece of Edwardian doggerel or an original W.C. Bourton? My guess is that Wag wrote it about Ethel.

As I told you, my mother would have opened the memoir and flicked through a few pages, but she lacked the will to press on. Having discovered a lot more about my uncle, I had a better reason to persist. Bad grammar, atrocious spelling, dense paragraphs, tedious details, lists of names were a definite deterrent. You would think Wag had a whole lot in common with Mr Pooter. Getting through a whole page could take a while. And then you would stumble across something that was like discovering a seam of gold in a clapped-out mine.

I was interested in what Wag said about horses. In the First World War, he rode the lead horse of six that pulled a field gun. During that last week of his life, he told me that Shrapnel, the horse with whom he had been partnered since the very first day in France, was shot dead from beneath him. Wag survived. He was good at that. Like me.

Unlike anyone else in my family, I was also good at school. I could concentrate, even when other boys were flicking blotting-paper pellets. I was good at sport, in spite of my mother's insistence when I was about seven that I wear iron and leather splints to cure my knock-knees. At Dulwich Prep School, I won the gym prize, was made captain of cricket and was a top-scoring inside right on the football team. My parents were keen that their boy should excel academically, and put me down for Dulwich College. The problem was, in order to obtain the necessary grant to cover the fees I had to pretend to be a resident of Streatham. Upper Norwood, where we lived, was outside the school's catchment area. My father did pay the rent on his mother's flat in Streatham Hill so he was able to produce the right documentation. But until we moved to Dulwich Village, the deception meant that for years I was forbidden from inviting a friend home, and frequently got muddled with my geographical whereabouts.

Deception, deviousness and duplicity were not the monopoly of only one side of the family.

My father changed his name from Adolf to Alfred. He hated to be called Alf. Fred was fine. Before the Second World War, he sang with a band called Harold Beam and his Sunshine Boys. I have a couple of his black vinyl 78rpm records, crackly and scratched from those old needles. One is called 'Happy And Contented', the other 'Ah, But Is It Love?'. He performed under the name of Fred French – once or twice, so it's said, with the Crazy Gang. While I was growing up he could still do a turn, including a soft shoe shuffle. I liked his light tenor voice, modelled on Al Bowlly. But showbiz wasn't for him. Or the other way round. A job in the foreign department at Lloyds Bank was a safer bet, and that is where he stayed until he retired and took up picture dealing.

What motivated Wag to pursue his life of crime remains mysterious. When he and Ethel came to supper at our house he always presented himself as a model citizen. There were no obvious clues in the books my uncle wrote. What he did reveal in them was that he left school, aged fourteen, in 1911 and got a job at Peek Freen's Biscuit Factory. This mainly seems to have involved carrying dirty overalls to the laundry. I found out that another sister, Annie, also worked there but nobody ever mentioned her when I was growing up. All I know is that she packed biscuits. After six months, Wag was offered promotion to the bakery by a Mr Nunnerley. The prospect was too exciting to accept.

The next job was in Great Dover Street. Wag was going up in the world – engineering, earning 7/6 a week, working a lathe. He had to get to work by six a.m., hitching a ride at Smithfield Market for the last stretch of his journey from Brixton on a horse-drawn butcher's van. By the time he got home, after a twelve hour shift, he'd say it was just about time to go to work again. Then there was a brief spell at a leather warehouse in Bermondsey before my uncle found his true vocation. In the *Daily Chronicle*, Wag spotted an ad for an apprentice engraver at Thomas Sanders & Sons, 42 Wardour Street.

He discovered he was good with his hands, patient and methodical. My mother always said he had a real eye and could duplicate anything. Dexterity and sight – essential talents for an engraver.

His house in Surbiton contained some beautiful objects – for instance, an original David Roberts oil painting of the great temple at Abu Simbel. As a fan of that greatest of orientalist artists, I always coveted this. My father, neither an orientalist nor sentimentalist, made sure it fetched a more than decent price at auction. Maybe I'll try to find it and buy it back one day.

There were some ornate Berber coffee pots that had belonged to Sir Ronald Storrs, who was Governor of Jerusalem during the period of Lawrence of Arabia. Quite a lot of Lalique glass, a set of grotesquely delicate netsuke, and a very good pair of brown suede brogues that I still wear. They're a snug fit. I walk like Wag, in one of his incarnations at least.

In terms of general décor, I have to conclude, my uncle played a game. In his modest living room, a horrible plastic bowl decorated with sunflowers was placed next to a delicate eighteenth-century cut-glass decanter. A quality Persian carpet clashed with a strip of Axminster in the hall. He either had eyes to see and didn't look, or he was deliberately throwing everybody off the scent. Or was it Ethel's influence? Perhaps he loved her too much to acknowledge that, while he had taste, she had none.

What intrigued me more and more was the true nature of the relationship between my mother's favourite brother and sister. Would the memoir reveal that Wag was in love with his own sister? Did he try to hide that not only from Ethel but from himself too? Was my uncle a master of disguise or simply a man, like many others, who had his secrets?

CHAPTER 6

Wag

I had my first proper fight when I began work as an engraver at Thomas Sanders. With a fellow apprentice called Bert Lockner. He accused me of giving the receptionist, Queenie Green, a more than old-fashioned look and challenged me to meet him outside after work. There are lots of alleys around Soho where disputes could be settled in private, shady courts where dark deals and murky deeds are done to this day.

Of course, I had had my fair share of scraps at school. When some boy, Tubby Martin, bigger than everyone else in our class, pinched my treasured marble collection, he thought he could put the frighteners on me. I knocked him down on his fat arse. And took his stash of multicoloured glass balls. The playtime sweet treat he had secreted in his shirt pocket, I ate in front of him, slowly. I never liked the taste of Fry's famous Turkish Bar, but I wanted to make him suffer.

Bert Lockner thought he was tough too. He liked to swagger around, thinking we all admired him. Queenie Green didn't have eyes for this little twerp, any more than she did for me. We were both far too junior for her. She had set her cap at Mr Furlow in Accounts, with his smooth, black, brilliantined hair, eau de cologne and two-toned shoes.

At six o'clock sharp, we left the building and made for Fountains Court. It was a dank January evening, dark at four thirty. A few shifty punters were abroad, but the 'models' on the first floor up those narrow staircases were not doing a roaring trade just yet. I was learning so much so fast.

'Aren't you going to take your jacket off?' Bert asked.

'Too cold,' I said.

'Sissy,' he replied, flicking a hand out at my tie.

That irritated me. It wasn't as if he had even landed a blow, but I didn't like the gesture one bit. I hit him hard in the solar plexus with my left, and crossed with my right as his chin came down.

Bert Lockner fell flat on his back and banged his head. I contemplated kicking him in the ribs, but decided against it. Instead, I knelt down beside him.

'You all right?' I asked.

His pale blue eyes were watering. 'I slipped.'

I tried to help him up.

'Don't touch me.'

'Suit yourself.'

A couple of waiters walked by, talking loudly in Italian. They took not the slightest notice of us. This was everyday life in Soho. I liked it. My knuckles hurt, though, from their sharp scrape with Bert's jaw.

'We'll say no more about this.' Lockner was up on his feet again, and trying to wipe some mud off his jacket sleeve.

'As you wish. No skin off my nose.'

'But if I catch you . . .'

'Oh, do give it a rest, Bert. Try not to be such a prat.'

'I'm warning you.'

'Are you asking me to hit you again?'

Bert looked around him.

'Let's forget all about it and go. OK?' I offered.

'You won't tell anybody?'

'Mum's the word.'

'Cross your heart?'

This was worse than school. I made the sign. 'And hope to die,' I said.

CHAPTER 7

Jack

My dad liked to box. He taught me the basic moves while I was still at prep school, in the garden at our house in Upper Norwood. We often used gloves. He showed me how to tuck my chin into my left shoulder and keep my right-hand guard up. I had a good left jab, and could put all the technique into practice, as long as I wasn't being hit back. That is the hard bit about boxing. When someone is punching you, it's difficult to keep your head and return fire.

Uncle Wag often joined us for Sunday lunch, and was keen to watch me go through my paces. Most relatives have to pretend to be interested in such displays, but Wag's applause seemed genuine, without revealing that he knew anything about boxing himself.

At Dulwich College, after three matches against inferior opponents in the inter-house boxing competition, I reached the final of my very light weight against an older boy called George Curwin, who had represented the school at fisticuffs more than once. The first round I surprised him. I was fast, moved well and hit quite hard for my height and build. I won it easily.

In my corner, a friend who was no slouch in the ring himself, warned me, 'Next round he's going to come for you. Keep on your toes, keep out of range, keep that left in his face.'

I tried. For a short while I outmanoeuvred my opponent, dodging, ducking and flicking out the jab. But when Curwin caught me with a sharp right to the head, followed by a pummelling to the body, I went into a trance. There was no pain. He kept on hitting me, and I forgot to fight back. The cauliflower-eared referee had to intervene.

'You fought a good fight, son,' Curwin's father said when I left the ring. I hadn't. I lost. I could have done better. I never boxed again. But who knew George and I would meet on different sides of the law one day?

Dulwich College was founded by the Elizabethan actor Edward Alleyn in 1619 for twelve poor scholars. It was funded by money from bear pits and whorehouses. When I turned up at the junior school in 1952, pupils were not allowed to wear collar-attached shirts, and were instructed to keep the middle button of their jackets done up at all times, except when they were removed during break. Only prefects were allowed to keep theirs open.

The College of 'God's Gift' encouraged the manly virtues. We swam naked in a freezing, dilapidated open-air swimming pool – 'Towels off, boys!' – and we were expected to join the Cadet Corps. Conscription was still in force. My father, who had served without particular distinction in the RAF during the Second World War, thought it was a good idea to get started early. 'That way,' he said, 'you'll be graded officer material immediately when you do your national service. You won't have to do all that square-bashing like your poor old dad.'

I hated the Cadet Corps uniform. The material was so abrasive I wore pyjamas under my trousers. Unfortunately, after one of my gaiters worked loose, this ruse was discovered and I was put on defaulters' parade for two weeks. But the sneers from our CO continued for months. I suppose I deserved them. However, I can still present arms and do a correct about-turn should my country call on me to serve.

The week after I heard national conscription was going to be jettisoned, I resigned. The CO, a Mr Turner, who doubled up as Deputy Head, also lived just over the road. He insisted on an informal meeting with my parents. 'Jack may only have one more year at school. But to quit now is bad for morale,' Turner said over a dry sherry. 'Bad for your son, bad for the school.'

It made no difference. My father was always deferential towards authority, but he had no love of the armed forces, and saw no practical reason why his boy should stay on. I had scored highly in my Empire Range test, with a very heavy Lee Enfield rifle. In the RAF section for my last year, with smoother uniforms and slacker invigilation, I had even flown a two-seater plane for a minute or so.

The teacher in charge of the RAF section was also my form master, a willowy young man, a bit like Dirk Bogarde. He too affected not to approve of my decision to hand in my uniform. 'I'm an aesthete like you, Armitage,' he said. At that time, I wore a waistcoat and was an ostentatious fan of Baudelaire and anything fin de siècle. 'But I've learned to give orders and to take them.'

'Hypocrite lecteur,' I said. 'Mon semblable, mon frère.'

How on earth my mild-mannered Uncle Wag wore the uniform and followed orders without complaint and survived those three years in hell at the front, I shall never know. He didn't seem to be particularly brave or strong. He never bragged about his achievements. He never boasted about anything. But then, as I learned later, there were some things he did in France that would not look good on anyone's record.

CHAPTER 8

Wag

From a tram top on my journey to work, I saw the excavated skeleton of a Roman boat in the low-tide mud by the Houses of Parliament. One night in 1913, walking along Regent's Canal, Halley's Comet blazed briefly across the sky. And my half-sister Ivy Matilda was born – such a fragile little thing. She was the first and only addition to the family after Father had died of tuberculosis in the nick, three years earlier.

A new man had appeared in Beatrice's life. He was Greek. A builder by profession. God knows how he inveigled his way into our mother's affections. She had always despised Trade, even though none of her children ever managed to improve themselves.

My mother was too posh to go to the lavatory. God knows how she squeezed her bladder so tight, but I never saw her excuse herself in a public place. It was something ladies didn't do.

At this time we were living in a draughty, damp pile in Brixton, not far from the railway line. At least the new man in Mama's life wasn't strapped for ready money. He dealt in cash. No receipts. The house stayed warmer than usual in winter, roast meat was always on the table of a Sunday, pies and stews during the week, fish on Fridays. Michael was the Greek's name. He had a ready laugh and didn't get in the way. We tolerated him, just as easily as we had let our father go.

Stavros we called him. It was a cheap joke. He played up to it, even put on a funny Greek accent from time to time, although he spoke as well as any of us. Mama was very keen on proper elocution. Any slide into south London lingo when we were children meant a rap over the knuckles. 'Be anything you like,' she said. 'But never be common.'

She never spoke about her own line. But if she was top drawer I am a pygmy's uncle.

I may have described my family as a collection of ne'er-do-wells, presided over by a tyrannical matriarch, but, for a sustained period, in a number of different houses, we were very happy all together. If new arrivals to the family, male and female, were not the highest of achievers, they would fit in immediately. There was the tall, bookish Aubrey St John, an editor with the publishing company of Chatto & Windus. He married Florence, one of my showgirl sisters. He brought books home, which nobody read.

The other male addition to the Bourton clan plighted his troth with the batty but beautiful Aurelia. Ernest Worsley looked like a bald-headed eagle in a suit. He was an accountant of little account who held down his job, was never early or late, and had a laugh that echoed up from his toes. When Ernest was amused, it was a sign from beyond that all was well with the world.

Jago was my favourite brother. Dashing, handsome, with wild black hair, he led astray the local women. He was like catnip. They couldn't leave him alone. And Jago played the field with a casual abandon that only made him more successful. How he found time to earn a living, I shall never know. After leaving school early like me, an apprentice engineer, he decided to work for himself. He did a bit of plumbing, decorating and, later in life, radio and television repairs. He had the knack of restoring machinery with half the original components.

For some strange reason, Jago sacrificed this life of Riley

to pop the band of gold on to the left finger of a bright and busty babe called Molly. She worked in a dress shop in Streatham High Road, and was a snazzy dancer with a laugh like a foghorn. When she and brother-in-law Ernest let rip, you had an auditorium response more rich with mirth than a whole audience could deliver in the Trocadero Music Hall down the road.

I am giving you a glimpse now of our lives after I returned from France. There was a side to our peculiar family that bound us together – a muddled but supremely generous spirit that no one who lived in any of our many houses will ever forget.

With almost no money, we survived. How my mother managed to feed not only her own brood but a constant stream of guests and hangers-on remains one of the key unanswered questions of the universe. She didn't have to refer to holy writ nor to hunt through a recipe book to achieve the miraculous. But the feasts she conjured up from nowhere, her roasts, her pies, sweet and savoury, were legendary. Even as a child, I remember the sound of the clank of bottles, the sweet pop of a cork, the hiss of a beer cap being opened.

At Christmas, our extended dining table almost burst through the walls into the always neglected gardens. And the sound of revelry could not be muffled by the misty dining room windows.

On a grey cold evening, 25 December 1915, at a place called Cambrin, sitting at a long trestle table, I chewed on a leg of stringy chicken and sipped a tot of rum. A private with an accordion played 'I Wouldn't Leave My Little Wooden Hut For You'. I thought of my sister Ethel, of the dimple on the back of her hand when she took mine in hers.

I got into a spot of bother over the dinner that celebrated the nativity of our Lord Jesus Christ in Bethlehem, the child in whose blessed name we fought this ridiculous war. At the farm where we were billeted we saw a number of chickens roosting in the trees. I was not a country lad. As a child, my mother had taken us to the seaside once or twice. We had wandered along the pier at Brighton, and we had watched the hills and forests of Sussex roll by from our third-class carriage in the steam train that carried us from Victoria. I knew what cows and sheep looked like. But I was a city boy, comfortable in the smoke. It was odd to find myself now in the middle of a vast spread of churned-up pasture in northern France, with gunfire rather than birdsong in the background. Everything was arse about face.

As the youngest and most recent recruit, I was ordered to climb up one of the leafless hawthorn trees and bring back a chicken for the pot. It was my first kill. I hit the unwary bird on the head with the butt of my rifle. It fell to earth without so much as a squawk. Briefly, I was a hero. The following morning, Lieutenant Wainwright summoned the men together to say that M. LeCoq had reported the loss of one of his chickens.

Gunner Watson snorted. We hadn't heard the farmer's name before, but we all understood now why Watson found it funny. It was impossible not to crease up.

Lieutenant Wainwright kept a straight face. 'LeCoq wants an apology and twenty francs.'

'That's a bit steep, isn't it, sir?' said Wood.

'So it was one of you?' Wainwright scanned our faces.

I stepped forward.

'Gunner Bourton.'

'Yes, sir.'

'I cannot let this action go unpunished.'

'Yes, sir.'

'Report to my tent at 1800. Meanwhile, you men had better

divvy up and find those twenty francs. LeCoq is not a man rich with the spirit of Yuletide.'

At least Gunner Watson had a laugh before he died. He was the first man in our battalion that we lost. Hit by splinters from a 5.9mm shell a few days later.

We could only raise fifteen francs and a few centimes between us. 'Sorry, sir,' I said.

Lieutenant Wainwright was only a couple of years older than me. But he had the confident manner of his class. 'You're an engraver back on civvy street, I believe, Bourton. Stand at ease.'

'Yes, sir.'

'Any good?'

'Yes, sir.'

'Then perhaps you can be of assistance to me.' Wainwright, who was sitting on a fold-up canvas chair, bent down to smooth a piece of non-existent mud from his left boot. 'In exchange, I'll take care of our friend, the farmer.'

CHAPTER 9

Jack

During the Second World War, my father Fred was in RAF Intelligence, stationed in Scampton, Lincolnshire. He was a naturally secretive man, and, even in later years when it no longer mattered a damn to anyone, never spoke of his wartime experiences – except to say that he played a lot of cricket when he was shipped off to Burma towards the fag end of 1944. The Japanese, of course, are not renowned for their skill with willow bat and red leather-bound ball. By the time Leading Aircraftsman Armitage arrived in Chittagong, the war in that part of South-East Asia was more or less over. I don't think my father heard a shot fired in anger.

At Scampton, he was mentioned in dispatches for his work on the Dambusters Raid. He also got a mention in the Lincoln town hall register, because his only son, Jack Reuben, was born in that cathedral city in the summer of 1943.

By 1945, my mother was back living in London, so I have no misty memories of a bucolic childhood under the flat Lincoln sky. I've never visited the East Midlands since.

Husband still on inactive service on the other side of the world, and short of cash, a perennial state of affairs on all sides of my family, Ivy was obliged to share cramped quarters with her mother-in-law, Alice Augusta, in Streatham. Everything was straitlaced about my paternal grandmother, including her pink corsets. Her thin grey hair was always tucked in a roll into a tight headband. Her lips could zip shut in an instant as a sign of disapproval. As far as I could tell, she disapproved of almost everything except Max Miller. 'He's a cheeky chappy,' she would say. That is what everyone said who didn't understand the music hall comedian's salacious double-entendres.

Two women in one kitchen is never a good idea. My mother put up with these conditions for a while, then decamped when a vacancy arose in what became the last Bourton family home – the Old Rectory.

A room became available when my mother's half-sister Annie died in a bombing raid. Annie was the one who worked at the Peek Freans biscuit factory, the sister no one can remember much about. The night some bastard German dropped his lethal load over Shaftesbury Avenue, she was dancing with her fancy man at a club called Sylvano's. She was good at the jitterbug. It was her birthday.

There are quite a few Bourtons dotted round South Norwood Cemetery, including Annie. You need a genealogical chart to keep track of this sprawling family. I was eight when Grandma Beatrice died. It was my first funeral. Was I the only person not to cry? I remember thinking that it was just as well there had been no rain that day or we would have been standing in a quagmire of tears.

A stone angel with one broken wing stood solemn guard on the right side of Grandma's grave. How deep it was. Looking down, as I followed the other mourners in throwing down a single daffodil on to the coffin, I hoped I would not fall in.

Beneath a shady cedar, mauve and white crocuses brought a little spring cheer into this desolate day.

At the wake in a nearby church hall, the sobbing ceased. As the booze circulated, soaked up by triangular egg and cress sandwiches on pappy white bread with the crusts cut off, tragic faces began to transform. Auntie Rose fell over. A stranger in our midst, invited and transported by Violet, laughed so much I thought he would explode.

With my favourite cousin Oliver, I looked on incredulously at the behaviour of these adults. 'They're all drunk,' he said. 'Fancy a slug?' Picking a half-empty glass of warm white wine from one of the tables, he downed it in one. 'That's how you do it. If we were in Russia we would have to throw the glass into the fireplace.' But we were in Streatham. 'Of course, they only drink vodka.'

Oliver was two years older than me. And at least twice as clever. 'They tried to kill Rasputin with vodka.' I didn't know who he was talking about. 'Poisoned vodka. Didn't make a scrap of difference to Rasputin. He downed the whole bottle.'

'In one?'

Oliver glared at me. 'They stabbed him and shot him and pushed him under the ice.'

'Why?'

'Because he was a bad influence on the Tsarina, stupid. Because he saved her little boy. He had haemophilia. When the Bolsheviks shot the whole royal family, they discovered the girls had pictures of Rasputin in the lockets round their necks. Somebody cut off his willy. They keep it in a bottle in a museum in St Petersburg.'

I didn't follow any of this except the bit about the willy.

'He was extremely smelly. Like you.' Oliver grinned. 'Let's eat all the cake and be sick.'

Even my mother's eyes were dry now. She was talking animatedly to Oliver's mother Connie. Connie was her cousin, which made Oliver my second cousin. I hope you're keeping up. Connie's husband Captain Hugo Craden-Walsh had put in a rare appearance for this solemn occasion, and was swaying slightly.

Uncle Ted sat down at the piano and played a couple of slow, reverential tunes, then accompanied Florence and Violet in a close harmony rendition of 'Hold Your Hand Out, You Naughty Boy'. Even at my tender age, this all seemed quite inappropriate for a funeral. But it was fun.

The bleak old church hall thrummed with life.

There was some clapping of hands, clinking of glasses, and the room grew quiet as Uncle Wag climbed up on the wooden stage. He was a small, neat man who didn't look short. Reserved in manner, he wasn't the kind of jolly uncle who pinched your cheek and laughed his bad breath into your face. But he always paid special attention to me, as if he were really interested in anything I had to say. No one ever explained to me why his nickname was Wag.

'As the oldest of the family, I think I should say a few words.' It was clear even to a boy of eight that my uncle wasn't entirely comfortable with public speaking. 'I came through the First World War without a scratch. Well, not exactly . . .'

Aunt Ethel, pale and serious, gave a nervous cough.

'We have come through a second conflict.' Uncle Wag's voice grew in strength as he spoke. 'Again, not exactly in one piece.' Was this a reference to Annie? 'We have had our ups and downs as a family. But one person held us together . . .'

A hush held the whole room in a cocoon. I could hear my own breath in my nostrils. A single tear slid down my mother's cheek, and my father slipped his arm through hers.

'Beatrice Leonora Bourton was the most remarkable woman any of us will ever know.'

It occurred to me that Aunt Ethel's expression at this moment was as beatific as if she had seen an angel appear on the wooden podium.

CHAPTER 10

Wag

My trade goes back a long way. Primitive man carved patterns on ostrich shells. In the British Museum you can see engraving on bone and ivory, dating back to the Middle Stone Age. I often went there during my short lunch break. It was a bit of a dash from Wardour Street, but I only ever focused on one or two exhibits at a time.

The Sanders building was nothing if not antiquated – a wooden structure that had been converted into offices and studios in the nineteenth century. Before that, Number 42 Wardour Street had been a coaching inn called the Jolly Brewers, owned by the Regency pugilist Jim Belcher. Butcher turned boxer, Belcher had had a good run in the early 1800s, but, after losing an eye at a game of racquets, his career in the prize ring was stymied. These days, the stables of Belcher's Jolly Brewers were packed with boxes rather than horses. Protruding from the upper landings, the wooden pulleys installed to haul up visitors' huge trunks had never been removed.

'I'll show you something, if you like,' Queenie Green said to me one evening. She had been hanging around for Mr Smoothydrawers, but apparently Arthur Furlow had other things on his mind than the doe-eyed little receptionist.

I had been working late. Practice makes perfect, as Mother never tired of saying. And I was an attentive student. I had learned how to use a tool called a burin to make designs on steel-faced or copper plates that could be used for book illustrations, reproductive prints, security-sensitive papers and banknotes. Another technique, 'repoussé' – yet I never learned a word of French at school – involved hammering a malleable metal from the reverse side to create a design in low relief. I discovered I was able to copy almost anything. Give me a blank sheet of paper and my mind remained an empty quarter. Ask me to duplicate a design or a document and I could oblige, almost with my eyes closed.

'Come on, Mr Swat.' It was not that I hadn't noticed. Queenie Green was a very attractive young woman. Her glossy blonde hair she kept tucked up in a smooth bun, and she wore neat print frocks, which emphasised the way her hips swung when she walked. I had noticed her all right. But, after the incident with Bert Lockner, I had decided to keep myself to myself and get on with my job.

In the early days, as the most junior member of staff, my job involved fetching the boss Mr Edward a regular jug of beer from the nearby Hop Pole pub in Wright's Lane. It was an opportunity for me to roam the streets of Soho. I had got to know a number of locals to nod to – Mr Harmsby who owned Vanderbilt's Picture Framers, a delivery boy who worked at Wolf Bros Papermakers, and Joe Studley who tuned all the pianos at Warne's on Carlisle Street. I loved the bustle. And I was becoming a dab hand with that burin.

It was like an electric shock when Queenie Green slipped her hand into mine. We paused in the gas-lit corridor next to the boardroom, where the names of previous bosses and the most celebrated Sanders craftsmen had been embossed in gold on double mahogany doors.

'We shouldn't go in there, should we?' I whispered.

Queenie smiled. 'Who says we can't?' She turned the handle, and in we went.

A portrait of the founder of the firm, Thomas Edward Sanders, was encased in a heavy gilded frame. He exuded hair and confidence. You could be forgiven for thinking that the smell of burning Cuban tobacco leaves still drifted from the cigar he gripped in his right hand.

'Do you want to see something?'

I was coming to the conclusion that Queenie was a bit of a one.

Pulling back the chairman's seat from the head of the polished rectangular oak table, she knelt down and rolled back the thick Persian carpet to reveal a trapdoor.

'Go on then,' she said.

'Go on, what?'

She pointed to a brass ring: 'Open it.'

I obeyed. If a monster had jumped out baring jagged teeth, I would not have been surprised. A ladder led down into the darkness.

From a compartment in the glass-fronted drinks cabinet, Queenie withdrew a large flashlight.

'You certainly know your way around this place,' I said.

'Go on then.' Queenie directed the yellow beam of the torch into the dark space below, and I did what I was told.

'Don't you dare look up my skirt,' Queenie said, as she followed me down the wobbly ladder. 'Thank you,' she added, as I took her arm to help her down the last couple of rungs. 'Aren't you a real gent.'

I wasn't sure if she was sending me up. She shone the beam under her chin and smiled at me like a deranged ghost. I noticed for the first time that her blue eyes glimmered with intriguing hints of violet.

'What do you think this was?'

Around a smallish circle, behind an elaborately carved

balustrade, four rows of raised seats led up to a gallery that stretched round the whole chamber.

'It's a cockpit,' Queenie said. 'Excuse my French.'

I felt myself going hot in the shadowy cellar.

'From the old days. They don't do it any more. Horrible idea, don't you think? Cockfighting. It was outlawed some time in the 1840s. So Arthur, Mr Furlow, tells me. He knows his history.'

Good luck, I thought. Poncey, know-all git.

I tried to imagine what it might have been like, back in the day – hot, sweaty, loud, betting men from gutter to gentry glued to the spectacle of spurred gamecocks in their fight to the death.

Queenie turned to me. 'So was that interesting or what?' she said.

'Very interesting,' I said.

She turned off the torch. I felt the warmth of her body and her breath on my cheek. Then she slipped her tongue into my mouth.

CHAPTER II

Jack

My cousin Oliver Craden-Walsh and I liked to play Nazis. These were the days of jingoistic comics like *Boy's Own*, as well as the old favourites *Dandy* and *Beano* and strips from America like *Captain Marvel Junior*. Whenever we spotted Oliver's new stepfather, we would cry, 'Donner und Blitzen! It is ze accursed Englander.' And make a dash for it.

Oliver hated his stepfather. When forced into a real-life encounter at the breakfast or dinner table, he would only bark like a dog in response to anything his stepfather said. There were attempts to make him change his ways – bribes, tears and threats. But, as far as I know, Oliver never answered Winslow with a human word.

I had stayed the night with my cousin when my parents went for a weekend with some friends in the country – a dinner-dance at a hotel in Guildford. So I was witness to the curious scene at breakfast.

'When the dog has finished with the marmalade . . .'

Oliver emitted a low growl.

'When the dog has finished with—' A loud bark greeted Winslow Compton as he grabbed the jar of Robinson's medium cut from his stepson. He hesitated for a moment, glared at Oliver, then began to smear his toast with a knifeload of orange preserve.

The barking intensified.

'This is intolerable.' Compton's red face turned an alarming shade of mauve. He pointed to the door. 'Out!' he shouted as one might to a disobedient pet. 'Get out. And don't come back until you can behave yourself.'

As he finished his breakfast, the wicked stepfather's blood would have curdled at the desolate and dangerous howls of the Hound of the Baskervilles as Oliver and I ran down the stairs.

In a roofless shed at the end of his garden my cousin had rigged up a Western saloon, decorated with the skull of a dead moose. There were plenty of filched bottles, not all completely empty, to stick on the single shelf. We had passed the days of dividing into Cowboys and Indians and now preferred to wrestle or play football on the threadbare lawn. One day, he goaded me into drinking all the sour wine, the Dubonnet, the white vermouth and the foul-tasting Drambuie. 'If you don't run round the garden one hundred times,' Oliver told me, 'you'll die.'

'What about you?'

'I'm immune.'

'Like Rasputin?'

Oliver fingered the small scar on his right cheek, the result, he said, of a knife fight with some dacoits, out of their minds on opium. I didn't believe anything he said, but it was always entertaining and sometimes true. 'The Pig's last wife' – Oliver only referred to his stepfather as the Pig – 'committed suicide,' he told me.

I was panting hard after thirteen circuits of his lawn and felt dizzy.

'You can give up now.' Oliver got bored with the game he had played on me. 'Yes, Mrs Pig committed suicide. In the Queen's Hotel.' This was a sprawling, rather tatty Edwardian edifice on Church Road, Upper Norwood. 'She took an overdose of rat poison, slit her wrists and hanged herself from a hook in the bathroom with a dressing-gown cord.'

Suddenly I was violently sick. And Oliver laughed his head off.

The last time I saw Oliver, he more or less saved my life. But some canker gnawed at him. I often blamed those tabs of acid in the sixties for starting the rot. Or was it his childhood, as with so many of us (or maybe all of us) that both formed and ruined him?

Like Uncle Wag, and all his siblings, Oliver and I were brought up by women. Father figures were largely absent. How did that affect our perception of the universe? We were not tied to apron strings. We had the freedom of the garden. We made treehouses, swung from ropes, dug pits for smaller children. I also learned to dib a leek from my mother, and how to hang wallpaper. She did all the DIY at home. What on earth was my dad doing? He was rarely at home. He wasn't working, that's for sure. On the rare occasions I called the office, his assistant Davidson always replied, 'I'm afraid your father is hors de combat at the moment.'

If I had ever had a son, I wonder if I would have followed in this same tradition of paternal neglect.

When Uncle Wag got home from his first evening out with a girl, he confided to me, his mother was waiting up for him.

'What time do you call this?' Beatrice emerged from the living room as soon as she heard the key turn in the lock.

Uncle Wag liked to keep things close. His business was his business. But he made an exception for me. I had just told him about the first time I decided to spend the night out with a girl. I had telephoned home, and, for once, found my father. 'Come home immediately,' he ordered. I ignored that and returned the following day. Neither of us ever mentioned the subject again.

I was the same age as Wag had been – seventeen and a bit.

' "Where have you been?" Beatrice was fuming.

"Working late. With some mates."

She sniffed my breath. "You haven't been drinking. You've been with someone." '

'I remember blushing,' Uncle Wag told me. 'But feeling quite proud of myself. Not that I was ever the world's greatest lover.'

I really didn't want him to elaborate. He didn't.

'Oh well,' he said. 'There we are.' Uncle Wag poured us a second glass of sherry.

'It was the most exciting night of my life,' Wag continued. 'London was such a magical city in those days. Gas lights gleaming on the Thames when we crossed the river. There I was, on the bus with this beautiful young girl, her leg pressed up against mine, all the way from Vauxhall to Clapham Junction. I wonder what ever happened to Queenie Green?'

CHAPTER 12

Wag

'You have never done this before, have you?' Queenie said.

In the half-light from the red-beaded bedside lamp, she let me watch her unroll her stockings from a black suspender belt. Her lace underwear was red. 'A scarlet woman,' I could imagine my mother saying.

'You had better not make any noise,' Queenie had said, as we walked up the narrow staircase. I recognised some black and white engravings, done on the cheap, of Piranesi's nightmarish classical ruins. I couldn't help but straighten one as she opened her door on the top landing. 'My landlady is deaf, but she'll go mental if she finds I've brought someone home.'

I took the initiative and kissed her hard on the lips. '*You're* a bit keen,' she said.

Queenie slipped her dress over her head, and slid under the brown crushed-velvet coverlet.

I stood still, at the foot of the bed.

'Are you joining me, or what?'

I undid the laces of my black shoes, and put the pair, socks tucked into the heels, neatly underneath the chair on which Queenie had dropped her dress. I wondered if she could hear the thumping of my heart, and worried about the state of my underwear. My pants were fresh on this morning, didn't have any holes in them, but they were not new. And I wasn't brave enough to remove them in front of her.

There, it was done. Jacket, shirt and tie off. Queenie smiled as I climbed in next to her. We lay side by side in silence, not touching. Then I rolled over and kissed her again.

'Do you have a johnny?' she asked me.

'A johnny? Sorry, I don't,' I said. 'I hardly expected . . .' I had never been to bed with a woman before. With all those females in the family, I had never seen one naked. Queenie sat up and pulled her bodice over her head. She undid the pins in her hair and shook out her golden tresses. As she did so, I noticed dark stubble under her armpits, and wondered if she bleached her hair.

'Then I guess we'll just have to be careful,' Queenie said. 'I don't keep a supply by my bedside.'

Under the sheets, I removed my underwear and kicked them over the edge of the bed.

We were both naked now. There was no turning back.

'Who is she?' my mother asked. We had transferred from the foot of the stairs to the kitchen, where she made us both a cup of cocoa. 'Some girl at work,' I said.

'Is she pretty?'

'Very.'

'Nice?'

'Don't know yet.'

'Older than you?'

'I suppose so.'

'I wonder what her game is?'

The cocoa was still too hot to drink. I prayed the interrogation wasn't going to be too specific. I shrank inside at the memory of my first attempt at sex. Even if Queenie didn't have a supply of condoms in her bedside table, she did pluck out a neatly ironed white cotton handkerchief, embroidered with a single red rose, to wipe the sticky mess from her thighs and belly. 'There, there,' she said. 'Don't worry. These things happen. We'll do better next time.'

'Where does she live?' my mother asked.

'Clapham Junction. Near the station.'

'How did you get home?'

'Walked.' Our latest house wasn't very far up the hill on the Common.

My mother tutted and shook her head. We were now able to take sips of our drinks at the rectangular pine table. Burnished copper saucepans lined the walls. A long wooden hanger above our heads could be pulled down with a piece of thick cord to dry the laundry over the large cast-iron coal-burning range cooker. This was the warmest room in the house, where the family gathered together most frequently, although Beatrice always insisted on supper at a properly laid table in the chilly dining room. 'I don't mean to pry,' she continued. 'I was worried about you.'

In spite of her best efforts, Beatrice's offspring did not have a good record with the opposite sex. In later years, Rose ran off with Josephine's fiancé and had an illegitimate child before her lover ditched her. Ted got his second girlfriend Mildred pregnant and did the right thing. God knows how many affairs Florence had with unsuitable men, before she married the most unsuitable of them all . . .

But I was Beatrice's first child. She felt she had a duty to protect me. She was right. I learned fast, but I was only seventeen. And very green.

My father Leonard Bourton came from a good Dorset family, who had land and property, and lost the lot. He had been expected to train as a barrister but ended up as a travelling salesman. He was rarely home but whenever there was a sustained visit, Leonard usually said goodbye to his wife in the knowledge that she was pregnant again.

He contributed nothing to the upbringing of his children. Nothing except debt and shame. And, after he died, there were rumours that our father had another family in Tulse Hill.

He must have had extraordinary charm as well as vigour. Although Mother seemed to be the most sensible and practical woman, a certain type of man turned her head. She was a fool for love.

Wormwood Scrubs was my father's home from home. Mother never let any of us visit him in prison, although she remained loyal to her husband all his life. A talent for spending other people's money got him into regular trouble with the law, and he never seemed to learn his lesson. I must have inherited Leonard's criminal tendencies, but, fortunately for me, I never got caught.

My mother yawned, concealing her open mouth behind her hand. 'I was worried about you,' she said again. 'You could have called.'

The sound of crying from an upstairs room prevented any further interrogation. I recognised the thin wail of Aurelia, never a good sleeper. 'I'll wash up.' Picking up my mother's cup, I kissed her on the cheek, and could smell her favourite Yardley's powder. 'Sorry, Mama,' I said. 'I'll let you know next time. If there is one.'

CHAPTER 13

Jack

I had better luck with women than my Uncle Wag did – especially when I was initiated into the secret rites of sex.

My first kiss, when I was about seven, was with Sylvia Pearce, behind the garden roller. My parents and I were living in a three-storey house in Upper Norwood, which was divided into three flats. We had the basement, ground and garden. Above us, Captain Wood, retired, shared his life with his sister, whom we knew as Mrs Johnson. Perhaps she wasn't really his sister. We found her very rough compared with the perfectly mannered, well-spoken ex-Fusilier. They had a little plot, like an allotment, at the end of the garden. Every time we went away for our summer holidays, to Bognor or Bournemouth, the Woods moved their fence forward a fraction. How did they think we would not notice? But neither my father nor my mother cared too much, and Oliver and I welcomed the opportunity of improving our chances of scoring a direct hit on Mrs Johnson with a Taylor's Gold pear from a neighbouring tree. It was more fun than kissing Sylvia Pearce.

More often than not, as we spied upon the couple from our leafy shelter, we only lobbed a little unripened fruit in their vicinity to see if it was possible to distract either from their hoeing or pruning. But when my cousin hit Mrs Johnson on the bum as she was bending to pull up an early lettuce, she responded with a most satisfying yell.

At first, the good captain's sister was unable to spot the perpetrators in their hiding place. But uncontrolled giggles helped her track us in the tree. 'Come down from there, this minute, you rascals,' she screeched. 'Or I'll bring you down with a ruddy 'ook.'

It was worth the punishment Oliver and I received later. No sweets for a week, banishment from the far end of the garden for three days, and, most grisly of all, the formal apology to Mrs Johnson. 'Or I'll bring you down with a ruddy 'ook,' became our catchphrase of the year, suitable for all occasions.

In the fifties, kids were free to roam. The gardens in Upper Norwood were huge, but a regular haunt for Oliver and me was Crystal Palace Park. Down by the lake, the concrete statues of prehistoric monsters were all painted brown and grey in those days. A gigantic bear hugged a tree, two iguanodons stood together on an island. Dragonflies hovered over the stagnant water, from which a plesiosaur was always on the verge of climbing. And it was possible to wander round the foundations of the Crystal Palace itself – Joseph Paxton's monumental cast-iron and plate-glass building that had been moved to the park after the Great Exhibition. A couple of mossy sphinxes still gazed out from the ruins over the wilderness of untended parkland.

'I was there, boy, with your mother, when the palace burned down in 1936,' Uncle Wag told me. 'You could see the flames for miles. And my mother took me there when I was a young 'un when they had the Festival of Empire to mark the coronation. Now what have they built? A bloody television tower.'

Wag would not allow a television in the house. He and Ethel listened to the Third Programme on his antique radio. 'Listen to the quality on that,' he used to say, having turned the whistling dial from the Home Service to the correct frequency. 'You couldn't do better in a concert hall.'

In my youth, I can't say I much enjoyed my visits to Wag and Ethel's house in Surbiton. My uncle was proud of his roses, which he always made sure were well manured. The stench from the garden could be overpowering. It didn't seem to bother him. Maybe it was a nostalgic reminder of the days when the local countryside had not been despoiled by more dreary suburban houses and streets identical to his.

I don't suppose the house where I spent my first night with a woman was more than a mile away from the flat Uncle Wag's Queenie had rented. I was still at school. So was Angela. She looked a dirty old man's dream in a uniform that was some sizes too small for her. And Angela was a big girl. These days I would call her jail-bait.

One afternoon, my mother surprised us in the kitchen. My first real girlfriend was sitting on my lap obscuring me from sight. 'Where's Jack?' Mum asked.

'Mum, this is Angela,' I muttered, embarrassed. 'We were just leaving. I'll walk her home.'

Angela's parents had a place on Hayling Island, and went away most weekends. Usually, daughter went too, but on this particular Saturday she had been invited to a classmate's party in Clapham and was trusted to behave herself.

I did better than Wag in the sense that at least I phoned home, even if I didn't obey my father's instructions to return immediately. And Angela was well prepared for a long and sleepless night.

CHAPTER 14

Wag

I told them I was experienced with horses. If you tell people something with sufficient confidence, they will believe you. So they made me the lead rider of a team of six light draught Vanner horses which pulled an eighteen pounder gun, mounted on two wheels. A driver rode the left-hand horse of each pair. There was me, Johnson and Booth. The gun carriage was equipped with shrapnel shells, which contained 374 spherical bullets – effective, supposedly, up to three hundred yards from the burst.

I was a natural. Horses liked me. Maybe it was my smell. Or the fact that I was short and unthreatening. I only had to watch someone saddle up once to know how to do it myself. And it wasn't hard to pick up the knack of harnessing the gun.

My horse Shrapnel was an old hand. He still carried a piece of metal in his neck, which is how he got his name. Shrapnel didn't rear at the sound of gunfire, nor if a shell exploded in our immediate vicinity. Perhaps he passed his calm on to me. People thought I was brave. I wasn't. After two weeks' basic training on Salisbury Plain, the new recruits moved from practice to the real thing across the Channel. But not everyone adapted as quickly as I did once we were over the water.

We lost Watson, as I mentioned earlier, on the very first day of the campaign in northern France. He was blown to bits leading the team to my left. We just continued forward, as we had been ordered, and set up positions.

The idea was that our concentrated artillery fire would support the infantry. We were probably better at blowing up the tangled networks of barbed wire. On occasion we got lucky and succeeded in preventing the Huns from advancing from their trench positions. Luck rather than judgement can prove a valuable advantage.

I have been partially deaf in one ear ever since going to France. I had never heard such a din. But sometimes I felt almost sorry when the noise stopped. My head was in quite a muddle after my life changed direction, and, as for many other misfits and bounders, the war had come along at just the right moment.

When I enlisted, Mr Sanders said I could have my old job back when I returned, and Queenie said she would wait for me. I believed one of them. Or maybe both, because Queenie also had a vested interest in me.

'I've got this friend,' Queenie had said one evening in the Hop Pole after work. 'He's in a spot of bother.' She took a contemplative sip of her gin and tonic. I stuck to beer. Spirits were something I never got the hang of, although I swilled down anything I could lay my hands on during the Great War for Civilisation, as it's called on my gold medal with the winged Greek angel on it. 'We, I mean I, thought you might be able to help.'

The once white ceiling of the Hop Pole was covered in a yellow varnish of nicotine. The smoke from countless pipes and cigarettes formed a pea-souper all round the bar-room tables.

Queenie took a quick puff of her Capstan Full Strength and stubbed it out on the glass ashtray. She knew I didn't like the smell of cigarettes on her breath or on her clothes. 'It wouldn't be strictly legal . . .' she continued. 'But there could be something in it for you.' Her eyes flickered over my face.

'Some government security bonds have gone missing at the office. This friend of mine sort of mislaid them. They need to be replaced. Soon. I've got the serial numbers.' Queenie fiddled with the packet of cigarettes, but didn't take out another gasper. 'It would be a matter – fairly straightforward for someone as clever as you – of knocking up some copies, so no one will notice when they do the audit next week.'

I wondered if her Mr Furlow had anything to do with whatever fiddle it was.

'Do you think you might be able to help?'

Frankly, I didn't know what to think. I had pinched a few bob at home from the wallets and overcoats of our theatrical boarders, even the odd sixpence from my own mother's purse. I had sneaked a sherbet fountain from the sweetshop counter when the owner's back was turned. The boy revolutionaries Nat Devlin and I once broke the window of a greenhouse in the immaculate garden of a man Nat told me was a big shot in the City. 'It's the class war,' he said. 'We are making a statement.' The shattering glass certainly made a very loud noise.

I had no particular moral conscience to hold me back. But until that moment in that seedy pub, neither had there been an opportunity for me to commit a real crime.

'I would need the correct hallmarked paper,' I said.

Queenie smiled at me, as though I had just presented her with a fistful of diamonds. 'You could have them tomorrow.'

I took a slow gulp of my bitter. 'How much money does this involve?'

Looking around her, as though there were the slightest possibility of anyone being able to hear us over the babble of the crowd and the thumping piano, Queenie's words were barely audible.

'Did you say two thousand pounds?' I asked.

'Shhhh!' Queenie scowled.

'So, what would be in it for me?'

That smile again. It promised me Aladdin's Cave and heady nights in the harem.

'Isn't that enough?' Queenie asked, after failing to receive an immediate answer.

'More than any man could dream of,' I said eventually.

'Plus seven and a half per cent,' she added.

'Fifteen per cent,' I said.

'I am not authorised . . .' Queenie tapped her fingers on the shiny table, and smoothed a tiny piece of ash on to the wooden floor. 'Ten per cent.'

'Twelve and a half per cent,' I said. 'Give me the paper and I'll have the job done by Friday.'

CHAPTER 15

Jack

When he wasn't playing golf with clients of the bank, my dad liked to hunt around the auction rooms. His own father had been an amateur collector. As the unacknowledged curator of bits and bobs of family heirlooms I still have five large, slightly mottled watercolours by the Irish Royal Academician Claude Hayes on the walls of our house. These paintings were acquired when they were young and fresh in the 1880s by my grandfather Roland Armitage. Hayes was good at big Norfolk skies with a farmer on horseback, a couple of sheep and a haystack. My favourite picture, which exudes an appealing melancholy, is of a sailing boat, lying on the long, cold beach at Dunwich. There is a hint of blue among the voluminous cloud before the tide comes in.

None of these paintings would fetch much at auction these days. But I would never want to sell a single picture my father left me – not even the unauthenticated watercolour sketch of Joshua Reynolds's *Strawberry Girl*. The finished oil hangs in the Wallace Collection. It is a portrait that reminds me of someone I loved and lost. She looks haunted, as I still am by the memory of her.

My father, although often absent in my early childhood, behaved a bloody sight better than Wag's. When I was older, apart from teaching me the rudiments of boxing, he took me to either the Gaumont or the Century in King's Parade to see all the latest cowboy or pirate movies. I grew up with John Wayne, Errol Flynn, Cornel Wilde, Burt Lancaster and Ricardo

Montalban. I even liked the blond dwarf Alan Ladd. Anyone who could run, jump and fight appealed to me. And that could include women – like the flame-haired Maureen O'Hara and the raven-tressed, pouting Yvonne De Carlo. When my father and I went to the pictures my mother always stayed home, preferring to read a book.

I was also happy to trail along with my dad round the dusty spaces of Harrods Depository over Hammersmith Bridge or to Bonhams in Battersea, salerooms in Cheam or as far afield as Woodbridge, where we always stayed the night in a haunted vicarage. The Reverend Aspinall – my father had no truck with religious orthodoxy but liked the company of this robust and eccentric family friend – had a collection of pipes, Oriental daggers and music boxes. Everything was uninsured. 'They are perfectly safe here,' the white-haired Anglican priest told me on my first visit. 'Look.' Just by the entrance door on a shelf, an object was covered by a green velvet cloth, next to a giant severed hand made of teak and inlaid with not very precious stones. 'From Burma,' the reverend said. 'Buddhist. Karma.' I still don't know exactly what he was trying to tell me.

'Take off the cloth.'

I must have been about twelve. I was easy with adult company, having decided, years ago with Oliver, never to try to understand grown-up behaviour.

I unveiled a human skull.

'That is the Reverend Blackstone,' Aspinall explained. 'Born 1599. Like that bastard Cromwell. Beheaded by the Lord Protector in 1649. The day he signed the King's death warrant. Blackstone stays here. Keeps an eye on the place. If even a speck of my dust should be carried out of that front door, without my consent, the skull would scream the place down. Want to try?'

'No thank you, sir.'

'I don't need a dog. Or a burglar alarm. Not with the good Reverend Blackstone.'

'Did he live here?'

'Still does. Quiet as a mouse. I have even seen him in the garden, sitting on that bench by the plum tree. And he flits around from room to room. You'll probably spot him during your stay.'

I never did. Disappointingly.

I liked the idea of the screaming skull. My Uncle Jago's son Luke kept a skull too (although I never heard it utter the merest squeak) on a Black Magic altar in his dark bedroom, decorated with cabalistic signs and lit only by candles. The oldest of my football league of cousins was a disciple of the Beast 666, the bald-headed magus and drug fiend Aleister Crowley. 'Do what thou wilt shall be the whole of the law.' Luke was enormously fond of quoting the Satanist's most famous dictum. He frightened me when I was little and I only dared stand in the doorway of his room at Lewin Road. These days, he runs a small cattery in Birchington where scratching posts are more important than sex magick with the perfect, compliant Scarlet Woman.

As a young man, I sought neither refuge in God nor comfort with the devil. Sunday school was not on the agenda. The Reverend Aspinall was the only representative of the Church who made me think there could be more to life than the here and now. I liked his stories of Cavaliers and Roundheads. The past, for him, was more alive than the present.

Once a year at Dulwich Prep, there was a mock general election. My father never voted anything but Conservative. My mother was a floater. It was all a yawn to me. I voted for the Labour Party, simply because the rest of the class were true blue. In the fifties, no one was clever enough to consider inventing an alternative like Screaming Lord Sutch's Monster Raving Loony Party.

My only flirtation with politics came about because of that young woman who reminded me of the girl in the Reynolds painting. Giesele Karpfinger. A German. She was an ardent communist. We went to Moscow together in 1972, during the good old days of the USSR, saw the November parades at the Kremlin, queued for hours to pay homage to the yellowing, embalmed corpse of Lenin and drank a lot of firewater.

My cousin Oliver introduced me to her at one of the scruffy dos he gave in north London in the late sixties. His early obsession with the Mad Monk Rasputin had matured into a romantic affair with the great revolutionary Trotsky, the man whose face had been obliterated so carefully from the Soviet record as Giesele and I discovered as we studied the photographs in the Lenin Museum. God, it was cold out there. I had a scarf, a woolly hat and a leather overcoat, but I froze my balls off on the streets of Moscow. How massive that city seemed, compared with Ye Olde Village Tea Shoppe of London.

Giesele and I stayed, shivering, in the grand and threadbare art nouveau Hotel Metropol, built before the Revolution, but nationalised in 1918 by the Bolsheviks and renamed the Second House of Soviets. Nowadays I believe it has a pool and a gym, but retains the glorious art nouveau chandeliers, the mosaic-lined elevators and the opulent stained-glass ceilings for the oligarchs, crooks and tarts who replaced the idealists and criminals of yesteryear.

For myself, I never joined the party. But I did go to Oliver's parties in Crouch Hill. His dingy flat was lined with agitprop Mayakovsky prints and photos of the dashing young Trotsky, as well as one of the old one, head bandaged, after he had been fatally wounded with an ice axe by an undercover NKVD agent. There was also a massive poster of Eisenstein's *Ivan the Terrible*. It was an original, picked up in a junk stall in Portobello Road, but curling round the edges now and badly stained from its position near the stove in the filthy kitchen.

I was always fastidious and hated to see something of value and quality so criminally neglected. I offered to take the poster off Oliver's hands, but he declined. I respected property, but did not necessarily consider that the owner had exclusive rights to it. Of course I was not a communist, but it was the anarchist Pierre-Joseph Proudhon who made the amusing observation that property was theft. So I had no compunction about taking the poster off Oliver's wall one day when he had gone out for beer and appropriating it for myself.

I don't suppose, for one second, that Uncle Wag dithered with any theoretical or ethical considerations when he decided to forge those documents. He saw an opportunity. He took advantage of it. Nor was my own transition into a brief life of crime really driven by a conviction that the proletariat was brutalised and exploited by bourgeois capitalists. I was not greedy. Nor was my dear uncle. We just had a more pragmatic attitude to right and wrong. Legitimate business can be conducted with characters who, quite consciously, break the formal laws of the land. Bankers do it all the time. Wag understood that. So did I, from an early age.

CHAPTER 16

Wag

There was a disbelieving expression in Booth's eyes as he lurched into me, blood pulsing from a bullet hole in his shoulder. Strangely, under the circumstances, it reminded me of the look in Queenie's eyes when I stuck at a whacking twelve and a half per cent share in forging those documents. That first deal turned out to be more of a trial run – to see a) if I could do the job and b) to check I could keep my mouth shut afterwards. I passed on both counts. More work had followed before I went off to war.

The German soldier Booth and I had disturbed that night on our way to the latrine must have been lost or desperate for a crap. Or both. Perhaps he was a scout, come to do a recce on the enemy position. Like the 17th Battery, Second Indian Division, Jerry never seemed to know either what was going on, or where he was on the map. Commands were issued to move forwards, backwards and sideways. We all fired when we were told. Sometimes, quite probably, on our own men.

I was lucky. The Kraut's Luger jammed when he tried to shoot me as well, while still trying to pull up his trousers with his left hand. I didn't have time to help my comrade Booth and ignored his groan when he fell to the ground. My main thought was to grab the German's gun, which I did, and wrested it from his hand. As the soldier struggled, his trousers slid further down his ankles.

The fellow was more concerned with covering his embarrassment than saving his life. With one kick, I knocked him off the wooden slats that covered the stinking pit, and down he fell into the shit. When his head popped up, I shot him twice, and he disappeared from sight. It was my very first kill and I was surprised how easy it was.

I kept that gun with me throughout the war. And used it again. It never jammed for me. Back in Blighty, too, I had cause to use it again in peacetime.

They gave me a medal for kicking that German into the excrement, and for carrying Booth back to our camp. He was invalided off to a field hospital. 'Thanks, old man,' were his last words to me. 'I would have been in the shit myself if it hadn't been for you.'

He never returned to the unit. Apparently, gangrene set in. Pity. He was a good bloke.

Lieutenant Wainwright offered me special privileges after I did that job for him, following the chicken incident. And a couple of others afterwards. He needed papers to take some unauthorised leave. Had a French floozy in Nancy he was sweet on. Good luck to him. He cancelled my debt to the farmer with the unfortunate name and paid me for other work. I was happy to be supplementing my soldier's paltry pay, even though there was nothing to spend it on here and absolutely no guarantee I would make it back home. It was just a little extra insurance.

There was a fair amount of dosh in my London bank account already, rather more than a young engraver might normally expect to have. After a few more jobs for Queenie's mysterious friends, I had opened accounts with more than one bank, and made sure that my mother had some spending money while I was away fighting for King and country.

'I won it at the races,' I told her. 'Had a tip from a chap at work.'

'I wouldn't like you to get into gambling, William.' Mother

could not conceal her concern. 'It is the slippery slope. Look at what it did to your poor father.' Leonard's name was rarely mentioned, and his stretches in jail were never alluded to. Prison was one way, perhaps, of avoiding the trenches. I hadn't thought of that.

'I promise, Mum.' There was only a week to go before the 17th Battery was due to be shipped off to Le Havre on December 15th, 1915. 'Don't suppose I shall be playing the horses while I'm in France. I've got to ride one, though. Into the Valley of Death.' That wasn't a very good joke, and my mother's face crinkled up with worry.

I had just returned to our new house in Brixton after basic training on Salisbury Plain, where I had developed a taste for umbrella field mushrooms. You could almost see the fungi squeezing out of the damp earth in the misty dawn. After a night's guard duty, I would pick a crop, while rooks squawked from the bare oak trees, and share them with my friend Vernon Hotchkiss. We had been at primary school together in Camberwell. Hadn't learned much, either of us. He had become a commis waiter at the Café Royal, where Oscar Wilde once held court among the red plush.

In his new catering role, there was not going to be much opportunity for Vernon to experiment with haute cuisine. But the memory of those mushrooms, fried in sizzling bacon fat, still makes my mouth water.

I shall never forget the sight of Stonehenge looming up before us in the early evening, as the new recruits returned from a long hike with heavy backpacks towards our barracks. The wintry sun cast its low rays through one of the Neolithic bluestone lintels towards our marching feet. Did any of us feel connected to an ancient English past? I don't know. But, then stuck in France, shrapnel whizzing round my head, rats gnawing at my boots at night, perhaps I did experience something. It wasn't exactly patriotism. But I was proud to be English. I didn't much care for Germans. Like most of my comrades, I remained as clear about the rights and wrongs of the conflict as I was about the whole mystery of existence.

I felt as if I'd died there, that would be fine with me. Except that I should have liked to have seen my mother again. And Ethel, of course. Ethel in particular. I never cared deeply for Queenie. She was a rite of passage. I knew she made use of me. Though I was a willing accomplice. And my life would not have been the same if I had never met her.

Everything you do has its repercussions. You don't know that when you are young. Everything connects.

CHAPTER 17

Jack

My father wore a bowler hat to the bank every morning. Fred was the image of the conventional city gent. But after paying his dues to temporal authority in Shoreditch, he would put on magnifying headgear to help him enhance the signatures on paintings of dubious origin he had acquired on his rounds of the auction rooms. I also suspect that during his period at Lloyds he assisted various clients in shifting money to foreign parts in ways that did not strictly adhere to the punitive financial restrictions of the period.

Apart from defaulters' parade, as a result of being caught wearing pyjamas under my corps kit, I had no problems with the discipline at school. I was never beaten, never punished. The dog never ate my homework. I simply kept out of trouble.

Other boys actively preferred confrontation. One boy in my form I particularly admired was called Stuart Hamish McPherson. At assembly, no matter what the hymn, he always sang the words of 'Do You Ken John Peel?'. And when our class received a very rare visit from our diminutive headmaster, I remember McPherson calling out, 'Mind your head on the doorknob when you go out, sir.'

But the biggest tearaway, and my closest friend from Dulwich Prep days was a boy called Linklater. He was always known as Link, though his Christian name was Andrew. His father owned a second-hand motor saleroom in Streatham. The Linklater motif, familiar in the advertising pages of the *South*

London Chronicle was of two hands, in the ten past two position on a driving wheel.

At preparatory school, Link had been considered to be a bit rough. It wasn't as though people still sneered at 'trade', but second-hand car dealers were considered to be synonymous with dodgy. Plus – a schoolboy with real money in his crocodile-skin wallet was a target for the envious and for bullies.

Dulwich College Preparatory School had a 'house' system based on Red Indian tribes – Ojibwas, Chippeways, Deerfoot and Mohicans. Link frequently referred to himself as the 'last of the Mohicans'. And he could have met his end at the tender age of ten, before I rescued him from a good kicking by a blood-crazed renegade band of short-trousered Deerfoot braves. Five boys had set upon him by the bicycle sheds after a game of football. One was waving Link's wallet, whooping and doing a war dance. I grabbed it off him. Still in mud-encrusted boots, I made good contact with some enemy shins and Link scrambled to his feet. He was no coward. No longer totally outnumbered, he also showed he could be useful with his fists. When I think of that film *Shane* and the fight scene in the bar, I'm Alan Ladd, the small, buckskinned gunfighter, and Link the battling farmer, played by Van Heflin. Side by side, the two men rout the baddies, triumph over superior odds and smile broadly at each other.

'Thanks, Kid,' Link said, wiping a smear of blood from his cheek as the Deerfoot war party beat a retreat.

'Armitage,' I said. 'But you can call me Jack.'

No one picked on Link again. He was never popular. That did not bother him one bit. We became friends. Through two schools and out the other side. He always called me Kid.

The Linklater family lived in a mansion on Leigham Court Road. The garden was the size of a park. Where I had a small toy jeep to pedal up and down the lawn as a little boy, for Link's twelfth birthday his father gave him a real live two-seater motorcar. That is how I learned to drive, tearing round my best friend's grounds.

For his eighteenth birthday, which was celebrated in the Locarno Ballroom on Streatham High Road, someone gave Link a gun. I think it came from his Uncle Sid, who was, Link confided, friends with a gang run by the two Richardson brothers, who worked out of Camberwell.

'It's a Webley Mark VI.' Link let me break open the revolver, which he removed in a leather pouch from the well-polished walnut chest of drawers in his bedroom. 'I keep it with my socks. The smell will keep snoopers well away.'

There were six .455 cartridges in the cylinder. 'Used to be standard service issue until 1947.' Link spoke with the authority of a gunsmith. 'And I have two spare packets of ammo. Keep them underneath my Aertex pants.'

I snapped the barrel shut.

'Careful with that.' Link took the pistol from me. 'The safety's not on.'

Like most boys, I had fired an air rifle, and once nearly fainted when I thought I had hit a pigeon. 'What are you going to do with this?' I asked.

'Kill me some bar, Kid. What do you think?' drawled Link in his best Fess Parker Davy Crockett impersonation. 'You never know when it might come in useful.'

For Link's eighteenth birthday bash, my father suggested I wore the plain black jacket I still had from school and borrowed his bow tie. But Link's short, fat, Brylcreemed dad insisted on hiring me a proper dinner jacket from Moss Bros. I was embarrassed. My father said, 'We cannot possibly accept that,' but Mr Linklater insisted. 'A man's got to be properly dressed,' he said, clapping me on the shoulder. 'You've been a real mate to my son. I respect that.'

Link wasn't the only nickname in the family. Mum was known as Bummy Mel. She had been christened Annabel. I'm not sure if Linklater Senior was ever dribbled with holy water at an Anglican font, but as a joke his mates baptised him in the name HL when he and they were old enough to know better. It was the fault of a fortnightly children's TV programme called *Whirligig* which featured a puppet called Mr Turnip. It was, very briefly, his son's favourite show. Mr Turnip's side-kick was an actor named Humphrey Lestocq, always referred to as HL.

Humphrey Linklater was nobody's stooge, although some would argue he was a puppet for Eddie and Charlie Richardson. And when those two gentlemen played a joke on you – you knew it. And it was never very funny.

Humphrey Linklater was no comedian either. However, I never saw him without a smile. It was as distinctive as his trademark waistcoat and suit.

'Aren't you Jack Armitage?' Her long, straight hair was the colour of copper. In the glittering glow of the Locarno Ballroom, the slim young woman's single-strap silver-sequined dress dazzled almost as much as her smile. Her pale shoulders were neat and angular.

'Do you remember me? Sylvia Pearce.' It was just about possible to make out her name above the sound of Cliff Richard's 'Move It' and the hubbub of well-oiled and well-assorted guests all trying to extract every last ounce of the Linklaters' outrageously generous hospitality.

It was the first time I had seen Sylvia Pearce since we had

grappled tentatively behind the garden roller in my back garden a decade ago. She had an impish grace when she was seven. Now she was stunning.

'Shall we?' It was impossible to talk, and I did know how to jive. So did Sylvia. She was supple in my arms, swift on her feet, twirled with a smile that ignited the dry tinder of desire inside me.

As the record ended, we kissed.

'Are you with anyone?' I looked round for a burly boyfriend.

She shook her head in time with Elvis, who was now singing 'All Shook Up'.

'Nor me.'

We danced some more.

Link weaved his way over to us, arm round a red-haired girl who was popping out of her green satin blouse.

'This is Sylvia,' I shouted.

He looked at his companion. 'Amelia.'

She looked put out. 'Camilla,' she pouted.

Link gave her a big smacker on the lips. 'Sorry, baby,' he said.

'Fabulous party!' Sylvia had to shout that twice in the birthday boy's ear.

'Why don't we go somewhere?' Link exaggerated his words so we could lip-read.

'You can't leave your own party,' I bawled.

'I can do what I bloody well like.' Link's cheeks flushed red.

Lonnie Donegan was now singing 'My Old Man's A Dustman'.

'Who chose this bloody awful music?' Camilla slurred.

'Who do you think?' Link's lower lip protruded belligerently.

'I need the little girl's room.' Camilla staggered away through the reeling throng on the dance floor towards the red-illuminated Ladies sign.

'I think she loves me,' Link said, with a huge grin. 'God, I'm parched.'

I mimed drinking a glass to Sylvia, and she nodded back.

Link beckoned us to some back stairs. The lurid chic of the ballroom was replaced by black lino and the smell of floor polish and carbolic. After one flight, Link pushed open a door that led into a small, ill-lit bar. A number of men in suits sat at green baize tables playing cards. A few more, sunk in deep brown leather armchairs, sipped contemplatively on tumblers of Scotch.

There was one man at the bar. He was staring into a gin and tonic, and blowing smoke rings from a fat cigar.

Link clapped him on the shoulder. 'This is my favourite Uncle Sid.'

'All right, my son?' Compared with HL's broad smile, Sid's reminded me of a snake, if snakes could smile. 'Enjoying your party?'

'This is my great friend . . .'

But Link's uncle's eyes were fixed on my companion.

'Hello, Sid,' said Sylvia. 'Fancy seeing you here.'

CHAPTER 18

Wag

I was not properly educated, whatever fantasies my mother entertained about class and quality.

Everything I learned, apart from basic mathematics and reading, I taught myself.

The only two people in our family who ever got a proper education were Jack and his cousin Oliver. But Oliver went off the rails, poor boy, his life blighted by his parents' divorce.

Jack is the clever one. My mother would have been so proud of him going up to Cambridge. He doesn't flaunt his knowledge about the place. He is calm, methodical and observant. Who would have imagined, when he was a shy, curly-haired boy on Ivy's lap, that we would have grown so close?

One afternoon in 1915 young Mr Edward asked me to come into his office at Sanders. He sat at an embossed leather desk, complete with silver pen and ink tray, photograph of his family and heavy ledger book all arranged neatly before him.

'You are a good worker, Bourton.' He didn't ask me to sit down.

'Thank you, sir.'

Sanders cleared his throat and looked up at the beamed ceiling. 'It has been brought to my attention,' he said, 'that some equipment has gone missing . . .'

'I hope you're not suggesting . . .'

'I know that you often stay late, Bourton.' He moved his ink tray a fraction to the left, then moved it back to its original position on the desk. 'You might have seen something, someone . . .'

I distracted myself by trying to read some of the titles in the bookshelf behind my boss. 'What exactly has gone missing, sir?'

'Sheets of metal.' Sanders coughed into his hand. 'And some cash from the safe.'

I didn't even know the whereabouts of the office safe, but I had a pretty good idea who did.

'One hundred pounds in five pound notes, to be precise.'

'I wish I could help, sir.' Was I under suspicion or not? It was hard to tell from this interrogation.

Mr Edward rose to his feet. 'I am sorry to trouble you, Bourton. I am obliged to ask every employee about this. We have a reputation here for absolute security. You've not been with us long, but I'm very happy with your dedication to your work. I'm sure you can be trusted. Continue in this direction and promotion will be swift.'

As far as I had seen, nothing was swift at Thomas Sanders & Sons. It would be time to move on soon. 'Thank you, sir,' I said.

Sanders shook my hand. 'Run along then, there's a good fellow.' He walked me to the door. 'Keep up the good work.'

Queenie looked over at me as I returned to my workroom and picked up the flat graver for fill work on some lettering on a new bond issue. My hand was as steady as ever.

'Was it you who took that money?'

I checked the top of Queenie's head. Her roots were

definitely darker than the blonde hair that tickled my naked chest.

'What do you take me for?'

I didn't answer that.

'They are on to us over the missing metal,' I said. 'We should have replaced it. That was really stupid.'

Queenie Green's room in the Clapham boarding house had not become our little love nest exactly; but we did meet there on a fairly regular basis. It would be churlish to say that our relationship was not pleasurable for me. Queenie had helped me take that crucial step out of boyhood.

She rolled on to her front. 'There is another job they want you to do.'

I caressed her smooth bottom. 'No thanks. I'm calling it a day,' I said. 'It's not worth the risk. Besides, I don't think I'm going to be working at Sanders much longer.'

'Does that mean you're going to ditch me?'

The landlady's clock on the first-floor landing chimed eleven.

Running my hand up Queenie's back, I planted a warm kiss on her neck.

'No, that has nothing to do with it,' she murmured. 'You don't really think I pinched those fivers, do you?'

'Of course not.' I gazed at the one picture on Queenie's bedroom wall. It had a black silk scarf draped over one corner of the elaborate gilt frame. It depicted a steamboat sailing under a bridge. The boat and the parapet above the river were artfully decorated with strips of mother of pearl. On the bank, a man unfurled a fishing rod, and two carriages traversed the four-arched bridge. Underneath on a little plaque it said: 'Souvenir de Mayence'.

'We can't go to France but why don't we go away somewhere else?' I suggested, rather dreading Queenie might agree.

'After this one, last job,' said my pretty accomplice.
'I told you, I'm finished with all that.'
'They won't like it if you do a bunk, you know.'

CHAPTER 19

Jack

The motto of Selwyn College, Cambridge comes from 1 Corinthians 16:13. As translated in the King James Version of the Bible, it reads: 'Quit ye like men.' Be brave.

The Right Reverend George Selwyn (1809–1878) founded this not very attractive red-brick college and went on to become the first Bishop of New Zealand. Initially, the majority of applicants to his college had wished to study theology. I was reading English.

You did need to be brave. It was not the syllabus that daunted me at Cambridge, but the ratio of men to women – 10 to 1. Aged nineteen, hormones raging, the study of literature did not satisfy all my desires. Rules and regulations more suitable to a nineteenth-century prison colony were rigorously enforced. To distinguish town from gown, students were supposed to wear full academical kit outside their halls of residence. Elderly proctors in mortarboards, accompanied by college porters (known as bulldogs) in top hats, gave chase to any young man suspected of leaving his gown behind in his study.

If caught in your rooms after hours with a person of the opposite sex, an undergraduate could be sent down. At least this punitive rule was extended equally to the women's colleges. The rumour was that in Girton, if a young woman was visited in her room by a gentleman, even in the afternoon, her single bed had to be dragged into the corridor.

It was like being banged up in Colditz. I became adept

at climbing into second-floor windows after being locked out until a young man from Wigan called Doughty sawed out one of the prison bars in a downstairs window at Selwyn, but I only discovered this easy access to the outside world after curfew towards the end of that long, frustrating first year. After that, I lived in digs in a dustball attic in Silver Street, adjacent to Queens' College. There was a front door key you could pull out on a string from the letterbox, so no more need to climb in after curfew, but it didn't solve the problem of the dearth of female company. So I was grateful to have the company of Sylvia Pearce.

That first year, most Friday nights, I caught the train to Liverpool Street, changed on to the Central Line, then took the Northern for the journey south to the Oval. It was only a short walk from the tube station up Kennington Road to the Georgian terraced house where Sylvia had her bijou basement flat.

I didn't ask what she got up to during the week, as long as she was able to free her diary for the weekend for her desperate visitor from the East Anglian fens. Number 72a was no dank student dive. The deep red sofas were decorated with ethnic cushions. Sylvia had Tiffany lamps and a beautiful glass-fronted credenza, where she kept the drink. I had never seen such a range of bottles, except at Link's. Alcohol didn't really agree with him, although he drank plenty of it. He preferred purple hearts.

'There.' After a long embrace, during which I had to fight back the desire to tear off her clothes, Sylvia poured us both a glass of Dom Pérignon. 'Tell me about your week.'

> 'I wonder, by my troth, what thou and I
> Did, till we loved?'

John Donne and the Metaphysicals were Top of the Pops for me at that time.

> 'Were we not weaned till then?
> But sucked on country pleasures, childishly?'

I lingered suggestively on the word 'sucked'.

'So why aren't you getting the benefit with those clever young things at Newnham? Isn't their college just across the road from yours?'

'Seriously,' I said, 'if you saw some of those women looming out of the mist, you would run for your life.' I refilled our glasses and continued.

> 'If any beauty I did see,
> Which I desired, and got, 'twas but a dream of thee.'

'Is that still the same poem?'

'Yes. Do you know who I mean when I say C.S. Lewis?' I asked her. 'You know, the Narnia stories?'

'Come on, Jack. You know perfectly well we're not great readers in my family,' Sylvia said.

'I've been going to hear him lecture on Malory. About Lancelot as the first tragic hero of the English novel. Now I have to write an essay.'

'That explains it. So you've come to me for help. What do you fancy eating tonight?'

'I just fancy you.'

Although there was a more than respectable kitchen, with a mixer, a rack of knives, silver cutlery and Royal Copenhagen china, I never saw Sylvia so much as cut a slice of bread. After a long and languorous morning in bed, I often made us scrambled eggs with a couple of slices of Cracker

Barrel Cheddar on the side. But that was about it on the cooking front.

'How's Sid?' This was an area of Sylvia's life around which I tiptoed with the utmost delicacy. I now knew that Link's uncle had set her up in this flat. He was associated with two of the biggest villains in south London – Charlie and Eddie Richardson. They had a thriving scrap metal business in Camberwell, and a number of other interests as well. In spite of Sylvia's assurances that Sid was well out of the way in Marbella, I feared the day when her bedroom door would crash open and I would see that reptile standing there with a couple of thugs who would slice me to shreds with their razors.

But there were some risks worth taking and I didn't mind going without supper.

CHAPTER 20

Wag

The first punch caught me round the side of the face. Arthur Furlow held my arms behind me, while the other fellow went to work on me.

'You snot-faced little git.'

As I was wandering home after work on a Friday night, after my last tryst with Queenie, Thomas Sanders's chief accountant and this bloke I had never seen before dragged me into the alley that connects Dean and Frith Streets.

I absorbed the full force of a punch in the breadbasket.

'Now you . . .' The rat-faced bastard who seemed to be in charge of the rough stuff caught me round the throat. 'You had better start listening. You can't stop now. If you don't do exactly what we tell you, I'll see to it personally that every single bone in your right hand is broken in two. You'll never work again. Is that clear?'

To show how clear it was to me, I head-butted him, and followed up with a sharp kick to the balls.

'Fuck me,' Furlow grunted, as I elbowed him in the guts. I was not Jim Belcher, but I had been in a few fights since early days in the playground. Two against one are reasonable odds if you're not afraid.

Unfortunately, I did not have it all my own way. This was not Ratface's first fight. I might have caught him with a lucky kick, but he came back quickly, hurling himself at me, this time with a knife in his hand. I managed to catch his wrist, but he was wiry, and slipped out of my grasp.

Furlow yanked me by the hair at the precise moment that his partner tried to stab me in the neck. Fortune favoured the underdog. I heard the blade snicker through the shoulder padding of my jacket. Flailing round, I punched Ratface in the ear. He reeled back.

This was a fight I was never going to win. I made a dash for it.

A bunch of revellers were wandering out of Gennaro's. I barged into a woman and sent her flying. Staggering at the impact, I managed to keep my balance. 'Sorry!' I gasped – more polite than Ratface, who knocked the woman over again as he came charging after me down Dean Street. There was no sign of Furlow. Maybe he was as bad at running as he was at fighting.

'Hey! What do you think you are playing at?' I heard someone shout.

In a dingy doorway that smelled of urine, I squeezed myself into the shadows. Ratface dashed past, heading towards Shaftesbury Avenue. I returned at a modest pace the way I had come. On the corner of Brewer Street, I bumped into a puffing Arthur Furlow.

He did not look so brave now that he was on his own. 'You're in big trouble, Bourton,' he blustered. 'You can't muck about with us. You had better do what you're told or—'

I hit him again; as hard as I could, in the solar plexus, and left him vomiting against the wall of a chemist's shop.

An elegant couple passing by shot Furlow a look of disgust. 'That's the trouble with Soho, darling,' the woman said, tightening her grip on her escort's arm, 'it's full of drunks.'

It seems totally daft to sign up as an under-age recruit in the army, but that is what I did. I had my reasons. Furlow and Ratface had not got the better of me yet, but the threat of further violence convinced me that I would be safer in the trenches than on the streets of Soho.

'I trust your decision has nothing to do with our little chat the other day.' Mr Edward shook me by the hand as though I were an unknown visitor in the greeting line at a reception. 'Do come and see us when you get back.'

After the Battle of Mons in the last week of August 1914, many young men had decided to enlist. At that time no one in our family was old enough to be eligible or daft enough to sign up. We knew about the war with Germany, but believed the thing would be over in a couple of months. Yet by late September 1915, a few months after I joined up, nearly two and a quarter million men had exchanged their jackets and trousers for khaki and hundreds of thousands had died. And there was no sign of an end to the bloodshed.

You were supposed to be at least nineteen. But, as I discovered, if you didn't have flat feet, one eye and a dose of the clap, a firm signature was all that was required to get you enrolled.

My mother was distraught. 'I don't understand.' I had never seen her cry so unashamedly. 'You're just a boy. My boy. It's not as though you have to go.'

I didn't give her the 'Your country needs you' speech. Or remind her of the unprovoked assault by a German U-boat on the *Lusitania*. Everyone was crying, and I was only off to Salisbury Plain for basic training. The assassination in Sarajevo of Archduke Franz Ferdinand had had about as much impact on us as a haggis exploding in Auchtermuchty. On the other hand, when Germany invaded France, every newspaper carried more or less the same headline: England could be next. That put the wind up a lot of people.

Ethel was the only one of my siblings who passed no

judgement on my decision to join up. Of course, she didn't know my real reasons for going. After training as a nurse, my favourite sister had been helping to patch up wounded soldiers who had been shipped back home from France for some time. She must have seen some terrible sights, but she never went on about it. There was a gravitas and modesty about Ethel that set her apart from her hysterical drama-queen sisters, Florence and Violet.

Queenie had been absent on my last day in the office. A touch of flu, so the sour-faced temporary replacement claimed. Queenie had avoided me since I told her about the incident with Furlow. In my crisp new uniform, I decided to pay her one last visit. On my way down the hill to Clapham Junction, I marched to an imaginary drum.

No one answered the doorbell at Number 106. I tried the brass knocker. A woman wheeling a big black pram stared at me as though I were about break the ground-floor window. A rag and bone man clattered past. I wondered that his skinny brown horse had the strength to pull both driver and cart. The darkness of the evening gathered its cloak around me.

Standing back on the pavement, I could have sworn I saw the curtain twitch at Queenie's window. I banged and rang alternately.

Never give up, as my old mum used to say. A shrivelled old crone in a pink apron opened the door, and wedged herself in the crack.

'Is Queenie in?' I asked.

I might as well have been speaking Urdu. The landlady, it had to be her, gazed at me blankly. I knew she was supposed to be deaf, so I repeated my question very carefully and pointed upwards.

'She's not well.'

'I know,' I said. 'But can I please see her?'

'She's not taking visitors.'

I tapped my tunic. 'I am off to the front any minute. I wanted to say goodbye to Queenie.'

Perhaps patriotism flourished like the aspidistra in parts of south London. The landlady beamed and opened the door. 'Come into the parlour,' she said. 'I'll go and get her. Who shall I say it is?'

'Wag,' I said.

She stared at me.

'William. William Bourton. A friend from work.'

I listened to her footsteps disappear up the stairs, while I wandered round the ground-floor room. Pink and white striped wallpaper provided an eye-watering background for a good quality mezzotint engraving of Henry Fuseli's *The Nightmare* and another one by the same artist, *Lady Macbeth Seizing the Daggers*. What odd choices.

'Hello, Wag.' Queenie's face was pale. A bloody bandage covered her right cheek. 'Look what you made those bastards do.'

CHAPTER 21

Jack

One Sunday, before I caught the eight fifteen train back to the seat of learning, Sylvia and I had lunch with Link at the Spaniards Inn on Hampstead Heath. Why he selected this venue was a mystery. Perhaps it was because it was far from prying eyes in the Deep South.

Hand in hand, Sylvia and I strolled through the Vale of Health on our way from the Tube. Karl Marx used to take his family there of a weekend. D.H. Lawrence lived with his wife Frieda at Number 1 Byron Villas when my Uncle Wag was dragging that eighteen pound field gun in France. North London was like another planet for someone from our neck of the woods. For all the grand houses in Streatham, Dulwich and Upper Norwood, the bucolic gentility of this area was something else.

Cherry blossom lay like confetti on the dewy grass.

'The lovebirds.' Link stood to embrace Sylvia. The dark, oak-panelled room of the Spaniards Inn was packed, but my old friend, as always, had secured a good table in the corner. We shook hands. 'Hi, Kid.' I always liked the way he said that.

There was a pink glaze like faded warpaint beneath both his eyes. He looked as though he might have been partying for a few days without sleep.

'I need you to do something for me.' Link had been jittery throughout lunch, and only played with his roast chicken. Sylvia had hoovered up her meal, as though she had been kept on bread and water for a week in solitary. I was still eating.

'What do you think of the wine?' he asked.

It was a Châteauneuf-du-Pape, not something I drank very often in Cambridge.

I raised my glass to Link, then to Sylvia, and took a long, appreciative sip. 'Revolting,' I said.

Link reached down under the table and passed me a brown briefcase. 'Take that with you, will you?' he said. 'Keep it safe for me.'

The case, smelling of new leather, was surprisingly heavy.

'What's inside?' I asked. 'Gold ingots?'

Link looked at me coldly. 'You really don't want to know.'

Sylvia took out a mirror and checked her make-up. She shot me a warning look and shook her head.

'Have you finished, sir?' Our friendly young waitress extended a hand towards Link's plate.

'Thank you,' he said. 'Yes. Any pud, you two? They do a good trifle here. Sticky toffee pudding?'

'I'm stuffed,' said Sylvia.

'Coffee?'

'Nothing for me,' I said.

'Nor me,' added Sylvia.

'Just the bill then,' Link said to the waitress. 'You'll never guess who I saw the other day? Stuart Hamish McPherson.'

'Flob on him, Muck,' I said, repeating the regular cry of form 2B. One of our old classmate's celebrated skills had been spitting. The other was a rude noise he made by squeezing both palms together. 'Sorry, sir,' he would say to the teachers. 'Just passing wind.'

He could not keep out of trouble. 'Remember RI?' I said.

Of course, Link remembered. He snorted. Even Sylvia had heard the story before. But we were struggling for conversation this lunchtime. Asked to select some instructive lines to read out loud from the Bible, McPherson had managed to find in the Book of Isaiah references to Nob, a eunuch, and the inevitable breaking of wind.

'He's only on some bloody training scheme for Unilever,' Link said. 'Still, not as bad as studying English Literature at some poncey college in Cambridge.'

Link's dad had slipped me a sealed beige envelope containing £50 in crisp £10 notes when I received the news that I had been accepted by Selwyn College. It was always my impression that he had wanted his son to go to university, but, clever as he was, Link could not be arsed to do his homework. He simply followed his father into the business, even adopting HL's signature three-piece suit.

I was wearing a faded, stained, brown corduroy jacket, the cliché image of a student.

'Can I make a contribution?' When the bill came on its white plate, it was only right to make the gesture.

'Don't be daft, Kid.' Link reached into his old crocodile-skin wallet. 'I'm loaded, aren't I?'

'And dangerous to know,' said Sylvia.

'Look who's talking.'

Sylvia did not return his smile.

It wasn't easy crossing the narrow road outside the Spaniards Inn. Back in 1585, a tollgate had marked the boundary with Finchley. This afternoon, there was an unbroken procession of Sunday afternoon traffic.

'Can I give you two a lift?' Link's grey E-Type Jaguar was parked against a grass verge further down the Heath.

'Thanks, mate,' I said. 'We'll wander back.' The low spring sun was blinding behind Link, almost obliterating his silhouette. I raised his leather briefcase in farewell.

'Careful with that or there'll be hell to pay.' Link stuck out his right thumb. 'I'll be in touch,' he said.

We heard his car door close, and the sound of the ignition. 'He's in trouble, your friend,' said Sylvia, 'isn't he?'

CHAPTER 22

Wag

It could have been an entrance to the underworld kingdom of Hades. The Greenwich Foot Tunnel stretched under the Thames from Greenwich to the Isle of Dogs. There wasn't a soul inside. Just the sound of my new army boots echoing off the glazed white tiles.

Out on the street I had to ask a passer-by for directions to the Newcastle Arms on Glenaffric Avenue. East London was unfamiliar territory to me. But, according to Queenie, this was where I would find her good friend and mine, Arthur Furlow. Regular as clockwork of a Saturday, apparently, he would drink two pints in the saloon bar of the Newcastle and eat sausage, egg and chips.

Furlow looked startled when I sat down on the bench seat beside him. 'Don't let me interrupt you,' I said, resting my half of bitter on a square cork mat. 'I won't be staying.'

'Thought you had gone for a soldier . . .' Furlow looked me up and down, inspecting my spanking new uniform. A group of dockers, dressed up for the evening, were getting a few in before the football. No one was bothered about two blokes in the corner.

'Better not let your food go cold,' I said. 'My battalion's shipping out from Dover tomorrow. Didn't feel I could leave without saying goodbye to you.'

'What do you want?' Furlow was sweating. I could smell his brilliantined head.

The beer was good. Rich and cool. I wiped my lip. 'If you so much as touch a hair on Queenie's head again, I will make sure that you regret it.'

'You and whose army?' Furlow summoned a flash of bravado. 'After a couple of weeks over there, who says you'll even be around?'

'I'll be back. If only to come and get you.'

Furlow cut a slice of Wall's finest pork sausage and made an ostentatious show of chewing it with his mouth open.

'Didn't your mother teach you any manners?' I clamped Furlow's jaw shut with my left hand and pressed the sharp blade of the burin I had pinched from Sanders against the pulsing jugular in his neck. I'm a mild man, but when my blood rises I can turn nasty. 'As I was saying . . .' I removed my left hand from his mouth and wiped it on the shoulder of his blue serge suit.

Furlow coughed up a gobbet of masticated sausage. 'Please take that thing off my neck.' A bead of blood trickled down to the collar of his clean white shirt.

'I promise you,' I said, 'as God is my witness, I will come back for you . . .'

Removing the sharp blade from his throat, I plucked out his red silk tie with a flourish and sliced it in half.

I doubt if Furlow would have looked more surprised if I had stabbed him in the throat. 'What did you have to go and do that for?' he said. 'I bought that tie in Jermyn Street.'

'Be thankful it wasn't your finger,' I said.

Furlow picked up the remains of his tie. 'They only wanted to frighten you a bit. Both of you. There's a lot of dosh at stake here. I'm just a guy in the middle.'

I slid the burin back into my uniform top pocket and buttoned it up.

'Make sure you tell your friend.'

'I don't have any control over him.' With a shaky hand, Furlow took a swig of his pint.

An old gentleman in a shiny grey suit, a thin roll-up stuck to his lower lip, pulled up a chair by the upright piano at the far end of the bar. It was more or less in tune, as he hammered out 'It's A Long Way To Tipperary'.

As I stood to go, I tipped the remains of Furlow's lunch over his smartly pressed trousers and poured the last of my beer over his head. 'If I hear a whisper that anything has happened to Queenie, I swear I'll come for you.'

One of the first things I was asked to do on reaching my quarters in somewhere called Beauvaire was to assist in the construction of stables for the horses. The Battle of Loos had been fought some months earlier. Local kids played among the Allied guns. To them it didn't feel like war at all. More like a game of soldiers.

We built the stables out of local brick and then covered them in white tarpaulin – as it turned out in full view of an enemy observation balloon. The Germans waited until the building work was completed, then blasted the whole lot to buggery. My contempt for the officers who ordered the work to be done cannot be expressed here.

Pure chance kept me away from the firing line. Picket duty. So my bullet-riddled corpse was not lined up on the ground for burial alongside Les Bradin, Chris Radley, Bill Marniet, Sid Broffman and 2nd Lieutenant Everest. Many brave and loyal horses were lost that day too.

Some weeks later we were lucky the wind changed direction. Having been softened up with a deafening mortar attack that lasted more than an hour, we would have been helpless against the tear gas unleashed by the Germans. Our mob had only the most rudimentary protection against chemical attack – something called a Hypo helmet, which was little more than a khaki-coloured flannel hood soaked in special protective chemicals. We also were instructed to piss on the cloth since the ammonia was supposed to offer protection against the chlorine. It was comic, I can tell you, to see our men prepare for a gas attack.

Can you believe, at the beginning of the war, we didn't even have mortars? Jerry on the other hand was well equipped and made the most of his superior strength. Needless to say, our lot had precisely nothing at all with which to resist the Germans' latest attack. When the mortars had done their bloody work, Jerry came at us pell-mell from their trench position opposite our ineffective dugout, screaming and shooting.

Everyone's experience of war is different. For me it was like walking through a dream. I was a witness to the murderous mayhem, deafened by the noise, but my pulse remained regular, and, on this particular day, I was totally focused on keeping the horses calm.

A surprise counterattack from our own chaps saved us from more or less certain death. As we made our retreat slowly down a rutted highway towards the ruined town of Chaprin, poor old Shrapnel had his left hind leg blown off. I was hurled on to the road next to a big crater, where a solitary human arm poked out through the mud and ice.

Apart from a cut to my forehead from a sharp stone, only my palms were grazed as I tried to break my fall. I hadn't the heart to shoot Shrapnel myself. Hotchkiss refused to do it too, even though I pleaded with him. Only Johnson had the guts.

On one of my campaign medals, the sun shines on a Greek rider who is mounted on a proud steed, its left and right legs bent in classical symmetry. On the reverse side, round the

King's head some lettering spells out 'Georgius V Britt. Omn. Rex Et Ind. Imp'. I don't suppose the designer ever saw horses as intimately as I have seen them, sleeping with them in the hay, sharing the oats from their nosebags, witnessing their warm bodies shattered by mortars and machine-gun fire.

That evening I helped bury Gunner Lock, Driver Edwards, Johnny Glover and an old bloke who really was called Tommy Atkins. He was forty-five. But I only shed tears over Shrapnel.

CHAPTER 23

Jack

'Could you please explain to me exactly what the bloody hell I'm doing here?'

Link was gazing at a poster of Lenin in my cousin Oliver's top-floor flat in Crouch Hill.

'Thought it was time for you to meet a different class of person.'

I was still sponging off the state. I had done a bit of desultory job-hunting after leaving Cambridge, but fancied the idea of becoming a great movie-maker. It was not hard to obtain a postgraduate grant in those days, and I had been offered a place at the London School of Film Technique, which operated out of an old warehouse in Covent Garden. At least half the students were American, eager to avoid the draft and I soon became friends with one draft-dodger in particular, who shared my passion for film, Tyler Cohen. For the time being I was happy to be back at my parents' place in Dulwich, and to visit Sylvia when I felt the need for a bit of sex.

My old school friend offered me a swig of Macallan from his silver hip flask. 'Don't know how you can swallow that stuff,' he said, gesticulating at the bottles of Hungarian Bull's Blood on the kitchen table.

The sweet scent of marijuana hung heavy in the air. Oliver's guests had not come here for fine wines but to plan an anti-Vietnam protest the next day. Many were sitting on the threadbare carpet, passing spliffs around. I was sticking to the rotgut. Even inhaling Old Virginia tobacco never agreed with me.

Link was wearing an open-neck white shirt, grey trousers with a neat crease and a soft black leather jacket, which clearly had not fallen off the back of a lorry nor been made from reconstituted plastic. His only concession had been to abandon his usual waistcoat on that warm October afternoon. 'It will be a red rag to the bullshitters,' I had warned him on the phone.

'What ho, comrades.' Oliver joined us. Summer and winter, he affected thick black spectacles and a polo neck of the same colour, a style popularised by Colin Wilson, the author of *The Outsider*, which was already a decade out of date. 'Welcome to the Revolution. Oliver Craden-Walsh at your service.'

Link shook hands with my cousin. It was the first time they had met. Oliver had gone to Alleyn's, another school in the Dulwich area, until he was expelled for trying to burn down the library. This failed act of arson was not motivated by a hatred of books, he claimed but because the school failed to stock Marx's *Das Kapital*, Engels's, *The Condition of the English Working Class in England*, and, in particular, Trotsky's *The Revolution Betrayed*. Oliver really did care about the struggle of the working class even though his surname was double-barrelled.

'What good are the works of G.A. Henty and Harrison Ainsworth to a student of world history?' I remember him ranting when I was about fifteen. 'Who needs 15 million pages from Samuel Richardson on the rape of Clarissa?'

To the undisguised distress of his mother and the equally undisguised relief of his stepfather, the rabid Hound of Crystal Palace abandoned his family home for a squat in Elgin Avenue, then to the outer darkness of Crouch Hill. There he was able to pay the derisory rent, thanks to his job as a postman. The crumbling house with its peeling porticos was owned by a Czech émigré, who had left Prague just before Alexander Dubcek's attempt to reform the worst repressions of Soviet rule during the Prague Spring.

He had evidently never finished unpacking. The stairs were lined with rolled carpets, dusty oil paintings, three monumental porcelain chinoiserie jars, a garden rake and scythe, cardboard boxes bulging with leather-bound volumes, ancient kitchen scales with brass weights, and a *Howea forsteriana*, its leaves now as dry and grey as the dead earth in its ornate art nouveau metal pot. That was just some of the stuff. On the first and second landing on the way up to Oliver's garret, two statues kept an eye on the many visitors who were able to negotiate a path to the top. Jaroslav Makovec had been a dentist, so he said, back home – and an ardent amateur collector of junk.

The landlord was not present at Oliver's party. From the rambling late-night political debates I had previously enjoyed in his *Old Curiosity Shop* of a living room, I'm not sure he would have approved of the rash of copies of Mao's *Little Red Book*, which had become the mini Bible of aspiring activists across Europe. It could easily be stuck, like a wallet, in the back pocket of your jeans. I spotted at least three copies among Oliver's comrades.

Mao Tse-tung's socialist dictums were stolid rather than enquiring but the new young, middle-class lefties of Harold Wilson's Britain liked the bite-sized slogans. 'Political power grows out of the barrel of a gun' became a familiar chant. However, as far as tomorrow's protest was concerned, the weapon of choice was marbles. And maybe firecrackers.

'There is going to be trouble tomorrow.'

Link's blue eyes hardened. He knew more than my cousin would know in a million years about 'trouble'. In fact in case of trouble, Link always carried a pair of knuckle-dusters. There had been a dip in second-hand car sales and HL had diversified into both fruit machines and scrap metal. In south London, from Camberwell and Peckham Rye through Forest Hill as far as the wastes of Catford, to the grimy edges of Battersea and beyond, that meant dealing with the Richardsons.

If Charlie and his brother were not best pleased with the behaviour of a client or a bad debt or simply with the way someone looked at them, there could be 'trouble'. And trouble hurt. Even if the rumours of victims being nailed to the floor were an exaggeration.

'I thought it was supposed to be a peaceful protest,' I said to Oliver. President Johnson's Tet offensive had united across Europe a very vocal student opposition to US policy in Vietnam. A smallish demonstration, including nearly all the guests in Crouch Hill, was scheduled to take place the next day at the LSE, before marching to the American Embassy in Grosvenor Square. And I, with a couple of fellow London School of Film Technique students, was going to be there to film it. Hearing about the rally, I had seen an opportunity, hastily adapting my script for our final film exercise about a nice south London boy who goes off the rails to include some genuine documentary footage.

Link handed me his Webley, complete with silencer. He had promised to lend it to me for one scene to be shot on a piece of wasteland in Peckham. The two student actors required for a retributory punch-up did not have to study hard for their roles. One, a black ex-paratrooper, was called Nicholas Hunt. 'Whatever you do,' he said, '*never* call me Nick.'

The other guy, Jason Strauss, could have been an Apache warrior in modern dress. Both did the occasional job for HL – like making sure a customer never defaulted more than once on a payment.

In return, I had brought Link the briefcase he had given me for safe-keeping on Hampstead Heath. Of course I had opened it against his orders and had been taken aback by its contents: several bars of gold indeed; contraband no doubt; and some official-looking certificates that seemed to be some kind of government bonds. God knows what Link was mixed up with now. I was relieved to hand it back.

'This march is about peace,' Oliver said. 'But we need to make a stir. There is no point in just waving placards and chanting. People need to be made aware of what is really going on in Vietnam.'

'What *is* really going on in Vietnam?' Link was finding it hard to disguise his irritation with my cousin.

I quoted Adrian Mitchell's poem:

> 'I was run over by the truth one day,
> Ever since the accident I've walked this way
> So stick my legs in plaster
> Tell me lies about Vietnam.'

'It's Stop the Draft Week in America.' Oliver was not in the mood for verse or jokes. 'It was the CIA who killed Che Guevara, you know.' The Cuban revolutionary's body had been found a few days earlier in Bolivia.

'They did for Brian Epstein too,' Link said with a barely disguised sneer. 'Did you know that?' Back in August the Beatles' manager had, apparently, committed suicide.

'Do you have any beer?' The striking young woman with straight blonde hair had a strong German accent. 'I don't like the wine,' she complained. 'And I don't like dope.'

'This is Giesele.' Oliver perked up. 'Giesele Karpfinger. Meet Jack Armitage.'

CHAPTER 24

Wag

June 1917. It was nice to sleep in a real bed, even though the mattress was hard. How strange it was not to be scratching for lice, to feel clean, to wear pyjamas.

I shared the ward at Gower Street University Hospital with ten other wounded men, most in a far worse state than me. It was a miracle that the bullets that had torn a ragged path through my right thigh had not left me a cripple for life. I was luckier than the bloke next to me, who had to get used to a stump after gangrene set in.

A weary doctor with cold hands removed the bandage over a gash just above my right ear. A breakfast of warm sweet porridge oats made Gunner Bourton a cooperative patient. I could have been in the Ritz. Such luxury. I didn't have to do anything for myself, except go to the toilet. 'Don't touch that scab,' the doctor told me. 'Even if it itches.'

I was used to obeying orders, whatever I thought.

My first visitor was Ethel. Pristine in her nurse's uniform, she held my hand and wept silently. 'Indestructible, that's what I am,' I said. That is what I believed. But so, I guess, did the other poor bastards who were mown to bits around me.

'Is that your bird?' Hopkins, the infantryman in the next bed, asked me when my sister left the ward and waved goodbye in the doorway. 'Bit of all right, isn't she?'

I could have knocked the bugger off his crutches. But how was he to know?

My mother and Jago were the next on the duty roster. There were more tears. 'Surely they won't send you back?' Mother said.

'As soon as I can walk properly.'

'Don't walk then,' said Jago. 'Can't you just do a good limp?'

I punched him lightly in the chest.

Mother fumbled in her bag, and brought out a small dish wrapped in muslin. 'Your favourite,' she said, as if my nostrils could have failed to detect the scent of damson and plum.

'Don't suppose the scoff was much good out there . . .' Jago really did not have the slightest clue.

'Sausage, egg and bacon for breakfast,' I said. 'Ginger biscuits for elevenses. Two mugs of splosh. Roast mutton for lunch with roast potatoes – not as good as Mother's though –; crumpets toasted over an open fire in the afternoon.' I was warming to the fantasy. 'Champers and caviar at six on the dot, after a hot shower. We all dress for dinner there, you know. Turtle soup, choice of pheasant or Dover sole, and Eton mess to finish. But nothing, nothing in the whole wide world to touch your pie, Mama.'

My only complaint about the month I spent in that hospital was the visits by the padre. But the sermon from a fellow patient who accosted me whenever he could grab the opportunity were even worse. Private Ronald Longridge was a trunk in a wheelchair. And, once he had wedged his way next to you, it was hard to dislodge him.

'Look what is happening in Russia.' Longridge's grey eyes would assume a visionary gleam. 'They are not putting up with those Romanovs any more. People are taking power into their own hands. That is what we should be doing here. Shoot the King. And his tart of a wife. Come home. You know how many men were lost just at Tannenberg?'

No, I didn't. And I didn't want to either. 'You believe what you want to, my friend,' I said.

'You'll just do what you're told.' Longridge's look of scorn did not bother me one jot.

CHAPTER 25

Jack

Standing on the roof of a car in Grosvenor Square, Nagra sound recorder slung round my neck, I pointed a woolly directional microphone towards the angry crowd.

> Hey, hey, LBJ –
> How many kids did you kill today?

The chants were angry, but anarchy was not loose upon the streets. Via Trafalgar Square, ten thousand people, mainly students, led by the London head of the Vietnam Solidarity Committee, Tariq Ali, walked in an orderly fashion to the American Embassy.

Our cameraman, tall, elegant, unfluffable Alex Tompkins, was ready, Arriflex on his shoulder. And my co-writer/producer/director Tyler Cohen was beside us. We had taken up a position right at the front of the square, clambering on top of a parked Vauxhall Victor.

Nowadays, the police call it kettling. When you confine a large group of men and women in a smallish space, something is going to blow. The rhythmic repetitions of 'Ho, Ho, Ho Chi Minh, We shall fight and we shall win' had been replaced by 'Kill the Fascist Pigs!'

The police were prepared. When they brought on their mounted officers in two lines in front of the hideous concrete and glass embassy, the day was decided. It was marble and cracker time. In the front line, I spotted Oliver and Giesele, an old Etonian anarchist called Doyle and a morose Irish fellow traveller who went under the name of Boggy. It was Boggy who rolled the first marbles towards the horses' hooves to make them lose their footing.

I didn't see who flung the first few firecrackers. One louder explosion caused a well-trained horse to rear up, and, as the animal came back down, one of his hooves caught the head of a young woman. She toppled over. The horse trampled on her.

Shouts turned to screams. Bottled rage flared into frenzy. Here we were at the Winter Palace in St Petersburg, the revolutionary mob, provoked beyond endurance, determined to overthrow Kerensky and his lackeys. Exhilarating images of the scene, conjured up by Sergei Eisenstein's film *October*, flickered in my mind.

But this wasn't being staged for a film. Fifty years later, on this dry October afternoon, Alex, Tyler and I were the only people there to film a real-life event in leafy Grosvenor Square. None of the batteries of cameras and microphones we see today had been drawn up in serried ranks to exploit the situation for worldwide twenty-four-hour news. But then this was not exactly the Russian Revolution.

A group of protesters tried to drag the injured woman to safety, while others, who had witnessed the accident, surged forward, consumed with self-righteous wrath at the brutality of the police.

The cordon buckled and held. Batons came out. Hard blows were dealt on unprotected heads.

In full view of the large gilded bald eagle on the embassy roof, two helmeted policemen were dragged off their horses. The crowd howled like a lynch mob. Bottles were hurled, along with branches of wood snapped from trees and bushes in the square. I adjusted the volume on my recorder, while Alex zoomed in on faces contorted in fury. The car we were standing on started to rock as bodies, propelled forward by the general surge, were shoved against it. Tyler staggered, but kept his balance.

'I've got to change the roll,' Alex shouted above the din.

More glass was shattering now at the edge of the double line of blue. A Coca-Cola bottle hit me in the small of the back, and rolled off the roof of the Vauxhall and into the gutter. I looked round to see who had chucked it.

'Sorry, mate,' shouted a whiskery Trot in a donkey jacket.

While Alex rummaged in his leather shoulder bag for another can of film, more missiles were thrown – clods of earth, CND placards, broken poles from Viet Cong flags. We were directly in the line of fire, and there was no way Alex could safely remove the short end of black and white film in his changing bag.

We clambered down from the car roof into the human maelstrom. At that moment, taunted beyond endurance, the mounted police charged the enemy.

It was the first time in my life that I was really frightened. The horses were massive. The grim expressions on the faces of the riders confirmed they meant business.

I was one of the first across the green parkland of the square, relieved to discover there were no railings to climb over. I lost sight of Tyler and Alex, aware only of the panic of fleeing protesters all around me. A boy and a girl, holding hands as they ran, were trampled on by the horses. Their screams were ear-piercing.

On the other side of the shrubbery, I drew breath, and made sure my Nagra was still working.

'Dat was fun, vasn't it?' A strongly accented German voice spoke beside me. I looked round into the gleaming green eyes of Giesele Karpfinger. 'Schwein,' she added.

CHAPTER 26

Wag

'There are ghosts here, I swear to you.'

'Don't be daft, Aurelia.' I had been given two weeks' convalescent leave. My sister and I were having tea in the kitchen of the Brixton house. She had brought out our best blue and white Doulton china, normally reserved for birthday celebrations.

'I see them in the street. I hear them in the dark.'

For a while Aurelia had been a disciple of the late Madame Blavatsky but it didn't make much sense to me when she tried to explain about Monads and astral projection. She was more at home with table rapping and mystic vibrations in suburban villas with the curtains drawn.

'I have seen enough dead bodies to last me a lifetime,' I said.

She covered my hand with hers. 'I know, darling. It must have been terrible for you. Don't listen to the ramblings of your silly little sister.'

'What is this tea?' I asked. 'Better than the slop I have been used to swilling down.'

'It is only Darjeeling.' Aurelia had the strangest brown eyes, with a faraway twinkle. 'But it's from Fortnum's. This boy I know gave me a packet for Christmas.'

'I expect he did.'

We both laughed.

'He's called Ernest. Not very bright. But I like him. He's kind . . .' She poured us both another cup from the teapot, which was decorated with a scene of birds flying over a pagoda. 'Oh, I nearly forgot.' She went over to the bread bin and opened a small paper bag containing a couple of scones. 'Toasted?'

'As they come,' I said. 'What a treat.' To be home was bliss. The only thing missing was the presence of Ethel, my angel, who had returned to her nursing job in Yorkshire. I was proud of her sense of duty but could not help feeling bereft.

Aurelia cut my scone in half and laid a big smear of butter on both sides. 'That should help fatten you up,' she said. 'You're thin as a rake.'

The front door banged shut, there was some rustling in the hall, then Mother joined us in the kitchen. 'Mmm,' she said, spotting the special china. 'Tea party. Be an angel and pour us a cup, will you? I'm gasping.'

On the marble table top by the cooker, she removed some shin of beef and ox kidney from her wicker basket.

'Potato pie?' I was salivating already. You can keep your smoked salmon and your larks' tongues. I always loved my mother's potato pie, a pot full of tatties infused with the intense flavour of onions and meat with a thick suet crust. I had dreamed of it while chewing down my bully beef and jaw-breaking biscuits in the trenches.

Mother smiled at the big smacker I planted on her cheek.

'Can I peel the potatoes?'

'You put your feet up, Wag.' Aurelia finished her scone, and washed up plate, cup and saucer in the sink.

'I could get used to this,' I said. 'Life of Riley.'

'Hello, darling brother.' Florence flung her arms around me and left a smudge of bright red lipstick on my nose. 'What a day I've had. Any more of that tea?'

'Sorry.' Aurelia had poured the last drop for Mother.

'There's nothing else for it.' Florence came back from the

living room with a bottle of Gordon's and some Schweppes Indian tonic. 'What the doctor ordered.' She fetched four tumblers from the cabinet by the door, and poured great slugs of gin into the glasses.

'It is a bit early for me,' Mother said. 'But why not? It's not every day we have my dearest boy sitting here with us.'

I was not a member of the Temperance Society but nor was drink a demon that possessed me ever. It was easy enough to watch what it did to other members of our family.

'Chin, chin.'

We clinked glasses. In the trenches near Ypres someone had told me that this toast was Japanese slang for penis. I tried to forget that as we drank.

'Bugger! Sorry, Mama.' Florence covered her mouth. 'I forgot the lemon.'

'We haven't got any,' Aurelia said.

'I'll put it on the list.' Mother raised her glass. 'To my wonderful children,' she said.

Florence displayed her emotions on her face like the flashy costumes she wore at the Café de Paris, where she was doing a short run in a cabaret. Reaching for a white handkerchief, she made sure her thick mascara did not run as her eyes filled with tears.

'To our wonderful mother,' I rejoined.

The gin was gone in no time at all. I opened a bottle of red. Our supplies (often by the case) came in the main from Florence's many after-the-show dates with a series of well-heeled admirers.

'Chin, chin.' My chorus girl sister was speaking a little more slowly now. 'That's what I was going to tell you. There might be a part for me, quite a big part in *Chu Chin Chow*.'

'Will you be Ali or Baba?' I asked.

Florence ignored that. 'They want me for the part of . . . of . . . Bloody hell. Can't remember her name. Oh, I know – Zahrat. Zahrat Al-Kulub.'

'Is that the lead, dear?' Mother asked.

Florence batted her eyelashes. The room went quiet for a moment. We knew all about her auditions.

'Open Sesame,' I said.

'Hope so.' Aurelia had finished peeling the King Edwards.

'Ted should be back later. And Jago,' Mum said.

The smell of onions frying slowly was intoxicating, as if I was not intoxicated enough already. It was time to slow down, especially if that potato pie was to be savoured fully. I was glad nobody asked me about life on the front line. I kept the horror of what I had seen for my nightmares.

'I had a drink with Frederic Norton the other night,' Florence said.

'Who's he when he's at home?' Aurelia asked.

'Don't you know anything? He's the composer. He's the man who wrote the music. He reckons I've got a big future.'

There was an almighty crash from upstairs. Aurelia looked at me meaningfully. 'I told you,' she said. 'Ghosts.'

CHAPTER 27

Jack

'I don't know what you see in her – stuck-up German cow.' Link stretched back in the LSFT basement viewing theatre in Shelton Street. 'Your film is crap, by the way.'

'You're probably right.' I hadn't shaved for a couple of days, after working through two successive nights in a cutting room on Wardour Street. I felt, looked and smelled like a derelict. Giesele was complaining that I was ignoring her. 'I don't vait for any man for ever,' she had snapped down the phone. 'And certainly not for some boy vit his silly film.'

'What about all that searing political comment? Or did I miss something?' Link asked.

The unique scoop footage we had shot in Grosvenor Square on the day of the anti-Vietnam protest turned out to be on a roll of bum film. The allocation of stock by the school had been insufficient for our purposes, so Tyler and I relied on the kindness of strangers. We learned to beg, borrow and steal.

You get what you don't pay for in life. I could have wept when we saw the first rushes. Some so-called 'short ends' we had carried away in triumph from the British Film Institute were well past by their sell-by date. Balloons of light burst along the edges of the frame. These flashes were punctuated by bursts of interference, an invading mass of dots, as though our signal were being jammed from another planet.

The only solution was to make that real-life violent protest outside the American Embassy into a dream sequence, intercut with the central love scene.

In a cold basement flat in Archway, we had tried to persuade our stars to remove their kit. Tyler and I had decided that we couldn't mess around. We were not re-making *Brief Encounter*.

Our male star was very reluctant to go naked. Our leading lady on the other hand was merely continuing a scene she had been playing at home. We had had to drag her out of bed with her boyfriend earlier in the evening. I'm not sure if she even bothered to put on her pants and bra.

'I promise you,' Alex tried to reassure our anxious actor, 'you won't see anything you shouldn't. Bit of tit and bum, that's all.'

A fire was burning in the grate, and, between takes, Bob, our gaffer, held a two-bar electric heater over the couple to prevent a massive outbreak of goose bumps. The idea was that the flickering glow from the burning coals would provide the limited illumination. We soon found that was impossible to achieve naturally. Having upended Bob's bicycle, we cut out some black paper and attached it to the rear wheel. With a light placed on the carpet behind, if we wiggled the wheel backwards and forwards, the desired visual effect was achieved.

The only problem was how to do it without laughing. Courageously simulating the utmost passion as they rolled about the bed, Daniel kept his genitals clutched tightly between his legs. Bob and I had to stuff handkerchiefs into our mouths to stop the spluttering.

'You'll never get that past the censor,' Link said.

What did he know? Before the end of term, when all the final year students' films were screened, I did take the precaution of showing our 15-minute effort to John Trevelyan, Secretary of the British Board of Film Censors. He was famous for 'not shrinking to use the scissors, especially when it came to protecting the young'. I'm still not sure how I managed to secure an appointment.

That afternoon, sitting through *The Game Chicken*, a rubbish title for which I take full responsibility, with the Censor was an unnerving experience. Trevelyan, not for one second without an untipped Senior Service Fine Virginia cigarette between his thin lips, refused to sit down, and prowled around the tiny viewing theatre, pausing occasionally to stick his foot on the armrest of one of the uncomfortable chairs.

The end titles came up, followed by some chinagraph squiggles on the celluloid. A last beam of light from the projector beat against the blank screen, and the electricity was switched back on.

'Well . . .' Trevelyan walked slowly to the front. 'Yes,' he said.

I swallowed.

'I don't think I have any problems with that.' He tapped a long piece of ash into his hand.

'We weren't setting out to shock anyone,' I said. 'We just felt it was important to be truthful.'

'There are many ways of telling the truth, young man.'

I reflected that it was often a very good idea to say as little as possible.

'You have my blessing,' Trevelyan said. 'Thank you for showing me your film. I think you have talent.'

I stood to shake his hand. The censor was over six feet tall and I felt like one of Snow White's little friends. 'Thank you, sir,' I said. 'I much appreciate your taking the time to . . .'

He clapped me on the shoulder. 'Good, good,' he said. 'Must get on. The devil drives.'

'You really serious about this German bint?' After the screening, Link had driven me back to my parents' place in Dulwich. I could not afford a flat of my own, not even to share digs with a group of fellow scruffbags.

'I wouldn't necessarily say serious.' We were drinking some Bells and water, courtesy of my generous friend. 'Seriously, though, what did you think of the film?'

'I liked the punch-up.'

He was right. Nicholas Hunt and Jason Strauss were the most authentic ingredients in the whole bloody movie. Only on screen for three minutes, they brought an elegant, natural conviction to the fight scene.

'You can't go on living like this,' Link said. He didn't mean I was living rough. My parents owned the leasehold on a big house in a desirable area, and my room was as elegant as a rich bachelor's apartment in Albany, with nice paintings, courtesy of my dad, books and heirloom ornaments. But I had no spending money, apart from the odd windfall from a poker game with friends.

'You're right,' I said. My parents never raised objections if I brought a girl home but it did mean tiptoeing about the place at night. And Giesele, my new, radical girlfriend, was scornful of her bourgeois lover. 'A man of your age does not live with his Mutti und Vati.'

I did not comment on the fact that Giesele was happy to bank the regular cheque from her own Mutti, which kept her in soft suede Biba boots and long purple dresses. She also ran a small convertible Volkswagen.

'You could do the odd job for me, if you liked,' Link said. 'Bring you in a few bob.'

'No questions asked,' I said, putting a finger to my nose.

'I mean it.' Link put down his glass on the inlaid Moroccan side table. 'Family firm. Proper office. Filing cabinets. Secretary. Prime location in Camberwell Green.' He snorted with laughter.

'Makes the Civil Service sound exciting.' To please my dad, I had sat the Civil Service exams in a draughty hall near Burlington Arcade and was set to start work in the Home Office after completing my film course.

'We set up companies. And we sell goods.'

'That you don't strictly own.' I had heard about this scam some time ago from Sylvia. The Richardsons were coining it with 'long firms' – businesses that existed solely to buy goods on credit, without any intention of repayment.

'It's a thought, though, Kid. Isn't it? Money for old rope. Frankly, our personnel don't compare too well with a gang of monkeys.'

I wondered what Sylvia was up to. I hadn't seen her since my head was turned by Giesele. Whatever fire had burned in our hearts had imperceptibly fizzled out. We never had a row or anything. Nor had Uncle Sid put the frighteners on me, although he must have been tipped off that his mistress had a friend. Maybe HL made sure I was all right. I don't know. I didn't like to ask.

'Think about it anyway. You can't even afford to take the Kraut out to dinner.'

My ideologically committed girlfriend liked her scoff. For all her razor-sharp cheekbones and svelte figure, Giesele had stubby little fingers, like the good middle-class Fräulein that she was. To distract any critical observation of these hands, a strip of red varnish was only applied in a thin line down the centre of each fingernail.

She would not grow into a plump Hausfrau hanging out with me. However, thanks to a bit of decorating work for a neighbour, I was able to take Giesele for the occasional restaurant lunch. It was a long way from her flat in Onslow Square to the Old Friends in Limehouse, but, as far as I knew, this was the best Chinese food in London – fresh, exotic and light on the monosodium glutamate.

The surroundings were not what you would call swish, but no one – even someone as contrary as Giesele – could deny that eating there was a genuine gourmet experience.

She adored east London. 'It is so real,' she said. 'Not like where your parents live in ticky-tacky land.'

I wondered what her mother's house in suburban Gütersloh was like.

I took Giesele on a tour of the East End and told her about the opium dens in Limehouse, described in Dickens's *The Mystery of Edwin Drood*. We also visited the Grapes, disguised under another name in the opening chapter of *Our Mutual Friend*.

I avoided the Blind Beggar in Whitechapel, where Ronnie Kray murdered George Cornell, a valued associate of the brothers Richardson, and main supplier of the pills that were turning my friend Link into a jittery wreck. With a 9mm Luger, Kray shot his old pal just once through the forehead.

There were tons of witnesses in the pub that night. Someone even recalled Cornell's last words, 'Look what the cat's brought in.' But no one came forward to testify. The police were obliged to let Ron go free.

Giesele was wary of Link. They didn't like each other. Unlike her, he came from a genuine proletariat background. He was at odds with the system. But he had as much time for card-carrying lefties as for someone with an advanced case of bubonic plague. Somehow or other, a truce was maintained when we went out as a foursome, and Giesele was always animated with Link's latest girlfriend Rachel. Rachel had come up the hard way. Council estate in Peckham, father a trade union foreman at Surrey Docks in Rotherhithe, student activist at the LSE and working now for Release, an agency providing bail services for people arrested for drug offences. Rachel ticked all the boxes. God knows what she saw in Link or vice versa. Maybe animal magnetism did the trick. Maybe she didn't know what Link and his dad got up to. Maybe it turned her on.

Gott knows what Giesele saw in ze accursed Englander either. And why on earth did I put up with her? I had been seduced for a while by the romance of those two indomitable idealists Lenin and Trotsky. And that fantasy bound Giesele and me together. We were fellow travellers in a Soviet dream world. But in the end my lack of funds was a problem.

It was impossible to pretend any longer. Whatever political cause my German girlfriend pretended to espouse, she wanted what she called a 'real man', and she certainly wanted a relationship that did not involve going Dutch.

Things came to a head when I got lost navigating our route back from the Old Friends.

'Vot dat!' When Giesele got really angry, she spoke like the caricature of a German. 'A Londoner who does not know his London.'

I'd had it with her put-downs and her sniping.

'Why don't we pull in over there? I know exactly where we are,' I said.

Giesele stamped on the brake, but kept the motor running. Her most kissable lips were clamped together.

'Well, goodbye,' I said, and climbed out of the car. I did not look back. Somehow or other we had found ourselves near Victoria Station. It was only three stops to Herne Hill and a brisk walk home.

I vowed we'd never speak again.

CHAPTER 28

Wag

The peeling paintwork on Number 106 was in a worse state than it had been the last time I came to call on Queenie Green. I knocked on the red door and rang the bell. But Mrs Carstairs, the landlady, had a brand-new hearing aid, and it was almost with a sense of relief that I heard that her tenant had done a runner, leaving a month's rent unpaid.

'I remember you, though. Wounded, eh?' Mrs Carstairs had also been kitted out with new false teeth. Her unexpected smile had an alarming regularity, and the dentures sparkled in the gloom of the narrow hall. 'Do come in.'

The living room had not changed at all. 'You seem a nice young man,' said Mrs Carstairs. 'What possessed you to get mixed up with a floozy like that?'

I sat down in one of the deep, brown velvet armchairs next to the fire. 'I expect you would like a nice glass of sherry . . .'

After yesterday's hammering at home, I wasn't too sure, but I appreciated the thought. 'Thank you,' I said.

Queenie's ancient landlady unstoppered a cut-glass decanter on a silver tray that stood on a table next to the chair opposite mine. She was obviously not averse to a tipple on her own.

'Are you home for good?'

I wasn't in uniform, so this was not an unreasonable question. 'I go back to France the week after next.'

'Poor devil.' Mrs Carstairs savoured the manzanilla then swallowed it down. 'I've never been to Portugal,' she mused. 'Don't suppose I ever will either. Don't expect I'll be going anywhere much. Although I do have a sister in Croydon.' She laughed to herself. 'Has it been awful?'

'I can think of things I would rather have been doing.'

'I'll bet you can . . . I've got a travelling salesman in there now,' she said. 'In your friend's old room. He's away half the time and pays on the dot.'

'Do you know what happened to Queenie?'

'She never wrote to you?'

'Not really. No. It wasn't like that.'

'Wasn't it?' She refreshed her glass. 'Would you like . . .?'

'No, thanks.'

'Put hairs on your chest.'

I had noticed how often people now used clichés in their conversation. Was this because no one wanted to confront how brutal and bitter the world had become? My family, including my mother, was guilty of the same offence. Words had become a sort of bandage.

'I read all that guff in the papers about tactical advances and our brave boys. You were wonderful. I know you're brave. You don't have much choice.'

'Unless you're in High Command,' I said, 'and that lot don't seem to have the first idea about what's really going on.Queenie didn't leave a forwarding address, by any chance? Sorry. That was a stupid question.'

'Hah. Any envelope that comes addressed to her, I chuck on the fire.'

'I don't blame you.'

'Can't see what you saw in her. Nice young man like you.'

I wasn't so nice. And Queenie Green had been a very important part of my education, even though she had introduced me to a side of my character I did not particularly want to advertise.

'You deserve better.'

Oh yes, I thought to myself. Ethel's face swam into my mind.

'I think,' Mrs Carstairs said, 'that she might have got married. Can't remember his name. Nasty piece of work too, if you ask me.'

'Furlow?'

Mrs Carstairs gave me a long, hard look. 'Yes, that was it,' she said. 'Furlow.'

CHAPTER 29

Jack

Sometimes I rang Giesele's number, just to hear her voice. I always put the phone down when she answered. She must have known who it was, but she never called me back.

It was the sixties. You could do anything you liked, except, in my case, find the right woman. Tyler Cohen, my friend from film school, and I started our own company – Karma Films. God knows how we came up with that name but we had great plans to produce a feature film. Neither of us had a bean. I was on the National Assistance, collecting forty-one shillings a week from Brixton Labour Exchange. And Cohen's dad in Stockbridge, Massachusetts, was fed up with financing his draft-dodger son.

We hired out for the BBC as sound recordists from time to time, but never earned enough to fund two seconds of our own film.

It was Link who came to the rescue. It was his idea to talk to his dad about providing the finance for our film. I had proved I could be trusted when I had looked after that briefcase.

But nothing is for nothing. In return for old man Linklater's substantial capital investment in Karma, I was being asked to front a business operation I knew to be fraudulent.

'There is an element of risk in this, Kid,' Link said. 'I'd be lying if I pretended there wasn't. But, in the unlikely event the Old Bill does come knocking at your door, we will take care of you.'

'You mean I might go to prison?'

'We all might.' Link gave a crooked smile. 'But we also have plenty of bent coppers on our side.'

'What do I have to do?'

'Sit in a little office in Camberwell Green. Talk to a few people. Sign some papers. Doddle.'

Why did I agree? It wasn't out of greed, or because of unrequited love for a woman, any more than it was for my Uncle Wag when he made the decision to forge those documents and break the law. I saw a chance. And so I took it. I became a part of south London's most notorious Non-Ferrous Scrap Dealers' empire. Charlie Richardson may have been arrested the day England won the World Cup, but a long prison sentence failed to interrupt his business expansion. Charlie's brother Eddie was already inside along with his friendly enforcer, 'Mad' Frankie Fraser. They had been sent down after convictions for GBH in the so-called 'Torture Trials'. The Richardsons had held their own elaborate kangaroo court cases for anyone who crossed them. If the evidence wasn't going to plan, Fraser would use a pair of pliers to extract the accused's teeth, without anaesthetic. To obtain the right kind of confession, electrodes from an old wind-up battery were attached to the genitals of the man in the dock. Verdicts were rarely in doubt and sentences severe.

The business arteries of south London had become clogged with what the brothers called 'long firms'. The game plan was simple. A company would be set up and proceed to conduct normal business for a few months. Lines of credit would be established. 'Your job is to win the trust of the suppliers,' Link told me. 'You have the voice, the manner, Kid. I think we would like you to be handling top of the range – de luxe washing machines.' Link ignored my look of absolute horror. 'That kind of merchandise. At a certain moment, we stick in a very large order, sell the lot and disappear.'

'I just want to make films,' I said. To my father's distress, I had called the Home Office to say I had decided against taking up my position. Curiously, my first job would have been with Immigration and Prisons.

'Do you actually like what you do?' I asked Link.

He shrugged. 'I'm twenty-five years old. I have made more money in two years than my old man did after a quarter of a century of graft.'

Linklater Senior had erred only slightly from the straight and narrow during his time as a second-hand car dealer. It could have been a matter of adjusting the odd logbook or faulty speedometer. A hire purchase agreement might have needed the occasional adjustment. It was only around the beginning of the sixties that a substantial loss of market share encouraged him to throw in his lot with Charlie Richardson. And now HL was running the whole show, together with his number one son, my old friend.

'But what do you want to spend it on?' I asked. 'More cars? More babes? More drugs?'

I knew the late, unlamented George Cornell had kept Link well supplied with purple hearts, Dexedrine, uppers, downers and God knows what else. I wondered who his dealer was now.

Link shrugged. 'Who wants to live in the real world?' The expression on his face was one I should prefer to forget. It was that of a man who had maybe had a fleeting glimpse of paradise, only for it to be replaced by a hellscape created by Bosch, where mutilated corpses hung on torture wheels, hellfire raged and malevolent monsters stalked the earth.

CHAPTER 30

Wag

That morning, before the bombardment started, I picked a bunch of snowdrops.

It was good to be back. I don't think.

My horse Charlie was pleased to see me. He was the only one left from the original team. Somehow, Lieutenant Wainwright had survived too. Some people have the knack. He could have stood naked in a howitzer storm singing 'Roses Of Picardy', and remained unscathed.

August, September, October, November – nothing but rain. I got through Passchendaele somehow or other, and I met up with an old friend.

After sheltering in a pillbox captured from Jerry, our team was making its way across a wider than usual duckboard bridge. In the dank mist from the water's edge, stumps of blasted trees stretched to the horizon.

Someone should have spotted the enemy dugout. A whole bunch of greatcoated Fritzes in their metal helmets erupted before us like devils from the pit. We were taken completely by surprise. I saw Brewin, Brewer and Bulford go down. But not the fourth B for Bourton. I was immune to bombs and bullets. Somehow I grabbed one of the Jerry's rifles as we engaged and pulled the trigger. He hit the muddy water with a splash.

The action was bewildering. Crouching down, I fired my newly acquired Mauser into the melee. It was hard not to score a direct hit. Our Lee Enfield rifles were all right as far as they went, but they got clogged with mud and grit. The captured weapon I was using was more reliable, but it only had five bullets. I was done in a trice. When a screaming Jerry dervish ran at me with his bayonet, I shot him point-blank.

He fell on top of me, hot blood spouting from the hole in his face. It was not the most pleasant experience of my service career. A fusillade of bullets splintered the duckboard. Whose side they came from was anyone's guess. I detected a whiff of garlic sausage from the ruined mouth of my assailant as I rolled him off my body.

Shells exploded in the grey air above our heads. Hot burning metal hissed in the water and clattered on to the planks. 'Help me!' I heard one of our chaps shriek. But there was nothing I could do. I shot again at anyone in stone-grey serge. Then ran out of ammunition. If I came through this in one piece, I found myself reflecting, I should scavenge around the Hun corpses for some bullets.

At a crouch, I made a dash for a gap in the barbed wire. A number of my comrades were heading in that direction, so I presumed I wasn't running straight into the arms of Jerry. A man fell in front of me, clutching his left shoulder. Bending down, I grabbed hold of the bloke's right arm and dragged him to his feet. Another bullet hit him from the back, and his legs buckled. A strength you don't possess can appear in situations of mortal danger. I hauled my comrade on to my back and staggered onwards over the pitted mud until we toppled together into the safety of one of our trenches.

I was winded by the fall, but cushioned by the body of the man I had saved. His eyes flickered open. 'Thanks, mate,' he croaked.

'Well, look who it isn't,' I replied. 'Hello, Lockner, my old fellow apprentice. How's tricks? Seen Queenie lately?'

CHAPTER 31

Jack

'Take a seat, son.' 'Monkey' Rawlings had the raspingly rough voice of a navvy, who smoked a packet of cigarettes before coughing his way through breakfast. 'I've heard good things about you. So you're the Professor . . .'

Monkey Rawlings was not what you would call a snazzy dresser. His green and yellow check jacket was too big on the shoulders, and the open-neck white shirt looked as though it could do with a wash. Whoever cut Rawlings's dark, unkempt hair would not have been allowed scissor room near either of the slick Kray Brothers. He looked as though he had been dragged through a hedge backwards. I could hear my grandmother Beatrice saying that. Rawlings' eyebrows were wild. Curly black tendrils sprouted from his earlobes and nostrils.

The few villains I had encountered before, like Link's Uncle Sid, took exaggerated care with their appearance. The Krays, in particular, were considered to be a couple of poncey wankers, as interested in their tailors and cultivating showbiz connections as in extending their nefarious business empire.

All I knew about this man was that he took care of business when Link's dad was out of town. This was not, as I understood the invitation, supposed to be an interview, more a kind of getting-to-know-you session.

'We don't run a graduate trainee scheme here, you know,' Rawlings said.

If I hadn't been sure what direction this chat was going to take, I was now beginning to have a rough idea.

'You may think that we're just a bunch of diamond geezers here, but I can tell you, Jack' – I didn't like the way he emphasised my name – 'that we take our work extremely seriously. And we encourage our employees to do the same.'

The office, above a betting shop in Camberwell Green, revealed very little about the business of the occupant. On one sludgy cream wall, a rectangular spiral-bound calendar featured a red Lamborghini. That was it for décor.

'HL's boy assures me,' Rawlings continued, 'that you bring very special gifts to the table.'

'But you have your doubts,' I said.

Rawlings directed his icy gaze at me full blast. 'HL is in Monte Carlo at the moment, as you know.'

I didn't know.

'Before his unfortunate arrest, Charlie was moving us out of the basic scams. We made a packet out of the long firms and warehouse insurance, but people are getting wise to that stuff.'

I was beginning to wonder if the person who had invited me to join the company knew the whole range of the Richardson operation, or was this werewolf simply bullshitting me?

'Have you got a passport?'

'Of course.' In 1961, before I went up to Cambridge, I had spent seven months in Paris, thrilled to escape the serene sanctuary of Dulwich Village for a city where Algerian dissident paramilitaries were throwing grenades out of windows and exploding parked cars with plastiques.

'We have these connections in Cape Town . . .' Rawlings did not elucidate further.

'Do you mean smuggling diamonds in frozen fish?'

'Oh,' Rawlings said. 'So you do read the papers . . .'

We both knew perfectly well that this story had not been reported in the press. But Sylvia Pearce had confided in me once upon a time. I felt a twinge of regret about Sylvia, remembering how she and I had cackled in bed at the thought of Charlie Richardson's grandiose ambition to diversify overseas.

'Do you know anything about perlite?'

'It is what my mother taught me to be.'

He shot me a sharp look. 'You a comedian? We have interests in perlite mining. And have you heard of BOSS?'

'I wouldn't like them knocking at my front door.'

'I don't think they usually bother to knock.'

BOSS was apartheid South Africa's shadowy Secret Service.

The interrogation continued.

'Do you have any connections with the Metropolitan Police?'

'I reported a missing cat to them once.'

'It is of great importance to us to maintain the most cordial connections with Scotland Yard.' Rawlings picked at his ear and excavated some wax. 'You have an old school friend, George Curwin.'

'I would hardly call him a friend. He pulverised me once in a boxing match.'

'Well, Curwin is a rising star in the force. He is the sort of officer we would like to cultivate.'

Rawlings got to his feet. He was an enormous man. I noticed the hair on his knuckles, and reflected that I would not like to encounter him on a night when the moon was full. It was bad enough in the daylight.

'Can I offer you a drink?' He pointed to a full bottle of Johnnie Walker.

'No thanks,' I said.

'Good.' Rawlings wandered over to the window. 'I'm teetotal myself. Doesn't agree with me.'

I made an effort to smile.

'Yes,' he said. 'You might like to run into Curwin one day.

Have a bit of a chat. Maybe invite him to one of our clubs. The Reform at the Elephant and Castle. Introduce him to a few people . . .'

I was beginning to wish I had not refused that drink.

'You parlez français, don't you?' The way Rawlings's patter zigzagged around was disconcerting.

'I have spent some time in France.'

'So you can get by?'

What any of this had to do with becoming a front man for a long firm was a puzzle. It wasn't like the Civil Service interview, where I had been asked very specific questions about dock strikes and whether it made financial sense to keep large numbers of troops in foreign parts. I had studied my *New Statesman*, but was still inadequately prepared. For all the notes the board took, they must have paid as much attention to my answers as Monkey Rawlings did now. How else would I have been offered the job in the Home Office?

Rawlings returned to his seat and cracked his knuckles. 'Well, thanks for coming here today, Jack. Good of you to spare the time. We will talk again.'

He didn't seem to be interested in shaking hands and I was relieved to make my escape.

As I caught the Number 36 bus on the other side of the road, I looked back at the first-floor office. Monkey Rawlings was standing at the window. I couldn't tell if he was looking at me or staring into space. Either way, the menace in his stance made me shiver.

CHAPTER 32

Wag

On December 17th, 1917, somebody found two Christmas puddings at an abandoned Allied dump near Amiens. We couldn't wait until the 25th to eat them.

The local train station, wherever we were, was still functioning, but the church was in ruins. We'd received supplies, but no balm for the spirit – not that I ever believed in any of that stuff. Yet there was a lull in the fighting on Christmas Eve. We played football. I was stuck in goal, and froze my arse off waiting for the other side to kick the heavy leather ball in my direction.

A couple of officers from HQ pitched up to watch. There was nothing spectacular to applaud in our 12–3 victory against a team of peg-leg Frenchies, but the two English supporters clapped politely as we trudged off the uneven wasteland pitch.

'Nat!' I said in surprise to the tall young man in a captain's uniform. 'Is that really you?' Even with the neat Max Linder moustache, it was unmistakably my old friend Nat Devlin. The boy revolutionary. His steely grey eyes locked briefly on my face, then bored right through and out the other side.

There I stood, lowly Gunner W.C. Bourton, the Invisible Man, smile freezing on my lips.

'I say, old chap . . .' His accent had smartened up since our newt-hunting days on Tooting Bec. 'Fancy a snifter at the Mess?'

He wasn't talking to me but to his fellow officer.

They marched straight past me without another look towards the station, where the officers' living quarters were rather more luxurious than the Nissen huts where the rest of us cannon fodder hung out. But after months in earthen dugouts, none of us was complaining.

Years later, at Victoria Station, I encountered Nat Devlin again. As the train jerked forward in the direction of Brighton, I was nearly thrown into the laps of the couple opposite. I was about to apologise when I saw who it was.

There were only the three of us in the carriage. Devlin and the woman I assumed was his wife were travelling second class. She was neat and pretty, with a bow-shaped brooch on her grey two-piece suit. Costume jewellery, I observed. Devlin had exchanged his peaked cap for a brown trilby with a black band, boots for Church's brogues.

I looked him up and down.

Devlin shifted uncomfortably in his seat, staring out of the grimy window as we rattled across the Thames.

I continued to stare at him. Resolutely, he refused to catch my eye.

At Herne Hill, Mr and Mrs Devlin changed carriages.

'Arsehole,' I said, as my childhood friend was closing the door.

I shared my wodge of Christmas pudding with Bert Lockner. It had grown lukewarm by the time I located his bed in the sick bay he shared with eight other poor sods.

'Should have brought my other set of teeth,' he said, as he chewed his way through three spoonfuls. 'Thanks, mate. Where's the brandy butter?'

'I used it to glue the sole on my boot.'

'We could save the last bit for Jerry. At twenty paces, you could kill a man with this.'

'How's the shoulder?'

'They haven't sawn it off at least.'

I had to hold the plate for him to eat his Yuletide treat. Lockner's left arm was in a rough plaster cast.

'And your leg?'

'Still there, I think.' He demonstrated that both limbs were in working order under the sheets. 'Would you like to sign my arm?'

'I don't have a pen.'

'I say, Bourton . . .' Lockner looked as though he were about to deliver a deathbed confession. 'That hiding I gave you back in Soho. I hope you don't hold that against me. We're mates now, aren't we?'

I stared hard at my fellow apprentice from Thomas Sanders & Son. He wasn't having me on. He evidently believed that he had been the victor in that fight. I patted him on his good shoulder.

'Here, you finish it.' Lockner handed me the plate. 'For a while there, I thought this might be your revenge.'

Cold or not, hard as a cannonball, the pudding did remind me of Christmas at home, reminded me of carols, a warm fire, all the family gathered together. My darling Ethel. In a minute, Lockner and I would be pulling crackers and putting on paper crowns.

'What lies at the bottom of the ocean and shivers?' Lockner did his best to enter the spirit even without a motto to unfold.

'I give up.'

'You're not trying very hard. A nervous wreck.'

We both laughed. I laughed a lot. I laughed until I choked. Tears filled my eyes.

'It wasn't that funny,' Lockner said.

I laughed even more. At that moment, the whole sick bay started to rock with the helpless mirth of people who did not have the faintest idea what they were laughing about.

The shelling began again the following day.

CHAPTER 33

Jack

'Make way!' Uncle Wag cried. 'Make way! Make way for the Great Panjandrum!'

My happiest childhood memories are of Christmas at the Old Rectory.

I have a vision of my uncles Wag, Jago, Ted and Aubrey carrying Beatrice Leonora Bourton out of her bedroom on their shoulders in an embroidered campaign chair.

For a moment, I thought my grandmother was crying, but they were tears of happiness that rolled down her rouged cheeks.

Carefully, the three sons and one son-in-law lowered their treasured burden at the head of the long table. The silver cutlery sparkled on the starched white tablecloth. My own mother had contributed the holly and red berry centrepiece. Oliver and I, more of a hindrance than a help, had hung up the wreath on the studded oak front door of the rectory.

Because of the numbers, Christmas lunch was served spilling over from the dining room into the high-ceilinged hall.

Many celebrations and dramas were enacted in that entrance lobby. Those old walls absorbed the memories more deeply than the participants did. It is easy for human beings to jumble events together and contradict each other about what really took place.

On wobbly ladders, the men had hung lurid paper chains from one corner of the room to another. Aesthetically, especially with the addition of a riot of multicoloured baubles, the decorations were probably over the top. But for a small boy, they spelled magic.

Until my Uncle Wag explained the origins of the expression some years later, I was under the impression that the 'Great Panjandrum' was a turbaned Eastern potentate. Such a character could have played a leading role in a comic opera by Gilbert and Sullivan. In fact, Wag told me, the name was used to describe a massive explosive-laden weapon designed by the British military, but never used in battle during the Second World War.

The front door opened, introducing a gust of cold air and Auntie Florence, arms laden with bags. There was no way my mother's sister could ever avoid making an entrance. 'Sorry, darlings.' All the bags fell on the floor at once, spilling a mass of parcels. Helping her pick them up, I smelled the sweet scent of gin on her breath.

Auntie Rose emerged, pink and sweating, from a door that led down to the kitchen. Her pinned-up hair was hidden by a silk scarf. Flour and gravy stains smudged the yellow and red daisy design on her apron. 'I need a drink,' she cried. 'It's like an inferno down there.'

'Cocktail, champers, pale ale?' Uncle Aubrey appeared at her side like the most attentive sommelier.

'I could murder a port and Guinness.'

Aubrey grimaced.

Fresh from draining the blood of a bat at his satanic altar, Luke appeared at the top of the stairs.

'The Prince of Darkness,' whispered Oliver.

For all his bravado, I knew my cousin too was afraid of Jago's strange son. But there was nothing weird about his sister Nancy. She was busy, putting the finishing touches to the table with the addition of water glasses and the place names she had written out carefully with her new ballpoint pen.

Uncle Wag made sure Grandmama had a champagne cocktail – always her preferred tipple before the Christmas dinner was carried in. Oliver and I were given our special glasses – the last two remaining from the original set of ten – embossed with red-combed cockerels. There might have been a dribble of sweet vermouth at the bottom of our drinks, but the main ingredient was R. White's Fizzy Lemonade.

'I'm putting you next to me,' Uncle Wag said. 'Is that all right?'

'Thanks,' I said. Wag always made an effort to talk to me, and sometimes helped out when I couldn't finish the meal on my plate. It didn't seem to matter how much food he ate, my uncle never put on weight.

'It was the war,' my mother used to say, as if that explained everything.

Immaculate in a crisp white blouse and navy blue skirt, Aunt Ethel circulated with the smoked salmon on brown bread and butter and the jellied eels. It took me years to acquire the taste for fish. Smoked haddock haunts me still. During a long period of my childhood, sick successively with scarlet fever, whooping cough and measles, haddock was one of the few things I could bear to eat. I could not force it past my lips now if you stuck electrodes to my genitals.

Jellied eels I have never mastered either. It was a tradition at the Bourton Christmas to serve them as a starter. Smoked eel with a smear of horseradish sauce I can handle, but the thought of cold, gelatinous chopped eel boiled in vinegar can still make me heave.

'Close your eyes and think of England,' Uncle Wag advised, the first time I was required to participate in the ritual.

At the top of Electric Avenue in Brixton, before the High

Road and the big department store Bon Marché opposite, the last of the market stalls specialised in cockles, whelks and live eels. You placed your order and the fishmonger cut up the slowly writhing creatures before your eyes. I was repelled and fascinated.

'After I got back from France,' I remember Wag telling me, 'I became obsessed with eels. The extraordinary journey they make from the Sargasso Sea across land and water all the way to Electric Avenue. Like me, they are survivors.'

To end up chopped into pieces on a fishmonger's stall, I thought, unable to follow my Uncle Wag's train of thought.

A case study would probably have revealed that, apart from Wag himself plus his inscrutable brother Ted and the reliably game Jago, there weren't many takers, and quite a lot of jellied eel got chucked away. The only other person I ever saw try a taste was Ethel, perhaps as a loyal tribute to her brother because he had survived the war and retained a superstitious taste for this not very Christmassy dish.

It was Ethel who made sure that the younger generation was not neglected. Sausages roasted in honey and mustard were a standby treat for Oliver and me. 'Don't spoil your appetite,' Ethel warned as my cousin and I enjoyed three in succession and sucked the stickiness off our fingers. There was no danger of that. The glistening roast never arrived on the table before three o'clock. And when I say roast, I mean roasts – a turkey, a goose and a joint of sirloin, just to be on the safe side.

Uncle Aubrey opened another bottle of champagne with a loud pop. Rose clapped her hands. 'Back to the front,' she said, making sure she took a refill with her to the kitchen.

'I'm on my way,' said Ethel. 'Reinforcements.' Ethel didn't do jokes. That was as near as I heard her get.

'Come and talk to your Grandmama.' Beatrice's regal manner was intimidating. I sat down beside her. 'Tell me about school,' she said.

My mind went blank.

'What are you studying?'

'Vertebrates.' I shuddered at the memory of an end of term class with a biology teacher of cadaverous appearance called Cridland – known to all of us as the Dreaded Crid. I had not been concentrating on his endless drone, until I realised he was pointing a finger at me.

'Armitage! Wake up, boy!' he shouted.

I stared at his vulture's beak of a nose.

'Perhaps you would like to tell the class if you include yourself among the vertebrates?'

'I'm not entirely sure, sir.'

This response provoked a general snigger.

'Would you say that you were spineless, Armitage?'

I was lost. After that Cridland wasted no opportunity to make me the butt of his pedantic jokes.

Later, I made sure to bone up (you see how catching bad puns can be) on the subject. I vowed not to be caught out and humiliated again.

Behind me, Oliver was playing with his yo-yo. One elaborate flick knocked over my special cocktail glass, which shattered on the floor.

'Oh no,' cried his mother, kneeling down immediately to scoop up the pieces. 'I'm so sorry.'

'Be careful, Connie,' said Grandmama. 'You'll cut yourself.'

Florence scuttled off for a dustpan and brush.

'It doesn't matter, darling. I never liked those wretched cockerels anyway. These things happen.'

'Sorry, Gran.' Oliver looked mortified. 'I didn't mean to.'

'I know you didn't. Now then, we need to find another special glass for Jack.'

It was part of the Christmas ritual that the three youngest cleared the table. Everyone was supposed to do their bit. Although most of the Doulton plates contained only a few remnants of the turkey, goose and beef, the crispy roast potatoes, sprouts and peas, there were congealed lumps of parsley and thyme stuffing, bread sauce and smears of cranberry to scoop into the waste bin, before stacking the plates by the side of the sink in the scullery for Ted and Wag to do the washing-up later.

Luke didn't lift a finger. I assume, at sixteen the oldest of the cousins present, that he felt he was too old and that the task itself was demeaning to a devotee of Aleister Crowley. In retrospect, I'm surprised that the Grand Panjandrum did not insist that Luke participate. Nor was it ever expected that my dad do anything to help, except sing some of the old songs later. He had been brought up by his mother to expect women to wait on him hand and foot and my mother seemed content to carry on the tradition.

The following day, we were due to visit my other, paternal, grandmother in Cricklade Avenue for Boxing Day. I cannot say I ever looked forward to it. Nan, as she liked to be called, was a competent cook. For the four of us – my father was an only child – we always had a huge joint of ham, with mash and parsnips. Perfectly edible, but there was never any sense of the kind of joyous excess we experienced at the Old Rectory.

On top of the stove at the rectory, a portable metal baby bath kept at least four home-made Christmas puddings simmering in warm water.

When Wag and Jago set light to the brandy and carried in

the pudding with the blue flame licking around the serving bowls, we, who were about to receive, saluted it with clapping and cheering. Nothing particularly special happened that day. But our whole family was together. Christmas was simply the happiest time of my year.

CHAPTER 34

Wag

It wasn't easy to find the right materials to do the kinds of job that Lieutenant Wainwright asked me to do for him. I didn't ask what he wanted with all those forged papers. It wasn't my business. I took the money. I kept my hand in. I also kept records in a secret code. But I did wonder if he was running quite a little business selling unauthorised leave to those who had the money to buy it.

I didn't want any special favours from my officer. I didn't dodge the action. The longer the war continued, the more confident I felt that I would make it home in one piece.

When we found an old printing press and all sorts of equipment in the basement of a bombed-out newspaper office in some shithole town near Ypres, you would have thought it was Wainwright's birthday. He literally rubbed his hands together. 'As soon as we get back to Blighty, Bourton, I think we should set up a little business together. I have a lot of contacts, and you, Gunner, are the cleverest fellow I have met in my whole life.'

Whether any of the other chaps had a clue what we got up to, I don't know. I was careful. And Wainwright made sure I had the opportunity to work in his billet, whenever we were lucky enough to have a roof over our heads and something better than a flickering candle for light. Maybe people thought I was his bum boy. Such speculation didn't bother me one way or the other.

On a dew-soaked July morning, I found myself well behind

the front line and took my new horse Charlie for a ride. Fancying myself as a country gent, I spurred him to chase a fox. After a mile or so through beech woods, the animal gave us the slip. The big guns and shells had not devastated this little paradise yet. I wandered into a walled garden, and hitched Charlie to a plum tree by an asparagus bed that had gone to seed.

I stroked Charlie's muzzle and talked to him about nothing in particular. His ears flapped backwards and forwards. It is vital to strike up a relationship with your horse. He is more important than any of your human comrades. Charlie was a handsome beast, with a black coat and a shiver of white lightning on his forehead. During the few days we were not fighting or trudging to a new irrelevant position, I made sure he was combed and as glossy as a horse could be. He would never replace Shrapnel in my affections, but I tried hard not to let on.

I sat down on a bench and contemplated life. Not really. I have never been one for profound meditation on the state of the universe. I hadn't informed Charlie, but I knew we existed in pure hell. He wouldn't have argued with that.

A white dove fluttered down and bobbed round in the long grass. It was so peaceful. Maybe I had been gassed and didn't realise it. I saw a wooden cross with my name and initials on it. I swear to you this is true. A slight breeze rustled the branches of the trees then all was still.

At the sound of a door opening, the dove flew away.

A young, fair-haired woman walked out of the house, carrying a glass of water. She smiled as she handed it to me. 'Anglais?' she asked.

'Nicht Allemand,' I replied. The water was cool and refreshing. 'Thank you,' I said. 'Merci.'

'Qu'est-ce que vous faites ici?'

We had reached the limits of my vocabulary.

She extended a hand and led me inside. A loaf of brown bread lay on the kitchen table next to a slab of cheese. 'Vous avez faim?'

It was no good. I couldn't understand or speak the lingo.

She was very pretty, with freckles under her cornflower eyes.

I put down the glass on the table.

As if it were the most natural thing in the world, she kissed me gently on the lips.

I was aware of the heavy scrape of my boots on the uncarpeted stairs as I followed her up to her bedroom.

Without a word, she undressed, and I did the same.

I was back in camp by 0900 hours. That was well within the curfew set by Lieutenant Wainwright. I spent the rest of the morning working in the stables with the other two members of our gun team. We didn't have much to say to each other. The smell of the straw and the horses was sweet.

I can tell you now that that was the only day in the whole bloody campaign, maybe in my whole life, that I didn't think about Ethel.

CHAPTER 35

Jack

'Je ne comprends pas, monsieur.' The attractive young hotel receptionist looked embarrassed to be asking the question. 'Qu'est-ce que ça veut dire – ce "Bonegrinder"?'

This was what my partner in Karma Films, Tyler Cohen, had scribbled on his registration form in the space marked 'Profession'.

Before my three-year sentence to the penal institution of Cambridge, I had spent seven months in Paris. I still spoke good French. It was testing, nevertheless, to translate 'Bonegrinder'. I couldn't manage the answer without laughing. Tyler, whose grasp of the language was college standard, started to laugh too. I felt the kind of hysteria I used to experience in class when McPherson managed to find that extended sequence in the Bible when the words 'an eunuch' were repeated every other line. Tears filled my eyes and my voice became strangulated.

'Et vous êtes "Impresario"?'

Well, sort of. Tyler and I were in Monte Carlo to scout locations for our film and to discuss a possible script with Link's dad. He was still holed up in the principality, in the Hôtel de Paris next to the Casino.

In the end, even the receptionist had the good grace to join in the laughter. She made the executive decision to abandon sense in favour of having our bags taken upstairs.

In our recently acquired company car, a Vauxhall Estate leased at a knockdown rate from the Linklater garage, Tyler had undertaken the lion's share of the driving. We had booked in at the Hôtel Terminus de Nice in Monte Carlo, which offered the most reasonable prices for a week's stay. Conscious of the fact we were earning no money yet, Tyler and I agreed that we could not afford two rooms.

At Film School, students and teachers had been wary of my sharp-tongued Harvard-educated friend. He wasn't interested in politeness or small talk. It wasn't as though we knew everything. Neither of us objected to being shown how to load and operate a camera, or how to splice film. However, when our teacher started giving instructions on how to audition actors and suggested that the first question should always be, 'What would you say is your forte?' Tyler suggested that he could manage without any more advice, thank you.

'But I'm your tutor,' came the reply.

'So why don't you toot off?' said Tyler.

But Tyler and I simply got on well. We shared a double room in Grenoble on the way down. He didn't snuffle, snore, speak in his sleep, and we each kept to our side of the bed.

In Monte Carlo we had two singles, two armchairs and one desk. No problem.

'I have to abandon you,' I said when we had unpacked. 'Sorry about that. I've got a hot dinner date with Linklater.'

'All right for some.'

My partner knew I had a private business arrangement with our primary financial sponsor and didn't ask any probing questions. What he didn't know was that I had gone through customs carrying a bag with a false bottom stuffed with £20,000 in used notes. Monkey Rawlings had supplied me with the carefully aged leather hold-all.

While Cohen was in the bathroom, I transferred the money into an old blue duffel bag.

'See you later.' I banged on the door.

'Don't worry about me, Jack.' It was our special catchphrase.

It was a leisurely stroll down towards the port. The bag on my shoulder made me look like a hitchhiker, but I was wearing a decent, slightly crumpled suit and tie. No one refused me entry at the elegant Belle Époque hotel where HL was staying.

This was not the first time I had visited Monaco. For a period after Paris, I had a girlfriend in Grasse, in the hills behind Cannes: Geneviève. I idly considered looking her up this time, but the affair had not ended well. The Côte d'Azur was familiar to me, still glorious before the Croisette became jammed with hookers and cars, before that most gracious, uniquely beautiful coast was turned into a honky-tonk.

'Ah, Monsieur Armitage. Suivez-moi, s'il vous plaît.'

It was not necessary for the maître d' to show me to my host's table. There was only one man in the dining room, in the far corner, sitting by the window.

HL stood as I approached, and we shook hands.

'Un apéritif pour monsieur?'

I could see HL was having a Bloody Mary.

'La même chose,' I said. 'S'il vous plaît.'

'Et une bouteille de Puligny-Montrachet soixante-un.' I had assumed that Link's father spoke no French, but Humphrey Linklater's French accent was better than his English one. 'Where on earth did you find that terrible bag?' he asked me.

'It's all there,' I said.

In those last days of the sixties, capital controls were still in operation in Britain. At one time, as I recall, you could only legally take fifty quid out of the country at any one time.

'You're a cool customer, Jack. Good lad.'

My Bloody Mary arrived and we raised our glasses to a successful operation.

'I'll slip the evidence upstairs.' HL rose to his feet. He

made no concessions to Mediterranean style. He still sported the three-piece suit. Grey worsted this cool February evening. Better quality, I observed, than he used to wear. 'I have a safe in my room. Don't trust the management.'

An elderly couple were shown to a corner window table at the other end of the restaurant, but the grey, flamingo-like woman complained about a draught, and they were moved to a more central position.

'See anything you fancy on the menu?' HL said when he returned. 'The lobster is good.'

I was still in cheap independent mode, and, as soon as I spotted the price, had scanned further down the menu.

'If you like it, have it.'

'Lobster it is, then,' I said.

The bottle was uncorked. Linklater Senior took a single sniff and pronounced the wine excellent without testing any further. 'We will have it later,' he added in French.

'Anything to start?'

'No, thanks.'

The waiter took the order and we finished our apéritifs.

'So where are we with the film?' HL asked.

'Nowhere really.'

'Script?'

'Outline only. This chap, bit of a loser, has to deliver a package to a place in the south of France. Doesn't know what's inside, or what the game is . . .'

'Sounds familiar.'

'Beautiful locations.'

'I'm thinking of moving out here permanently,' HL said. 'Time I did something a bit different. Rawlings is a safe pair of hands. I don't have to breathe down his neck. And my boy's no slouch either. The problem is the missus. She can't speak the language. I bought her this Linguaphone set, even hired a personal tutor. She can't get her brain round it. Clever woman, my wife. Funny, though. When it comes to foreign, she just goes into a tizz. I don't get it. I like it out here. Beats Streatham any day. It's all going downhill there now anyway. But Mel says she doesn't want to leave her friends and family. I tell you, I wouldn't mind if I never saw any of them again.'

In all the years I had known him, this was the longest speech Link's father had ever made.

'When did you learn French?' I asked.

'During the war,' he replied. 'I was in Chartres under cover with the Resistance . . .'

I tried to hide my surprise at this revelation.

The lobster arrived, and we were both offered bibs. When HL accepted, I followed suit. Just as well – as I cracked my first claw, hot, buttery juice squirted on to my chest.

'Dangerous work, this.' HL smiled, as he secured a sliver of succulent white flesh with the two-pronged fork.

For some reason, I found myself thinking of Mad Frankie Fraser extracting a gangland victim's tooth with a pair of pliers. I didn't let that ruin my appetite.

'Script needs a bit of work then,' HL said.

'We haven't got started yet. It'll come.' I spoke with a confidence I didn't feel. Tyler and I were a couple of amateurs who had got lucky. In our dreams we would be making a multimillion-dollar epic about the great explorer, linguist and pornographer Sir Richard Burton – in exotic locations with a cast of thousands. Here we were, however, in Monte Carlo, producing a movie to order. A sort of vanity project for Linklater Senior. But it was a start. We were not being obliged to work our way up from the floor. We would give HL what he wanted: a distraction from the cares of crime.

'Have you been to Eze?' my business partner and patron asked. He looked vaguely embarrassed. 'Could be a good location . . .'

Years ago, Eze used to be a fortified stronghold under the jurisdiction of the House of Savoy. It was more famous now for the *jardin botanique*, a collection of cacti and panoramic views.

'Villefranche too. I like it there.' HL was getting into his stride now. 'Marvellous round the port.'

I took another glug of wine.

'Young Cohen,' HL said. 'He know anything about . . .?'

I shook my head.

'Good lad.' It was the second time he had said that.

'Excellent wine.'

'Glad you like it.' HL signalled for another bottle. 'You work hard all your life. There comes a time when you want to appreciate the good things. The air down here suits me. And the tax situation does have very considerable advantages. Did you know that there is a branch of the Grimaldi family in England who believe they have more right to the throne than Rainier?'

HL was revealing sides to his character I had never suspected.

'And how's my boy?'

'Haven't seen him lately.' The truth was that the last time I ran into Link, he was completely off his tits on drugs.

'I worry about him.'

I wondered if my dad ever worried about me . . . Not much, I suspected. He was obsessed with his salerooms and outwitting the antique dealers' ring. My mother, on the other hand, wore a look of perpetual anxiety, especially since I had moved out of home. However, she never asked me any searching questions about how I could afford my new flat in Notting Hill, which I was sharing with Cohen, courtesy of Karma Films. You know in life what you wish to know.

'He's not interested in the cinema. Don't know what he is interested in.' HL was still musing about his son. 'Money. I suppose he takes after his old dad. My fault.'

A few more people had reduced the sepulchral hush of the large dining room. I don't suppose anyone there was under fifty. Many would be popping round to the Casino afterwards. Before the war, that elegant building had entertained an equally elegant clientele. But now it catered to a more common sort. I wasn't too impressed the only time I had tried my hand there at roulette. A lot of Italians in shiny mohair suits were chucking their money around. I lost the stake I arrived with, then cleared off. That was in the days when I was hanging out with Geneviève, who worked in a parfumerie near Grasse. One weekend she had introduced me to her friends in Monte Carlo as her fiancé. Our days were numbered after that. I preferred her sister anyway – Martine – but she didn't look at me twice.

'You must have the crêpes Suzette,' HL said. 'They're better than the ones they do at Verrey's.'

Did he imagine that his son's old school friend indulged in fine dining on a regular basis? Or was he just showing off?

It was like a conjuring trick. Flames, posh pancake, smart service. The taste wasn't bad either. And the Puligny-Montrachet was going down a treat. I could get used to this.

'Would you like to come with us tomorrow?' I kept my fingers crossed under the table.

'Can't manage that, I regret,' HL said. 'Couple of things I need to attend to. Now I have that cash. Maybe the day after tomorrow. There're a few places I should like to show you. What do you make of Rawlings?'

'Monkey? Wouldn't like to bump into him on a dark night.'

HL smiled. 'He's a tough cookie. Clever though. Cleverer than Charlie probably.'

'But not Eddie,' I almost said, though what did I know? I had never met either of them. In the photos I had seen in the papers, the younger Richardson brother looked like a regulation thug.

'Charlie is a force of nature.'

We had a grappa each. 'Cauterises the wounds,' HL said. 'Just the one. Always does the trick, if you have had a few.'

I felt pleasantly woozy.

'If you could have any car in the world, what would you choose?' HL asked out of the blue.

'An Hispano-Suiza.'

My host and patron downed the last of his grappa. 'The V-12 or the HS-9?'

'The Dubonnet Xenia.'

'You're pulling my leg . . .'

'I know nothing at all about cars,' I confessed.

'Goering had two, you know,' HL said.

'And Hitler only had one,' I joked. 'More than Goebbels. He had no balls at all. One day I'd like to hear more about your war.'

'One day maybe I'll tell you.'

We shook hands after a coffee in a cosy little bar, where the ancient pianist played some anodyne contemporary standards interspersed with the occasional melody from yesteryear. 'Thank you very much, sir, for a most enjoyable supper,' I said.

'We will do it again.'

'I'd like that.'

'Bring Cohen if you like.'

'He'd like that.'

'There might just be another little job I need you to do.' HL escorted me to the lobby with its extravagant, domed stained-glass ceiling. A fat man, with a chihuahua under his arm, was shouting the odds with a hotel porter. 'You should come out again for the Grand Prix in May.'

'Absolutely, if it fits in with our shooting schedule.'

A uniformed commissionaire opened the door for me and touched his peaked cap.

'You need a cab?' HL asked.

'No thanks. I'll walk.'

We shook hands again.

High on its ridge, the lights of the ancient Grimaldi palace glittered above the harbour. I wondered if Princess Grace was at home. And I wondered what on earth I was doing out here.

CHAPTER 36

Wag

We had run out of ammunition.

The enemy had no such problems. I don't remember being on the receiving end of such a severe pounding before. Dank earth, smoke, gunpowder and the overpowering stench of blood clogged my nostrils. The noise filled my head. It was impossible to imagine a time when the revolving world was not juddering from an endless series of explosions. God knows what Charlie and those other poor horses were making of it.

At Verdun in one day, 7,000 horses were killed by long-range shelling on both sides, including ninety-seven destroyed by a single shot from a French naval gun. It was as well we did not know such things at the time. Ignorance can help keep a man sane.

It was Porchester who spotted the grey-green cloud of gas, seconds before his head was blown off.

'Just as well it wasn't phosgene.' Nurse Webster had a soft spot for me.

'Just as well I had a mask.' It hurt to laugh.

And the wind had changed direction at the last moment, after Jerry opened his canisters of chlorine.

'Just as well I never took up smoking,' I said.

'Good strong lungs.' Nurse Webster never told me her first name. She had curly black hair, although I only saw her once without her nurse's hat. I remember her twenty-eighth birthday. We had tea and cake in the ward.

My lungs were damaged. I would never run the mile now, nor would I return to the front. You would not hear me complaining about either. I felt lucky to be alive. And to be out of there for good.

After a week in Nell Lane Hospital, Manchester, I had been moved to a big convalescence home in Northenden. My skin and vision improved rapidly. I dropped a line to Nurse Webster and promised to come and visit her. She was nice. She liked me. She wrote back and signed the letter Maggie with an X beside it. But I didn't fulfil my promise. I was fixed on getting home. And seeing Ethel again.

When I finally got there, to my disappointment, Ethel wasn't there to greet me. She was still doing her duty in a hospital in Yorkshire. I received quite a welcome from the rest of the family. But for all the tears and all the laughter, a sense of unease permeated the house.

The sights and smells of London were a distraction: the organ grinder and his monkey, the muffin man balancing his tray on his head, the sheer joyous bustle of the city after the grisly remorselessness of daily horror in France. The absence of danger made it easier to sleep at night. Yet memories of Charlie and all those poor horses that I had seen suffocating in the mud haunted me. And the image of Porchester, blood spouting from his headless torso, tormented me in waking dreams.

I wondered if Lockner had made it home. The bullet wounds he had received were bad, but I feared it was the Christmas pudding that could have done for him.

It was clear there was something they weren't telling me. The day the Armistice was signed, my mother finally came out with it. 'Ethel's engaged.'

It felt like a mortal blow. I coughed behind my hand and tried to catch my breath.

'Who to?'

'A doctor. Cornish. Walter Cornish.' It sounded as though Mum was reading from his CV. 'Seems like a decent fellow. Well spoken.'

'Funny, she never told me about him in her letters.' There was no regular Royal Mail delivery service where I had been but occasional letters from the family did arrive from time to time in grimy, crumpled envelopes. Ethel had been my most faithful correspondent. I was never much of a writer myself. I hadn't seen her since I'd arrived back in Blighty. The news of her engagement hit me like another dose of gas.

Florence sensed my distress and did her best to cheer me up. Together, we bought my first demob suit for £7 at Newman's the tailor in Coldharbour Lane. 'Laurie gets all his stuff made here.' My outfit came straight off a dummy in the window. The trousers were a bit long. 'I'll take them up for you, darling,' Florence said.

'Who is this Laurie fellow?'

'Oh, just someone I know. Fantastically talented.'

The next time I would buy a new suit, it was made to measure in Savile Row. With the money I had littered around the place, I could have dressed like Burlington Bertie. But I wasn't letting on to anyone just yet how well-heeled I was.

Modestly dressed, I reported back for duty at Thomas Sanders & Sons in Wardour Street. Mr Edward gave me my old job back, and increased my salary by a couple of shillings a week. They were hard up for experienced male staff. Lockner, I discovered, would not be rejoining the firm. Apparently, he made it all the way to the second Battle of the Marne, where a surprise Allied victory turned the tide of the war. But Lockner was one of the many who lost their lives.

I really liked being back at work there. It took my mind off things – like a certain person's impending marriage.

Ethel was working in a private hospital in Whitby. Not a place I had ever visited. With that Cornish fellow, apparently. Eventually, I did receive a letter from her. It had been written while I was still on the other side of the Channel and had been redirected from France via Manchester before it finally reached me at home.

My beloved brother,

I have missed you most terribly. It has been a nightmare not knowing if you were alive or dead. The news you read in the papers does not tell the half of it, I know. And the stories you hear from people who have been over there, you would rather not hear.

I can't tell you how lonely I have been.

I like my job, though. We have to work long hours, but it is worth it. And they do a marvellous fish and chips down by the port. I don't suppose you have had a battered haddock for a good long while. Or your favourite jellied eels. I never cared for the taste of them much myself, as you may remember.

You will have heard by now about Walter. I should have preferred to tell you myself, face to face. But I am stuck up here in the frozen north.

He is a good man. Kind and generous. And I think he will make a good husband.

You know how I feel about you, Wag. Please understand why I have said yes to Walter's proposal.

Your loving sister,

Ethel

CHAPTER 37

Jack

It wasn't anywhere near as famous as the Thomas à Becket in the Old Kent Road, where England's greatest heavyweight Henry Cooper trained in the boxing ring upstairs, but a number of useful fighters worked up a sweat in a back room of the Perseverance off Camberwell Grove.

The smell from the urinals in the Gents was pungent. Perhaps it was down to all that testosterone. Monkey Rawlings had just beckoned me in to show me a small handgun taped to the inside of an old flushing cistern in the second stall, the only one that had a lavatory with an unbroken seat. 'Just so you know it's there, Jack.'

Apparently there were a few other firearm stashes in various clubs and pubs around town, in the unlikely event that Rawlings or whoever would be the last man standing, ready to shoot his way out of trouble.

How had I come to this? I didn't know who I was any more. Was I a film producer, making a film about French gangsters to rival the Nouvelle Vague movies I so admired? Or was I really here as a lackey of the notorious and all-too-real Richardson gang?

'Didn't think much to that new bloke, did you? Powder puff.' Rawlings was referring to a not so young tearaway called Eric Waterman. I had known him, from a distance, in my Upper Norwood days. El went to the local primary, Rockmount, and was admired for his skill with an air rifle as well as with his fists. He had shot out every street light on the Northfield estate where he lived.

He was a relatively new recruit to the Richardson empire. Waterman had had his successes as an amateur middleweight and had even managed an interview with Our 'Enery's manager, Jim 'the Bishop' Wicks. Now Eric's minders reckoned he might still make them a few bob on the professional circuit – not the legitimate kind, not at Earl's Court nor the National Sporting Club, but in garages and derelict office blocks. With bare knuckles.

'He's past it,' Rawlings said while washing his hands. 'Could be useful handling a little local difficulty, but I wouldn't stake any dosh on him. It's that jab. Look.' He held up his big right hand, palm open. 'Hit me there.'

I popped him with a tentative left.

'Harder than that.'

I tried.

'Better,' he said. 'For a little bloke. Here, let me show you.'

I held up my right hand. His left hand snuck out and hit me twice in succession. The blows stung.

'The looser you clench your fist, the quicker the punch.'

He hit me again. That one really hurt. 'See. That's what you have to do. The tight fist does the damage. You turn it at the last moment . . .' – he demonstrated in mid-air – 'when you bang them on the jaw.'

The lavatory door opened behind him. If the bloke was desperate for a pee, having considered the scene, he decided to hold it until later. He beat a hasty retreat.

Rawlings and HL seemed to have other plans for me than as a bare-knuckle fighter. But since Link had suggested the idea of my fronting a long firm, there had been no further mention of the subject. Instead, I had been used by his father's outfit as a currency mule, and that was about it. 'We want you to make another trip to Monte Carlo shortly.' Rawlings hadn't given me a precise date, but it looked as though it might coincide with our plan to get Karma Films' first film on the road. Tyler and I were producing a 'short', as a sort of calling card, to send round festivals to show how young and talented we were. Perhaps, I swanked, we could even get the movie into the cinemas as a supporting feature. It was all pie in the sky. But HL was happy. And he was paying.

Monkey Rawlings was less happy with me.

'What have you done about finding that old school mate of yours, Curwin? I haven't seen the two of you hanging out yet.'

'I'll see what I can do,' I said. But I had no intention of putting myself out for Monkey.

The script for our short was not much more elaborate than the one I had first outlined in Monte Carlo, but it had some good jokes, an attempt at mystery and two actors who were prepared to accept a modest salary for a week in the south of France.

Though I say it myself, I had demonstrated a genuine talent for organisation. I secured a deal to use the facilities of a local studio, la Victorine, a couple of French soundmen, a script girl of a certain age, and a production manager called Bernard.

We had not made an auspicious debut at Studios la Victorine. HL had driven us to the gates in the hills above Nice Airport. 'Sorry, lads,' he said. 'I can't come with you. Er . . .'

'Pressure of work?' Cohen used one of our all-purpose catchphrases for any occasion.

We got out of HL's Citroën DS, feeling like a couple of prats, and walked towards the gates.

The guard there eyed us with suspicion and asked if we had an appointment. We tried to bluff our way in, but he firmly barred our way.

We ambled about outside the gates for a bit then I said, 'We can't do this. Let's go.'

It took us about an hour to walk back down to Nice Airport. From a telephone booth near Departures I called the Victorine, was put through immediately to the studio manager, Antoine Arnaud, and arranged a meeting for the following day. Don't ask me why we didn't do things properly the first time round.

When Monsieur Arnaud escorted us round the standing set that had been used for François Truffaut's *Day for Night* I was dazzled and felt the magic must be rubbing off on me. Carné's *Les Enfants du Paradis* had also been made there during the German occupation. Many of the 1,800 extras had been Resistance agents using the film as daytime cover. I wondered if HL knew about that.

Bernard the production manager found the most extraordinary location for our main interior work.

In the foothills behind Nice stood a ruined Moorish mansion, once the property of the extended Grimaldi family. From the peeling walls, portraits of resplendent aristocrats stared disdainfully at common visitors. The house was owned by an eighty-year-old antiquarian called Madame Emmenot. She had thin, self-dyed orange hair and wore dark glasses day and night. One of the lenses was cracked. She pinched our soundman's Gauloises whenever she had the chance. 'Regardez-moi ça,' she said to me when I did the initial reconnoitre with the suave, leather-jacketed Bernard. 'C'est un Titian.' From underneath a Madame Récamier-style chaise longue, she dragged out the picture of a voluptuous young woman, swathed in richly coloured drapes.

Then she pulled out the bottom drawer of her Louis XVI writing desk, and waved an uncut emerald in my face.

'Why doesn't she sell them?' I asked my production manager.

He shrugged his shoulders and made that pouting 'pfoof' noise, used exclusively by the French.

'Vous savez, monsieur,' said Madame Emmenot, 'qu'Hitler himself came 'ere. They accused me of being a collaboratrice. What could I do? Une femme on her own?'

Apart from the cigarettes, she was happy to take our generous offer for the location work, and to tuck into the packed lunches prepared by the studio.

One morning we lost a whole day's shooting.

'Monsieur Jacques!' Our antiquarian hostess was distraught. 'On m'a volé. Mon émeraude. It was right here!'

I got down on hands and knees and poked around for her emerald in the dust underneath the chaise longue in her living room, with a disapproving-looking Grimaldi the silent witness on the wall.

'Are you sure you didn't put it somewhere else?' I won't do the whole sequence in French.

'It was him.' Madame Emmenot pointed at HL, who had just arrived to check, as he liked to, on our daily progress. 'I don't like him. I don't like his face. He did it. I'm calling the police.'

I caught a glimpse of the hard man behind HL's bland features. 'I wouldn't do that if I were you, madame,' he said firmly. He sounded so much more convincing in French than he did in his own tongue.

'Thief!' cried Madame Emmenot, slapping HL on his plump belly.

'I assure you, madame, there has been some mistake.' Humphrey Linklater kept his temper. 'And you're the one who is making it. Now let us be calm and go over the facts.'

'You have stolen my emerald.' Madame Emmenot jabbed

her finger at him. 'You are a thief. I see it in your face.' She was panting now and I worried she might have some kind of seizure. 'You think I am a silly old woman, but I know a thief when I see one. Thief! Thief!'

The studio's French sound recordists were looking on sheepishly.

'This won't take a minute,' I said. 'Why don't you go off and have a coffee?' There was a café nearby and nobody liked going into the old lady's filthy kitchen any more than they did to her antiquated lavatory.

'Please sit down, madame,' I said, taking her wrinkled hand in mine and guiding her to a tapestry-covered wing-backed armchair. 'I'm sure your emerald is here. And we will find it.'

Tyler came in from the Victorine. 'Any luck?'

'Tell everyone to go home,' I said. The shoot we had planned for today involved the participation of Madame Emmenot. She and I had rehearsed the lines for her brief dialogue sequence with our hero, and she was word-perfect. But there was no way I was going to be able to coax a performance out of her after this ugly scene.

HL glared at me as though this were all my fault. On hands and knees we covered every inch of floor. Dust and God knows what else stained the knees of Humphrey Linklater's smart trousers. The palms of his hands, which he kept clean so fastidiously, looked like those of a car mechanic. Dust unto dust.

'Oh, how uncomfortable this is!' Madame Emmenot sprang to her feet. 'Cette chaise . . .' She felt behind her under the cushion and brought out the emerald. 'Ah,' she cried. 'Le voilà. Pourquoi?' she said to HL. 'Why did you put it there?'

Predictably, our glorified home movie was a flop – a series of non-sequiturs ending in an anticlimax. All the script's post-modern irony and understatement added up to bugger-all, without a strong plot or violent emotions. All the things we should have done, we didn't do.

HL did not seem fazed by our failure to find a distributor, nor that no single respectable review ever emerged from the festivals at Cork, Edinburgh and New Delhi, where our film was shown in competition. I still have the chintzy scroll from the Delhi Film Festival to remind me that once I had ambitions to be someone entirely different.

The second-hand car dealer turned scrap metal merchant turned gangland boss, however, seemed to feel he had a good return on his investment. HL loved being on set, was deferential towards the actors, took unashamed delight in seeing all his favourite Côte d'Azur and Monaco locations included, and enjoyed hosting suppers for the crew at the Hotel Terminus de Nice, where the house rouge, Vin Bernard, cost two francs a bottle. He was a real gent, and never confronted us with our failure.

The man who financed Karma Films and this rotten picture may not have got his money back but HL did maintain his hold over me. Even if I wasn't ever actively involved in walling up a dead rival of his in one of the cement supports on the Hammersmith flyover, I did smuggle out two more large dollops of cash in £50 notes to Monte Carlo for him. But I never did get to go to the Grand Prix.

CHAPTER 38

Wag

I somehow thought I might see him there. After all, what Wainwright and I had in common was a talent for remaining alive. It was as though only the two of us existed in the dense crowd that attended the unveiling of the memorial to the Royal Artillery on Hyde Park Corner in October 1925. Even with all the hats and umbrellas, which obscured people's faces during the interminable service of remembrance, I spotted Wainwright, my former commanding officer, immediately.

At a Lyon's Coffee House near Marble Arch, we celebrated our reunion with lukewarm milky coffees.

'Do you know,' Wainwright said, 'after all those years, I haven't the foggiest idea what your Christian name is.'

'Nor I yours,' I said. 'William.'

'Harry.'

We shook hands.

'People call me Wag.'

'Why?'

'Long story.'

'You don't look like much of a wag.'

I toyed with a piece of dry sponge cake, and popped it in my mouth.

'I'm not.'

'Wag . . . What does it stand for? Wartime Artillery Genius?'

A light steam from all those damp coats merged with a mist

of cigarette smoke. We could have been in the trenches again, although the Corner House décor had the edge on mud and rotting timbers.

Wainwright didn't smoke either. We were a couple of clean-living boys.

'What are you up to these days?'

'Same old, at Thomas Saunders.'

Wainwright raised a quizzical eyebrow. He was wearing a smart suit with a dark blue tie in a Windsor knot and a well-cut white shirt.

'Is that a Prince of Wales check?' I asked, admiring his suit. 'Do you remember? We saw him once. The Prince. Can't remember where we were exactly. Near Amiens, I think. He inspected us. From a motorcar.' It had shot past at about twenty miles an hour, but I did catch a glimpse of David Windsor's pale, anxious, handsome face.

'He was awarded the Military Cross for that. Bastard.' Wainwright shook his head in disgust.

'All I remember is that we had been under attack for three solid days, and then we get this order to clean our kit and form up in ranks for some visiting general. We had buried half the troop, so there weren't that many of us left. And you're telling me that our brave little Prince received a decoration for sitting in the back of a car? I didn't know. Bastards, the lot of them.'

'And it is our job now to redress the balance, wouldn't you say?' Wainwright said.

During that long stretch at the front, I had learned only one good thing: don't trust your officer, trust your horse. With the exception of Wainwright, who had a more subversive personal agenda, I had always steered clear of officers. If I had allowed myself free rein to vent my feelings about their tactics, general behaviour and the punishments they meted out to their own men, I could have run amok with a gun.

'It's good to see you, William.' Wainwright's eyes twinkled. 'Not sure I'm going to be able to call you Wag.'

'William is fine,' I said. 'It is my name, after all.'

'Well, William,' said Wainwright. 'We return to a land of opportunity. I would not have expected you to join the dole queue. But I don't suppose your job is paying you more than a pittance. Money isn't everything in the world, but it does have its uses.'

'Where are you living now?' I asked.

'Eaton Mews. You?'

'Brixton.'

'This coffee really is terrible,' Wainwright said. 'Do you fancy something a bit stronger?'

It was totally unexpected when my sister Josephine died. 'It's just a bit of a cold,' she said one evening. 'I've got a terrible sore throat.'

I made her a hot whisky with honey and lemon. It didn't do any good. She was gone within the week. Spanish flu, spread by close quarters and massive troop movements, killed millions. Miraculously, no one else in the family was infected.

Martin was the next to go. He was hit by a police car in a chase following a jewellery robbery in Hatton Garden. Nothing to do with Martin. He never got on the wrong side of the law – except for that one time. I suppose we could have sued for compensation, but nothing brings back a life. Martin was only crossing the road.

I pray he got to the other side . . .

Despite miraculously not losing any sons to the war, it seemed the Bourton family was lurching from one tragedy to another. Jago's firstborn died next. My mother didn't approve of her youngest son's choice of wife. Molly was brassy, no mistake about that. She looked like a barmaid. Red lipstick smudged her teeth. A son was born within seven months of signing the register at Brixton Town Hall. But little Edmund died before he reached the age of one. They didn't try to have another child for some time after that.

For me, however, there was some good news during this period. Ethel's fiancé Walter Cornish was offered a posting in Cape Town, South Africa, and, to my joy, my beloved sister decided not to accompany him. She broke off her engagement and returned to London. Had I been a religious man, I would have said three 'Hail Marys'.

CHAPTER 39

Jack

What was it, I wonder, about my family and the law? I was not the only person who transgressed. My dear Uncle Wag of course, not to mention my maternal grandmother's first husband; and cousin Oliver's penchant for hard drugs.

And then there was my mother Ivy, who waged a lifetime's war against insurance companies.

Looking back, I blame Sanger's Circus. My mother and I had spent a hot afternoon in the big tent on Tooting Common. In those days, a child could still thrill to the sight of lethargic elephants, toothless lions, overdressed monkeys, clever dogs and the occasional sea lion who did the clapping for you. Then there were the mournful clowns in their hideous make-up, the sequined acrobats and the horse acts.

The smell of sawdust in our nostrils, brass band honking in our ears, my mother and I went to look at the animals in their stalls after the show.

It was a palomino stallion I had admired in the ring. He could rear up on his hind legs, even take a gracious bow. When my mother stretched out her hand to pet his muzzle, the horse bit the diamond off her engagement ring. He must have thought it was a cube of sugar. He also must have had very strong teeth. Or the setting was weak. Or it wasn't a genuine diamond my father had given his bride-to-be back in 1939.

My mother was distraught. The circus people claimed they

had poked through the dung afterwards, but there was no sign of a precious stone. The insurance people didn't believe the story, and refused to pay.

From that moment on, my mother began a relentless, lifelong campaign of guerrilla warfare against insurance companies. At the slightest damage from a water overflow one Christmas or the 'loss' of a handbag and camera while on holiday, my mother would lodge a claim. The stained carpet would not be replaced. Decorators would submit estimates for repainting, wallpapering, repairing floorboards. But whatever repair was necessary, she did it herself. She would not surrender to any insurance company in the land and she would pocket the reward.

After a brief sojourn in borstal, the sentence passed for his failed attempt to burn down Alleyn's school library, my cousin Oliver flirted constantly with alternative values. The worst crime he ever committed in my eyes was to take out a subscription to the communist newspaper, the *Morning Star*. However, he could have been done for possession of Class A drugs. For a while, after the marijuana and demonstrations period, he dabbled with cocaine and heroin. 'I have this great supplier,' he told me. 'Only the purest stuff, I promise you. It is safer than booze. I'm not addicted.' His hazel eyes were like pinpricks when he told me this, and he nodded out later in the middle of a sentence. Oliver was still obsessing about his beloved Trotsky and claimed to be compiling notes for a book about the great revolutionary's last years in Mexico.

He moved to Cambridge. 'I'm off drugs,' he told me. 'I'm going to get my head in order and finish my book. And I've got this job at Heffers.'

I even went up to see him from time to time and we visited some of my old haunts together. Rules had been relaxed. Mixed sex colleges had appeared. Oliver lived with his landlady, an American woman. 'She is seventeen and a half years older than me,' Oliver said. 'But I love her. Kate is the most extraordinary person.' He never introduced us.

Oliver developed a sleeping disorder. He couldn't sleep at all. He tried listening to a tape of Tibetan gongs, swallowing a hot, milky drink before bed, reciting poems in his head, counting backwards from a million. It got beyond a joke. A number of different doctors were consulted. Pills like benzodiazepine were made available on prescription. They didn't work. He tried primal therapy. At one stage, he found himself in a kibbutz in Israel, making regular excursions to the Sinai Desert to scream his head off. Still he couldn't sleep.

Then Oliver discovered a new guru – Timothy Leary. This Berkeley-educated professor believed that psychedelic substances could be more helpful than therapy. For his sustained advocacy of the mind-expanding properties of the *psilocybe mexicana* mushroom, later synthesised as LSD, Leary saw the inside of twenty-seven prisons round the world. It all sounded like nonsense to me.

Oliver started calling me 'man', and tried to explain the eight-circuit model of consciousness whereby humans could become accustomed to life in a zero- or low-gravity environment.

When Leary died of prostate cancer in 1996, several grams of his ashes were sent to outer space in a Pegasus rocket, which remained in orbit for six years until it burned up in the atmosphere. Oliver died of an aneurism, and his remains lie still in a stone urn at Golder's Green Cemetery.

However, the person who worried me most at this moment was my old mate Link. He was going off the rails. His daily intake of amphetamines was beginning to make him twitch. Then he would swallow other multicoloured pills to help him balance.

'You're supposed to be his friend,' Monkey Rawlings said. 'Can't you do anything?'

'Yes,' I said. 'But I'm not his keeper.'

'He'll get us all nicked if we're not careful.' Rawlings's concern for his boss's son was not altruistic. 'He's a loose cannon, that boy.'

Most of the work I did in the adjoining office to HL's Mr Reliable was legit. I checked accounts, dealt with lawyers and edited correspondence, such as it was, to make sure it didn't sound completely illiterate. I made the acquaintance of a curious group of people – from Neanderthal enforcers and spivs at the betting shop to a couple of sisters, twins, who had a flower stall in the market. They loved the Richardsons. 'People say they done the most terrible things,' Betty would say (she was older by one minute than Doris). 'Well, they might have crossed the line once or twice. But only with them as deserved it. All that stuff about nailing people's heads to the floor. That's rubbish. That's the papers for you. They're just a couple of naughty boys.' And the sisters would shriek with laughter.

'The trouble is.' Link and I were having a rare heart-to-heart. 'My dad doesn't like me.'

'Don't be daft,' I said.

We were having an early evening nip of Scotch in Link's new Knightsbridge pad. It was in an old red-brick mansion block, but all the apartment's fixtures and fittings were spanking new. Concealed spotlighting, glass coffee table complete with neatly stacked *Motor* magazines, a fridge the size of a wardrobe, a couple of signed R.B. Kitaj prints on the magnolia living room walls.

'He used to live opposite us in Dulwich, you know.'

'Who did?' Link asked.

'Kitaj.'

'Who's he?'

'Him.' I nodded towards the paintings – one was of a naked woman's back.

'Oh, him,' Link said. 'Load of rubbish, if you ask me.'

'All the kids used to like to babysit for him. Had the biggest collection of porn you've ever seen.'

'You know I think my dad would have preferred to have had you as a son. An academic. Not a moron like me. I can't concentrate. Never have been able to. Not like you. I couldn't sit down and read a book. I have to be out there, doing something.' Link poured himself another drink and gestured towards my glass.

'No thanks.'

'I work my arse off, Kid. You know that. But he prefers hanging out with you in Monte bloody Carlo.'

'I don't think we will be doing much more of that.' There was a new project Cohen and I were working on: an adaptation of Bernice Rubens's Booker Prize-winning novel, *The Elected Member*. What a terrible title. Almost as bad as our Film School effort, *The Game Chicken*. But Cohen identified with the story. It was all about a conflicted Jewish family. I was out of my depth, but went along for the ride. It was not set on the Riviera.

Michael Hastings, the playwright, tried his hand at a draft script. Neither Tyler nor I could make head or tail of it. We got a chap called Tudor Gates to have a go. Can't remember much about the result, except that we always referred to the author as Georgian House.

My film-making career was in limbo.

'I think we should go to Sybilla's tonight.'

'Fine with me.' This Mayfair disco nightclub was owned by

a group of people including the Beatle George Harrison and the Australian disc jockey Alan 'Fluff' Freeman. The Kray Twins provided protection.

The first time I went there, a little while after it opened in June 1966, I was Link's guest. When it was time to leave, the doorman helped me on with my very ancient grey overcoat. Both arms disappeared into the lining. Red-faced, I was unable to leave a tip.

This time I was kitted out in a sharp black velvet suit from Rupert Lycett Green's trendy shop Blades . As Link commented when I gave the outfit its first public airing, 'You think you look like the dog's bollocks.' And I did.

There was a ridiculous superstition between the two of us that if 'California Dreaming' by the Mamas and the Papas was among the first three songs played on arrival, we would be all right. That did not necessarily mean pulling a bird. We were not always on the hunt, although I had found no girl I particularly liked after abandoning Giesele at Victoria Station. But you did need someone to dance with.

On the disco floor, Link was in a league of his own. Whatever he was on added a little extra pizzazz to his twists, twirls and hand gestures. He was electric. You couldn't take your eyes off him. I could jive all right, and go through the motions of the Locomotion, could even do the Madison, but Link was spectacular. His body entered the music. He was transported.

My friend gave me the thumbs-up. Mama Cass was doing her stuff. 'All the leaves are brown . . .' It was going to be our night.

The place was packed. I clocked the comedian Lance Percival from *That Was the Week That Was* with a silver-haired nymphet, and Michael d'Abo, the lead singer from Manfred

Mann. He had been at Selwyn when I was there, but was more interested in music than education. He didn't show up for the second year.

There were some other, less salubrious characters I recognised lounging at tables or at the heaving bar. They preferred to keep their names out of the papers, but liked rubbing shoulders with the fast crowd.

We found a table for four in a quieter side room. Two people were already sitting there and were halfway through a bottle of Veuve Clicquot. 'Hello, Jack,' said Sylvia. 'Long time, no see.'

I bent to kiss her on both cheeks.

'This is my friend George.' The man stood. He was about my height. Sleek black hair was combed straight back. He had an olive complexion, and there was something about him that was familiar.

'Hello, Jack,' he said as we shook hands. 'Remember me? Curwin of the Upper Fourth.' He went into a boxing crouch. 'George. Detective Inspector George Curwin to you.'

I glanced over at Link, who shrugged his shoulders to indicate, 'Nothing to do with me, mate.'

The Animals sang 'We Gotta Get out of This Place'.

'Fancy a dance?' I said to Sylvia.

CHAPTER 40

Wag

A lot of people blamed Winston Churchill. His decision as Chancellor of the Exchequer to reintroduce the gold standard made the pound too strong for the export market and the price of coal fell.

Mine owners did not want to see their profits fall. So they cut miners' pay.

'Try living on their wages before you judge them.' King George V's royal response did not prevent the inevitable confrontation – but a ten-day strike hardly brought the country to its knees. Those miners who got their old jobs back were forced to accept lower pay and longer hours.

We had to wait a few more years for things to get really bad for the rest of us. On Black Tuesday, October 29th, 1929, the US stock market collapsed. Worldwide economic recession followed.

But a couple of smart operators in London experienced no problems with a shrinking of the money supply. There was always a market for false papers, and Wainwright and I had a new speciality – passports. Businessmen in trouble often needed to leave the country in a hurry. Assets needed to be shifted from one place to another. Speed was of the essence. No one wanted to doodle around and argue about our exorbitant fees.

All the negotiations were handled by Wainwright. After a full day's engraving at Sanders, I would take the bus to the workrooms I had rented in an empty house near Exmouth Market. The landlord was delighted to ask no questions and to receive his money in cash at the end of each week. Mr Anonymous got on with his job there, methodically and meticulously, often late into the evening.

'I am sorry, Bourton,' Mr Edward said to me one day. 'But I'm going to have to let you go.'

I wasn't sorry. The only reason I had hung on in Wardour Street was for the cover it gave me. Even though I was Sanders' top craftsman, the salary was derisory. I never complained, never asked for more. I was the perfect employee.

It turned out that, like so many traditional Soho businesses, Sanders had to cease trading. The old place was torn down, along with other wooden buildings in that Soho street. British Gaumont Pictures built a big office there instead. Out went Clarkson's the wigmaker and Rayner's the pork butcher, who sold the best pease pudding and faggots in town. The dray horses disappeared who used to carry milk from the dairy at the top of Broad Street, where William Blake had worked as an engraver a century earlier. Even the snuff stall outside the Blue Posts public house moved on. That is the bit of history I remember, the little insignificant, personal bit.

Every single family business collapsed, including Johnson's the chemist, and you would have thought there was always a demand for pills and plasters. Those reassuring large coloured jars were packed away in crates and boards were nailed up over the windows.

Rinola's, which had been a favourite restaurant of the boy King Edward, closed its doors after one riotous evening when a whole bunch of us drank the place dry and slurred our last, tearful farewells.

The world moves on. I was prepared.

On behalf of my mother and the rest of the family, I put

down a deposit on a house in Streatham – an old rectory, complete with tennis court. Must have been a very sporty vicar who gave the sermons back in the day. I could have bought the place outright. Flashy was never my style, though. Never draw attention to yourself. That was my policy.

My siblings were just about earning their keep. People still needed cheap and serviceable clothing, so old Ted hung on to his job in Croydon. Jago was on call night and day to fix people's broken toasters or whatever household electrics had failed. Nobody was buying new stuff. Florence was resting. In her line of work, this was not an unfamiliar situation. Ivy modelled underwear for a firm in Bond Street. And Aurelia's clientele for her spiritualist séances increased exponentially with anxiety about the dire state of things.

On the whole, the luck of the Bourtons was good, for a change.

I didn't breathe a word about getting the bum's rush myself. Every morning I went off to town at eight o'clock. But I was home more often at a reasonable time in the evenings, now I could spend my day on more remunerative work in Exmouth Market.

Ethel devoted herself to private nursing, a job that was always in demand. I met her at Marylebone Station, when she returned from Whitby. We took a taxi all the way back to Brixton. What an extravagance.

'I think I would shave that off if I were you.' Those were my sister's first words to me after at least a year and a half. I had grown a moustache. It didn't last another day.

She didn't stay home long, though. Not long enough for me. She was the same old Ethel. Pale and distant. Sometimes, I thought of her as a ghost. She returned to haunt me but I could not touch her.

'Do you have any regrets about not following Cornish?' I asked her on one of the rare occasions we were alone together. Mother had complained of a headache all day, and retired to her room without touching a morsel of the lamb stew she had prepared for supper. I volunteered to do the washing-up. Perhaps the rest of the family were so gobsmacked at this suggestion that they all had to go and have a lie-down.

'Sometimes I do wonder if I did the right thing,' Ethel said.

That was not the answer I wanted to hear. 'Have you heard from him?'

'He is not that sort of man. Too proud.' Ethel finished the drying-up, and folded the damp dishcloth neatly over a rail on the cooker.

'Do you miss him?'

She looked at me solemnly. 'Not as much as I missed you when you were away.'

My throat went dry.

'Has there been anyone in your life?' Ethel asked.

'No. Not really.' I did wonder occasionally about where Queenie was now, and every once in a while I thought about the woman in the farmhouse in France and whether the whole thing had been a dream.

'I've been offered a post in St Mawes,' Ethel said. 'In Cornwall. Ward sister. It's a step up. A nursing home for retired generals. Top brass.'

'Aren't there any good jobs in London? I mean, do you always have to go so far away?'

Ethel never answered a question if she didn't feel like it. 'How is your work?'

'Fine.'

'I've never seen anything you've done.'

'It's not really for bringing home. Gun decorations, that kind of thing.'

'You haven't had enough of shooting?'

'I wouldn't do it, but I've got nothing against killing pheasants, if that's what you mean.'

'It is a miracle you're still here.'

'Couldn't leave you by yourself, could I?'

She smiled at me. Whenever I think of Ethel, which is every single day, I remember that smile.

The telephone rang. We only had the one, out in the hall. It was Wainwright. 'I know it is a bit late, William,' he said. 'But I think you had better come round.'

To get over to Eaton Mews by public transport at ten thirty in the evening was a tall order in those days. But cabbies were desperate for trade and on the lookout for any custom to help keep the wolf from the door. Plus, there was hardly any traffic.

At 10.57 precisely, I knocked on the blue door of Harry Wainwright's mews house.

'Thanks for coming.' Harry didn't look overjoyed to see me. 'Come in. What'll you have? This is Chief Inspector Baker, by the way.'

A tall man, still wearing his raincoat, rose to his feet. 'Good evening, Mr Bourton,' he said. 'I have been looking forward to meeting you.'

CHAPTER 41

Jack

A chorus of boos greeted the end of the second round. Already bleeding from a cut on his right eye, Eric Waterman slumped on his stool, while his corner man went to work with a cotton swab soaked in epinephrine.

'Your man is in big trouble, isn't he?' Curwin shouted above the general din. We were at a table right up at the front of the Lonsdale in Southwark. Waterman's minders had secured permission from the Boxing Board of Control for their boy to go pro. This was his first shot. But, boy, had they found him the wrong opponent. Lean, hard, half a stone heavier, 'Tiger' Kelshall from Trinidad looked to me as though he could be the new Randolph Turpin. Kelshall used the same wide-legged stance favoured by the former middleweight champion of the world. His reflexes were like quicksilver, and he could punch with both hands.

Waterman was nobody's pushover. Somehow, he got through the next round, hanging on, and got in a few digs to his opponent's finely toned body.

'I can't take any more of this.' Link's girlfriend Rachel picked up her drink and handbag. 'I'm off to the bar.' For those too squeamish to watch a couple of bruisers beat the Bejasus out of each other, the Lonsdale supplied a cosy retreat away from the ring, with light music, magazines and attentive staff. 'You don't have to come with me,' Rachel said to Link. 'I'll be OK.'

Sylvia, on the other hand, had no qualms about staying to watch. Her eyes gleamed and she twisted a lock of her red hair in her fingers as she watched the action. I wondered if she was still Sid's mistress.

I remembered my father coming home, slightly the worse for wear, the night Randolph Turpin defeated Sugar Ray Robinson in London. It was on July 10th, 1951, eleven days away from my eighth birthday. 'What a fight.' My dad sat down heavily on my bed. 'Fantastic. Never seen anything like it. If only you'd been old enough to come along.' He stood up and demonstrated the Turpin style. 'Bang! Bang! Boomph!'

Waterman reeled from an explosive combination of lefts and rights to the head. Somehow, he managed a riposte of his own to Kelshall's chin. The crowd roared.

'Come on, El!' Sylvia shouted. I reckoned Eric must have been a conquest of hers at some stage of our young lives.

It looked to me as though Curwin had his eye on her now.

Turpin had never recaptured his moment of glory. Only two months later, he lost his title to Robinson in New York. By the end of his career, my dad's hero had to resort to professional wrestling. He got mixed up with the wrong people. It was a familiar story. The pub he acquired in Llandudno failed to get him back on the road to recovery, and on May 17th, 1966, Randolph Turpin shot himself.

'I reckon that last round was even,' Curwin said. Waterman had managed to go five without being counted out. I was never sure exactly how the points system worked. But we had score cards on the table, and Detective Inspector Curwin was marking his assiduously.

The bell rang for the sixth. Kelshall attacked with a flurry of blows. Waterman covered up well, and then appeared to trip slightly, butting his head against his opponent's. Kelshall stopped in his tracks.

Waterman unleashed a savage left below the West Indian's heart and followed it with an uppercut to Kelshall's chin.

Curwin and Sylvia, the whole baying pack of boxing fans were on their feet.

Kelshall hit the canvas with a bang.

'Ten, nine, eight . . .'

Every spectator at the Lonsdale shouted down the seconds with the referee, who was crouched over the prone body in the centre of the ring.

It was all over. Sylvia and Curwin went into a clinch, and danced up and down as though it were New Year's Eve.

From corner man to manager, Kelshall's team rushed over to their protégé, and a doctor was called.

Blood still dripping from his right eye, face bruised, Eric Waterman spat his gumshield into the cheering audience, climbed up on the first rope, and waved both gloved fists in triumph.

Link and I clapped.

'That was a turn-up for the book,' I said.

'Not really, Kid,' he replied, with a wink.

CHAPTER 42

Wag

'There really is a ghost in this house,' Aurelia insisted. 'I don't care if you think I'm barmy. But I am telling you. This time there really is.'

We were unpacking all the boxes, having moved into the Streatham rectory that would remain the Bourton family home even after our mother died.

Not so long ago, the ghost in our last house had proved to be a neighbour's black and white cat, which crawled in through an open upstairs window and dislodged a vase.

'I checked with the previous owners,' Aurelia continued. 'You can make fun of me all you like.'

Rose and I settled back in a couple of armchairs in the chaos of the half-unpacked living room and prepared for Aurelia to complete the story. 'It wasn't the vicar,' she said.

'She was quick, but the vicar was quicker. Nobody knew he was there,' sang Rose.

'He was a banker. Went bankrupt.' Aurelia checked to see if there would be any further interruptions. 'He hanged himself in the attic.' She gazed upwards.

Suitcases, old tea chests, a metal trunk, some books and a standard lamp without a shade we had stored that day in that capacious loft area. No bitter chill when we shifted the stuff there suggested that we were trespassing in some unholy place. No mocking laughter echoed round the supporting beams of the roof. There was no hidden door either, shrouded in cobwebs, that led to the secret room where the past had been buried alive. But that first night at the rectory, Jago and Molly were awoken in their top-floor bedroom by what sounded like a scuffle, followed by a crash. Then silence.

The next morning, in his striped pyjamas, Jago went up to the attic to have a peep. The standard lamp had been knocked over. No stray cat scuttled past him through the door. No tramp had crept in to find a place for the night. No sudden gust of air from a non-existent window had caused the lamp to fall.

'We'll call him George.' Jago became an immediate convert. 'I don't think he means us any harm.'

Aurelia was happy with that. She did not believe in exorcisms. 'Obviously,' she said, 'he likes it here. He wants to stay. Good luck to him.'

From that day on, if there were any noises or unexplained breakages, people used to say, 'It's just old George.'

For me and Wainwright, the only apparition who materialised with monotonous regularity was Chief Inspector Baker. How he had got wind of our little operation was never clear. But he was on to us. And the copper wanted a bit of the action. Initially, to keep his mouth shut, he told us it was for the Police Benevolent Fund. But, as time went on, Baker started introducing some new clients himself. We even did some work for some of his colleagues at Scotland Yard.

In fact, after the initial shock of his appearance at Eaton Mews, Chief Inspector Baker's arrival on the scene resulted in a significant increase of revenue for our thriving business. It became a regular thing to have a drink with him at the pub. I even had to confess to myself I enjoyed his company. One day I invited him back to Streatham. After that he started spending a lot of time hanging round the rectory on the slightest pretext and soon I noticed he had his eye on my sister Violet.

Before I knew it they got married. Commander Hastings of south London's finest was best man, and the guard of honour was composed entirely of the men in blue. We were legit at last.

I had a bent copper as my brother-in-law, and half the force as my new mates.

To keep up appearances, it was time to get another lawful job. In fact, I had taken steps to get myself re-employed a little while before Violet plighted her troth. There's a design you can still see on the stock of a J. Purdey & Sons rifle – two ducks and a drake, a tree, hills in the background, curlicue scrollwork. I did that. 'The finest craftsmanship', as they say in their advertisements.

Athol Purdey, with his sons, James and Tom, carried on a gunmaking tradition that stretched back to 1798, when the first James Purdey became apprenticed to Thomas Keck Hutchinson, who forged Damascus barrels out of old horseshoes. Horseshoes made the toughest steel, so it was thought, on account of all that trampling on metalled roads.

I worked out of Purdey's in Mayfair for more years than they would probably want to remember. My hand never lost its sureness of touch. I was a phenomenon.

Decoration was my trade. A Purdey shotgun is unique. Even in my day, one would sell for more money than many people could make in a year. Look at their over-and-under action bases with fine scroll engraving on the walnut stock blank. A pheasant flaps out of the long grass. That was me too.

Fancy designs were not always required. Sometimes, all that was necessary was gold lettering and numbering, acid-etched to give a gun its unique look. The toffs who bought such beauties were interested in driven game and sporting clays, not in the fine art of murder.

Collectors from all over the world have bought my work, although no individual craftsman takes the credit. But for my own amusement and for the record, I always left the concealed initials EB in my designs. It can take a while to spot them. I am a cunning little fellow.

CHAPTER 43

Jack

While I was growing up my parents seemed to lead parallel, separate lives – my father spending most of his time at work, my mother focused on her family. But having jumped at the chance of early retirement from the bank, my father developed a new passion – for travel. As a family of three, we had barely been abroad together, but he and Ivy now found a new togetherness and went off on regular adventures to France, Spain and Portugal. They were usually accompanied by two other retired couples, friends of my father's from his wartime training days at Scampton.

The three couples bought flats in the same apartment block in the fast-developing resort of Calpe, near Alicante on the Costa Blanca. We had some jolly holidays there. I remember a hot July when Uncle Wag and Aunt Ethel came out to stay. I had to give up my room for them and sleep on the couch. Even though they were already quite elderly, they knew how to put away the cheap red wine like the rest of us.

When they weren't entertaining friends or family or watching the days drift past from their balcony overlooking the sea, my parents rented the place out. There was inevitable wear and tear. Walls and woodwork needed a touch of paint. When my father invited me out to help him get the Calpe flat into shape for next year's season I jumped at the chance. Karma Films was in terminal decline and I was not ready to accept that my life was ruled by a criminal gang. My mother offered to stay behind in Dulwich; she realised I would relish the opportunity to spend some time alone with my dad.

In early November, it was still warm enough to swim in the Mediterranean. Goats wandered across the undeveloped wasteland in front of the spanking new white towers that had been erected on the scrubby terrain near the salt flats. If you didn't have any pesetas at the little restaurant down by the port, it didn't matter. 'Pay now, pay later, ees the same,' said the old boy who ran it. We never failed to settle up.

My father and I painted and decorated, ate paella and rotisserie chicken and, to start with at least, were in bed with a book by ten most nights.

One night we went to the circus. It was a tatty display, with a moth-eaten bear, some midget acrobats and a dog act. I was reminded of the debacle of my mother's engagement ring. It wasn't very exciting and my father suddenly remembered that this was the night of the European heavyweight title fight at Wembley between Henry Cooper and the Spanish champion, Jose Urtain.

Boxing was a passion my father and I had always shared and we wandered down to the El Toro bar to watch the match on their television, which was mounted on the wall next to a huge poster of the matador Luis Dominguin.

Five minutes before the boxers climbed into the ring, a scuffle broke out in the bar. A fat Dutch bloke called Joost, who had the flat above ours, got into an argument about the price of a gin and tonic with the owner, Ramon. A couple of blows were exchanged before two German men separated the squabbling pair.

The room divided off into Spain v the rest of Europe.

'Ridiculous.' Joost had only the slightest accent. 'The bastard has added a ten per cent surcharge just so we can watch his bloody TV.'

He and the Germans had joined our table. 'You can have some of our petroleum, if you like . . .' My father pushed the bottle of Campo Viejo towards Joost.

The Dutchman made a face. 'No thanks. I want to see the whole fight,' he said. 'That stuff sends you blind.'

'Prosit.' The Germans raised their pints of lager.

'Klaus.'

'Und Hans.'

'Jack.'

'Und Fred.'

We all shook hands.

A huge cheer from the Calpe locals greeted the arrival of their man in the London ring.

We drowned them out when Henry acknowledged the roars of his home crowd.

In the first round, Urtain butted Cooper above the right eye. Blood poured from a cut. The skin on Henry's forehead was like paper. It was a problem throughout his boxing career.

Joost leapt to his feet. 'Did you see that?' he shouted. 'That was deliberate. Cheat!' he shouted towards the bar. 'All Spaniards are wankers.'

The Germans made the Dutchman sit down.

Cooper's cut man set about repairing the damage.

The next eight rounds were a lesson in the fine art of pugilism. Henry Cooper's left jab was legendary. Deservedly. By the eighth round, Urtain was black and blue. He couldn't breathe through his nose, his left eye was closed. Courageously, he came out for the ninth, but his corner threw in the towel. Henry Cooper, Great Britain's finest, was European champion again.

El Toro went wild. Joost threw his wicker chair at a bunch of local fishermen, who had gesticulated in our direction. One of the waiters, normally the most attentive of Ramon's staff, went to remonstrate with the Dutchman, who lashed out with his elbow. Some Spaniards from an adjoining table entered the fray.

Calmly finishing their third pint of beer first, Hans and Klaus stepped forward. They were big men. Punches were given and received.

My dad looked at me. I looked at him. It was back to the fight in *Shane*. Ramon and a group of his compadres surged over. Anybody not a subject of Franco's Fascist Republic was an enemy. I watched my dad adopt the Turpin stance, and was impressed with his sharp left jab into the face of the first Spaniard who tried it on with him. A young chap who worked at the grocer up the Avenida Gonzales came at me with a bottle. I ducked at the last moment, and he only hit me on the shoulder. It hurt, though.

I banged him once in the midriff. Then the right cross to the chin. The old routine. Always worked.

A whistle blew. It was like a freeze frame in a movie. In the doorway of El Toro stood two policemen in their funny hats. Behind them, the Mayor of Calpe and Link's Uncle Sid.

At Sid's villa by the landmark peñon near the port, Joost and Ramon, arms round each other's shoulders, toppled into the floodlit swimming pool.

'Bloody hell, Jack. Fancy meeting you here.' Sid Mullin swirled the ice against the rim of his cut-glass tumbler, and sipped his Chivas Regal. 'Reckon we got there in the nick of time.'

The long, heavy oak table in Sid's baronial living room had been pushed against the wall. My dad was dancing to Marino Marini's classic rendition of 'Piove' with a young Australian woman called Edna. Earlier, by popular demand, she had performed a pas-de-deux with Sid's gay housekeeper or lover, I didn't know which. As the famous Tchaikovsky ballet music began, she had introduced their act as 'The Dying Duck'.

The applause as the couple took their bow went on for about five minutes. Enemies had become friends. Sid was the hero of the hour. He had invited everybody from El Toro back to his villa. Including the police and the mayor. The man was an example to us all.

'I didn't know you had a place out here,' I said.

'Didn't know you did.'

'Not quite in your league.'

The paintings were truly terrible. Huge, lurid, abstract swathes of reds, yellows, purples over rough surfaces of sand. At least Mullin did not display a penchant for sad-eyed boys with donkeys, like so many other expats. Black metal chandeliers dangled from the ceiling. Deep white couches were already stained with red wine. Sid didn't seem bothered.

The sound system, top of the range, belted out a stream of contemporary hits, interspersed with fifties pop. Michael Holliday crooned 'The Story Of My Life'. He was rumoured to have had a homosexual affair with Freddie Mills, world light heavyweight champion from 1948 to 1950. Only a few years before, Mills had been found shot in the head in his car, parked in a cul-de-sac behind the failing nightclub he owned in Soho.

At his funeral in Camberwell New Cemetery, Henry Cooper was one of Mills's pallbearers. Holliday was already dead of a drug overdose. Ronnie Kray was not among the mourners, although he was supposedly one of the boxer's lovers.

The Dave Clark Five's pounding 'Glad All Over' made the whole villa vibrate. Catatonic revellers were roused from their slumbers to stomp and jerk their arms about on the polished parquet. I noticed my father and his new Australian lady friend had slipped away.

'I met Freddie Mills a few times,' I told Sid.

'I expect you did,' said Sid with a conspiratorial smile.

'Yes. He used to come to Brockwell Park Lido. I was a Herne Hill Icicle for a year. I must have been mad.' That sometimes meant breaking the ice on the open-air pool. 'There was this old bloke. Bernard Parkhouse. He never missed a day's swim. Still going when he was ninety-three. Freddie Mills always came for his birthday.'

'Didn't do him much good,' Sid said.

'Who?'

'Freddie. Should have been a bit more careful.'

At the sound of breaking glass, Sid turned his head like an uncurious tortoise. 'Bloody animals,' he said.

I was quite keen on the idea of going home. There was no one at this bunfight who appealed to me. Was I going to hang around for my father? God knew what he was up to. I had never thought of him as a ladies' man. Yet when I thought of it now, there were some evenings when he would come home late, wearing an inscrutable smile. It was always the same procedure. The front door would slam. The bolt would be slid home. This would be followed by a long exhalation of breath.

If my mother and I were in the living room, he would gaze at us for a long moment, and say, 'I love you both.' Then he would make his way slowly upstairs to bed.

Whether Mum would check his collar for lipstick smudges or sniff his body for musky odours, I never knew. And I never asked him what he got up to with Edna that night.

'I wonder if you could do me a favour, Jack?' Sid said.

Here we go, I thought.

'You still friends with Sylvia?'

'Oh you know, I've only ever seen her socially,' I said. My armpits felt damp although the heat of the day had gone.

'There's a little something I'd like you to give Sylvia when you go home.'

I finished my expensive, silky Scotch and put it down on a glass-topped side table.

'Yes. I'd be most grateful to you. Don't declare it, though. I think the duty might be a bit excessive.'

'Right,' I said. 'Of course, Sid.' I was a trained man, after all.

'I could get it for you now, if you like.'

'We're not off until Saturday.'

Sid nodded contemplatively. 'I have to be away myself. To Tangier. Tomorrow afternoon. Can't stand Morocco. What a dump. Corruption and camel shit. Never do business with an Arab,' he added. 'Why don't you come upstairs now, and I'll pass it over.'

I wasn't too keen on the idea, but had no choice other than to follow our host to the first floor. We had to step over a few bodies. There was a squeal and the slam of a bedroom door as we wandered down the landing. A suit of armour stood guard below a tapestry of a group of mounted soldiers charging towards a distant castle defended by turbaned Moors.

Sid reached into his trouser pocket and pulled out a heavy key-ring. 'Can't be too careful out here,' he said. 'Thieves everywhere.'

Unlocking the door at the end of the corridor, he led me inside. A four-poster bed was draped in white cotton. Papers and leather-bound ledgers were arranged neatly on an antique desk by the window. A life-size statue of a classical nude held aloft a burning torch, like the Statue of Liberty, casting the only light in the room.

Sid unhooked a gilt-framed oil painting of an eighteenth-century galleon firing a broadside at an invisible target, laid it on the floor and twiddled the dial of a wall safe. 'Here you go.' He handed me a slim rectangular case. 'Keep it safe, son.'

My life, I reflected, was pathetic. I was a well-educated smugglers' mule. Failed film-maker. Useless article. I despised myself. It was time to change my life.

CHAPTER 44

Wag

To be frank, I was chuffed with myself. The family had settled in happily in the big old rectory in Streatham. There were to be no more early morning bunks from bailiffs, as we had been obliged to do in Peckham Rye, Camberwell, Tulse Hill and Clapham Common.

No one in the family was used to a permanent home. For years, Mother never knew when we might have to do a runner. If funds dried up, as they always did, on went her hat in the early hours. We would wait by a crack in the door for Ted to bring round the hired van, then it was all hands on deck to stash away our possessions in the back before the sound of the milkman's horse could be heard at the far end of the street.

We were once caught after one of these flits. Mother looked as though her underpants had fallen down in Buckingham Palace when the bespectacled representative of the landlord tracked down the Bourton Mob to their new hidey-hole in Tooting.

Shooing the man into the living room, Mother dealt with the situation on her own. He emerged grim-faced, but with the official papers stuffed back in his shabby black briefcase.

But now, times were good. I even had the tennis court fixed, not that anyone played on it with any regularity. With shrieks and giggles, Florence would prance around on the red clay surface with the occasional admirer. I hit a few balls with Wainwright on one of the rare occasions he visited the house. The two of us were careful to keep our lives and business arrangements separate.

Wainwright had been coached as a young man. It showed. No amount of industry from a fit, keen competitor will make much of a game against someone who knows how to position their feet and strike the ball correctly with those heavy wooden racquets. I resolved to take some lessons.

The decision to retain a regular gardener was also my idea. No one had ever bothered, in all the big houses we had occupied over the years in south London, to devote any time to the usual acreage outside. Lawns grew thick, bushes became swollen and blowsy. Weeds obscured the banks of lupins, and bellbinder climbed up standard roses and choked the blooms to death.

No one else took much interest in whether the herbaceous borders flourished, nor if the pear and apple trees were pruned.

There was a decorative wooden gazebo outside the court area. It had two cramped changing rooms, whose damp floorboards had warped and needed replacing. Some criss-cross slatting above the window was also rotten with woodworm, and would break off in your hand if you so much as touched it. The green woodpecker, who was a regular visitor, liked it there a lot. That sharp beak would have to find nutritious grubs elsewhere. It was time to get to work on making good.

On top of the roof, a rusty weathervane depicted a man aiming his shotgun at the sky, watched by a spaniel with its tail erect. The metal creaked in its socket when the wind blew.

I know Mother appreciated the effort I put in to both house and garden, as she did my financial contribution. After expressing initial concern that I might be on the same slippery slope as a certain Leonard Bourton, she accepted that the gambling I claimed was responsible for the regular infusions of capital was a no-risk venture for her oldest son. 'We have a syndicate,' I told her, 'with a very clever system. Don't ask me how it works. There is this chief accountant at the office, brilliant at working out the odds and with some very useful connections at a number of stables. We don't win every week. That is impossible. But everyone contributes a portion of their salary. We're never going to lose our shirts. And we stay ahead of the game – sometimes making very substantial profits indeed.'

'You swear to me that there is nothing illegal, Wag?'

'On my honour, Mum.' I hated lying to her, but what else could I say?

'I don't know what we would do without you,' she said. Tears filled her grey-blue eyes.

When I pulled up in my new red and black Austin 7 that warm June day, my mother clapped her hands. 'I can't think of the last time I had a holiday.'

White cherry blossom clogged the gutter outside the rectory. I secured the handbrake. Wainwright had given me some useful driving lessons over the last month. You didn't need a licence in those days. You could weave all over the road before you got the hang of double declutching, a tricky process of changing gears that no modern driver could manage.

Ethel emerged with her suitcase. 'Here.' I took it gently from her and slid the case next to mine in the boot.

'We're only going to Burgh Island,' I said to my mother when Jago and Ted appeared, carrying her huge trunk between them. 'Not Timbuktu. For two nights.'

'You can't be too careful.' Mother folded her arms across her chest. She looked magnificent. Tiny, defiant, the only reason our funny family stayed together. When she died, that all-embracing love died with her. 'Who knows who we might meet?'

We knew that Noël Coward and Gertrude Lawrence had recently stayed at the swish Devon hotel we were heading for. Famously, Agatha Christie later used it as a setting for two novels, *Ten Little Niggers* and *Evil Under the Sun*. I tried reading that last book, but what I never understood was, if Hercule Poirot was so clever, why couldn't he speak proper English?

Mother sat beside me in the front, bolt upright, like the chaperone for a courting couple. Ethel made herself comfortable in the back seat.

Our route to the West Country took us through the wilds of Reading and Andover. We stopped at a deserted pub called The Cricketers, not far from Stonehenge. It seemed another lifetime since I had done my basic training on Salisbury Plain before setting off for the muddy hell on the other side of the Channel.

Ethel persuaded our mother that it was a good plan to make use of the facilities after we had finished our ploughman's lunches. And I scoffed down a Scotch egg for the road while the women were gone.

We slowed briefly at the prehistoric stone circle, but did not stop to explore.

As a golden sun began to turn hazy in the softening blue of the late afternoon, I parked by the seafront and our little group took the towering sea tractor across the flooded spit of sand to Burgh Island which was cut off by the incoming tide. On arrival, a couple of spotty youths escorted our luggage in a metal pram.

'What an adventure.' It was, I realised, quite a rarity to see Mother so relaxed and full of smiles. Her role as head of the family had taken its toll. The lines on her face bore witness to that.

There wasn't a lot to see, but the three of us, Ethel and I each holding one of Mother's arms, wandered slowly round the craggy island. It made a nice change from Streatham. We looked at the cold, green sea, listened to the seagulls, breathed in the fresh air, didn't say much.

'How is your room?' I asked my sister at our early supper under the circular stained-glass ceiling of the hotel's dining room. We had dispensed with cocktails in the bar, and instead I had splashed out on a bottle of Heidsieck.

'Cheers.' Ethel raised her glass. We clinked flutes and drank. 'Huge,' she said. 'The bathroom is bigger than our whole house. I could drown in the tub.'

'Don't do that, dear,' said Mother. 'Always wear your waterwings.'

I remembered swimming with my comrades in an icy, fast-flowing river near Ypres during a lull in the shelling. All those skinny, white naked bodies. So vulnerable, so alive, so expendable.

Other guests began to arrive as we finished our first course. Everyone was dressed up to the nines. My stiff white shirt was beginning to dig into my neck. Maybe I had put on a little weight recently. Too much easy living. All fingers and thumbs, I had had to ask Ethel to tie my black bow tie before she took my arm down the sweeping staircase to supper.

'You smell sweet,' I said as my sister's dexterous, slim fingers fixed the knot and made sure the ends were even.

'It's Shalimar,' Ethel said. 'Walter gave it to me.'

I managed not to wrinkle my nose.

A string quartet played a selection of Ivor Novello tunes, including 'Keep The Home Fires Burning' and 'The Land Of Might Have Been'. When they finished with 'And Mother Came Too', we all laughed.

A few couples hauled themselves on to the dance floor for a leisurely breather between courses. The band obliged with some slow waltzes. All very decorous.

After cracking her way through the crème brûlée, our mother decided to forgo the coffee and brandy. 'Time for my beauty sleep,' she said. 'Thank you, Wag. That was a real treat. I can't tell you how much I appreciate your thinking of your old mother.'

I sipped Ethel's brandy, having drained my own glass a little too quickly.

'Thank you, Wag.' Ethel covered my hand briefly with hers. 'This is sweet of you.'

'We haven't finished yet.' It was only ten o'clock. 'Do you fancy a dance?'

'Just the one then, before bed,' Ethel said. She looked luminous. The most beautiful woman in the world. My sister.

I was careful not to hold her too close, but, try as I did, I could not stop trembling.

CHAPTER 45

Jack

It was the first time I had been searched in customs. With increasing irritation, my father looked on as a busybody official in a short-sleeved white shirt and with two Biros in his top pocket laboriously removed from my case every item of dirty underwear, every crumpled shirt and paperback book, even checking the spines of *Brideshead Revisited* and *Ten Days that Shook the World*. Sand from my swimming trunks pattered down on the desk at Gatwick Airport.

'Do we look like a couple of criminals?'

I wished my father would keep his trap shut. They had finished with him in a matter of minutes. Had I, perhaps, acquired some taint from my current dodgy dealings which left an invisible dye observable exclusively to professional upholders of the law?

'Would you mind unzipping that, please, sir?' The procedural politeness was beginning to unnerve me.

From my washbag, the customs man undid the stopper of my shaving foam, sniffed, counted out each silver-foiled wrap of Codeine, and looked twice at the Imodium tablets. I could have done with a couple of them now. My bowels were feeling loose.

Practised hands slid around the corners of my case, but they did not discover the false bottom.

'Thank you, sir. We're sorry to have kept you.' The customs officer gave me a long, hard stare, as though I might break down suddenly and confess.

'About time too,' my father said. 'We've got a train to catch.'

'And we have our job to do, sir. Thank you for your patience. You're both free to go.'

'What do you suppose all that was about?' asked my dad, as we clattered through East Croydon on our way back to Victoria. 'Thank God they didn't catch me on the way out with those extra pesetas.'

Monkey Rawlings had supplied me with two cases when I first took out the bundles of cash to Monte Carlo: one big one with a false bottom for the secretion of paper money, and another, with a small hidden compartment for a tiny case or package containing something of considerable market value. I gave thanks to him now.

Monkey wasn't so pleased with me when I told him I wanted to jack it in. 'You don't need me here,' I said. 'Surely you can find some other tame clerk who knows how to add up and spell . . .'

The Lamborghini on the wall calendar had been replaced by a November Aston Martin, gun-metal grey like James Bond's.

Monkey Rawlings cracked his hairy knuckles one by one. 'I suggest,' he said, 'that you reflect on this decision. Running scared, just because you've had a little brush with customs . . . By the way, have you seen Sylvia?'

As a matter of fact I had a date with Sylvia in Kennington that evening, the first in ages. I didn't expect to stay long, just in case it got back to Link's uncle. I wasn't totally clear where Sid's interests lay. He maintained his mistress in some style. He knew I knew her. But he had a houseboy in Spain. I concluded he got about a bit.

'I just don't want to do this any more,' I said. 'It's no reflection on you or anyone else. I have an MA from Cambridge. I do some mindless office work here and smuggle money and jewels. It doesn't look good on my CV.'

'Have you talked to HL?'

'Not really.'

'Good. Let's keep it between ourselves for the time being.' Rawlings gazed towards the window. 'With Ron and Reg Kray inside, and no sign of early release for good behaviour, the world is our lobster.' He banged his hand on the table. 'Do you know, Jack, that someone poured boiling water over Frank's feet in the nick. That's not very nice, is it?' It was hard to follow Monkey's thought patterns, but I assumed he was referring to the Richardsons' enforcer Mad Frankie Fraser. 'You've never been inside, have you?' He didn't wait for me to respond. 'They allow him to wear slippers now because he's got a few blisters. I can't believe it. The world's gone soft.'

'It is time I found a proper job,' I said.

'You have a proper job,' said Monkey. 'Don't think what you do is a real job?' He looked as though he would take great pleasure in strangling me. There were red flecks in his eyes. 'Don't think you can get away from us now. You need to keep softening up that copper friend Curwin of yours. Find out something that we can use. To reel him in. In the meanwhile, we're watching you. We take our work very seriously here, Jack my lad. I've told you that before. It is a matter of life and death.'

So far my efforts to secure legitimate employment had resulted in a big, fat nothing. I worried about my ability to pay my share of the rent on Blenheim Crescent if I gave up my job for HL, even though after the recent cash windfalls I was better off by a million miles than my flatmate Tyler. Like me, Cohen had accepted that we were never going to cut it in the great wide world of movie-making. Only skilled technicians like Alex Tompkins, our camera operator, were in demand. He had just been signed up for a stint in Jamaica on an independent film about a black gangster.

Tyler had begun writing slick pieces about pop for *Rolling Stone*. He knew his rock from a hard place. He had also met this nice English girl whose parents owned a pile in the country. Chloe seemed to like Cohen's sour take on life. And he abandoned his studious inverted snobbery about the British class system once she invited him to share her bed in Earl's Court. He didn't even curl his upper lip at the fact that Chloe edited the books page for *The Lady*.

Going through the motions, I had answered an ad for a job in sales and marketing at a big magazine group. In the test for the shortlisted candidates, I suggested, as part of a promotion in a family travel magazine, give-away crayons to highlight routes on maps. I was surprised that such a ludicrous idea secured me an interview in an office on Fleet Street, opposite the spot where London town is divided from the City by the cast-iron statue of a dragon.

'I believe you know my son,' said the managing director after I had taken my seat in front of his wide mahogany desk.

'Stuart? The last I heard he was doing a training scheme at Unilever,' I said.

Norman McPherson gave me a proud parent smile. 'He works here now, with me. He was a bit of a slouch at school, I know that. I don't mind saying that I was seriously worried about him for a while.'

'Do give him my best.'

'I will. I will indeed.' McPherson folded his hands together. 'I'm not one for the old school network. Came up the hard way myself. But when you meet an old Dulwich boy, you have a pretty good idea about his character and staying power.'

I wondered how a man like this held on to his job.

'If you were to take up a position here' – Stuart Hamish McPherson's father lanced me with his probing executive stare – 'I would expect your total commitment. Sometimes we may stay as late as six o'clock, throwing ideas around.'

I nodded enthusiastically.

'As you see, Jack – I hope I may call you Jack?'

'Of course.'

McPherson extended his arms. 'As you see, these offices are extremely well appointed. But when you commence your labours here, you must not necessarily expect a carpet beneath your desk. That is something to be earned. However, I hope you will keep your dignity.'

I telephoned McPherson's secretary the next day to say I was joining the Fleet Air Arm.

'Look what the cat's brought in,' said Sylvia. I heard the echo of George Cornell's last words to Ronnie Kray.

'Lovely to see you too.' We managed the regulation kiss on both cheeks.

'How was Spain?' Sylvia didn't seem to give a stuff one way or the other.

'Here, this is for you.' I handed her the rectangular velvet box. Sylvia did not inspect the contents. I had taken a look earlier, of course. De Beers would have kept the necklace under armed guard.

'It was a bit boring for the first few days,' I said. 'But after we met up with your friend, we knew everyone in town.' It was true. 'Everyone' turned out be a motley bunch, true denizens of the Costa del Crime – a striptease dancer from Bromley called Adele, who was hanging out with a bloke called Martin, known to his close associates as 'Jelly', because of his skill with explosives. There was also the female impersonator Alan – 'Call me Alaine' – whose Shirley Bassey was indistinguishable from the real thing, except Alan had better arms.

I had fancied an American divorcée who looked like Marilyn Monroe, but she wasn't too impressed by the English suitor who threw up in El Toro after the seventh too many gins and tonic.

During our last few days in Calpe, Klaus and Hans introduced me and my dad to a group of timeshare operators, building developers and pool designers. They came from all over the shop. After Monte Carlo, I was glad to have a chance to give my French a workout with an extremely glamorous, slightly older French photographer, who was pausing for a moment in Calpe before heading south for a Condé Nast travel shoot at the Alhambra. But time ran out on that dialogue, and she was not looking for a one-night stand.

'It was fun,' I said. 'Wish you had been there.'

'I don't much care for Calpe,' Sylvia said. 'Bit of a dump. Can't understand why Sid likes it so much. I prefer his place in Madrid.'

My hostess wasn't offering champagne as she had in the good old days of not so long ago. 'Are you still seeing that German bit of stuff? Stinkfinger or whatever her name is?' she asked.

'I'm not seeing anybody.'

'Me neither.'

'What about Curwin?'

'Don't be silly, Jack. He's a policeman. And he is not on the take. From Sid or me or anybody else. Whatever Monkey thinks.'

We took a leisurely stroll through a bottle of Meursault – not top of my list of white wines. There was not a lot to talk about, so we went to bed early.

CHAPTER 46

Wag

After returning from the war, many ex-soldiers found it difficult to adapt to civvy street. No more orders, no more bombs. I knew some chaps who actually missed the excitement of the trenches. Yet at least you did not fear death when advancing twenty yards from one side of the road to the other, even though motor traffic became more frantic.

Wainwright and I had made the most of our opportunities – in France, and now back in England. We were not traumatised by the past or the future. Even the Blitz didn't cramp our style.

Curiously, my first glimpse in 1917 of a huge reconnaissance Zeppelin, silhouetted against dark clouds, still feels more like science fiction to me than watching the Apollo landing on the moon. At the other end of the scale, how mysterious was the tiny crystal set radio my brother Jago made – with its tuning coil of copper wire, capacitor and earphones. I can see his grin now when we got our first signal and tuned in to a radio station where the unintelligible speaker could have been a Martian.

We take change for granted. Inventions unimaginable in my youth propel the world forward. And so much that made life tangible and precious has been lost for ever.

Now I forged passports for a living. What would Ethel have thought if she'd known? Her loving, devoted brother, Tory-voting, non-smoking, unadventurous William Charles Bourton had been a habitual criminal since before he came of age. She would never have agreed to come and share her life with me away from the family in Streatham. But she did.

It wasn't that I was fed up with living with the rest of the Bourtons. It gave me great pleasure to have provided them with a home as grand as the rectory. But I had a dream that one day I would live alone with Ethel. Just her and me.

'People will talk.' My brother Ted rarely expressed an opinion. He remained inscrutable behind those heavy glasses. 'You will have separate bedrooms?'

'Of course,' I said.

'I mean, I am not suggesting . . .' But he was.

Even Mother gave me an odd look when I told her about my plan to move out. 'We will miss you both,' she said.

'Surbiton is not far away.'

'It is if you don't have a car.'

'I'm over forty years old, Mother. Don't you think it is time to have a place of my own?'

'But does it have to be with your sister? Shouldn't you be settling down with some nice young woman?'

'Maybe. I haven't met one.'

Mother did not press me on this.

When I suggested the idea to Ethel, she didn't seem to find the idea peculiar at all. We had always all lived together. No doubt there were neighbours who found it odd that such a large family should choose to live as closely together as a caravan-load of Romany travellers.

There was a quiet understanding between me and Ethel. Things did not have to be spelled out.

In spite of my secret life and the brutalising experience of war, I never considered myself a worldly man. My darling sister Ethel knew what it was to deal with other people's pain, but she retained an ethereal innocence throughout her life. How did she imagine that my earnings as an engraver could have helped buy the rectory and now the place in Surbiton? Did she think that a little overtime made it possible to trade up from my original Austin 7 to a Daimler two-door drophead coupé? Churchill did his electioneering from the leather back seat of the very same car.

Ethel knew that I was a keen amateur photographer. She would no more have dared open the door of my first-floor darkroom than she would have considered disturbing me while I was sitting on the lavatory. She kept our new house spick and span, but the attic where I had my printer, technical equipment and office was also strictly out of bounds.

As with everything in my life, I was self-taught. I had saved up for a Kodak Brownie before the war and graduated to a 35mm Leica. Say what you like about the Germans, and I hate them to this day, they know how to make a decent camera. The lenses developed by Professor Max Berek were pure genius. One, the Summarex, was called after his dog. This must have amused him in the same way as it tickled me to conceal Ethel's initials in every gunstock engraving I made.

For my professional photographic work, all I had to do was aim, focus, click and develop. A clear portrait was all you needed to stick in a passport.

I wish I had not sold those pioneering pictures by Henry Fox Talbot I collected after the war. Nephew Jack would have appreciated them, even if he would not have been the slightest bit interested in the photoglyphic engraving process invented by Talbot in the 1840s. I was obsessive about technical detail. Jack had a good eye. Better than mine. But he did not have the patience or the capacity for taking pains that I possessed. He had to move quickly. His instincts were good, which has kept him out of trouble. And he was of invaluable help to me when

I came to the conclusion that my days as a crook were well and truly over.

'I think we should lie low for a bit,' my brother-in-law Chief Inspector Baker advised. The three of us were standing round Wainwright's Eaton Mews fireplace. A row of gold-embossed stiff invitations from Lord This, Lady That and Sir Somebody Another were arranged neatly on the marble mantelpiece. It was clear why Wainwright supplied most of our contacts. The new crowd of customers who came via Baker were not usually as well connected as Wainwright's but had hard currency to dispose of quickly in pursuit of personal safety.

'There're people sniffing around, and I don't like it,' Baker said.

'Cops?' Wainwright asked.

'Not exactly.'

'Inland Revenue?' Wainwright tried again.

In his role of detective inspector, when Baker came round to Eaton Mews, he always kept his mac on. He refused to take a seat, and would prowl around like a man who has been promoted from downstairs without having acquired even a smidgeon of upstairs etiquette. I don't mean he blew his nose on his sleeve. But, for an officer who must have found himself in a lot of tricky situations, he was unable to disguise his unease in these surroundings. He patted his thinning, sandy hair. 'We just need to take care,' Baker said. 'That's all I'm saying. We have had a very good run lately. I don't want to compromise that.'

'Can't you give us a few more clues?' Wainwright asked.

'There's this bloke called Darby Sabini.'

I had read about him in the papers.

'He's an Eye-tie from Clerkenwell.'

'Yes, yes,' said Wainwright, as though everyone knew that.

'Do you want me to tell you or not?'

'Sorry, Detective,' Wainwright said. 'I'm listening.'

'Sabini has his sticky fingers in all sorts of pies. Not just the gee-gees, dogs and the betting shops. He's got judges, politicians and policemen in his pocket. Word gets around. We're a small operation, but Sabini can't bear not to be in on the action. I don't know about you, but I don't fancy being done over by one of his boys.'

Rather like the Richardsons, years later, and their blood feud with the Kray Twins, it was common knowledge that the Sabini family waged war against the Cortesi Brothers from the Elephant and Castle. 'In fact, I have been meaning to ask you . . .' Baker stared at me. 'Did you get your name from "Wag" McDonald by any chance?'

'Never heard of him,' I said.

'He's been running the Cortesi show for a while,' our insider on the force replied. 'With his brother Wal. Wag and Wal. Couple of mean buggers.'

'I had a chat with that Cortesi once about a bit of business,' said Wainwright. 'Nasty piece of work. Nothing came of it.'

'So did you get your name off him?' Baker continued. 'I mean Wag . . . It's a funny sort of a name.'

'Maybe he got his name off me?'

'Don't make a joke of it. McDonald is no joker, I can tell you. I have heard the rumours. The Sabinis think your name is a tribute. That it means you're a McDonald creature,' Baker said.

'So what are we going to do?' I asked. A cold wind blew down my spine.

CHAPTER 47

Jack

'*Ab ovo* . . .' Link's girlfriend was reading out the rejection letter I had just received.

'Ab-latative absolute!' Link said. At Dulwich College, this was his answer to any question about Latin grammar. 'Measure of difference.' Sometimes he'd be correct, and the rest of the class would applaud derisively.

'*Ab ovo*,' Rachel continued, 'you will never acquire the necessary skill to become an editor at this company.'

'You see,' said Link. 'I told you. Stick with me. We're branching out, Kid.'

Undaunted by my previous experience of job-hunting, and in defiance of Monkey Rawlings, I had been for an interview with an Austrian-born publisher, who had fled his country of birth in 1938. He had seemed impressed with my Cambridge pedigree, my experience as a film producer and my ability to speak French. 'I would offer you a job,' he said, 'but we have had to close the upstairs offices because of a leak in the roof. Here,' he said, passing me a French edition of a book by Jacques Soustelle on the Maya. 'Why don't you translate a couple of chapters of this, and we will talk further in a month.'

Rachel continued with the letter. 'Your execrable translation and complete ignorance of the history of Mexico . . .'

I took back the letter from Rachel. 'I only applied for a job in sales,' I said.

'That publishing bloke is an astute judge of character, if you ask me,' Link said.

I wasn't giving up. Inspired by my Uncle Aubrey, book publishing seemed to be a good career choice if I couldn't make it in films. That morning I had spotted an advertisement in the *New Statesman* for a position at Penguin Books. I kept quiet.

The Waterman's Arms in the Isle of Dogs was beginning to fill up. My Uncle Wag told me it had been a rough place in his day, when it had been called the Newcastle Arms. 'I had to put the wind up someone there once. A real bastard,' he told me.

Since then, the pub had been acquired by the writer, broadcaster and alcoholic Daniel Farson with the aim of transforming it into a music hall. A group called the Levity Lancers performed there. They reminded me of the Temperance Seven, who, with a unique touch of deadpan humour, played imitation twenties' jazz. With frontman 'Whispering' Paul McDowell, the Seven had managed two Top Ten hits.

A few months earlier Link had decided to go into music management. The Levity Lancers were his first signing. They never made a record. They never got anywhere. But the new man on the block had more luck with Birds of a Feather – five girls: bass and acoustic guitars, drums and two singers. They even shared the stage, on more than one occasion, with Elton John, made three albums, and proved a good return on investment.

Both Link's acts were appearing tonight. Doreen, the dark-haired lead of the all-female group, came over before the show and gave him an ostentatious smacker on the lips. Rachel didn't care for this particularly, but understood we were doing showbiz here. I preferred the peroxide blonde vocalist, Eileen, and screeched her name like a teenager with the rest of the audience when she hit the thrilling high notes or gave that trademark wriggle of her hips. On the occasions when Rachel did not accompany us, Link would also burst his lungs calling out for Eileen. But neither woman showed the slightest interest in us as men.

In the fifties there was a famous London impresario called Larry Parnes. He had the Midas touch, transforming the lives of a number of louche young men. He gave them some unforgettably naff names: Vince Eager, Johnny Gentle, Dickie Pride, Duffy Power, Lance Fortune, Terry Dene. Parnes paid these guys a weekly wage, but no royalties. Fame and fortune could not be guaranteed. However, a few performers like Marty Wilde, Georgie Fame and Billy Fury had cause to be thankful to the 'Beat Svengali'.

Unlike Parnes, Link had neither the sexual imperative to groom young men for stardom, nor the professional nous to really exploit his select few clients in the pop business. In this, he was as unsuccessful as his father had been during his brief dalliance with the cinema and Karma Films. Nevertheless, as Linklater Jr said to me, 'Everything Dad does turns to gold. With me it turns to dust.'

We were joined by the glistening, plump-faced owner. 'Full house tonight,' Daniel Farson beamed. If only it could have been that way every night. A waiter followed him with an ice bucket and we were offered champagne all round.

'Francis was here yesterday evening.' The artist Francis Bacon was one of Farson's great friends. 'And Dionne Warwick.' I knew Freddie Foreman had been spotted there a few times too, before he was detained at Her Majesty's Pleasure like the Richardsons, the Krays and Mad Frankie Fraser.

The gay compère, Billy, was noisily masturbating the microphone on the small stage. 'I see we have got royalty here tonight,' he said. 'There are a couple of old queens at the bar.'

Three late arrivals squeezed into some chairs at the front. 'Hello, dear,' said Billy to one of the women as she removed her coat. 'How's the rash?'

Even though the routine varied little most nights, fat, squat Billy always squeezed a laugh out of his audience. The regulars waited for the moment when an unsuspecting American tourist would emerge from the toilets to be asked solicitously from the stage, 'Could you hear us while you were in there, dear?' Whatever the response, Billy's line remained the same. 'Because we could hear you!'

The Levity Lancers were going through their gig at a hell of a lick. We were reaching the moment when sustained hysteria would hit its peak and the long drive to the Isle of Dogs felt worth the effort. The lead singer removed his trousers, revealing skinny legs in a pair of black tights. With a flourish, he put on a matador's hat, and all those in the know cried, 'Spanish!' It may sound silly, but it felt rapturous. Impossible not to laugh like a drain.

Then we would all sing along to 'The Spaniard Who Blighted My Life'. This routine was interrupted by the arrival of a birdcage, which was placed over the singer's head and shoulders. Archibald Cable, I think his name was. From Swindon. A tender rendition of 'A Bird In A Gilded Cage' made a well-judged change of pace before the next cry would go up: 'Spoons!'

The drummer would then emerge from behind his kit and play a couple of carefully bent table spoons against his knee and up his body. Everybody would shout, 'Higher! Higher!' until he had climbed on top of the piano and was performing the percussion on his head.

'I've got to get those bastards on *Morecambe and Wise*,' boasted Link.

Farson rolled his eyes. 'Oh look. There's Babs. See you people later.'

After Eileen and Doreen finished their set, I beat a retreat. No doubt, their new manager wanted to discuss strategy with them about a new record, and about how to raise the Birds of a Feather profile. But the pop world held no appeal for me as a business opportunity.

Tyler and Chloe were clearing away supper when I got home. '*Boeuf en daube*,' Tyler said. 'You missed something.'

'Your French is improving,' I said.

'Hey, there was someone scratching about the door when we came back. He scarpered when he heard us on the stairs.'

'CIA,' I said meaningfully.

'Can't be. I'm in the clear.' He looked nervous.

Not so long ago the US Draft Board had tracked Cohen down to his London bolthole. He had thought he could dodge the draft by staying abroad but he was ordered to report to Ruislip Airbase to do a test and a physical. Tyler had gone into strict training. He stayed up for a week without sleep, took uppers, downers and smoked as much weed as he could lay his hands on.

On the day of reckoning, as he left for Ruislip, he was red-eyed, and paranoid off his head. I was instructed to wait by the telephone. Sure enough, the call came. 'I'm in the shit,' Cohen whispered.

'Where are you?'

'In a call box outside the base. I gave them the slip.'

'Are you mad?'

'I heard them talking. They are going to put me in a packing case and ship me off to Saigon.'

'Get back to the base this instant, you idiot,' I said. 'No one in their right mind is going to send you out there.'

'I need a lawyer.'

'No you don't. Go back to the base. Or you'll be in real trouble.'

Tyler did as he was told. They classified him 4F and gave him the name of a good shrink.

But I was surely the one in trouble now. Someone was definitely checking up on me.

CHAPTER 48

Wag

In an old book of fairy tales we had at home when I was young, I was haunted by the image of the terrifying gnome Rumpelstiltskin who, when his secret name is revealed, drives his right foot into the ground so hard that he sinks down up to his waist. Then he grabs his left foot with both hands and tears himself in two.

My own nickname Wag is a rather silly name. I never tried to hide it. But now, the idea that a leading south London gangster, of fearsome reputation, shared it with me became something of a worry.

I felt Wainwright and Baker sizing me up. Surely they couldn't suspect me of being a cuckoo in the nest? I had to trust them not to be swayed by the talk on the street. They knew I had nothing to do with the Cortesi gang.

One thing was for sure. The three of us were no match for two gangs of thugs whose lives were dedicated to organised violence. We were hardly likely to stride together down the New Kent Road with machine guns blazing at the combined forces of both the Cortesis and the Sabinis.

'Obviously,' Wainwright said, 'we can't just sit here and do nothing.'

Baker was still on his feet, the old Baker, prowling and uncomfortable.

'I think this is something for your lot,' I said to him. 'We have got to find a way of putting these buggers away, or encouraging them to blow each other to bits.'

Baker laughed humourlessly at this last suggestion. This

wasn't the movies. But in fact there had been a famous battle not so long ago between the two gangs outside the Duke of Wellington in the Waterloo Road. As I recall, there were seven fatalities. It became known as the Battle of Waterloo.

'How much do they know about us?'

'Enough,' Baker said. He paused by the mantelpiece and made a show of scrutinising all Wainwright's invitations. 'Maybe one of your distinguished friends had a few too many and gabbed . . .'

'And maybe one of your true blue colleagues was slipped a little something under the table for information received . . . It doesn't matter how the story got out,' Wainwright continued. 'It's how we deal with it.'

'Maybe the best plan is to pause our business for a while? Disappear from sight?' I was not the bravest man on the block, but nor the most fearful. After all, I had come through the bloodiest war in history. So had Wainwright. We knew how to keep cool under fire. But I had no desire for trouble if it wasn't necessary.

'We help people disappear all the time and cover their tracks.' The more I knew Harry Wainwright, and (for all our long association) that was not very well, the more I liked him. He was efficient, got on with his job, didn't flap, and was scrupulous with money. 'We should be the experts at it.'

'Except that we have no plans to flee the country,' I said.

'I wouldn't mind,' Wainwright said. 'Nothing much keeping me here. No wife, no family, no children. No nothing, really.' He poured us all a Scotch. 'But you're both family men.'

'Not exactly,' I said. I remained unmarried, but not, I suppose, unspoken for. And I had family responsibilities which I took more seriously than anyone imagined.

Baker, on the other hand, had recently become the father of a baby boy, Leo. My nephew, Leo the Lion, weighing in at seven and a half pounds with a fine head of tufty brown hair. Baker downed his glass in one, without adding water. 'It is beginning to look,' he said, 'as though yours truly is going to be lumbered with sorting out this mess.'

No one was arguing.

'Don't know why I bothered to come all the way over here,' he grumbled.

'For the pleasure of our company.' Wainwright reached for the bottle of Bell's. 'Have another one.'

'Don't mind if I do,' said Baker.

I stuck with the day job at Purdey's. Wainwright did whatever he did with his days, and we waited for word from Baker. It was an anxious time. I was jittery, nearly jumping out of my skin if I heard footsteps behind me.

For a while, I kept a beady eye open for suspicious figures lurking under lampposts. I instructed Ethel to keep the windows and doors locked and always tell me where she was going when she went out. I even contemplated adopting a disguise and slipping unobserved into the shabby streets of the Elephant and Castle to catch a glimpse of my nefarious namesake. But then I thought better of it.

And then one morning, the headline in the *News Chronicle* came as the perfect accompaniment to my breakfast fry-up. In the paper propped against the toast rack, I read: 'Sabini to Court'. My spirits rose. An illegal betting ring had been uncovered. Doping at Sandown and Kempton Park. After months of careful investigation, the police had raided a number of gambling clubs owned by a certain Mr Sabini, and a stash of evidence seized;

etc., etc. What was certain was that he would go down for a long time.

What about the Cortesi Brothers, though, and their immigrant mobster imports? There was no news of them in the paper. Nor of Wag or Wal McDonald, nor of another villain called Kimber, a close associate of McDonald's I had discovered from keeping my ear to the ground. His gang were the Brummagens, part of the wider association of the Elephant and Castle mob. We weren't in the clear if these characters were still at large. We weren't even in the clear if the whole bleeding mob was sent down. The tentacles of the underworld extend far beyond prison walls.

But it was a reasonable start.

CHAPTER 49

Jack

'Who's been a naughty boy then?' George Curwin stretched his legs on to the bright kelim carpet in Sylvia's basement living room.

Link looked at him, then at me, up at our hostess, who was uncorking some wine, and then at his feet.

Don't ask me why, but the three of us had been back to Dulwich College for an Old Boys' reunion. We were too young for that kind of nostalgia. Now we were trying to recover our equilibrium in the sanctuary of Sylvia's Kennington flat, where I also planned to spend the night.

'I didn't mean to. It just came out,' Link said. Before supper in the Great Hall, we had taken drinks with the other dinner-jacketed Old Alleynians and a selection of masters who looked just as dusty and dull as they had over a decade ago. Time had not withered them. They started out that way.

'Ah,' Link had said loudly, as the beak-like head appeared of our erstwhile head of biology. 'The Dreaded Crid.'

'I'm not sure he heard,' I said. 'And so what if he did?' I hadn't forgotten how he had humiliated me when I was at school by asking whether I thought I was a vertebrate.

Teachers do acquire an aura of imperturbability, as a defence against the supreme indifference to learning manifested by the bulk of their pupils and also as a bulwark against the boys' barely concealed contempt for their position of authority. It is quite possible that Cridland wasn't even listening. He asked us in turn what we were all doing now for a living, smiled bleakly at the answers as if his thoughts were elsewhere, then moved on to do his duty with another group of young Old Boys.

'What a ghastly existence,' I said, back at Sylvia's place. 'Imagine still having to sing the school song every day.'

'Or that dreadful rugby song.'

'And it's feet, feet, feet all the way.' Curwin had been a nippy fly half and also possessed a pleasing light tenor voice. 'And it's fall on the ball till you're black and blue and all . . .'

'Christ,' said Sylvia, handing round the glasses. 'Thank God I went to secondary modern.'

'For what we are about to receive . . .' Link raised the chilled wine to his lips.

'May the Lord make us truly thankful.' Curwin completed.

'*Quae de largitate tua sumus sumpturi*' – I took up the challenge with the eighth-century blessing learned at Cambridge – '*et concede, ut illis salubriter nutriti* . . .'

'Measure of difference,' snorted Link, and we drained our glasses.

'Public school tits,' said Sylvia.

'Never again,' I said.

We looked around for more wine. Curwin rose to his feet, a little unsteadily, and fetched the half-empty bottle.

'Go easy on that stuff,' said Sylvia. 'I've only got another three cases.'

There were times when I loved her to bits. There were times when I almost believed she loved me.

'So no girls allowed at these Old Dullard dos?' Sylvia had a lot of catching up to do on the drinking front. The class of '52 had a good head start. Although it would be fair to observe that Sylvia rarely let the second hand twitch very far past the seven o'clock mark in the evening without having a snifter of something or other.

'No girls,' said Link. 'No fun.'

'Never again,' I said once more.

'Did you see Mark Cousins?' Curwin said. 'He's a major in the Guards now. Zero out of ten in the brain box.'

'Best full back I ever saw,' said Link. I'm sure he never watched a school match in his life, and on the field had usually been too busy throwing mud at his own side to notice which way the ball was going.

'Look at that chap Curwin,' I said. 'The Fotherington Thomas of the Remove.'

'"Hello clouds, hello sky,"' Link said, quoting from the immortal Molesworth.

Unfortunately for me, Curwin showed no sign of being a 'gurl'. It would have been something to tell Monkey and get him off my back.

'And he's now a bloody detective inspector with the Met.'

'Bloody hell,' said Link.

'And look at you two lawbreakers,' said Curwin, the smile receding from his face. 'Or maybe better not.'

CHAPTER 50

Wag

This bloke had me up against the wall, with a razor at my throat. 'So what's your game?' he said.

With the blade against my Adam's apple, it wasn't easy to reply.

I had been walking down Streatham High Road from the station, minding my own business, as you do of a Friday evening after work. I had no plans. Ethel was away doing a week's stint at a children's hospital outside St Albans, and I had no desire to go dancing on my own or even to treat myself to Ronald Colman in *Bulldog Drummond* at the Regal. There was this book I was re-reading on Fox Talbot. Technical details about his photogenic drawing process were not everyone's cup of tea, but, as they say, I derived hours of harmless amusement from the great man's optical researches.

'I think you must be mistaking me for someone else.' The back of my head was scraping against the rough brickwork of Gleneagle Road. Street lighting barely existed there. To a passer-by, we could have been a courting couple in a clinch.

'I know who you are, Wag Bourton. Don't treat me like an arsehole, my friend, or I'll make sure you never sit down again.'

He had a grip on my left arm that informed me that my attacker was no amateur. If I offered any resistance, a fresh wide smile on my neck would be the last I would ever make.

'So,' he said. 'Let's have a little chat about your friend Harry.'

'Harry who?'

'People who know me . . .' I detected no hint of Italian in

my attacker's voice. However, this guy had to belong to either the Cortesi or Sabini gangs. 'People who know me,' the man continued, 'think I can fly off the handle. You can find out for yourself, if you like. So let me ask you one last time about Harry Wainwright.'

'He was my commanding officer in Flanders,' I said. 'A good man.'

'A very good man. A war hero. Like yourself.'

'Would you mind taking that thing away from my throat?' I said. 'It is difficult to breathe, let alone talk.'

He relaxed the pressure against my throat a bit, confident that I was not going to fight back or try to make a run for it. The bulky silhouettes of two men blocked both ends of the narrow street. On the High Road beyond, a red double-decker omnibus motored by, lights bright inside, commuters reading their evening paper or gazing blankly out of the window.

'You and your good friend Lieutenant Wainwright have been straying into enemy territory.'

I wondered if there was some sort of manual, where aspiring criminals could rehearse their elaborate dialogue. And did I detect a hint of Brummy in his voice?

'I'm here to tell you – you've hit the barbed wire. You have two choices. You cut us in or we cut you out.'

'Cut you in to what exactly?'

He shoved me back against the wall. The second bang to my head was particularly painful.

'There you go again. Just when we're beginning to have a nice conversation.' The thin edge of the razor was pressed more insistently against the skin of my throat. 'Try not to be a complete prat, Wag. You could be useful to us.'

So the plan was not to leave me bleeding to death tonight in Streatham Hill. That was a relief.

'We wanted to give you a message from Mr McDonald. Wag McDonald. You know who I mean?'

In the darkness, I was memorising the features of my assailant. He was a head taller than me. Hooded eyes that had no lashes. Flat fair hair, with a nose that had been broken by more than one fist. And he needed a shave. Perhaps that was why he carried a cutthroat razor.

'As you may have heard, there has been a bit of trouble recently in the Clerkenwell area. Mr McDonald is not displeased with this. There is a concern, though, that the Filth may be pursuing their enquiries elsewhere, poking their noses in where they don't belong.'

'I could talk more easily if you . . .'

'My name is Kimber, by the way. You may have heard of me.'

I nodded eagerly and he relaxed his grip on my arm and took a pace backwards.

'Are we beginning to understand each other? Good.' The hand that held the razor dropped to his side. 'We need someone with your expertise. Someone who can make sure that our papers are in order. It is Mr McDonald's view that you are the right man for the job.'

'Am I free to go now?' I asked.

'We will be in touch very shortly,' Kimber said. 'We know where you live, where you work, what time you take a shit.' I think he was exaggerating with that last claim. 'Don't even think of doing a runner. We will find you. We will burn your house to the ground. We will not leave one single, solitary soul alive. Do I make myself clear?'

'Extremely.' I tried to still my trembling knees.

Kimber smiled. Even in the shadows, it was clear he needed a better dentist, or a plate. I had never seen such crooked teeth. Like a shark's but not so pointed. 'So, put a sock in it, Wag

Bourton, and you'll come to no harm.' Kimber folded the razor and slid it into his right-hand pocket. 'Enjoy the rest of your evening. You'll be hearing from us.'

Thrown by this unpleasant encounter, I decided to pay a visit to the rectory, to check that all was in order there. Mother was sitting in the comfiest armchair in the living room, sipping a glass of Taylor's port. A fire was burning in the grate. The heavy green velvet curtains excluded any October draught from the French windows that led into the garden. Either side of a heavy black portico clock stood two Angelica Kauffmann vases. In spite of all our dawn flits, trips to the pawn shop and the inevitable breakages, those two vases had accompanied us to every single house I had ever known.

'You look pale, Wag,' Mother said. 'Maybe you would like to join me in a glass?'

She had poured the contents of her staple bottle of port into a heavy Victorian decanter.

'And what's that you've done to your neck?'

My hand went immediately to my throat. 'Cut myself shaving.' There was blood on my fingers. I found a handkerchief in my trouser pocket and pressed it to the cut.

'I worry about you,' Mother said.

I raised a glass to her. 'There's no need.' I swallowed the sweet liquid, and hoped it would slow my racing heartbeat. 'I'm fine.'

'You work too hard. Such long hours.'

'Helps pay the rent,' I said, pouring myself a second glass.

'They exploit you,' she said.

'Not really. I like my work.'

'Have you eaten?'

'I had a sandwich at my bench.'

'There's a pork pie in the larder. And some fresh tomatoes.'

'I'm not really hungry at the moment.' There is nothing like a razor to the throat to put you off your victuals.

Everyone else seemed to be out. Even without the customary hubbub of the usual occupants, the Old Rectory felt more like home than anywhere I had ever lived.

The kitchen was immaculate, which was an unmistakable sign that Florence had not been near the stove recently. Jago was the second worst offender. You could always tell by the trail of crumbs and abandoned knives if he had been in for a snack.

I had fetched the pie. Mothers like to see their children eat.

'So tell me about your day, Wag . . .' Mother settled back in her chair as though I were about to launch into an account of adventure on the High Seas and the discovery of El Dorado in the impenetrable jungles of a Lost Continent. I was hardly going to tell her of my encounter down the road with Billy Kimber and the so-called 'Elephant Boys'. 'You never bring anyone home,' Mum said. 'Isn't there some nice girl? Like that one you used to know at work?'

'She got married.'

'Probably just as well. I didn't like the sound of her.'

The image returned to my mind of Queenie unrolling her stockings the first night I spent with her. Apart from her and that brief, dream-like encounter in France, I had hardly been a man about town. The chaste love I felt for my sister was enough for me. But it was hardly a subject to discuss with one's mother.

'Good pie,' I said. I dipped each crusty chunk in a slurry of mustard and followed up with a slice of tomato. The aspic jelly was just right too. In food we trust.

Tonight, though, I would take my Luger from its hiding place under a floorboard by my bed and make sure it was in working order.

CHAPTER 51

Jack

'Do you think Curwin's on to us?' Link said.

'Probably. Doesn't mean he's going to do anything. But in any case, I've had it with this job. I don't want to end up in the nick. I'm getting out.'

I was clearing my desk at the Camberwell office. There wasn't a great deal to put in the cardboard box – a spare white shirt, a pair of Church's black brogues, an old Penguin copy of *Great Expectations* (I could hardly be expected to concentrate all day on columns of figures or on deciphering legalese) and a couple of pens.

There was a roar from the door. 'Where do you think you're going?' Monkey Rawlings marched in. 'I thought we had been through this before, Jack.' The menacing look on his face did not suggest that he was about to give me a farewell box of chocolates. 'When you work for the Richardsons, you sign on for the duration,' he snapped. 'You're a bright young man. I thought you understood. Just because Charlie and Eddie aren't here in the office does not mean they are not keeping an eye on things. We can't have you wandering about the place, knowing what you know. What did you think, Jack? That this was just a holiday job?'

Rawlings was wearing a dazzling new outfit today – a mauve shirt with a yellow tie clashed with a maroon jacket and red trousers. It was as though a naked man on the run had grabbed a bundle of clothes from a charity stall.

'Do you want me to write a formal letter of resignation?' I said.

Rawlings grabbed my arm. It hurt.

'Come on, Monkey.' Link tried to intervene. 'There's no need for any of this.'

HL's right-hand man turned on his boss's son with a snarl. 'When I want advice from a little git like you . . .' I could have sworn that his wild black hair crackled with static electricity. 'Put your things back in the desk, Jack.' His voice assumed the level tone of the man reading the shipping forecast. 'I have some papers I want you to look over.'

The red slashes underneath Link's eyes bleached away. 'I don't think you are giving the orders round here,' he said.

'Oh don't you, my son? I don't see your dear old dad around here anywhere, do you? And if I did, what the fuck do you imagine he would be doing about it? He's too busy feathering his nest in Monte Carlo and hanging round with tarts in the Casino.'

Link took a step towards Rawlings, but then thought better of it. He attempted a laugh. 'This is getting out of proportion, Monkey.'

Rawlings roughly let go of my arm. 'And don't call me "Monkey",' he said. 'Either of you. Ever. That name is for people I trust.'

'I phoned my dad,' Link said. We had gone to my flat.

It was worse than being at school, complaining about a sadistic teacher. Except that no boy I knew had ever squealed about the regular torments inflicted by a number of masters at my prep school.

'He's back on Monday.'

'I don't suppose he is going to let me off the hook, though,' I said.

'I'm sorry, Kid,' Link said. 'I got you into this. At the beginning, I thought it was mainly a bit of fun. And with the bonus of huge piles of cash. Frankly, I have been a complete and utter dickhead. I don't want to continue either, any more than you do. And I'm in far deeper. Maybe the music business is a fantasy of mine, but at least I'm the one making the mistakes. We're out of our depth here, Kid. And I doubt very much that my dad has the solution either.'

'Apparently, someone was ferreting round here the other night . . .' I said.

'Who was that?' Link asked. 'I say, Kid, have you got any gin? I feel one coming on.'

'Sorry, I don't. Stocks are low. I can offer you some red. Only opened yesterday.'

I poured us both a large glass. 'Tyler and Chloe came home to find some bloke trying to get into the flat. They didn't see his face or anything. He scarpered before they had a chance.'

'Can't have been Monkey. Sorry, I mean Mr Rawlings.'

For both of us, the memory of that encounter in Camberwell with Rawlings was a deep embarrassment. How pathetic we had been. How spineless. How perceptive that teacher Cridland had been about us.

'Cops maybe.'

'Surely not. Who knows anything about you?'

'Curwin?'

'Nah, he's just an old softie. Customs and Excise would have nabbed you at the airport if they had your number. It must be someone from the other side.'

'What other side? The Krays?'

'Ridiculous, I agree,' Link said.

'So who is the opposition?'

'Freddie Foreman's lot maybe . . .' Link was fumbling in the dark.

I was smaller than small fry. Who the hell could be interested in me?

'What about the Lambrianous?' Link looked almost triumphant to have come up with the name of another minor gang.

'What about the workers?' I said.

'What the hell are we going to do?'

'Get pissed, I suppose.'

'I have been doing this correspondence course,' said Oliver. His myopic blue eyes had shrunk behind his black, horn-rimmed glasses. Study may broaden the mind but it can ruin the eyesight.

'Who's a clever boy then?'

'"Life is not an easy matter,"' Oliver said. 'Trotsky said that . . . "You cannot live through it without falling into frustration and cynicism unless you have before you a great idea which raises you above personal weakness, above all kinds of perfidy and baseness."'

I clapped, with post-modern irony.

'Fitzwilliam have offered me a place. My old man went there, you know.'

'Very old school tie, comrade . . .'

Oliver had the good grace to look shamefaced. 'I guess it might have helped,' he said.

'Are you going to read History?' I had no interest in niggling him over preaching about the Workers of the World while making the most of the Old Boy network. After all spies like Philby and Burgess had dreamed of school while betraying their country.

Oliver had been back from Cambridge for a while in what he always called his 'gaff' at Crouch Hill. 'Things were getting a bit too hot with the landlady,' he said. 'And being a postman is more fun than trying to stop students pinch books in Heffers.'

My cousin and I were maintaining a steady pace along the Regent's Canal. We had passed Victoria Park, and were heading for the Grapes in Limehouse for lunch. The constant mutter of London traffic was muffled by the water and the barricade of houses and trees.

'I found out something the other day,' he said. 'When the Tsarina was trying to win a favourable press.' Oliver was talking about the Russian Revolution, as he always did. 'She dressed up in a nurse's uniform, in order to show what a good, clean, caring girl she was. It turned out later that a whole pile of nurses' outfits had been nicked by the prostitutes in St Petersburg. So when Alexandra's photograph appeared in the newspapers, it merely confirmed what everyone thought – that she was a great big tart.'

'Speaking of which, have you seen anything of Giesele lately?' I asked.

It was ages since the incident at Victoria Station. I had stopped the pathetic phone calls when I would put down the receiver as soon as she answered. But Giesele did still wander the gloomy passageways of my dreams and desires.

'Comrade Karpfinger?' Oliver mused theatrically, hand raised to furrowed brow. 'I saw her not so long ago getting out of a Bentley, owned by some rich film composer. Can't remember his name. Stanley someone. Another class traitor.'

'I don't go out vit Tory,' Giesele had told me when I said how much I had admired Harold Macmillan's sangfroid at the United Nations General Assembly after the Soviet President,

Nikita Khrushchev, took off his shoe and banged it on the desk. 'Could I have that translated?' the British Prime Minister had drawled.

'She hasn't come to any of our meetings for a while.' Crouch Hill remained an outpost for idealistic chatter, for a fit audience though few . . .

At Camden Lock, we had to take a diversion up to the road, before heading back to the peace of the canal.

'Vot dat?' As I looked around for the steps, I found myself saying in Giesele's aggressive German accent. 'A Londoner who does not know his London.'

'Do you miss her?' Oliver asked.

'No. Yes. I'm afraid I do.'

Ahead of us five young men sat on a bench. Two smoked cigarettes. One threw a pebble into the grey water. A fourth folded a newspaper and dropped it on the ground. And the fifth stood up as Oliver and I approached. 'Got a light?' he said.

'Doesn't look as though you need one,' I replied.

'Oh. Right.' He looked over at his mates. 'We're a bit short of change,' he said. 'Need to make a long-distance phone call.'

I reached in my pocket and handed over a couple of bob.

'I'm not sure that will be enough,' he said.

'Sorry, that's all I've got.'

I was looking around to see if there were any other walkers who might prevent a nasty incident from occurring. There was not even a nanny with a pram.

The other four youths formed up, two in front and two behind.

'Who's he?' The leader looked at my cousin.

'The Archbishop of Canterbury,' said Oliver, taking off his glasses. 'Who are you?'

'A friend of a friend,' replied the oily-haired young man.

They all wore black leather blazers, quite stylish, not those short jobs with studs the Hell's Angels like.

'Shall I tell you something?' Oliver said. 'I don't care if you're Frankie Valli and the Four Seasons. You're in our way.'

My cousin had the definite advantage of surprise, certainly as far as I was concerned. I didn't know he had it in him.

He grabbed the leader's arm and pushed him in the canal. As the second took a swing at him, my superhero cousin used the attacker's momentum to trip him up.

The least I could do was to deliver the old one two that had worked a treat for me in El Toro. As my opponent dropped to his knees, I joined Oliver in the fray. He had one bloke in a headlock, while kicking another assailant in the groin.

The last remaining ambusher clicked open a flick knife and came at me like he was at the Griffith Observatory with James Dean in *Rebel Without a Cause*. The sound of another splash as Oliver was clearing the towpath distracted my attacker sufficiently for me to grab his right hand and force the slim blade down with all the strength I could muster. He yelled as the point sliced into his thigh. I head-butted him, and over he went. The knife dropped on the ground and I kicked it into the canal.

Oliver was putting his glasses back on. Two humiliated punks paddled for the opposite bank. The remaining three decided to stay where they were, or had no choice in the matter.

'"Where force is necessary,"' Oliver said, '"it must be applied boldly, decisively and completely. But one must know the limitations of force – when to blend it with a manoeuvre, a blow with an agreement . . ." That's Leon Trotsky again.'

'Words for all occasions,' I said. That was the first time I had ever tried a head-butt. I wondered if I would have a bruise on my forehead later. 'I don't think there is much room for further manoeuvre here, do you?"

'I do not.'

We continued, at a slightly accelerated pace, our walk towards Limehouse.

'I didn't have a clue you could—'

'I would have gone bananas studying twenty-nine hours a day. I did ju-jitsu night classes in Upper Street. Near the King's Head.'

'Thank you, Grand Master.' I stopped and bowed.

Oliver bowed back.

'You saved my bacon.'

'A pleasure to be of service, comrade,' Oliver said. 'But, if you don't mind me asking, who are those people? What on earth have you been up to?'

CHAPTER 52

Wag

The event that had the profoundest impact on my life was the Great War. But I never consciously dwell on that time. My other memories are like layers of wrapping paper, with different designs, colours and textures. For instance, I recall that Mr Kirby who was the manager of the wig shop in Soho always wore white spats on a Thursday and a white rose in the buttonhole of his dark suit. When I contemplate those early days as an apprentice engraver, it is his picture that comes to mind. Yet I don't suppose the two of us ever exchanged more than half a dozen words.

Between Peckham, Camberwell and Clapham, I picture my little sisters. They always seem to be dressed in pink, running around the halls and up the stairs, shrieking, laughing and crying.

Then there is a more static image of my father – that long, pale face with the big dark eyes, staring at us from the back seat of a police van, before he was driven away. And my poor mother fighting back the tears.

Of course, there are many nights in the darkness when I only see blood and mud, and hear nothing but shellfire.

It is hard to think of the past in straight, chronological lines. Memories have a habit of circling round behind you, then popping up. Or, as a decade slides by, although you stare calmly across an empty plain towards a distant horizon, suddenly, like Genghis Khan appearing with his Mongol Army, an event occurs out of the blue that tramples quiet expectations into the dust.

My brother-in-law, Maurice Baker, was a practical man. It was fortunate he had found the perfect job, where a certain amount of criminal deviousness was crucial to preserving the rule of law. In a dawn raid, the Cortesi mob was finally rounded up. Irritatingly, not every single member of the gang found himself in handcuffs and followed the Sabinis to jail. Wag McDonald's name still did not appear on the charge list. I was also again sorry to hear no mention of Billy Kimber.

Nonetheless it seemed as though we might be safe for a while. Baker received a promotion and a special commendation for his role in keeping the city safe from marauding mobsters. As for Wainwright he treated himself to two Sèvres porcelain elephant vases, painted by Charles Nicolas Dodin. They looked very good in the alcove where he placed them, like relics in a shrine.

I was pretty sure I had not left my bedside light on in my bedroom. Ethel was still away. It was late. I had spent the evening with Wainwright at Madame Prunier's elegant fish restaurant in St James's. No jellied eels on her menu. But I was not complaining about the oysters. And the Welsh rarebit was better than the one they served at Wiltons round the corner.

I was not a registered bon viveur like Wainwright, nor did I become a member of the Fine Arts Society, but, over the years, I had gained access to worlds I never imagined when I started out in Wardour Street.

As an idle and amusing diversion, I acquired a collection of stevengraphs. Mounted on cardboard, these were little pictures, woven from silk, using Jacquard looms in Coventry. It was Thomas Stevens who came up with the idea of mass-produced memories. I bought my first one because it was of the pugilist James Belcher, which reminded me of my early days as an apprentice in Wardour Street. Sporting scenes were popular – from tennis to cricket. I added a depiction of the Crystal Palace; Lady Godiva; Dick Turpin's Ride to York on Black Bess; the *Lusitania*; another great boxer, John L. Sullivan, and the Declaration of Independence. I kept them all in a big, flat leather case in the top drawer of my bedside table – on which Billy Kimber, Wag McDonald's enforcer, was now balancing my Luger, pointing straight at my chest.

'Dirty stop-out,' he said. 'Thought you were never coming home.'

He had been lying with his greasy head on my pillow. That would have to go straight into the wash. I didn't question how Kimber had got in. After the incident the other night, I should have made sure that I started locking the door.

'What do you want?' I asked.

'I wouldn't mind a large Scotch.'

'I don't keep drink in my room, but I can go downstairs if you like.'

'You stay right where you are.' Kimber jiggled the barrel of the pistol towards my head. 'Where'd you get this?'

'Off some Jerry.'

'I didn't care for it out there myself. Came home early. Good gun, though. Why do people always hide their stuff under the floorboards?'

Frankly, I didn't expect anyone to go rooting around in my bedroom, and you would be an idiot to leave a weapon just lying about the place.

'I need a passport,' he said. 'Two passports. In a hurry.'

'Who for?'

'One for me, and one for Dicky Dolly.' I had an aunt in

the country who used to use the same expression. Aunt Dot. I don't even know if she was a real aunt. The Bourton family had relatives coming out of their ears.

'The game's up here, for the time being,' Kimber said. 'I'm off to Los Angeles. My friend and associate, Mr McDonald, also plans to join me. Do you know you share the same name? You must be an admirer.' He reached into his suit pocket and handed me a pristine passport. 'Apart from a day trip to Calais,' he said. 'I've never been out of the country.'

'There's no need for that.' I pointed at the gun.

Kimber kept the muzzle of the Luger pointing at my chest.

'I'm not much use to you dead.'

This was a point we did not explore.

'You'll need a new name,' I said. 'Who would you like to be? And we will have to make you look a bit different. I suggest you and Mr McDonald come to my office tomorrow. You know where it is.'

Kimber lowered the Luger. 'Have the kettle on at seven.' He stood up.

'I'd like my gun back, if you don't mind,' I said.

Kimber's smile exposed the terrifying teeth. 'Finders keepers,' he said.

'I'd like to hang on to it, if you don't mind. For sentimental reasons.' I grabbed my uninvited guest by the wrist, and tried to take back my Luger. Kimber resisted. We scuffled together in my bedroom. He was wiry and strong, but I wanted what was mine.

As we struggled, the barrel became stuck under his chin, and pressure from my grip caused him to pull the trigger. I gazed into his stricken eyes, and felt a corresponding dread.

Click. Not a deafening bang to wake the dead with a new arrival.

'It's not loaded.' I had assumed the intruder must have located the bullets which I kept in a large Toby jug on the shelf.

A bead of sweat ran down Kimber's forehead. 'Here.' He returned my weapon. 'I think this belongs to you.'

CHAPTER 53

Jack

'So you're a young man with connections, Jack. Now me, I'm a hard man. But I would never grass on one of my colleagues.'

Monkey Rawlings's smile was perhaps even more intimidating than his scowl. I won't tell you what he was wearing today, but it displayed his determination to avoid the dictates of fashion. The kipper tie had a zigzag pattern that made your eyes go funny.

The return of HL to London had not miraculously released me from bondage to the Firm. 'I'm sorry, Jack,' he said. 'I'll see what I can do.' I suppose that meant not a lot. He had to clear it with the Richardsons. The documents I continued to handle did not deal with the kinds of transaction that the average clerk would expect to pass every day on his office desk. Mind you, my quest for legitimate employment had also ground to a halt. The people at Penguin, out near the airport, had been friendly enough and had even invited me out for a drink. But that was as far as it had gone. No job had been offered. So I kept the Firm's books shipshape and my mouth shut.

'Connections? How do you mean?' I asked Rawlings.

The car of the month on the wall calendar commemorated a dank March – a white Alfa Romeo against a sky of azure blue.

'You know people who know people.'

'Not as many as you.'

'I'm just a bit of rough, Jack. We both know that.'

I sipped some water from a paper cup.

'Well, you don't know Charlie,' Rawlings continued. 'Things

could be worse in the Scrubs, but he's looking at a very long stretch. We all believe that an extended holiday abroad would do him a world of good.' The chap in the clown suit handed me a photograph of a cold-eyed man with a goatee beard and dark hair. 'As you know, they confiscate your passport when you do bird.'

'Is this Charlie?'

'One and the same.'

'Doesn't look like him.'

'That's the whole idea.'

'I don't know anyone who does dodgy passports.'

'I do.' Monkey Rawlings loosened his tie, and undid the top button of his shirt. Thick, black chest hair, like a ruff, was released above his collar. It was as though he were transforming into a werewolf before my eyes. 'But they're all doing time or have buggered off out of it.'

I passed him back the photo.

'See if you can come up with someone who will do you a favour,' he said. 'Ask around. Use your initiative.'

'Doesn't HL know anybody?'

Rawlings walked over to the window and wiped away the condensation with the palm of his hand. 'We have the same contacts.'

'But I don't have any.'

My bizarre boss turned like a beast at bay. 'I have every confidence in you, Jack.'

It was like being in someone else's bad dream. Unable to alter events or open my eyes and wake.

'I can assure you that Charlie will be most appreciative if you are able to help.'

'What about Eddie? Don't they both want to go over the wall?'

'We reckon one at a time is best. They're under constant surveyance. If Eddie comes out of his cell, the other blokes have to bang up.' He chuckled to himself, a strange, feral snuffling noise. 'Foreman, can you believe it, managed to persuade the warden to let him carve a chicken for his Sunday lunch. With a knife. A great big carving knife. As you know, wardens don't hand out bloody carving knives to any Tom, Dick or Harry but some people seem to be able to get away with anything. So Eddie wants to go to the kitchen to make a bit of toast. But Mr Foreman and the others aren't allowed to be in the same place at the same time with Mr Richardson, and have to go back to their cells like good little boys. When Freddie is ready to carve his Sunday lunch, there's no knife. I suppose it wasn't too hard to guess where it had gone. They found it eventually down the U-bend of Eddie's toilet.' Rawlings snuffled some more.

'Have you asked Link?'

'That boy can't tell his arse—' Rawlings checked himself. 'You public school blokes, you don't have the foggiest about what goes on in the world. It's quite simple really. If you cross me, there are repercussions. This is your task. This is an order. It's not a hard lesson to understand, and maybe it's time I taught you one, Jack Armitage.'

'Was it you who set those blokes on me the other day?'

Rawlings picked up the phone and dialled a number. Our conversation was at an end.

'So how is it all going at Linklater's?' My mother handed me a plate of neatly sliced gammon, and I added some roast potatoes and peas from the steaming bowls on the dining room table. After all those years as their lodger, it had been a while since I'd been home to Dulwich for Sunday lunch.

'Fine.' What does anybody say about a job they despise?

My father grunted. Working for a seedy scrap metal dealer in Camberwell was not what he had ever had in mind for his Varsity-educated son. His ears would pop if he knew how much I had earned since I started, a salary supplemented by a cut on the money-smuggling.

It wasn't just the three of us for Sunday roast at the Dulwich house. Uncle Wag had joined us, as he often had after the death of his beloved Ethel. He looked rosy-cheeked and prosperous, not bad for a man of his age. His dark green Harris tweed jacket was well cut. I noticed, for the first time, how neat the nails were on his elegant hands. And he was wearing some very smooth brown suede brogues with leather soles. 'We used to live in Camberwell Green,' he said. 'Wouldn't recognise the place now. Good potatoes, Ivy. Good as Mother's.'

My mum beamed.

'Not to mention Ethel's roasties,' he added with a sigh.

'Camberwell? It was another world then,' Wag continued. 'Not perfect, a bit shabby, but there was a graciousness on the streets in those days. No advertising hoardings. Quiet. No lorries and big red buses stinking the place out.'

'Horse-drawn chariots,' said my dad. He looked at Wag. 'Did you know that stevengraphs are back in fashion? I bought some at Bonhams the other day. I'll show you later.'

'I sold my collection years ago.'

'Pity,' said my father. 'I hope to make a few bob.'

Outside the bay window the yellow privet hedge was as immaculate as always. My father, not the keenest gardener during my youth, now took great care of front and back. Before the days of the motor mower, the sound of the old push and pull machine was a reassurance that all was well with the world, on Sunday anyway.

'Aren't you working with that Rawlings fellow?' Wag asked me. 'That's what I heard from someone the other day.'

'Not for much longer, I hope.'

'I used to know his father. The original missing link. Hairier than a Neanderthal. Joined the circus, if I remember correctly. He would have been locked up otherwise.'

'His son should definitely be put away. He works with the Linklaters.'

'You don't tell us much about your work,' my dad said. 'Have you got something else lined up?'

'Not exactly.'

I had a sudden thought. 'Did you ever run into the Richardson family?' I asked Wag. This was the first time I had heard my uncle mention that he had any connections with the south London underworld, and it had never occurred to me to ask him before.

'I wouldn't have counted them among my closest friends,' he said.

'They are just a couple of low-life crooks, aren't they?' My father only knew what he read in the papers.

'Few redeeming features that I can think of,' Wag said. 'Don't know where they got it from. Their father wouldn't have hurt a fly.'

'Wag, you never told me that you were in with these kinds of people . . .' Mum looked questioningly at her half-brother.

'I was never in with them, as you say. And now I live in the middle of nowhere. But I do keep my ear to the ground. I'm a south London boy,' Wag replied. 'You get to hear things. Obviously, I don't know every character on the block. But, I've seen some of them. Look at Fred here. Just because he works in the City doesn't mean his path hasn't crossed with entertainers . . .'

'Well, yes. It's true. I was friends with Nervo and Knox.' My dad was going back to pre-war days with the famous Crazy Gang when he thought he might have had a very different career than working in a bank. 'They lived just down the road.'

'And Monsewer Eddie Gray.' My mother was happy the conversation was moving into more comfortable theatrical territory. 'I loved the Crazy Gang.'

When I was about nine, my starchy Aunt Jess had taken me to a Gang show at the Victoria Palace. There was a moment when Bud Flanagan stuck a mop between the legs of his straight man Chesney Allen, and wiggled it about. Aunt Jess's pale complexion turned pink with laughter. 'It's a bit rude, isn't it,' she whispered to me, wiping her eyes.

'I knew your boss's father too. Willie Linklater.' Wag wiped his lips with a white napkin. 'He drove a tank during the war. They replaced it with a better version. Do you know what the first one was called?'

I was not a student of military history. Dad didn't have the answer either.

'Little Willie. Unfortunately for Linklater. After the war, he started dealing in old tyres, then restoring old wrecks, and worked his way up from there. Had an eye for detail. There wasn't a piece of machinery he couldn't fix. Don't know so much about his boy.'

'Mr Linklater put up the money for our film,' I said to the table in general.

'I didn't get an invitation to the premiere,' said Wag.

'You haven't missed anything,' I said. 'And there wasn't one.'

'Well, *I* liked it.' Good old Mum.

The entire cinematic oeuvre of Jack Armitage was in one can, stuffed away in a drawer in my bedroom.

'Once upon a time, when I was in my prime . . .' – Uncle

Wag paused to check he had our attention – 'there was this group of hoodlums called the Elephant Boys because they came from the Elephant and Castle. That was their manor. They were a right bunch. But there was this other lot too, and you never hear about them: they were known as the Forty Elephants. Terrifying. All women. Quite good-looking, some of them.'

Uncle Wag was revealing himself to be a rather more interesting character than I had ever imagined. Perhaps he and I had more in common than I thought. With the exception of the ebullient Jago, my other uncles were taciturn, to say the least. Ernest always looked as though he had wandered into a house of strangers and was too embarrassed to ask where the exit was. Ted exuded a more avuncular glow, but was unable or unwilling to communicate with anyone other than his wife. If he turned his bespectacled gaze on me, the myopic eyes aimed at my left shoulder, never at my face.

Uncle Aubrey I liked. But the Second World War did for him. When he came home wounded after Alamein, he took to the medicinal use of alcohol to stop the shakes. His old publishing job was no longer available. He and Florence invested their savings in property. They did up houses together, then sold them on. They had a son, known to us all as Little Aubrey. The drinking got worse. And dear, doolally Florence kept her husband company with the bottle. Their business collapsed, and so did Aubrey. After the last bout of the DTs, he never emerged from King's College Hospital. Now my nicest aunt ran a second-hand clothes shop near St Leonard's Church in Streatham. Occasionally, she picked up some smart fashion house labels, but the whole place ponged of poverty.

'You never told me about any Forty Elephants,' Mum said. 'They sound like something out of Fu Manchu.'

'There's a lot I never told you,' Wag said.

'So what did they do, these women?'

'The usual. Betting rackets. Bit of prostitution . . .'

'I have to say I'm shocked, Wag.' My mother was not expecting this kind of conversation at Sunday lunch. 'What were you doing with those lowlifes?'

'I wasn't doing anything. I don't believe it's a crime to know the people who live in your manor.'

'How's crime in Surbiton?' My dad refilled Wag's half-empty glass.

'No doubt there are things that go on there behind closed doors.' I noticed that my uncle drank very sparingly. 'But part of the charm is that nothing happens there at all.'

'Like Dulwich,' my dad said.

'I wouldn't be too sure about that. That Freddie Foreman has a place not far from here,' Wag said with a wink at me.

Mum was tight-lipped when I helped her clear up the plates and bring in the sherry trifle. She obviously did not like all this talk about crooks and prostitutes. I dreaded the idea that one day she might discover that her one and only son was also mixed up with that sort of person. But I was starting to see my uncle in a new light. Perhaps he could help me, point me in the direction of someone who could forge those passports for Monkey.

'Yes, that Linklater is not a bad sort,' Wag said at length. 'But I'm not sure if I care for some of his associates.'

My mum and dad had no idea that the chain of command at my office issued from Wormwood Scrubs. I began to wish I had never mentioned the name of the Brothers Richardson. I attempted to give Uncle Wag a warning look.

Fortunately, my uncle seemed to have recognised that it was time to change the subject. 'The stevengraph I wish I had kept is of the eighteenth-century pugilist Jim Belcher. There's a sentimental reason for that. But it is probably the rarest one you can find. There was a fire at the factory. The run was interrupted. I think there are only about two of the Belcher pictures left in existence. I would have given it to you, Jack. To remind you of your old uncle.'

CHAPTER 54

Wag

We were not mirror images of each other. The fact that we occupied the same space at the same time did not cause our atomic particles to combine or to implode. The coincidence of our nicknames did not have the slightest impact on the fabric of the universe.

Wag McDonald was at least a foot taller than me. Wavy, sand-coloured hair was carefully combed from a central parting, and he kept a brown moustache neatly trimmed. He looked like a refugee from an ancient daguerreotype. Had he sported a gold watch chain across his black waistcoat, he would have fitted quite happily into my collection of early Fox Talbot photographic portraits.

He and Kimber reported on the dot of seven at my workshop in Exmouth Market. It was a cool, misty morning. I had been up since before dawn, feeling a bit watery in my bowels. Although I had survived years of war in France, where the expectation of sudden death or mutilation was constant, I had lost that state of fatalistic indifference. I was surprised now to find myself feeling fearful.

Back in the generally unthreatening world of the metropolis, the endless parade of people was more like a diorama. You paid your penny, sat back and watched the show. In my criminal trade, I did have to engage with my customers – to doctor their documents, invent disguises and make-up, take their photographs. On the whole, though, I was not dealing with people who were hardened criminals. They were bankrupt bankers, aristocrats who could not repay their gambling debts, civil servants who had cooked the books, trusted employees who had salted funds away in foreign parts, and plain, greedy bastards who simply had an eye for the main chance. This lot was different, and a lot more terrifying.

'My colleague Kimber tells me you're a cool customer.' Jim 'Wag' McDonald's voice was soft and well-modulated. His stillness made me nervous.

Kimber handed over two passports. With his hooded, lashless eyes and broken nose, Billy Kimber was the more conventional image of a man at odds with the law. Curiously, I was more comfortable with him.

'Have you selected new names for yourselves?' I asked.

'Peter Piper.' Kimber laughed. 'Don't you dare say, "picked a peck".'

There was no danger of that, although the old tongue-twister now rattled round my head like a broken record.

'Maxwell Price.' McDonald's hard eyes dared me to smile.

Kimber drew out a piece of folded paper from the inside pocket of his baggy grey suit. 'It's all down there.'

'I hear,' McDonald said to me, 'that we have something in common . . .'

'Funny, that. How did you come by yours?'

'I cut the tail off someone's puppy.'

'Don't think I can compete with that,' I said.

I put the information Kimber had handed me next to the passports on my workbench, and wished my hand would stop shaking.

'Have you each decided on a look?' I asked.

'Butch Cassidy,' said McDonald. For a student of photography, which I was, there was a memorable picture of the notorious American outlaw taken in 1900. I could see exactly how to transform his English counterpart.

'Don't tell me you want to look like the Sundance Kid? He was his partner,' I said to Kimber.

'Why not?'

'With or without moustache?'

'With.'

'There won't be time to grow one.'

'I assumed,' said Kimber, 'that you would be able to supply me.'

I pulled out a long box from a tall box of drawers, where I stored a range of hairpieces, beards, even eyebrows. 'Moustaches, for the use of,' I said.

Kimber selected one.

'Mine had better come off,' McDonald said. 'Don't worry. I have brought my shaving kit. What do you think?'

'Depends how the police know you best. We could alter the shape and colour of the moustache, but I would say better off.'

'I like you, Wag.' McDonald clapped me on the shoulder, and an electric jolt crackled silently down to my shoes. 'Where's the . . .?'

I pointed to the bathroom door. We had all the facilities in Skinner Street.

'He likes you,' Kimber said.

It didn't make me feel any easier. We heard the hot tap make the hot water system groan and judder before the sink filled.

'Colour of hair?' I asked. 'Black?'

'I suppose so.'

'We can use a wig for the photo.' I reached into a drawer.

'When will everything be ready?'

'Day after tomorrow.'

'We have booked our passage for New York on Saturday.'

'Have a safe journey.'

Kimber looked pale in anticipation of the voyage, or maybe it was the early hour. Or maybe that was how he always looked. I had only seen the man in the dark or by artificial light. 'I get sick on a rowing boat,' he said.

McDonald emerged, rubbing a smooth upper lip and smelling of cologne. 'How do I look?' he asked.

'Like a new man.' I thought of a sleek scorpion.

'We will need to change the hair first,' I said. 'Side parting, I think. I can adjust the colour later.'

Obediently, the leader of London's most feared Cortesi gang returned to the bathroom. 'Better?' he asked, having made the necessary adjustments.

'Perfect,' I said. 'Who wants to go first?'

Kimber glared at me, as though I had asked a very silly question

'Does he know you're called Wag too?' asked Wainwright.

'He does. He is my number one fan.'

'Christ,' said Wainwright.

From the cobbled road to the white porticoed entrance, Eaton Mews was like a staging post for heavenly sanctuary after my nerve-racking morning with Great Britain's Most Wanted Man. McDonald had offered to pay for the passports. I couldn't tell if he was serious or not. 'They are on the house,' I assured him. In the 'your money or your life' stakes, I preferred my life.

'I never forget a favour, Bourton,' Wag said as he shook hands with Wag. I had never got round to explaining the origin of my own nickname. McDonald wasn't remotely interested in me. That was a relief. He just wanted a job done, without fuss. He had come to the right bloke.

'Good set-up, you've got here,' McDonald said. 'You'll be all right. I'll make sure of that . . .'

'Where shall I . . .?'

'Someone will be round to collect on Friday.'

'Six o'clock?'

'No slip-ups.'

'You'll need these too.' I gave both men a container with different coloured lenses. 'You'll have to practise wearing them so your eyes won't water too much. If we don't meet again . . .'

Wag McDonald's disconcertingly direct gaze stabbed me right in the pupil. 'I have a feeling that our paths will cross.' He gave my hand one last bone-crushing squeeze, then followed his henchman Kimber down the stairs and into the street.

Wainwright was wearing evening dress and was the immaculate image of the perfect gent.

'Well, that's the last of them, out of our hair for now. We can sleep easily now. But sorry, old man,' he said. 'I'm going to have to leave you to your own devices tonight. I'm going to the ballet.'

I had never seen the appeal of going to Covent Garden to watch men in white tights and young women prancing about in tutus.

There was a sharp tap on the front door. Wainwright was over in a flash to open it.

'Darling!'

If a spotlight had caught the woman in the white fur coat, framed in the doorway, I would not have been surprised. She was dazzling. Not pretty, but a face no one could forget. 'The taxi's running,' she said. 'We had better dash. Sorry, darling.' She cast an appealing glance in my direction. 'I can't bear to miss curtain up.'

'William,' Wainwright reached for his coat, white opera scarf and keys. 'This is Gertrude.'

'Miss Lawrence,' I said as I shook her white-gloved hand. 'It is an honour.'

'Can we drop you off anywhere, darling?' The most famous star in the West End of London was offering me a lift.

'It's all right,' I said. 'I'm going to walk.'

'Not all the way to Surbiton I hope,' said Wainwright, securing the latch.

'Have a good evening.' I held opened the door of the black taxi cab, and Gertrude Lawrence climbed in, flashing me a smile I would describe later to Mama as being like a sunburst.

On the corner of Belgrave Square, a flower seller gave me a good rate on a large bunch of white tulips. I didn't bring my mother flowers very often. And I did have a little something to celebrate, after all. I had encountered my evil double and survived.

CHAPTER 55

Jack

'It's Jack,' I said. 'I was wondering if I might come over?'

'I thought you might call,' Wag said. 'Any time you like, boy. I'm home all day.'

Frankly, I was in a blue funk about this passport business. Talk about amateur night. The only person I knew who would have more than the foggiest notion about obtaining false documents was Detective Inspector George Curwin, and I could hardly ask him. Sid was in Spain or Morocco or Buenos Aires. Sylvia was no use. Link claimed he had some contacts, but when it came down to it, he failed to produce the goods.

Was this some sort of test devised by Rawlings, I wondered, to see how ingenious the Cambridge MA could be? Or was the Firm genuinely at a loss in the forged papers department?

These days, courtesy of Linklater's, I was driving a mustard-coloured Daf. If you were out to impress the birds, this car was a non-starter – it sounded like a cross between a washing machine and a lawnmower. I believe it ran on rubber bands, but I never looked under the bonnet. On a good downward slope you could overtake pedestrians.

Next week, I might be revving a Porsche. It all depended on what was available. But cars did not interest me in the slightest.

Uncle Wag's house in Surbiton meant a slow journey, even if I could have worked up to the speed limit. The route from Notting Hill is meandering to say the least, and allowed too much time for thought. I was on my way to ask a sweet old age pensioner if, by the remotest chance, he might know someone who could help me do something completely and utterly illegal. It was madness. Even if he had just revealed he had some unexpected connections in the south London underworld.

Where were the cornfields of yesteryear, I wondered, as I parked my Dutch roadster in Wag's quiet, tree-lined street.

He had spotted me from the front room and had the door open as I walked up the crazy-paved path.

'If it isn't Jack the Lad!' We shook hands warmly.

Oh dear. He had been at the fertiliser again. The unctuous odour of manure had seeped into the house. The back door into the garden was open. How did this apparently fastidious man not notice the stench? He even invited it in. I have nothing against roses, but keep them pruned and fed with other less obnoxious chemical additives and no one is going to complain. As far as I knew, Wag did not compete at the church fête for prizes for his blooms. Maybe he had some bodies concealed under his ramblers and standards. I pitied his neighbours.

'Come and have some ginger beer,' he said. 'Or a sherry, if you prefer . . .'

'A glass of water will be fine,' I said.

Wag filled me a tumbler in the kitchen, then I followed him into the sitting room. The smell was not so bad in there.

Haltingly I confessed my dilemma. My uncle did not look surprised. 'So, Charlie and Eddie want to go over the wall,' he said, as though he were commenting on the state of the weather. 'They need passports in a hurry, and Rawlings has asked you to arrange . . .'

I took a large gulp of water. Pressure in the taps had made the liquid a cloudy grey, but it tasted all right.

'I can help you. You've come to the right place.'

You could have knocked me down with a feather duster, as my Auntie Rose used to say.

'Come with me,' he said.

On the first floor was his darkroom. My old uncle was not even puffing when we climbed up a spiral staircase into the attic. There was an area where he kept his engraving tools and general equipment. A long workbench with a vice, a saw, chisel, thin sheets of copper and a range of hammers.

A second connecting room contained a state-of-the-art enlarger and more photographic equipment, as well as an old Sanderson five- by four-inch plate camera mounted on a stand.

'There's a bit more to see.' Wag was like the curator of an ancient treasure house, delighted to have the opportunity to show off his secrets to a wide-eyed child.

We walked back down to the ground floor.

'After Ethel died, I had this installed.' In the dining room, hidden behind a collection of blue and white Spode plates on a big Welsh dresser, my uncle pressed a switch and a section of the wooden floor opened downwards. There were a couple of clicks, and a subterranean fluorescent light came on. 'All clever stuff,' Wag said.

Nimbly, he descended the ladder.

You did not have to bend your head. There was plenty of room. Wag led me down a lined concrete corridor into an enormous basement. Beside a long row of metal filing cabinets, stood an old Diebold's Special safe.

'Completely damp-proofed. You could survive a nuclear bomb down here.'

I looked round for the stockpile of water, corned beef and baked beans.

'If the big bang comes,' Wag said, 'I'm ready. I've had a good life, though. Wouldn't want to hang around down here for ever, waiting for the radiation to disappear.'

In a corner of the room, lights hung from a gantry on the

ceiling. A chair had been placed in front of a matte white screen, and two standing Kuhl lamps were positioned on either side. A Leica camera, slightly battered, rested on a table next to a twin lens reflex Rolleiflex.

'This is where I take the passport pictures.'

I was stunned. My uncle obviously had quite a business set up here.

Uncle Wag twiddled the dial of his safe, and tugged on the heavy handle.

I could see a mass of banknotes stored in one corner. From a compartment above, he pulled out a leather bag. 'Hope we won't need this,' Wag said, unwrapping a Luger pistol.

CHAPTER 56

Wag

My old friend Vernon Hotchkiss from primary school, the one I had shared field mushrooms with while training on Salisbury Plain, managed to survive the First World War. And the Second. Working in the Catering Corps helped a bit. The only action Hotchkiss saw was in the field kitchen. But bullets respect neither soldier nor chef. A stray round hit Vernon in the left arm in 1917, rendering him unfit for active service when hostilities with Germany recommenced in 1939.

In the meantime, he worked his way up from the Café Royal via the Hyde Park Hotel to running his own very swanky restaurant next to Quo Vadis in Dean Street, Soho. The greater bearded architect of the Communist Manifesto, Karl Heinrich Marx, lived in the same street above Number 28 during his formative intellectual years.

On June 28th, 1947, I took Ethel to supper at Hotchkiss's La Perla to celebrate my darling sister's forty-seventh birthday. It wasn't an age she wanted to brag about, but it was a great excuse to come up west for a slap-up nosh. Especially when your old friend runs the place.

We still needed our ration books. Though at least at home we never had to submit to powdered egg. An old woman called Daisy Trevor, who lived three doors down, kept chickens in her back garden. Miss Trevor made sure we were supplied with fresh eggs and the occasional bird, which she insisted on plucking herself.

Post-war London was a dreary place. It was a treat to eat

out. At the Old Rectory, I had dug a vegetable patch for victory. I became a dab hand at dibbing leeks. Potatoes thrived in the soil, and I always made sure to scoop up whatever manure the delivery horses left behind in the street. I was always rather partial to the smell. Runner beans were a success too.

Rhubarb flourished. I even experimented with asparagus, a plant I shall always associate with a farmhouse in France. But by the time the bed matured, it had already failed.

'That was the most delicious meal I have eaten in seven long years, Vernon,' Ethel said. 'Thank you.' The smoked eel and horseradish, asparagus in butter, steak Diane, champagne and fine wine had gone down a treat.

'Thank you for coming.' The owner had joined us at the table. 'There have been times lately when I wondered if I could afford to stay open much longer. But business is picking up again.'

We raised our cognacs and clinked glasses. 'Happy birthday, Ethel,' Vernon said. 'Great to see you both.'

Vernon Hotchkiss had gained weight but lost most of his curly, fair hair. For an ordinary south London boy, he had acquired the air of a confident man about town. I might have improved my vocabulary and ability to think in clear sentences, but my accent was nowhere near as polished as his. Shaw's Professor Higgins could have nailed William Bourton's south London accent in a trice. He would have to listen a bit harder to identify the origins of Hotchkiss's vowels and glottal stops.

'Do you know what I heard the other day?' Vernon said. 'Adolf Hitler is still alive. He and that Eva Braun got out of Berlin in a U-boat and they are living somewhere on the coast in Argentina.'

'I thought Hitler's body was identified in the bunker?' Ethel's pale features were slightly flushed. It suited her. Age had enhanced the contours of her face, the vivid blue of her eyes.

'The Russians have got the remains. They won't let anyone near.'

'Somebody told me,' I said, 'that a bloke called Ian Fleming got Bormann out of Berlin. He's had a facelift and is living in Hastings.'

'Who had the facelift? Fleming?' asked Ethel.

'Bormann, silly!' Immediately, I regretted flustering my sister.

'Bloody Germans.' Hotchkiss finished his brandy. 'The drinks are on the house, by the way,' he said. Le patron raised his hand. 'I insist.'

A flurry of post-theatre arrivals injected a shot of adrenalin into the restaurant. Waiters snapped to attention, the cloakroom attendant had to close the book she was reading, and Mr Smooth Vernon Hotchkiss glided over to kiss the hand of Gertrude Lawrence.

When she took her seat at the table opposite ours, the great star checked her audience. I smiled at her and inclined my head. Gertrude Lawrence beamed back, even though it was obvious she hadn't a clue who I was.

After Walter Cornish, there had never been anyone special in Ethel's life. Nor anyone in mine, come to that. Had we wasted our years, in longing or self-denial, or both?

There was the odd fellow who hung around for a while. Trips to the theatre and cinema, supper in Streatham (never a gourmet's delight). Ethel had rarely invited them home. Maybe the close-knit family put off potential suitors. Did we exude some kind of negative protective force field? I don't think so. There were intruders into the family, like Florence's Aubrey,

Jago's Molly, Aurelia's Ernest and Ted's Mildred, who made it through and stayed.

These days, no one could imagine such a household. Or someone like me who only severed the umbilical cord when he was middle aged.

Wainwright, though still single himself, couldn't understand why I had never branched out on my own. 'A young man like you,' he said, and this was back in the good old days of the Depression, when we made such a lot of money together. 'Fancy-free, loaded. You could have anyone.'

He couldn't have Gertrude Lawrence. I was dying to tell him I had seen her this evening. The two had had a brief affair, but people like her are married to their work. I understand that. In a way, engraving was my mistress. My comfort. My skill. The money was only ever a sideline, although a compulsive one. And it did come in useful.

Harry Wainwright invested his ill-gotten gains in a gold stone pile in Gloucestershire, just outside the village of Little Tew. He took up with a lurcher, and tucked hairy tweed trousers into long socks. I joined him once or twice on a shoot, but killing birds was never my idea of fun.

What he did on those long weekends in that vast mansion, I have no idea. Maybe he wandered round the place straightening the Old Master paintings or playing chess against himself? Of course, he did know vast armies of people. Wainwright's address book was the secret of our success. His house parties were lavish. But I never felt comfortable with the gaggle of guests. Although there was one young woman. I see her now in a red dress. She had these big brown eyes. She liked me. I could have tapped at her bedroom door in the still of the night. I wish I had. But not really . . .

If I could have Ethel to myself, that would be enough.

CHAPTER 57

Jack

There was not a sliver of space in the stiff leather briefcase for another bundle of hard currency. I only took the briefest glance at the contents before clicking the brass safety catches back on.

'The wages of sin,' said Rawlings. 'Good luck, Jack. I'd keep that case locked if I were you. Never know who you'll bump into out in the street. You wouldn't want to spill all that lovely lolly up Camberwell High Road.'

I was now a fully accredited criminal. With the help of my jolly old uncle. It was a bit like graduation day, but without the gown and fox fur.

'Charlie and Eddie would like to say thanks in person, and maybe they will one of these days.'

That was one side of the bargain I hoped would not come true.

'I knew you could do it, Jack. You're a clever boy. I'm impressed.'

When Rawlings handed over the photos of the two Richardsons (not two of the prettiest jailbirds you ever did see) he had asked me who was doing the key work. I couldn't say, could I? He respected that, although I have no doubt he put out whatever feelers he had to discover the identity of my mysterious master forger.

Like being a cop with an informer, you can't reveal the name of your grass, or the whole operation is compromised.

It was time to go home. I was going to drop off Wag's share

at his house and later I was meeting Link at his place. He had been down with the flu or something for a week.

'See you tomorrow,' I said to Rawlings.

'See you, Jack. Mind how you go.'

As I opened the door to an outer office, where our new secretary sat, Rawlings said, 'You can call me "Monkey" if you like.'

'Call me Ishmael.' Link coughed when he laughed. 'Bloody hell, Kid. You pulled it off.'

'You sure you're all right?'

'Never better.' Dark circles and a vampiric pallor did not encourage any confidence in Link's self-diagnosis.

'So you and Rawlings are best mates now,' he said. 'Who'd have thunk it? Don't suppose you're any more likely to tell me who did the job.'

'I can't, old man. I wish I could. You sure you're up for this evening?'

Curwin was giving a supper party, something neither Link nor I had managed in our bachelor existences. I had of course mentioned this invitation pointedly to my boss. Not that Curwin ever revealed any weakness that could be used by Monkey to put pressure on him.

The bell rang.

'There she is now.'

I had no one to bring. Sylvia was in foreign parts with Sid. Besides, I would not have wanted to take her with me. The occasional outing to a nightclub was OK. Sylvia was a terrific dancer. But there is a limit to the number of times you want to go to Sybilla's. Basically, we had nothing much to talk about. Sex is not enough.

'Hello, Rachel.' We kissed on both cheeks. 'You look great.'

'Glad somebody noticed.'

'Yes, you do,' said Link, too late.

Rachel was wearing a Mary Quant black mini dress. It could have been made for her. I wished I could find a proper girlfriend like her.

The table in Curwin's Battersea flat was laid for eight.

'This is Emma,' Curwin introduced his latest squeeze, who still had her apron on. 'She's in charge.'

'I'm in charge,' Emma echoed, imitating Bruce Forsyth's catchphrase from *Sunday Night at the London Palladium*. It was what you watched if you had nothing better to do on a Sunday night. I liked her immediately.

'And this is Bruce. Bruce Seton. A colleague of mine on the force.'

Curwin's guest rose to his feet. The process seemed to last for a couple of days. He was as tall as a house. We shook hands. 'Well, if it isn't Fabian of the Yard,' I joked. 'Television makes you look smaller.'

Seton gave me a withering smile. He had heard the joke before. Bruce Seton was the actor who had played the part of Detective Fabian on the telly. I had an encyclopedic memory for this kind of trivia.

'And I'm Miss Marple.' Bruce Seton's companion stayed where she was in her chair.

'Meredith,' Seton supplied her real name.

'Not really Marple?' I said. Might as well blunder in further. 'I thought your Christian name was Miss.'

'My surname actually is Christie.' Meredith slipped me a quizzical smile.

Rachel snorted with laughter. It broke the tension. 'I'm Hilda Baker.'

'Bugs Bunny,' said Link.

'Professor James Moriarty, at your service,' I said.

'The Napoleon of Crime!' everyone chorused, more or less simultaneously.

There was rat-tat-tat at the door. Curwin left us to our own devices, while Emma returned from a quick dash to the kitchen to check on the food.

I thought I recognised the sound of the laugh as George took the last guest to the bedroom to leave their coat.

'I think you know Jack,' Curwin said, when he came back into the room. The new arrival was looking into the hall mirror, straightening her blonde hair.

'Hello, darling,' she said.

It was like plunging in a broken lift from the very top of a tower block.

'Hello there, Giesele,' I said.

Cops, robbers and communists. It was a heady mix.

Emma could have won twenty-five Michelin stars for her cooking. Scallops and black pudding were served for starters. Giesele had been seated next to me, with Meredith on my left. I hoped my former girlfriend could not hear my heart thundering. When no one was looking, she quickly passed two slices of the blood sausage on to my plate. 'You know I cannot svallow dat stuff,' she whispered.

Giesele had no problems with the main course. It was Moroccan chicken in a proper tagine dish.

'George and I spent a fortnight in Marrakesh,' Emma explained, serving herself a discreet mound of couscous.

'Very moreish,' said Curwin. 'Or do I mean Moorish?'

He was unlike any policeman you could imagine.

'I ate the sheep's eye in Essaouira,' I bragged.

Now I had Giesele's attention. 'Vat made you do such a disgusting thing?'

'There wasn't a lot of choice. I was with this Moroccan girl and her family. I said I would eat one if someone else ate the other.'

'Showing off.' It did not take long for Giesele to get back into the old routine.

'Did you chew it?' asked Emma.

'A little bit. Like an oyster.'

'The last time I had an oyster,' Seton said, 'I was sick for a week. I'll never touch another one.'

'A policeman's lot is not a happy one,' said Link.

I don't remember much more about the conversation. There was a forest fire blazing next to me, and I was pretending I didn't feel the searing heat.

'Who vas this Moroccan girl den?' Giesele asked me quietly.

'She worked for Saudi Airlines.'

'And?'

'She flew away,' I said.

'Without you?'

'Without so much as a backward glance.'

'You should have eaten both the eyes. And the balls.' Everything Giesele said was a challenge. She changed tack. 'How is your family?'

'Fine. I don't live at home any more.'

'I should hope not.' Her lips were ripe, and those big, wide eyes were the most tantalising shade of green.

'I'm sharing a flat with Tyler. In Blenheim Crescent.'

Giesele made a face. She had never liked him.

'How did you come across Curwin?' I asked. 'I had no idea you two knew each other.'

'He interviewed me after a break-in at my flat. I liked him.

And I suppose he likes me. Ve have had the odd drink. But I was surprised when he asked me to supper tonight.'

'What did they take?'

'Vat you expect. Television. Jewellery. A ring my grandmother gave me. Apart from that, nothing of value. I can't recall how your name came up . . .'

It sounded to me as though Curwin's agenda had nothing to do with Giesele's burglary. I wondered, too, about the odd assortment of guests tonight. Was Curwin combining business with pleasure? What was he trying to find out? Was he after Link and me, as much as we were after him?

'I hear you two vere at school together. You public school boys . . .' Giesele's sharp little teeth were nibbling again at my extremities.

'What is that supposed to mean?' I could feel the old irritation begin to resurface. And the old desire.

'He seemed to know you very vell,' Giesele said. 'Clearly you're not a suspect. Although, quite frankly, it vouldn't surprise me to find out you had been poking through my things. You telephoned enough times.'

My face went hot. 'I'm sorry,' I said. 'I missed you.'

'I missed you too,' Giesele said, covering my hand with hers.

CHAPTER 58

Wag

It is a platitude to observe that everything and everyone dies. I have seen comrades blasted to bits beside me. I have walked across fields of corpses, seen body parts hanging from shattered trees, rivers clogged with men on their sluggish journey to the netherworld. And my poor Shrapnel.

Yes, my mother suffered the lacerating loss of three of her children before their time. Sister Josephine was the first member of the family to go, struck down by Spanish flu, followed by Annie, felled by a German bomb, then Martin, hit by a police car. Two stillborn boys were never mentioned. There was also the curious case of Michael 'Stavros' Andrews – the man who stayed for more than dinner. My respectable mother never married him; as it turned out, Michael played his brief part in our lives by fathering my half-sister, Ivy, then vanished into thin air.

Mother refused to consult the doctor. Every day she would put on her make-up, and clip on those heavy earrings that made her lobes droop like a Maasai warrior's. She would join whoever was up for breakfast in the kitchen, potter about a bit, sometimes summoning up the energy to pop out to the shops. But the tiredness and the ache in her lower back she was unable to disguise, from us and from herself, and more and more now, she took to her bed.

Ethel really liked the house in Surbiton, but she now felt her place was at home to nurse our mother.

'Your father wasn't such a bad man, you know.'

I was sitting in a green velvet chair beside Mother's bed, and squeezed her veined old hand.

My attendance at Father's funeral before the Great War had been dutiful rather than emotional. Ethel was the only one of his children who genuinely mourned for Leonard Bourton. It was her nature. Florence had cried too, but then she would weep at the drop of a hat.

In a crocodile suitcase monogrammed with his initials, Mama kept the clothes our father had worn to his last stretch in prison, his white handkerchief carefully ironed and folded on top. A wedding photograph of the happy couple was still on her bedside table along with the vase of fresh flowers we made sure were always there. The bride looked grave but Leonard Bourton was smiling broadly, as though he could see the Promised Land. With him, everything had been empty promises.

He made me a train once, out of wood and cardboard, with wheels from some discarded toy car. He was not a craftsman, but I treasured that engine. He never read me stories, though, or tucked me up at night. If he felt no particular bond with his own children, how strange to prefer the company of villains, to share a cell with another bloke instead of cuddling up with your adoring wife. Who would choose to slop out in the morning rather than be served a cup of tea in bed?

It is not as though I don't understand an addiction to breaking the law. But to be caught every time you do a job suggests Leonard Bourton must have had a screw loose or was simply an incompetent, compulsive loser.

Ethel and I probably received marginally more attention from our father than the rest of his large brood. Did he feel no responsibility for the seed of his loins, no love? It was a miracle I had not developed into a raving nutter like my namesake Wag McDonald.

'You've been a good son.' Mother's grip tightened on my hand. 'The best. I wish I could have done more for you all.'

'None of us could ask for more,' I said. 'After all, look – we're still here. With you.'

'You'll be head of the family.'

'No one takes any notice of me.'

We were quiet for a bit. The ormolu Empire clock between the two Angelica Kauffmann vases chimed a soft ten o'clock.

'Are you sure you shouldn't see a doctor?'

'Never held with them.' The eyes of the Grand Panjandrum glittered fiercely. 'Your father's father was a doctor, you know. A surgeon. Killed more than he cured, I shouldn't wonder.' It was a rarity for Mama ever to mention the past. 'I imagined we'd be living in a grand house, with grounds and servants. Not that I have been unhappy here, Wag . . . You won't remember, but when you were very little, our first-born, we spent a week in Brighton at the Grand. We had a suite with a balcony on the front. The sun shone every day. We didn't like to leave you, so we had room service. Lobster thermidor, Dover sole – the fish was so fresh you could taste the sea. At the end, there was some trouble with the bill. I suppose I should have known then . . . Marriage doesn't always turn out the way you imagined.'

There was nothing useful I could add to this subject.

'Do you think Ivy is happy?' Mum's youngest daughter via the late Michael 'Stavros' Angeleglou (or Andrews as he called himself) was her little treasure.

'Fred seems like a good bloke,' I said. 'And Jack's a nice boy. I wouldn't worry about them.'

'Florence . . .'

'Yes, I worry about her. But you've got to let her live her life. Aurelia's all right. And Jago and Ted.' All right was one way of putting it.

'Why did you never marry?' It wasn't the first time Mother had asked me that question.

'Never met the right person.'

'I remember someone called Queenie, from work.' Mother never forgot her name. There was, of course, no one else to remember.

'That would not have been a good idea,' I said. Queenie had vanished off the face of the earth.

'I hope Ethel made the right decision with that doctor . . . Now our Violet has done well, don't you think? Although I never thought anyone in our family would marry into the law.'

Sometimes, propped up in bed, Mama put me in mind of a beyond respectable German high duchess, yet she had led a far from conventional existence. And she was the unsuspecting mother of an unwanted criminal.

'Can I get you anything?'

'I know it sounds disgusting,' Mother replied. 'But I really fancy a hot Horlicks with a drop of brandy in it.'

As I walked into the hallway, Aurelia and Ernest were hanging up their coats. 'Just in time,' I said. They would be the second shift if Mother still wanted company.

Mother died that night, around three o'clock, the doctor said. Even if his patient had refused to call him, he had had to come eventually.

CHAPTER 59

Jack

My cousin Oliver died of an aneurism. Out of the blue. We had only spoken on the phone the previous week.

The service was being held at the Golders Green Crematorium. No priests, no organ music, no religion, no opiates. But we did have a rousing chorus of the 'Internationale' by the Red Army Choir as Giesele and I filed in with the other mourners.

'I still don't understand vy you don't speak,' she hissed. 'He vas the only cousin you liked.'

She was right. I should have spoken. My excuse is that I was afraid of cracking up.

Link and Rachel arrived. After a decade of sustained amphetamine abuse, Link was making a concentrated effort to put his house in order. He no longer looked as though his life was spent in a crypt. His hands were steady. I won't say my old friend was ready to climb Mount Everest, but he no longer looked like death warmed up.

Link and Rachel took their seats behind us next to Boggy, unrecognisable from the Trotskyite Irish hooligan of 1967, looking distinguished in a dark blue suit. At least, for old times' sake, he was sporting a red tie.

At the sound of 'The Red Flag', the congregation rose to its feet, and a woman with greying hair I had never seen before mounted the podium. She gazed slowly round the room while the anthem reached its conclusion.

'Good afternoon, ladies and gentlemen. My name is Kate . . .'

So this was the American woman with whom Oliver had lived in Cambridge.

'Kate Craden-Walsh.'

There was an audible intake of breath from the group of old friends. I was the only representative of the family present. Oliver had not spoken to his mother for years. My other cousins found him weird, and he had no patience with them.

'Oliver and I got married a month ago. I am sorry to make this announcement on such a sad day. As many of you know, my late husband lived his life on the edge. I truly believed I might help make him happy . . .' She took a deep breath. 'Oliver was so troubled and so passionate. I'm more than aware that many of his friends found his obsession with Trotsky ridiculous. But I admired it. I admired him. And now he is gone.'

There was a general shifting in our seats, as we waited for Kate to compose herself. She put on a pair of black-rimmed spectacles and cleared her throat. 'I should like to read you a few lines from Leon Trotsky. They were Oliver's personal manifesto. "As long as I breathe, I am filled with hope. As long as I breathe, I shall fight for the future, in which mankind, strong and beautiful, will become master of the drifting stream of his history, and direct it towards the boundless horizons of beauty, joy and happiness."'

Kate removed her glasses, returned them to her handbag, folded away the small sheet of paper, and rejoined the congregation, who applauded for a couple of minutes.

There were no more tributes, just one song – Woody Guthrie's 'So Long, It's Been Good To Know Yuh'. By the last verse, I had to reach for my handkerchief.

We didn't stay to shake hands with the wife or talk with old friends. Link saw my face and nodded. I had to leave. I was too choked to speak. If Giesele intended to reprimand me, she held back for once.

In her Onslow Square flat, she let me cry. I tried hard not to, but it was impossible to stop.

Eventually, I pulled myself together. 'Sorry,' I said.

'I did not realise,' Giesele said.

'Nor did I.'

'Would you like something to drink?'

'Sorry to have made such a display of myself.' I stroked Giesele's soft blonde hair and felt that tingle when I kissed her lips. Giesele Karpfinger was possibly the most exciting woman I have ever met. Sometimes I wondered if it was only possible for me to reach the highest erotic pitch with someone I didn't really like. Giesele was so combative and small-minded. Often I had to bite back my fury at her confident mantras about politics and human behaviour. At other times, fortunately, she made me laugh.

'To Oliver.' Giesele and I clinked glasses.

'I don't like cry-baby men.' That sounded more like my German dominatrix. 'I think you should have made an address at the funeral, and dat you should have spoken vit Oliver's wife.'

'I'll write to her. I don't know the woman.'

'You should speak to Oliver's mother.' Thinking of Kate, I was about to say, 'Which one?' but stopped myself. 'Do you think that might be enough good advice for now?'

Giesele put down her glass, took mine and put it on the table. The expression on her face didn't change, but her green eyes glittered. I stood up and grasped her extended hand as she led me into the bedroom.

CHAPTER 60

Wag

No one answered the bell. I banged on the door in Eaton Mews and found it yielded to my touch.

The living room was empty. The lights were on. Everything was in its place. The art books neatly stacked on the low, glass-topped coffee table. Wainwright's latest purchases, nicknamed 'Butch' and 'Sundance', had acquired a hidden spotlight on their shelf since my last visit. They were two Henry Moore bronze reclining figures, with tiny heads and holes where their stomachs should have been. My old CO had certainly become something of a collector.

'Harry?'

There was no reply.

The lights were on in the kitchen too, and the kettle still warm.

I closed the front door, and bolted it behind me. Then I thought, if there is someone here, I'll be stuck. I withdrew the bolt and picked up a poker from the grate before going upstairs. There was no point in tiptoeing.

'Harry?' I called again.

One of the paintings on the stairs – a small and jaunty Miró oil – hung askew. Harry, if he was still here, had not been alone. Like me, he was compulsive about his pictures hanging straight and his ornaments positioned just right. I adjusted the angle of the black frame and continued to the landing.

The bathroom door was ajar. I peeped in. Harry was not taking an early evening shower.

Nor was he taking a restorative nap in bed. Harry Wainwright lay on his back, blood pooled like an extra blanket around his stomach on to the quilted bedcover. I dropped the poker and bent over him. 'Oh, Harry.'

I looked around for a phone.

'Don't,' he gasped. His eyes locked with mine. 'Don't. It's too late. Clean up when you go. No one must know you've been here.' The effort of speaking exhausted him.

'Who did this?'

'Sabini's boys,' he croaked. 'They will be after you.'

'Give me their names.' I went quickly into the bathroom to fetch some towels and pressed one to the bullet wound in his stomach in a hopeless attempt to staunch the bleeding.

'Not too hard, William. It hurts, you know . . .'

'Sorry.'

'Luca Bellini and Fred Martin,' Wainwright gasped. 'You couldn't get me a glass of water, by any chance?'

I filled a tooth mug from the bathroom, and cradled my dying friend's head while he made an effort to swallow.

'God, I needed that. Thanks, old man.'

'Are you sure I shouldn't . . .?'

'Positive. Thought only a silver bullet would do for me. But I've had it.' Wainwright coughed and a dribble of blood escaped down his chin. I wiped it away.

'No one can trace a connection to you. I have made sure of that. Just do me one favour.' He winced with pain. 'I don't like to bring Pompey to town. It's too cramped here. Not fair on the boy. Will you look in on him from time to time? Make sure he's all right. My housekeeper will take good care, I know. Everything's paid for. But I'd feel happier if I knew . . .'

I gripped Wainwright's hand. 'Of course.'

He took a shuddering breath. 'I'm sorry we didn't get to know each other better,' Wainwright said. 'I should have liked to have been able to call you Wag.' He smiled and the light faded from his eyes.

I sat on the bed for a while and stared at a photograph of his beloved lurcher Pompey on the bedside table. For some reason the image of my horse Shrapnel swung into my mind. Then I bent over and kissed Wainwright on the forehead.

Outside it had grown dark. A police siren blared in the distance. I hoped they weren't on their way here. It was time to move, and there was work to do. I washed my hands, wiped the tooth mug clean, replaced the poker by the grate downstairs, cleaned every surface I had touched, and used a handkerchief to ensure no tell-tale fingerprints remained when I closed the door behind me.

The quickest way home was a taxi, but I couldn't take one from here. Cab company records would be checked by Scotland Yard in the murder hunt. People are not shot in Belgravia every day.

I had to get home fast, pick up my Luger, track down a couple of killers I didn't know from Adam, and wipe them from the face of the earth. Before they got me.

CHAPTER 61

Jack

'I cannot marry you. I'm sorry, darling.'

I had even brought the ring, which I put back in my pocket. Giesele and I were sitting by candlelight in a dark corner of a little bistro called La Poule au Pot in Ebury Street. She had finished her gigot of lamb with flageolets, and, like the trencherman I wasn't, I had waded through a whole steaming bowl of cassoulet. Only a morsel of sausage and two solitary beans remained on my plate. I could have eaten them, but I left them there, like lone survivors of a battle.

'You know Stanley also wanted to marry me,' Giesele said.

Stanley Heyman was a film composer, responsible for a series of florid scores that suited the mood of the seventies. 'What stopped you?' I asked.

'He was very talented. Rich. Very successful.'

'Like me.'

Giesele raised my hand to her lips. 'We would drive each other mad. You know that. You are too weak, too sensitive. I need to be with a man who is going to take charge.'

I drew myself up. 'Marry me then,' I said firmly.

'Quelque chose pour dessert? Monsieur? Madame?' The young waiter cleared away our plates.

Giesele shook her head.

'Non, merci,' I said.

The restaurant was full as usual. An office party was just warming up in a back room. A grey-haired man with a bleached-blonde young woman sat at an adjoining table. She looked as though she would rather be at home watching television. And a giggle of middle-aged women, immaculately coiffed and accoutred, seemed to be competing for who could tell the most squeal-inducing story.

For a moment, I focused on the outside world because I did not want to contemplate what was happening to me in mine.

'I think it is best ve don't see each other any more,' Giesele said.

'Best for whom?'

'Both of us.'

'Is there somebody else?'

'You know there isn't.' Giesele looked at me fiercely. 'And you. Do you still see dat scrubber?'

'Sylvia is a good, old friend,' I said.

'Vy don't you marry her then? I am sure she vould make the perfect wife for you.'

I thought back to a recent evening with Sylvia, Curwin, Link, Rachel and Giesele. Giesele had scrutinised a sapphire ring Sylvia was wearing. 'Vere did you get dat?' The question was not innocuous.

Sylvia's response snapped back like a challenge. 'You either spit or you swallow.'

I waved at our waiter for the bill. 'When do we start not seeing each other? Now?'

Giesele shrugged her shoulders. 'You don't even have a proper job,' she said. 'Vot do you think my mother would say if I told her I was getting married to someone who vorks at a scrap metal dealers and drives a second-hand Daf?'

She stood up, and draped a shawl round her elegant shoulders. 'You can come home vit me tonight if you vant . . .'

'I'll pass on that. I'll call you a taxi.'

I held the door open while Giesele gave the driver her

address, and I pressed a £10 note into his hand before he drove the love of my life towards Sloane Square and away down the King's Road.

Like our previous farewell at Victoria, there was no kiss goodbye.

CHAPTER 62

Wag

When I got home, I went upstairs to telephone Baker immediately. 'Christ,' he said, after he heard the news. 'I need to make a few calls. Stay where you are.'

Ethel was cooking my favourite supper when I came down again. I did not affect a maroon velvet smoking jacket or anything like that, but I did like to change my clothes as soon as I got home from town. I put on the fur-lined leather slippers my dearest sister had given me last Christmas, and hid the loaded Luger in the pocket of my black mackintosh hanging in the hall.

Ethel was cooking me calf's liver. I needed more iron in my soul tonight, and tomorrow. While I worried about Ethel becoming caught up in this awful mess, I also drew comfort from her presence.

'You look a bit pale,' she said. 'Are you all right?'

'Tummy a bit upset today. But this liver is perfect. Doing me good.' I could have been eating roast rump of radish. I chewed mechanically and tasted nothing.

I was not helpless in the kitchen, but my sister really did like doing the cooking and the housekeeping. My domain was the garden, with roses my newly discovered speciality. I dug in Gallica, which used to be grown in the Middle Ages for its medicinal properties. It later became famous as the Red Rose of Lancaster. I also liked the rangy, strongly scented Damask and the climber Noisette, which produces clusters of small pink blooms from spring to autumn. I experimented with Hybrid Perpetual, a staple of the Victorian garden, although I read in a second-hand copy of *My English Classic Rose Manual* by the Reverend Ward-Hill that a massive pink flowering in the spring was not certain to be repeated later in the year. So, as a precaution, I included the wrinkly-leafed Hybrid Rugosa, which, according to my second-hand bible, was not only hardy and prolific, but disease-resistant. Like me. In spite of the damage done to my lungs at the Somme, I never suffered a cold or a cough, unlike my more delicate sister.

I was not resistant, however, to guns and knives, and it was hard to put that thought from my mind. The news about Wainwright would come out soon. And I was next on their hit list. It was difficult to reconcile that thought with the evening's quiet domestic bliss.

'What have you been doing today?' I asked.

'Not much.' Ethel did voluntary work at the St Jude Hospice in Cheam, but had given up private nursing as a career to look after our house.

Ethel was an unworldly woman, as I have mentioned before, and never questioned how I managed to support the whole family. Our mother too had looked the other way. The same went for the rest of the family, who were happy to continue to fritter away their lives in the Old Rectory with a bit more room to knock about in now that Ethel and I had vacated the premises, until Aubrey and Florence, down on their luck, moved back home, with their pale, withdrawn son Little Aubrey, so the luxury of all that extra space was only enjoyed for a short spell. That house needed people. And so did George, the resident ghost. There is no point in haunting a place if you don't have an appreciative audience.

'I went to the library today,' Ethel told me.

And I saw a man die of a gunshot wound to the stomach today, I thought.

'I'm reading someone called Margery Allingham. *Police at the Funeral*. She has this detective hero, Albert Campion. He's clever, but not a clever dick like Hercule Poirot. A bit posh. You should try her one of these days.'

I had never been able to lose myself in a fictional universe. I couldn't see the point. Learning about roses from the Reverend Ward-Hill was another thing. I could concentrate on that, and retain the information.

Real life held more than enough drama for me.

'Then I had tea with Mrs Webster. Gill. At Number 17. The one who lost her husband.'

'An accident, wasn't it?'

'Yes. Last Christmas. He was standing on the platform of the Number 2 bus. He had been to Hamleys to buy presents for the kids. Had his arms full of parcels. The bus went round Hyde Park Corner. I suppose he couldn't hold on properly. He fell off and was run over by a lorry.'

I looked carefully at Ethel's face to see if she shared my thought that this was a ludicrous way to die. She didn't seem to, so I held my tongue.

'I'm knitting you a scarf too,' she said. 'So I have been quite busy.'

I helped her clear away, and insisted on doing the washing-up.

'There are some tinned peaches, if you fancy.'

'No thanks. I've done extremely well.'

We went into the living room. I wound the grandfather clock, the one I bought in pieces at the Cheam auction house. The brass hinges on the walnut door that opened to the pendulum were inscribed with the words 'In the possession of William and Ethel Bourton'. If I were killed, what would happen to Ethel? I couldn't bear to think about it.

The telephone rang. 'I'll get it,' I said.

Ethel was happy to continue with her murder mystery.

Gazing at my black mac in the hall, I picked up the receiver.

'Right,' said my brother-in-law, Chief Superintendent Maurice Baker. 'Here's the plan.'

CHAPTER 63

Jack

'I'm sorry to hear about Giesele,' Curwin said. He was up to date with my recent disaster. The man attracted information like fly paper.

We were at the Wembley Arena. Just the two of us. Curwin had called me earlier that afternoon on the off-chance. He said he had a spare ticket for Eric Waterman against an up-and-coming middleweight from Derry called Mulligan. This contender for the British title had wild red hair and a wilder left hook. He was one of those very light-skinned boxers whose flesh betrays every bruise and cut, but this boyo could absorb any amount of punishment and stay on his feet.

I hadn't seen Waterman fight for a while. 'I think Eric's got his work cut out for him.' Curwin and I were having a pre-match beer in the crowded bar. There was plenty of space around us. The usual punters could sniff the presence of copper from a hundred yards.

'That's what you said last time.'

'Last time I saw him he had a little help from his friends. Your friends.' At least Curwin had the grace not to give me a meaningful look. He knew perfectly well I 'worked' on the other side of the fence.

'No friends of mine,' I said. 'Waterman's since fought in Paris, Frankfurt and New York. Still unbeaten. Are you saying they were all fixes?'

'Come on, Jack.' Curwin surveyed the clientele assembled

tonight, bruisers in evening dress, jackals in smooth suits. 'You know what it's like out there.'

I spotted Monkey Rawlings in the mêlée. I hoped we would not bump into him later. He was kitted out in a dinner jacket with a mauve cummerbund. I was reminded of Fredric March in his most outrageous film role when he transforms from Dr Jekyll into Mr Hyde.

'To tell you the truth,' Curwin said, 'I'm thinking of getting married myself.'

'Everybody's trying to get in on the act.'

'Next May. I suppose you wouldn't consider being my best man?'

'You're pulling my leg . . .'

'No, Jack. We'd be honoured.'

I finished my beer and ordered two more. 'Wouldn't Inspector Fabian be more suitable?'

'Bruce is a good bloke. But I wouldn't say we were close. You and I go back a long way.'

'You knocked me about a bit once upon a time at school. Are you sure about this? Might not do your reputation any good.'

'You don't have form, Jack. I may not approve of your employers or some of your associates, but you're my friend, whatever happens.'

'All right, then. Yes. I'll do it. Of course. As long as Emma is happy with it.'

We shook hands as a bell signalled that it was time to take our seats.

Inevitably, Rawlings had tickets in the row behind us. But he kept his greeting to a wink and a quick smile. His teeth were not as ferocious-looking as the false set worn by Fredric March in the 1931 horror classic, but I felt a shudder go through me.

'The gang's all here,' said Curwin, score sheet at the ready.

There was an outbreak of applause as the actress Diana Dors made an entrance with her much younger new husband Alan Lake. At this stage of her career, she was on the blowsy side, but the sheen on her peroxide-silver hair blazed as brightly as it ever had. And the smile she threw to her audience knocked 'em in the aisles.

The spotlights heralded the arrival of the contender from Northern Ireland. We all had to stand up, as a big bloke squeezed past us to get to his place before battle commenced. 'Sorry, mate,' he muttered as he trod on my foot. He was followed by a mousey moll in an off-the-shoulder spangly dress. The perfume she wore was as strong as a punch on the nose from Our 'Enery.

Our Eric got a bigger cheer than the Irish hooligan, although one solid section of the hall kept up a chant for Mulligan. They didn't have the chance to shout themselves hoarse. The ageing Waterman (I'm talking here by boxing standards) started well, with a series of quick jabs which jolted the Derry guy's head back. Each time Eric connected, his supporters cheered.

They were not so happy when Mulligan hit the champion with a haymaker out of nowhere. Waterman didn't see it coming. He went down with a thump, and was counted out while struggling to his knees.

Coins and beer cans were chucked into the ring. The boos drowned the Irish contingent's cheers as Mulligan paraded around the ring, punching the air. There was nothing else to hit.

'Sorry about that, Jack.' Curwin crumpled up his score sheet and dropped it on the floor. 'Guess it wasn't Eric's night.'

There was a slow-motion stampede for the exits. After such a humiliating defeat, Waterman had every chance of ending up like the 'Horizontal Heavyweight' Jack Doyle, working as a potman in a pub in Notting Hill Gate.

Suddenly we were face to face with Monkey Rawlings.

'Well, hello there, young Armitage,' he said 'Aren't you going to introduce me to your friend?'

'Er, George Curwin, meet Mr Rawlings, who works with me,' I said.

'I know who you are, young man,' Monkey cut me off. Looking Curwin pointedly in the eye, he said, 'Always happy to help out a mate of Jack's, if you ever need it. You can call me Monkey.'

Curwin nodded politely, coldly, and then turned his back on him. I knew he could not be bought.

I was not as brave as Waterman. Or as good with my fists. I doubted I could go more than one round with Curwin, who still looked as though he could be pretty useful in a fight.

He and I were engaged in a different kind of contest. I knew he liked me, and the feeling was reciprocated. I respected him too. For some reason, Curwin wanted me back with the good guys. But what could he offer me? Immunity if I blew the whistle on Monkey, HL and their Merry Men? I could hardly confess I was engaged in the trafficking of forged passports with my very own good old Uncle Wag. Whoever would have thought it? It sounded like a joke. Although I was, as they say, laughing all the way to the bank.

CHAPTER 64

Wag

The heat from the hot water machine combined with the blaze of gas rings on the long stove misted up the windows of the Windmill Café (pronounced without the French accent and known to all as Nathan's) in Windmill Street in Soho. It was not too far from Scotland Yard, so Superintendent Baker could be at his desk on time after an early breakfast. I was partial to Nathan's fry-ups too and often met my brother-in-law there in the morning. It took me back to my old Soho days.

I had to rise at dawn to drive in from the Styx. It was easier to park in those days and there were no parking attendants prowling like bandits for easy prey.

'Best dog roll in town.' My brother-in-law wiped a dribble of fat from his chin, and I thought of Wainwright's last bloody cough.

My egg and bacon sandwich tasted of cardboard.

'Poor old Harry,' Maurice said.

The fresh tea could have been boiled bilge water. I pushed my white mug to one side on the Formica table.

'Can't find those bastards anywhere,' Maurice said. 'And, as far as I've heard, there are no fingerprints. Someone cleaned up pretty carefully.'

'That was me.'

'Good job.' Unlike me, Maurice had no trouble eating and drinking. In his line of work, if he were a sensitive plant like me he would have starved to death. 'You say Harry swore no one could trace us to him?'

'He didn't actually mention you.'

'Thanks a bunch.'

The café door opened, bringing a welcome breath of fresh air. Noting the full house, a young couple looked towards the counter. 'Sorry,' shouted Nathan. 'Try again in ten minutes. I'll save you a place.'

'I can't just pin it on the Sabini mob.'

'So what are we going to do?'

'It goes against the grain, I don't mind telling you.' Maurice patted his thinning hair. 'But we may have to handle this on our own.'

'What do you mean? I'm not a hitman.'

'You've fired a gun before, haven't you? Did you kill anyone?'

'Of course. But the war was different. We had no choice.'

My brother-in-law had not been called up, because he was in a crucial reserved profession.

'We don't have a choice now. Kill or be killed,' Maurice said.

'Anything else, gents?' Nathan Silver, second-generation immigrant from a big family who preferred London to Warsaw, rubbed down the table with a red and white dishcloth. 'Something the matter with that sandwich?' he asked, scooping up the mugs and plates.

'I wasn't as hungry as I thought. Sorry.'

'Another tea would be good,' said Maurice.

'Nothing for me, thanks.'

'One tea coming up.' Nathan kept his place moving at a fair old lick.

'I've got every grass, tart, bookies' runner and pox doctor's clerk in town on this case.'

'What about coppers?'

'Don't be stupid, Wag.'

'So what is the plan?'

'There's a full-scale manhunt going on to find Harry's murderers. We have to get to those buggers first so they don't land us in it.'

'How exactly are we going to do that? We've only got their names.'

Maurice leaned forward. 'Christ, Wag. Don't you think I've been doing my job? I know what they eat for bloody breakfast.'

'And when we find them?'

'Then we have no choice. They must be silenced. And we must stop them from getting to the family. For God's sake, if anything happened to Violet, to Leo, to the baby . . .'

To Ethel, I thought.

Maurice had a scar just below his left eye, and he had missed a minuscule tuft of stubble underneath his nose when he shaved this morning.

'You'll need a shooter,' said my brother-in-law.

'I have something at home. Untraceable.'

Superintendent Baker raised a sandy eyebrow.

'A Luger. Got it off a Jerry.'

'Any bullets?' He only half believed me.

'Enough.'

Maurice nodded like one of those toys that keeps bending its beak into a glass of water. 'You're a source of endless surprises, Wag . . . All right. Stand by your beds. If we don't get a result quickly, we're done for.'

'We can't kill everyone in Clerkenwell and the Elephant.'

'Don't worry. We know our targets. But I suggest you run Ethel over to the rectory first. It will be easier to protect them if they're all in one place. Just a precaution.'

The proprietor brought Maurice his tea. My brother-in-law looked up and smiled. 'Thanks, Nathan.'

'Good luck to you, Constabule. Always good to see you. Have this cuppa on me.'

It was the second time this morning I had driven down the Kingston bypass. It was nice having Ethel sitting up beside me.

The traffic was light. Sheep grazed in the sunshine. My sister tied a silk scarf round her head so she could enjoy the balmy breeze from the open window.

As we passed Robin Hood Roundabout, before turning up the hill from Richmond to Wimbledon Common, she said, 'Why don't we come here on Sunday for a walk? See the deer.'

I patted her knee. 'Good idea. We can check out the rose garden.'

'You and your roses.' Ethel smiled like a tolerant adult with a precocious child.

'Violet will be pleased to see you,' I said. 'And Leo. And you'll be able to help with the new baby.'

Ethel doted on our little nephew. He was so responsive and bright, even I, who had little time for small people, found myself making silly faces and animal noises. I had bought him a Meccano set for his last birthday, but Leo was not ready yet to assemble the red and green girders and strips. He preferred to use them as hammers or just for the noise they made when he upturned the box on the living room carpet.

'I really can't understand,' said Ethel, 'why it is absolutely necessary for us all to be put under police protection so suddenly, just because of Maurice.'

'He's a number one target for the Sabinis and the Cortesis since he helped close down their operations. These people are dangerous and unpredictable. One of their gang has just been released from prison,' I explained, making it up as I went along. 'It's highly unlikely that some Sicilian gangster is going to come all the way out to Surbiton to hold a Miss Ethel Bourton to ransom in revenge. But Maurice thought we should err on the side of caution. If we're all together in the rectory, it is easier to protect us.'

'Does that mean, when we go out, that we have to have a police escort?'

'I doubt that we will be there that long . . . We will have to ask Maurice.'

'At least it will be lovely to see everyone,' Ethel said. 'I don't get over there enough.'

After Mother's death, the traditional Sunday lunch continued to be faithfully observed at the Old Rectory. Jago's wife Mildred had taken charge of the kitchen. But sometimes Ethel and I kept the weekends for each other. Rather late in the day, it was like playing house.

On our last visit, I had noticed that jungle was beginning to reclaim the garden. What was the matter with my brothers? They lived there. Didn't they care what the place looked like? The toothless gardener had had to give up on account of a bad back. Overtaking a sluggish Rover with a smelly exhaust, I resolved to engage a replacement for raggedy Joe, who, for all his wizened features and missing teeth, was probably not much older than me.

I was tempted to stop off for a beer at the Sun on Wimbledon Common, anything to defer confronting the mission I could not dodge. Instead, we let the South Circular lead us inexorably to our destination.

'Hello, darlings!' Florence opened the door. 'Brilliant to see you, but what a fuss about nothing.' Powder and rouge could not disguise the ravages done to her face by drink and nicotine.

As I parked the Austin and brought our luggage into the house, a plain-clothes man on the other side of the street nodded to me.

Mop-haired Leo came romping down the stairs, brandishing an almost life-size monkey. 'This is Mr Bojangles,' he shouted.

'Hello, Mr Bojangles.' I patted the monkey on the head.

'Yook!' Leo could not pronounce his ls. He showed his new toy to Ethel. In delight, she picked him up and swung him round. It gave me a pang. Did she regret never having had her own child? Had living with me denied her that?

'Are you ready?' Maurice's process downstairs was more stately than his son's. He was followed by Violet, carrying their six-month-old daughter Linda in her arms.

'Give us a sec, will you?' I said.

'We have had to stick you in with George in the attic,' Violet said. 'I hope you don't mind.'

'We're old friends, that ghost and I. Where shall I put Ethel's stuff?'

'Her old room.'

Ethel was being chased round the hall by a demented monkey, roaring like a lion.

There was a semblance of order in the attic, even a light bulb that worked in the famous standard lamp, knocked over by George one night in his phantom struggle with whatever demons drove him to suicide.

I hung up a spare jacket and trousers in the dusty wardrobe, slid three white shirts, underpants and socks into a chest of drawers, folded my pyjamas under the pillow of my single bed, and unwrapped my gun.

I did not need to check that the chamber was fully loaded. Spare cartridges, just in case, I stuck in jacket and trouser pockets.

'We haven't got all day, Wag.' Maurice was prowling up and down in front of the door. We ran downstairs.

'Where are you going?' Ethel asked. 'I thought we were all going to stay together.'

'We have to see a man about a dog,' I said.

'Yes,' said Maurice. 'I need Wag's advice.'

Ethel looked alarmed but she didn't ask any more questions.

'Let's go into the living room,' said Violet.

How much did she know? I wondered.

Mr Bojangles banged his furry brown head against the back of my leg.

'See you all later.' I waved to no one in particular.

'We'll take my car,' Maurice said.

It was at Clerkenwell Green that Fagin and the Artful Dodger inducted Oliver Twist into the art of pickpocketing at the busy market which used to exist right where we parked the car.

Maurice told me that his sources had confirmed that the men looking for us would be gathered at this time in the back room of the Cock Tavern on East Poultry Avenue.

'By the way,' Maurice said. 'This is not happening. We are not here. I have discussed the matter in some depth with my good friend Commander Hastings. Officially, I'm on leave today. Gone fishing with my brother-in-law.'

A lorry drew up on the corner of Smithfield Market. Having opened the pavement door to the pub's cellar, a couple of burly blokes started to unload beer barrels.

'I didn't come this far to have my life ruined by a shitload of Sicilian immigrant bastards – or by the Metropolitan Police Force for that matter. I keep tabs on what is going on . . .' This brother-in-law of mine was turning out to be the most enterprising fellow. 'For insurance purposes, I have a whole dossier on Hastings. And a number of his top brass. Dodgy dealings and all that. Get this over and done with now and we'll be laughing.' Maurice's expression did not betray a hint of levity. 'In the back room of that pub, we will find the men we're looking for. Are you sure you're up for this?'

I swallowed hard and nodded.

'Let's get it over with then.'

The Cock was not due to open for another hour but the front door was unlocked. There was no sign of the landlord or any other staff in the bar. Tobacco smoke combined with the lingering odour of spilled beer.

I heard the click of billiard balls from the back room.

Maurice produced a regulation Webley. 'Don't worry,' he said. 'It has no serial number.'

I checked my own safety catch was off.

'Ready?' Maurice whispered, as his left hand reached for the door knob.

'Ready.' I took up my position, ready to charge in.

Outside there was a crash of falling beer barrels. Maurice flung open the door.

A stocky man, shirt sleeves rolled past his elbows, looked up from the green baize billiard table. His miscued white ball shot straight into the middle right-hand pocket. The second man had kept his jacket on, and was in mid gasp of his cigarette. They both froze as we entered.

Time stood still. In the war, I had only ever killed in self-defence. This scene at the Cock Tavern was premeditated. But then the image of Wainwright's bleeding body flashed into my mind. These guys had killed my friend in cold blood. They did not deserve to live.

The fellow in the jacket reached inside his pocket.

I hit my shirt-sleeved target fair and square in the head.

Maurice finished his man off with two shots. 'Yes, it's them,' he said, checking the bodies.

I had not heard so much as a footfall after we had fired our guns. The two delivery men now blocked our exit from the billiard room.

'It's all right, Wag,' Maurice said, as I raised my Luger. 'They're with us.'

CHAPTER 65

Jack

After providing passports for the Richardsons, I was finally able to stop working in HL's office. Monkey had lost his hold on me. I gave up any plan of finding a regular job in publishing and joined my dad on the auction circuit. He was good company and had learned a lot since he jacked it in with Lloyds counting house. I learned a great deal from him. Not just about watercolourists like Claude Hayes, whom his father had collected, but about more celebrated artists like John Cotman and the Norwich School. Dad was also interested in collectables like stevengraphs and netsuke. He taught me to be less impatient when on the hunt, to check the very last picture in a pile of old rubbish tilted against the wall.

I started buying, cautiously at first, but with increasing confidence. Where my father latched on to any painting with trees, cows and scudding clouds, I was attracted to more exotic scenes. Like Uncle Wag's David Roberts painting of Abu Simbel. Show me a ruin and a camel in the desert and I was a goner.

At the Harrods Depository on the river near Hammersmith Bridge, there was this very nice girl called Isobel, who would make your bids if you could not be present on auction day. That was extremely convenient. Except that Isobel had a queue of admirers who were not necessarily interested in any of the lots in the weekly sales.

My father and I did not just operate in London. There were funny little auction houses where we could pick up bargains from Tenterden to Portsmouth. Sometimes Mum came along too. She was astute on jewellery and started to specialise in exotic textiles from places like Sumatra and Surinam. It was both surprising and rewarding that you could buy so cheaply in one cluttered saleroom and sell so well in another.

My preferred venue, though, was what we used to call Harrods-on-Sea. The orange and white, faience-fronted building with its distinctive two cupolas made me think of pictures of Lutyens's far more distinguished Viceroy's House in New Delhi. Not that I had ever been to India. In the old days, this large and elegant Thameside edifice was used by members of the Foreign Service to store furniture and precious possessions, pending their return from postings abroad.

Before the nearby Castelnau pub closed its lunchtime session, I asked Isobel to join me in celebrating my acquisition of an oil painting I was convinced was a genuine Edward Lear. Over the course of the last few months, the two of us had indulged in mildly flirtatious badinage and this was not the first drink we had had together. Excited by my purchase, however, I was emboldened to ask her what turned out to be a life-changing question. 'Would you like to come out to supper this evening?'

'I thought you'd never ask.'

I liked the sound of Isobel's reply.

'Indian, Chinese, Thai, French, Italian?' The days of the ludicrously long jaunts to a Chinese dive in Limehouse were over. Food in London had improved immeasurably since the best choice of a spicy meal was an egg pulao at the Star of Pakistan in Lower Frith Street or a chicken cacciatore at the Amalfi in Old Compton Street.

'Whatever you fancy.'

I resisted the urge to make the obvious response.

'I'm easy.'

I resisted again.

We had another gin and tonic. 'I don't even know where you live,' I said.

'Royal Crescent.'

I had looked many times at Isobel's face. She had dark, wavy hair that was cut neatly at the base of her neck (had to be Vidal Sassoon), olive complexion, deep brown eyes, a straight nose and generous lips. At this moment, her features were coming into focus so sharply, it was like a magic mirror clearing to reveal who was the fairest of them all.

'What number?'

'Fourteen. The first floor. The one with a balcony.'

'Great. Shall I pick you up around seven thirty? If not exactly at seven thirty?'

'Bastard.' A bloke in a tan leather jacket slapped me on the shoulder. It was Dick Dawkins, special agent for the picture dealers' ring. 'You might have got something there,' he said. 'Can't think how we missed it. If that is a real Edward Lear, next time I see you I'll break both your legs.' He grinned. 'Cheers, Isobel. Watch out for this bloke. He's got his eye on you next.'

I did not bother this bunch, any more than my dad did. We were insignificant regulars on the auction room circuit, who had the occasional bit of luck. The ring of dealers had its own special targets. They did not pursue every knick-knack on the wall or on the floor or under the table. They were a syndicate who did not bid against each other for the good stuff at auction and would then quietly divvy up the profit between themselves later. It was a dodgy business, not strictly legal. Armitage & Son were tolerated as long as we trod on no one's toes.

'Good hunting,' I said.

Dawkins gave me an ostentatious wink and joined his mates

at the bar, who were discussing how to dispose of the plunder they had accumulated today.

'I'm not sure those people should be allowed,' Isobel said.

I wondered what she would make of me if she knew of my murky involvement with Linklater and friends . . .

If I could reserve a table, it occurred to me that Julie's in Portland Road was perfect for tonight. In easy walking distance from Isobel's place, tucked away in an intimate village enclave near the old Holland Park potteries, this honeycomb of discreetly lit alcoves was a custom-made cliché for romantic assignations.

I liked the way Isobel smiled at the suggestion of Julie's. 'I double-checked the provenance on your acquisition, by the way,' she said. 'I reckon it's genuine.'

The picture I had bought was an Egyptian scene. A parade of people on foot and on camels are protected from the fierce sun by a long and shady avenue of interlocking trees. The pyramids of Giza can be seen in the misty distance.

'I have a tiny watercolour of one of his parrots at home. I can show you later, if you like,' Isobel said.

'How pleasant to know Mr Lear,' as the artist poet wrote. How exhilarating to know Miss Isobel Weston.

'I have to dash,' I said. 'But I'll see you very soon.'

'You will.' Isobel got to her feet, and we walked out into the afternoon sun. If you looked to the left from Hammersmith Bridge, glinting green and gold over the river, you could have been transported back in time. The modern world was only traffic noise.

'I have a hot date with Uncle Wag,' I said.

'Who or what is an Uncle Wag?'

'It's a long story,' I said, leaning forward to kiss Isobel on both cheeks.

* * *

'They had the rope ladder over the wall and everything.'

'How do you hear all this stuff?'

My wicked uncle tapped his nose. 'I still have my contacts,' he said. 'Someone must have tipped off the prison governor. They let old Charlie do all the hard stuff and then nabbed him. Sadists. He'll be inside till he draws his old age pension.'

The other Richardson brother was out. That much I did know. In spite of the odd incident, which might have ensured an extended stay for some other prisoners, Eddie had been released. He didn't even need his new doctored passport, and had flown to Paris where les Frères Richardson were busy establishing a chain of sex shops, which also served under-the-counter cocaine.

I had heard all this from Link earlier in the afternoon on my way over to see Uncle Wag. 'I have definitely had enough of this lark, Kid,' he said.

'You and me both,' I replied.

'"Take Me Down" is at Number eleven in the charts.' This was Birds of a Feather's latest single. 'And I've just signed up this new babe – Lezley Lee. With a "z". She's fantastic. Makes Shirley Bassey sound like she's Whispering Paul McDowell.'

'Have you spoken to your dad?'

'The funny thing is,' Link said, 'that he wants out too. After all these years. The only problem is Mum. I don't blame her. Why would she want to go and live in Monte bloody Carlo? Why would anyone except my dad? It's like a sanitarium for old rich people.'

I couldn't solve the Linklater family's dilemmas. There was my own life to attend to.

Later, as Wag and I wandered out into the garden, in a rush of delayed excitement, I told him about my date with Isobel. 'She's quite something,' I said. 'It's early days, I know . . . I also bought a marvellous Edward Lear oil. At least, I hope it's an Edward Lear. Of Cairo. You'll like it. You'll like Isobel too.'

The roses had been well mulched in. There were no noxious odours this time, only the sweet scent of a cluster of white and pink roses in the afternoon sun. Wag must have cut the lawn earlier too. The rows were neat, and I spotted fresh green clippings on the compost heap in the corner of the garden. We sat at a round wooden table outside the kitchen. Once upon a time, I knew, corn fields stretched to the horizon beyond the wooden fence. Now rows of houses blocked the view of more rows of suburban semis.

'I'll always be grateful to you, Uncle Wag, for doing that job for those dreadful Richardsons. You got me out of such a hole.'

'I was glad to be of help.' Wag patted me on the shoulder. 'I stayed in that world too long. But then I wouldn't have had this place. Ethel would have been condemned to an early grave. I can't regret what I did.'

'The trouble is – they are all going to think I'm the man to go to now. Where all Monkey's usual connections failed, I came up with the goods.'

'It's not easy getting out,' Wag said. 'I know that all too well.'

CHAPTER 66

Wag

I won't say that my house in Surbiton was the Garden of Eden. And I had committed worse crimes than Adam ever did. Ethel was not my Eve. But I loved her more than I loved anything or anyone.

There was not a malicious bone in Ethel's body. But there was an invisible canker that gnawed at her.

'I ache a bit tonight,' she said one night after supper.

It was not long after we had come back from a visit to Australia in January 1957. We had spent a month out there, including four days with my nephew Randal in Brisbane. My athletic nephew had married a woman who got out of breath merely climbing up the stairs of their neat little house, which was situated not far from the Old Windmill in Wickham Park, built by convicts in 1828, Randal told us during our tour of the city.

Ethel had liked Australia. It did not assault the senses. She recognised the food. We spoke the same language, more or less. Having flown all that way, I had to see Ayer's Rock, but Ethel said she was too tired to come with me and watch the sandstone glow red at dawn.

I fetched a small footstool, and put it under her heels. 'Can I get you anything?'

'It'll be all right in a minute. I've noticed, around this time, it tends to come on of an evening.'

'We should get someone in to do the housework,' I said, although I was not unhappy that my sister chose to continue to look after the place herself. I didn't want some skivvy, however nice, poking her nose into my things.

Ethel picked up her book, *Judgment on Deltchev*. My sister had exchanged her addiction from crime to mystery and espionage fiction, and she liked to keep me up to the mark with the plots. Apparently, this latest one by Eric Ambler was about Stalin's purge-trials in Eastern Europe. Not my cup of tea. Searching for the page where she had left off, Ethel said out of the blue, 'Poor old Ernest. Hope neither of us gets like that. You must promise to tell me. If my mind starts wandering, and I keep repeating myself, just say, "Marbles".'

Aurelia's husband Ernest had been packed off to a nursing home. At least he didn't drool. But there wasn't much point in visiting him. He simply gazed into space and chewed the non-existent cud. If he was ruminating on anything, Ernest never explained. He never spoke another word. Poor Aurelia took it very badly. Her spirit guide Redwing was of no use. But she did not lose her faith. 'Ernest has simply travelled to another world,' she explained. Maybe he had.

'Have you been to see Edwina?' I asked. Edwina Green was our local GP. Bluff and brisk, you would have had to be in the last stages of the bubonic plague for her to consider scribbling a prescription. A good night's rest and plenty of fluids was her cure-all advice.

'About my marbles?'

'No, silly . . .'

'If it continues,' Ethel said, 'I'll have an X-ray.' My sister probably knew as much about medicine as Dr Green. After a month, she did go to the hospital. A malignant tumour was discovered in her abdomen.

Ethel received her sentence with the fortitude and courage that were typical of her. 'We can give you something for the pain,' the young doctor said, 'but I'm afraid there is not a lot we can do for you otherwise. I'm sorry.'

'How long has she . . .?' I asked.

'Impossible to predict. It might be three months. It might be a year.'

'I'll take the year,' Ethel said.

In some ways, that year was one of the happiest she and I spent together. There was a private clinic in Lausanne. I did my homework as soon as I heard the bad news.

'We can't possibly afford that,' Ethel said when I told her I had booked two tickets to Switzerland. 'And what about your job?'

'Bugger my job,' I said.

Don't ask me what Dr Kohn put in his syringes or in the drips that were inserted into the delicate veins of Ethel's arms, but bit by bit, the pain began to disappear.

Ethel had a private room in the clinic, and so did I. Right next door. There was no way I was going to return to a hotel in order to worry the night away.

I even ploughed through three novels, on the trot. Including a second go at *Great Expectations*. Ethel liked me to read to her in the evenings. It was comforting for us both. We laughed together and also shed a tear or two, especially at the scene in the gloomy prison, where Pip visits the dying Magwitch and tells him:

> *'You had a child once, whom you loved and lost. She lived and found powerful friends. She is living now. She is a lady, and very beautiful. And I love her.'*
>
> *With a last faint effort, which would have been powerless but for my yielding to it and assisting it, he raised my hand to his lips. Then, he gently let it sink upon his breast again, with his own hands lying on it. The placid look at the white*

ceiling came back, and passed away, and his head dropped quietly on his breast.

Ethel's vision became blurry, and she found concentration difficult, except during story time. About a month into the treatment, her pale skin turned almost translucent. Meanwhile, those wide blue eyes gleamed with a fierce brightness.

She liked me to brush her hair in the evenings, with the silver monogrammed brush she had brought from home. I could have performed this task for hours, but Ethel could not hold one position for more than a few minutes without discomfort.

I fed her when her hands trembled. The standard of the clinic's cuisine was as good as or better than most top restaurants, and there was an amazing choice of dishes. Ethel preferred the softer foods, things you could sift in your mouth rather than chew. I discovered a taste for dishes I never dreamed of eating in England, like steak tartare and globe artichoke.

'I'm not hungry,' Ethel would say. But I made her eat.

There were always crisply efficient nurses in attendance, but I remained my sister's faithful body servant. A bell was installed in my room next door, so Ethel could call me in the middle of the night if she needed me.

One night, it was a terrible scream rather than the bell that startled me out of a deep sleep. I didn't pause to put on slippers, and dashed next door.

Ethel was sitting up against her two white pillows, tearing at her hair like an inmate of Bedlam. 'Get it out, Wag,' she shrieked. 'Get it out!'

'Calm,' I said, lowering her hands. She continued to pant and her eyes were wild.

'Quickly!' she said. 'It's still there.'

Tangled up in her hair was the biggest spider I had ever seen – it had a juicy mottled green body with long legs. I had dealt with monster-size rats in the trenches, with minuscule lice and other bugs that crawl and fly, but there was something almost supernaturally unsettling about this harmless insect trying to extricate its eight legs from my sister's hair. It was not at all what you expected in a pristine, sanitised private room.

I grabbed hold of a couple of legs and squashed the spider's body between finger and thumb.

Ethel grimaced. 'That was disgusting.'

I must say I agreed. Plucking a piece of paper towel from a dispenser on the wall, I wrapped it round the insect's corpse and flushed it down the lavatory.

'You didn't have to kill it,' Ethel said. Typical woman.

'Would you have preferred me to have talked him down?' I asked. 'Or offered him a glass of milk?'

Ethel smiled. 'Thank you, darling. You were wonderful. You are wonderful.' She reached out for the brush on the bedside table.

'Here, let me do that.' I sat beside her and gently started to untangle her wild hair. As I did so, a sizeable tuft clung to the bristles.

Ethel's brimming eyes met mine. 'I thought I might have been one of the lucky ones,' she said.

Rather than suffer the slow indignity of gradual hair loss, Ethel decided it would be best to shave off all her hair. 'I'd like you to do it, Wag. If you don't mind.'

I used clippers, and kept a stiff upper lip as best I could, standing in a gathering circle of greying chestnut hair. (I kept one thick lock back in an envelope.) With my own cutthroat razor, I made sure Ethel's nicely shaped head was smooth of every last bristle.

My sister had her own special cream which I used to replenish the natural oils of the scalp. She liked me to massage her skin. 'It's very comforting,' she said. 'You have delicate hands for a man.'

Ethel had a couple of silk scarves that she wound into elegant turbans. That was beyond my natural skills. It seemed to me that I mourned the loss of her hair more than she did. I admired her lack of vanity, her resilience.

It was a struggle, though. She could not hide that, and I was glad there was refuge in sleep.

On days when Ethel felt strong enough, I wheeled her round the clinic's eighteenth-century gardens. Swans paddled on a series of formal ponds, linked by balustraded bridges. On the other side of an avenue of cypress trees, the snow-capped Alps loomed above Lake Léman.

If it was the slightest bit chilly, I made my sister wear the muff you can see in the photograph I carried with me the whole time I was at the front. In its double-sided case, the cut-out picture of Ethel in cloche hat, coat and long skirt, with me in uniform on the opposite side, brought me more comfort than a Bible, and it was a lot lighter to carry.

Words between me and my sister were never the most important thing. In many ways, our conversations were worse than mundane. We discussed ordinary, practical things. Ethel was not given to flights of fancy. During those months in Lausanne, I could have filled ten notebooks with the things we left unsaid.

CHAPTER 67

Jack

You could hear the squeak of boxing shoes from the upstairs floor, as well as an incessant hammering of the punch bags. Link and I were waiting for Monkey Rawlings at the Perseverance. The bar itself was empty. Sidney the landlord was wiping some glasses with a damp cloth, the usual Woodbine dangling from his lower lip. Every now and again, he would cough, and hawk up a gob of phlegm.

The door that led up to the training rooms opened, and Eric Waterman came out. A plaster was over his left eye. 'Usual, please, Sidney.'

The landlord was already pulling Waterman a pint of draught Bass.

'I'd like to get this, if I may.' I put down a pound note on the bar. 'And a couple more gins for us, please. One tonic.'

'Thanks, Jack.'

We shook hands.

'It is ridiculous, isn't it,' I said, 'that we've known each other since we were boys. I've followed all your fights and never said a proper hello.'

'Different worlds, I guess,' Waterman said.

'Would you like to join us?'

'Thanks.'

Link stood up.

'I know your dad,' said the former British middleweight champion. 'Bought a car off him once. Clapped-out old banger.

Exploded on me down the A40 at the junction of Old Oak Common Lane.'

'Sorry about that,' Link said. 'I can offer you a top-class discount on a light blue Cadillac Deville, genuine tree-wood dashboard and leather upholstery.'

'I suspect my days of fancy cars are over.' Waterman grinned.

'Bad luck about that fight with Mulligan,' I said. 'I was there. It was a lucky punch.'

Waterman took a contemplative sip of his beer. 'I have got a couple more fights lined up,' he said. 'Easier opposition. But I'm going nowhere fast.'

'You did all right,' said Link.

'Not bad for a boy from the Northfield Estate.'

'You must have made a few quid,' I said.

'I tell you,' Eric replied, 'by the time your manager's taken his cut and you've paid your trainer, your corner man and Uncle Tom Cobley, there's not much change left out of half a knicker. I haven't been able to buy my old mum a nice place by the swamp.'

We all turned at the click of the door opening. It was like the moment of reckoning in the last chance saloon. Monkey Rawlings stood still for a moment in the doorway, the cartoon villain of a B-feature Western.

'Losers' corner,' he said, walking over to our table. 'Lock up, will you, Sidney? This is a private function.'

The taciturn landlord stubbed out his fag, and did what he was told.

Rawlings pulled up a chair. 'You don't need to hang about,' he said to Waterman.

'I haven't finished my beer yet,' said Eric.

'Suit yourself.' The managing director of Camberwell

Green's leading charm school was dressed modestly, by his standards, in what might have been one of Arthur English's cast-off 'Wide Boy' striped suits.

Evidently, Link was having exactly the same thought. 'Play the music,' he said. 'Open the cage!' Those were the music-hall comedian's famous catchphrases.

'Are you trying to be funny?'

'I don't have to try,' said Link.

On the phone earlier, Monkey Rawlings had sounded as though he had finally come to terms with our mass defection. We had had the dire threats last time. Since then, I had at least done the firm some service. It was hardly my fault Charlie Richardson was still inside. Yet here was Monkey, gunning for a fight. He had obviously decided that it was necessary to teach us a lesson after all.

Eric Waterman was still in good shape. Next to him, though, the glowering Monkey Rawlings radiated menace. The spiv suit was an absurd disguise for the monster inside it, a creature from the real, live and mythical underworld whose bulky frame could barely be contained by the blue and white striped cloth.

'What's all this about, Rawlings?' asked Eric.

'None of your business, my loser friend,' Charlie Richardson's head honcho sneered.

'Seems that it is, now,' said Eric. 'Don't you call me that. Unlock those doors, will you, Sidney?'

From his right-hand suit pocket, Rawlings flashed a knife and nailed the boxer's right hand to the table. Link and I were on our feet in a second, as Waterman let out a roar of pain and surprise, knocking over our drinks which smashed on the floor.

'I'll take two of you with one hand behind my back. Oooh – look at the tough guy.'

Link had pulled on his brass knuckle-duster.

Out of the corner of my eye, I saw the landlord slip quietly upstairs and heard the lock click.

Face taut with pain, Waterman was trying to remove the blade from the back of his hand, while blood spilled over the table.

'Come on, Monkey . . .' I was circling out of reach.

'I told you never to fucking call me Monkey!'

'Oh no, you didn't.' This was worse than a pantomime. I continued to circle as though we were in an invisible ring.

Link rushed forward and took a swing at Rawlings. He failed to connect, and the Werewolf of Camberwell clubbed him round the side of the head with his huge right paw, and followed up with a lethal left to the jaw. I wondered if Rawlings had twisted his fist at the last moment, as he had once demonstrated in this very same public house.

Link tottered backwards and slumped to the floor next to the Gentlemen's lavatory.

'Your turn, Jack,' said Rawlings.

With a groan, Waterman yanked out the knife. His face was pale and his lips were tight as he bound a handkerchief round the gaping wound.

'Doesn't look as though you'll be winning any trophies for a while.' Rawlings unleashed a vulpine grin.

'Maybe not,' said Waterman. 'But I can still teach you a lesson.' His guard was up, and he moved forward quickly.

Rawlings was not a man to retreat. With a growl, he lashed out with his right again, only for Waterman to block with his left, shift inside, and use his damaged right hand to hit his opponent in the guts. Rawlings grunted, but kept on coming.

Waterman jolted the brute's head back with a powerful left jab, and another and another in a blazing sequence of punches.

I did not know what to do. In a Western saloon brawl, I

would have picked up a chair and smashed it over the baddy's head. But these were not stunt chairs. I didn't think I could lift one over my head. So I ran to the lavatory.

When I came out, blood was pouring from Rawlings's nose. One eye was closed, and he coughed up a front tooth on to the floor.

I released the hammer of the pistol that Monkey had concealed so long ago in the cistern of the bog with the unbroken seat. 'Doesn't look as though you need any help from me, after all, El,' I said.

I returned to the toilet and put the gun back where I had found it.

CHAPTER 68

Wag

My sister and I gave thanks to God and to Dr Kohn for her miraculous clean bill of health. 'Of course,' said Dr Kohn at the last consultation, 'I cannot guarantee that the cancer will not return. I am not a magician. But I'm very satisfied with the progress you've made.' He had the ascetic features of a monk and the wavy hair of a romantic composer, down to his starched white collar. Kohn's bill would have made the angels weep, but I was no angel.

I had funds in Lausanne and Zurich. More than enough to finance another course of intensive treatment for Ethel, should the dismal necessity arrive. And plenty to pay for a few days in Venice on our way home.

'It's too much,' Ethel said, although it was perfectly clear she wanted to go. 'We'll end up in debtors' prison.'

'What do you think I've been saving up for all these years?'

'I haven't the faintest idea.'

Frankly, nor had I. 'Neither of us has any dependants. I could leave my money to the Battersea Dogs' Home. But I would prefer to spend it on you. On us. We're celebrating a life regained, when all seemed lost. If that isn't worth writing a couple of large cheques for, I don't know what is.'

Ethel didn't have the inclination or energy to argue.

It had to be the Gritti Palace hotel, and a suite on the Grand Canal with a balcony looking over to the Santa Maria della Salute church. The little engraver from south London was turning into a talking guidebook. I swatted up every night and every morning, sometimes before breakfast, before our tour of the day. I was careful not to tire Ethel out, so I made sure she could have a sit-down whenever she felt like it.

'How are you feeling?' It was our last evening in Venice. We were having supper in the dazzling dining room of the fifteenth-century palazzo.

'My feet ache.'

'Pain anywhere else?'

'No. Thank goodness.'

Ethel reached out across the white tablecloth and grasped my hand. 'What would I do without you?' she said. 'My saviour, my dearest friend, my most beloved brother?'

We arrived home in time for Ted's funeral. A telegram had arrived from Jago as a porter was loading our luggage on to the hotel's motor launch. A heart attack, apparently.

'At least he didn't linger,' said his red-eyed widow Mavis after the service at St Leonard's.

I put my arm around her shoulder while she sobbed.

How drab and dusty the streets were. The soft autumnal glow of the Adriatic was replaced by a hard grey glare, as we drove in our black limousines in stately procession to South Norwood Cemetery, where my most inscrutable brother would join the members of our family already at their eternal rest. A crumpled newspaper was blown against the wheels of our car. Litter bounced along the pavement. A man in a cloth cap stared as we went by, his face as blank as a piece of old stone.

CHAPTER 69

Jack

As guests left their coats in the hall for the reception, Magnus Blunden played the grand piano in the vestibule. Magnus was one of the Levity Lancers, who had been persuaded by my best man Link to provide some of the musical accompaniment at the party, to celebrate the wedding of Jack 'the Lad' Armitage and Isobel Lettice Weston.

When the registrar read Isobel's middle name at Chelsea Old Town Hall, I heard it for the first time and laughed out loud. 'Lettuce? Why didn't you tell me?' I whispered.

'You would never have married me if you'd known.'

Isobel's mother glared in my general direction. Her husband remained bolt upright, looking neither right nor left. He was on parade. My father smiled and my mother looked agitated.

In spite of her mother's objections, Isobel had agreed. We didn't want all that hoo-ha of a church wedding, with its ridiculous costumes, ceremony and paraphernalia. We were determined to focus on a full-frontal post-marital celebration.

Some old mates were offended that only our parents, best man and a couple of other people had been quietly invited to witness the deed at the registry office. But that is how we wanted it, and we were the ones getting married – even though Sir Percival and Lady Weston were footing most of the bill for the knees-up at Searcys in Pavilion Road.

'Hello, darlings.' Aunt Florence was the first to arrive, her languid son Aubrey in tow. He managed a limp handshake and brushed Isobel's cheek with a kiss. This was going to be a long haul.

'Where's your mama?' Florence asked.

I nodded to the corner, where the two sets of parents were making heavy weather of the ante-prandial badinage. Sir Percival Weston CBE, DSO, MC had been Quartermaster General of the Army, but was now Governor of the Royal Hospital Chelsea, where three hundred or so elderly ex-soldiers, in their highly conspicuous red outfits, provided photo opportunities for tourists. Canons to the left, Pentaxes to the right.

Monkey Rawlings wasn't on my guest list. He had been invited to spend a year or two at Her Majesty's pleasure in Pentonville. No doubt he was meeting up with a lot of old friends and making some new ones. Someone had shopped him to the police. I can't remember what the initial charge was, some minor offence. But a lot more dirt came out at his trial. And neither Link nor I was implicated.

Perhaps there is a God who protects the not so innocent . . . Or perhaps we had our old school friend Curwin to thank.

As far as I know, HL didn't consult the heavenly father when making his decision to remain out of harm's way in Monte Carlo. He did finally manage to persuade his wife to join him, although he may have regretted that decision. Bummy Mel didn't like 'abroad', but decided to honour her marital vows and moan a lot. They were unable to attend our do, but a brightly polished second-hand Mini tied up with ribbon was delivered to our house.

Eric Waterman was one of the first people I invited. His boxing days were over. The knife wound he sustained in the Perseverance severed a ligament. He couldn't clench his right fist properly any more. But he was now working as a trainer at the pub's gym, and was confident that at least one of his young protégés was going places. He had a really nice girlfriend, called Heather, who was a Montessori teacher. Isobel and I saw a lot of them. The noble art held no appeal for either woman, but they didn't seem to mind if El and I rambled on a bit about the latest contenders for tawdry honours in the boxing ring.

'You've been and gone and done it now friends,' said Tyler, shaking me by the hand. 'Thanks a lot.' From the look on her face, it was clear that his girlfriend Chloe was twitching for him to pop the question. At a certain age, marriage can be like a pandemic.

'I am here for the duration,' I told Isobel, before the guests had started arriving. 'For richer or poorer. No matter what.'

We held each other tight, and I prayed that this wonderful young woman would last the course too, that she wouldn't find me dull and irritating, or find out about my former involvement with the underworld. Or run off with someone else. I had never shared my life with anyone before. I still had my secrets, though, and preferred to keep it that way.

I thought twice about inviting Giesele to the party, and did it anyway. She had not responded to the invitation, which was a relief.

I was sad Oliver wasn't there to see me married, but I invited some of the old left-wing brigade in his honour. Julian Doyle arrived with his wife, and Boggy, as well as a few more of the old Trotskyites. 'No marbles, no firecrackers,' I said. They handed over a pile of presents. 'And no *Little Red Books*.' I need not have worried. Each box contained a toaster and toast rack. Who said there were no jokes in the *Communist Manifesto*? Someone had remembered me saying that I would never get married because I already had a toaster.

Magnus played 'Some Enchanted Evening', but it was

beginning to get harder to hear the music over the increasing din of the crowd.

'Don't lose this, will you, girl?' Uncle Wag pressed a neatly wrapped gift into Isobel's hand.

Wag was looking frail. He had had a nasty dose of bronchitis in the autumn – the only time I ever knew him to be sick. My mum had nursed him, and stayed by his side in remotest Surbiton for the best part of a week.

I got him a glass of champagne and sat him down at a table, where he was joined by my mum and dad.

There was a long table for all the booty Isobel and I were acquiring for the marital home. Having wandered up and down streets of narrow houses in Islington, we had decided that west was best – the rooms were wider, even if the façades were not as gracious. We finally plumped for an 1860s south-facing terraced house off the grotty Askew Road, and, even though the previous owners had removed every single light bulb before they left the keys, Isobel and I remained happy about the deal when we moved our stuff in.

I spotted a large contingent of family and went over. My Aunt Violet's husband Maurice Baker was in a wheelchair.He had been invalided out of the force twenty years ago, after a person or persons unknown shot him in both kneecaps. He never complained about his crippling disability, and he was as nifty in his chair as a paraplegic Olympic basketball player. Violet had handled the situation well, too. They brought up their kids, went on cruises to Belize and the fjords of Norway. It helped, I suppose, that ex-Superintendent Baker had considerably more than his police pension to fall back on, or so Uncle Wag had let slip to me.

'Be lucky, Jack,' Maurice said. It was a line we always used whenever we met, although it was code for 'Watch out.' Charlie Richardson was the credited originator of the expression. It wasn't something you would want to hear him say to you, Wag told me.

After a flurry of greetings with aunts, nieces and friends, Isobel was careful to wipe the red lipstick smudges from my cheeks. I did the same for her.

'My lords, ladies, gentlemen, distinguished guests!' Link shouted from the top of the stairs. 'Can you please come and take your seats for the wedding feast? There are lists just outside the library to explain who you have the misfortune to be sitting next to.' A titter went round the room, and conversation resumed.

Link wasn't giving up so easily. 'Er hum!' he shouted again. 'Come on, you lot! It's time for a hot dinner, and we've got hours of speeches to come, so can you please come upstairs now and we can get this show on the road.'

Luke, Aubrey and two other male cousins carried Maurice up the winding stairs in his wheelchair, followed by an army of the extended Bourton family. I had packed them together in one corner. It was safer and they would be happier. Otherwise, Isobel and I had mixed and matched.

'Beat you to it,' I said to George Curwin, who had just shown up with Emma.

It would have been totally out of order for me to ask anyone but Link to be my best man. Curwin didn't appear to mind that I had not returned the compliment he had paid me.

'Keep that man on the straight and narrow,' Curwin said, after he had embraced Isobel.

'He doesn't need any help.' It was true. As a picture dealer I was the epitome of probity.

But when Sid Mullin and Sylvia picked that moment to join the happy throng, who could blame a police officer for speculating that shades of the prison house might still close around the growing boy?

CHAPTER 70

Wag

If Diana Dors could do it, so could I. Some time after her death from ovarian cancer in 1984, it was revealed that she might have ferreted away over two million quid in banks across Europe. She left the son by her first marriage, Mark Dawson, a note with a code that would reveal the whereabouts of the money. Her last husband Alan Lake was supposed to have had the key to unlock the mystery, but, after burning all his late wife's clothes, he did himself in with a shotgun.

Dawson tracked down a specialist computer forensics company called Inforenz. They identified the encryption as the Vigenère cipher. The company then used their own analytical software to suggest a ten-letter decryption key, DMARYFLUCK (short for Diana Mary Fluck, the actress's real name). Inforenz succeeded in decoding the whole message and linked it to a bank statement found among Lake's papers. But the precise location of the money remains unknown. There was speculation that the trail led to a second sheet of paper, but that note was never found. Very frustrating for all concerned.

If you look up 'Vigenère Cipher' you'll discover that it's a method of encrypting alphabetic text based on the letters of a keyword. No problems for me there, then.

After my darling Ethel deserted me for a better world, I rattled around the empty house. We had managed eight years together after her cancer was first diagnosed. I remain grateful for every day we spent together.

I was with her until she breathed her last breath, but I do

not want to talk about the day she died, except to say that I was holding her hand.

Having bought three pale A4 cloth-bound unlined books from Harris's the stationers in Charing Cross Road, I began the sort-of memoir you now hold in your hands.

This story was never intended as an autobiography, but I did want to leave a message behind for those who cared to look. And if I could no longer share my life with anyone, I needed to share my thoughts. So don't simply analyse the words on the pages, imagine you can hear my inner voice, as I'm talking to you now.

For three centuries, the Vigenère system resisted all attempts to break it. The original method was described by an Italian named Bellaso in his 1553 book *La cifra del Sig. Giovan Battista Bellaso* and then misattributed to this other fellow Vigenère. You see how we constantly get things wrong, how easy it is to subvert the truth and simply to make a mistake.

For the life of me I can't imagine how that 'wayward hussy', as His Grace the Archbishop of Canterbury once described Diana Dors, sat down and mastered the code that had defied even that distinguished mathematician, the Reverend Charles William Dodgson, author of *Alice in Wonderland*.

In a Caesar cipher, if you shift three places in the alphabet, A becomes D, B becomes E, and so on. The Vigenère technique consists of several Caesar ciphers in sequence with different shift values.

Are you following me?

To encrypt, a table of alphabets can be used, forming a tabula recta. I'm not going to go on much more about this. Once you know the trick, it's not that hard to follow. And, if you try to crack the code, the fundamental flaw you're looking for is the repeating nature of the key.

To entertain myself, I began writing, mixing fact with fiction, concealing within my story a code to unlock the history of my sometimes murky past. It was a sort of paper trail. Unnecessarily complicated. One volume would lead to the next and none of it would make sense without all three. The ultimate security, of course, was nothing to do with Vigenère. Who on earth would think of looking in these books for the records I kept of every single deal with Wainwright, and for the access codes to my accounts in Lausanne and Zurich?

The only truth I know, which cannot be put into words, lies beside me on my bedside table in a plain silver frame. It's a photograph of Ethel taken in 1920. She's in a nurse's white outfit, with a headdress that falls below her shoulders. It's a studio portrait, and carefully lit. My sister sits in profile. Her right hand supports her chin with the index finger pointing up. She looks quietly but radiantly beautiful.

CHAPTER 71

Jack

When Eileen and Doreen of Birds of a Feather sang their number one hit 'Losers' Corner' at my wedding, Link looked like he had won a million on the pools.

Uncle Jago and Aunt Mildred took to the dance floor. Even my ancient Aunt Rose joined in, and she didn't topple into the tables or sing out of tune. The younger crowd managed that without any help.

When Doreen performed a solo ballad, I plucked up courage to ask my mother-in-law for the regulation turn around the floor. It wasn't as bad as dancing with a sack of potatoes. She knew how to move. With ramrod-straight back and no give in her waist, Lady Candace Weston allowed her son-in-law to lead her in a slow shuffle for three eternal minutes, and was as relieved as me to return to the table where her husband was discussing Passchendaele with Wag. It was the first time I saw Sir Percival looking less of a stuffed shirt. My uncle gave me a knowing wink.

Isobel and I stayed up until three o'clock, opening our presents. We were not tired. Even the speeches had gone well. Link had avoided doing an excruciating best man special. Sir Percival kept it simple, and I thought I detected a tear in his soldier's eye when he recollected how his daughter as a little girl had existed for a year exclusively on chocolate biscuits. I do not think I made a hash of my bit either, although there was a moment when my mind went completely blank. When I dried, I gazed at all the expectant faces, took a sip of my wine, and thought, This is all right, as long as I don't stand here in silence for ever, these are my friends, they're on my side, they can wait a little bit longer. And then I was off again. I got a laugh. I did the sentimental, sincere bit, kissed Isobel and we both acknowledged the standing applause.

'Who's that from?' Isobel was keeping a list.

I had just unwrapped two silver-plated candelabras. 'George and Emma.'

'We'll have to think of something nice for them too when they get married.'

Salad bowls, vintage champagne (from those whose imagination was not equal to their generosity), Spode dinner plates, a statuette of an Egyptian figure that could be made into a light fitting but never was, two decanters, and an edition of The Book of Thoth, signed by the author Aleister Crowley.

'Guess who that's from?' I said.

'Luke!' Isobel didn't have to refer to her rolodex. She had met the family, and passed the test, where I had probably failed mine with hers.

Every time I gazed at Isobel, I thought how fortunate I was. The enchantment increased, and I was confirmed in my admiration when, on the day, she discovered a squiggle of biro near the hem of her white dress. Don't ask me how it got there. Her cousin Sophie had a theory about cleaning it off but it made the blue smudge spread further. 'Don't worry,' I said, not expecting to be believed for a moment, 'no one is going to look down there. They will all be looking at your face.'

Isobel didn't cry or freak out. She kept her head. And I

was right. Nobody mentioned the stain, even if they did spot it.

'I say . . .' Isobel had opened Wag's present. 'It's beautiful.' She clipped a necklace of perfect pearls round her neck, and took the card out of its slim black case. 'To dearest Isobel. My sister Ethel would have wanted you to have this. All my love, Wag.'

From a bigger parcel, I removed a single cloth-bound book. The card said: 'For my favourite nephew Jack and his lovely wife Isobel. Read, learn and inwardly digest. There are two more of these for you to find one day.' There were three Xs and Wag's signature.

I called my uncle the next morning to thank him for his generosity and also to see how he was.

'I've got cancer, angina and trench foot,' he said. 'Otherwise I'm fine, boy. But I need your help with something.'

On Saturday morning accompanied by Link, four big blokes and a lorry, we turned up at his house.

'Time to destroy my past,' Wag said. 'I should have done it years ago.'

The filing cabinets, the antique Diebold safe, every single container was cleared out of the cellar. Whatever incriminating photographs and papers Wag stored down there went up in smoke, no doubt to the delight of my uncle's neighbours. Their nasal passages must have adjusted to the manure cycles. No one had complained to him or the council.

'We can reduce this whole load to the size of a Rubik's cube,' said Link.

'Thanks, boy.' Wag clapped my faithful old friend on the shoulder.

With a belch of blue exhaust, the lorry disappeared down the road, its load concealed under a grey tarpaulin.

'Done and dusted,' said Wag. 'What say I take you boys to the Eagle for a spot of lunch?'

'Don't mind if we do,' I said.

In 1980 Charlie Richardson escaped from open prison. He didn't use the passport Wag had made for him immediately. He was 'on the trot' in London for almost a year, and was observed dressed up as Father Christmas, handing out presents to children to publicise his requests for parole. Curwin told me Richardson had also been spotted at a pub in the Old Kent Road, having a few swifties with some of the chief inspector's colleagues. Then he slipped over to Paris for a while.

Eventually he was nicked in the Earl's Court Road, and forced to serve the rest of his original sentence plus a little extra for the possession of drugs. Richardson was a man of influence, who, I'm relieved to say, I never had the pleasure of meeting. Somehow or other, he was allowed out on day release to help the handicapped. You couldn't make it up.

In 1990 Eddie Richardson was sent down for thirty-five years for his involvement in a seventy million pound cocaine and cannabis heist. He got out after twelve.

Things didn't entirely go the brothers' way. They fell out badly after Eddie accused Charlie of fraudulent business dealings. There's a joke in there.

Monkey Rawlings also qualified for early release. There were stories that he had gone to Hong Kong and was playing villains in Kung Fu crime caper movies. Stranger things have happened. Did you know that Wag McDonald worked for a while in Hollywood as Charlie Chaplin's bodyguard? That's a true story.

The three handwritten books of my uncle's memoir

remained, unread for years, at the bottom of a cardboard box in our attic, full of old letters, postcards, notes from Cambridge days, packets of family photographs and a pocket chess set. I did try once to concentrate on deciphering the text, but couldn't gather sufficient momentum. I didn't realise what was there. How could I? Just as I never discovered why he was called Wag. There are some mysteries that can never be solved.

I never tried to unlock the code he mentioned. Nor can I fathom why he included the doodle of the knight's helmet and crest below the poor but touching poem at the beginning of the first volume. Perhaps Wag was also the Guardian of the Holy Grail and was leaving yet another clue to an alternative Quest in addition to his secret, numberless accounts abroad. Who knows?

The fact is I didn't want his money. Isobel and I weren't rich. But we had more than enough to live on and we had each other. I was more than grateful for that.

Both of us wished our marriage could have been blessed with children. It wasn't to be. We discussed adoption after all the other possibilities had been explored. In vitro didn't work, and neither of us fancied the idea of a surrogate. It could have been my fault, of course. I had a low sperm count. But so did Curwin. And he and Emma managed to produce four boys in a row, enough to start a new police dynasty.

As we all know, there is no such thing as 'Happy Ever After'. Rachel lost heart with Link in the end. Fortunately, he never slid back to the amphetamines. Work became his drug of choice instead. He married Eileen from Birds of a Feather, but, after a year, she too ran off. The group broke up shortly afterwards. 'I'm finished with women,' said Link. 'Waste of time and money.'

Retirement in Monte Carlo suited HL so well that he had a heart attack. The last I heard of his wife Bummy Mel was that she was living in the Hermitage with a female companion, and wasn't in her right mind. Link went to visit her regularly. 'I've told her she can come and live with me,' he told me. 'I've got plenty of room. But, for reasons known entirely to her, she has decided to stay out there. I don't get it, do you?'

Sylvia married a titled toff and took up horse riding in a big way. I bumped into her once in the King's Road. From her accent you would have thought she had been born in Knightsbridge, rather than on Streatham Hill.

The word on the street was that Sid Mullin had taken over the running of the Richardson empire after HL and Monkey Rawlings disappeared from the picture, but maybe Sid had had enough of a life of crime. In any case, he took up permanent residence in Calpe with his friend Raoul. My parents sold their flat there after the view of the sea was almost entirely obscured by yet more high-rise development. They moved from Dulwich to an ooky-pooky house called the Dolphins on the edge of the green sward in Goring-on-Sea. You may remember that.

I never had to call on Uncle Wag's criminal connections, or his forgery skills, again. But Isobel and I met up with him a lot, and we became closer than ever. After his death, I saw no more of the sprawling Bourton family. And yet I feel a nostalgia for the idea of all those uncles and aunts and cousins. I am the last of the Armitage line. There will be no one else who will think back to the good old days that never were.

Isobel and I sit together in the evenings. We don't watch television much. She likes to read the art catalogues and check the prices. I never did sell the Edward Lear and don't care if it's genuine or not. Every now and again, we have a tidy-up. 'There's too much clutter in this house,' says Isobel. But I like our stuff. Everything on the walls or on the shelves, the sideboard or the desk reminds me of someone. My mother, my father, my grandmothers, the family – especially my Uncle Wag.

I am sorry Wag's grandfather clock doesn't tick any more. Maybe I should get it fixed.

The other day, having thrown away almost the entire contents of a cardboard box, including my definitive A-level essay on Lancelot as the first tragic hero of the English novel, *Le Morte d'Arthur*, I picked up the first volume of my uncle's memoir. The light cloth had faded to the colour of a shroud. It was a struggle to decipher at first. It was just hard work later. However, the book had its rewards. I learned a lot about a most extraordinary ordinary man, and I worked out, according to the Vigenère cipher, that if you began counting forward on the first row from the letters W, A, G, a whole new world could unfold.

Acknowledgements

First, I should like to thank my agent, dear old friend Caradoc King, for having faith in me and my writing.

Marianne, my adored wife, supplied the crucial criticism, which made me cut back the excess of detail, so that the novel moves forward at a sharper pace.

My children, Saskia and Jack, have not had a chance to read *Wag* yet, but have been right on the ball with an earlier novel *Minotaur*, and have only given me encouragement to continue writing. My sister Jane preferred the second in my Cretan Sequence, and I am delighted about that. *Wag* was an impossible challenge for her because of the autobiographical elements, which must have been a constant distraction. My sister-in-law Hester has been supportive beyond the call of duty.

While I bashed away at my book, I felt reassured by the presence in my life of Fanny Blake, Lizy Buchan and Terence Blacker.

My thanks also to the many friends who have commented, criticised or simply just been there. I could write another whole book about their kindness and love: Kaori O'Connor, Rina Gill, Chrissy Iley, Martin Buckley, Mark Booth, the very special Lauren Clark (not that you are not all special), Frank McLynn, Laura Morris, Rowena Webb, Lavinia Trevor, Jim Cochrane, Nadia Cameron-Blakey, Alan Brooke, Donald Kelshall, Carol O'Connell, Jonathan Gathorne-Hardy, Ruth Rendell, Dyan Sheldon, Daniel Metcalfe, Hugo Vickers, Kate Colquhoun and

Freddie (with his excellent soda bread and beaming smile), Ilsa Yardley, Geraldine Cooke, Will Sulkin, Tony Gooch, Stephen Weeks, Jane Wood, Jack de Lette, Tony and Martha Whittome, Janey King, Donald Spoto, Elsie Burch Donald, John Lahr, Connie Booth, Renata Zimova and Eleo Noreen Carson – Eleo's constant support and friendship have been so important to me. Have I gone on too long? I could say a whole lot more about you all, and how much your friendship has meant to me. Hope I haven't missed anybody out – if I have, you know who you are – you are all on my list of invitees to my memorial celebration.

Lastly, of course, we cannot forget Uncle Wag, whose nickname remains a mystery.

List of Supporters

Unbound is a new kind of publishing house. Our books are funded directly by readers. This was a very popular idea during the late eighteenth and early nineteenth centuries. Now we have revived it for the internet age. It allows authors to write the books they really want to write and readers to support the writing they would most like to see published.

The names listed below are of readers who have pledged their support and made this book happen, as well as the fiends listed at the front of this book. If you'd like to join them, visit: www.unbound.co.uk.

Sarah Adams
Catherine Addington
Clare Alexander and Guill Gil
Anthony Allen
Catherine, Majid, Farah, Romaissa and Iffah Amaioua
Tim Andrews
Elizabeth Armstrong
Jason Arthur
Patricia Atkinson
Gemma Avery
John Bald
Colette Baldetti
David Bann
Francesca Barra
Alison Barrow
Natasha Barsby
Jaimie Batchan
Francis Bennett
Thomas Bertram
Terence Blacker
Carole Blake
Fanny Blake
Margaret Bluman
Apostrophe Books
Mark Booth
Arabella Bosworth
Harriet Bourton

Neil Bradford
Jane Bradish-Ellames
T Broderick
David Bryan
Benjie Buchan
Edwin Buckhalter
Brie Burkeman
Anna Burtt
Charlotte Bush
Nadia Cameron-Blakey
Georgia Campbell
Maria Campbell
Daniele Carioti
Tiffany Chapman
Anya Cherneff
Ruth Cherneff
Russ Clapham
Lauren Clark
James Cochrane
Anthony Cohen
Kate Colquhoun
Richard Coomber
John Crawford
Annette Crossland
Alev Lytle Croutier
Deodata Blyth Currie
Jim Blyth Currie
Laura Deacon
Talisa Dean
Paul Dembina
Philippa Dickinson
Josceline Dimbleby
Trevor Dolby
Robin Dormer
Jenny Doughty
Susie Dowdall
David & Ann Dunlop
Robert Eardley
Helen Edwards
Lindsay and Carol Edwards
Richard Edwards
Miles Elliott
Robin Ellis
Linda Evans
Natasha Fairweather
Nigel Farndale
Peter Faulkner
Leah Feltham
Klaus Flugge
David Ford
Gary Frost
Reg Gadney
Hilary Gallo
Mark Gamble
Ramón García
Brenda Gardner
Jonathan Gathorne-Hardy
Adele Geras
Rina Gill
Jo Goldsworthy
H Gonda
Tony Gooch
Eleo Gordon

Lizzy Goudsmit
Frankie Gray
Christine Green
Helen Gregory
Jane Gregory
Anthony Griffiths
Jocasta Hamilton
Charles Handy
James Hannah
Anthony Heath
Andrea Henry
Nick Hern
Anna Hervé
Christie Hickman
David Hicks
Lisa Highton
Alex Hippisley-Cox
Penelope Hoare
Karen Holden
Wendy Holden
James Horwitz
Ian Hudson
Val Hudson
Bruce Hunter
Hermione Ireland
Virginia Ironside
Dotti Irving
Maxim Jakubowski
Patrick Janson-Smith
Kathy John
Tristan John
Oliver Johnson
Richard Johnson
Dean Kelshall
Donald & Cathryn Kelshall
Sara Ketteley
Yasmin Kidwai
Dan Kieran
Caradoc King
Janey King
Gilles Lafue
John-Richard Laher
Jane Lebowitz
Alice Lee
Jenny Lewis
Rowena and Ian Lindsay-Hickman
Tamasin Little
Jonathan Lloyd
Dr. Richard Lloyd
Laura Lonsdale
Leonora Lonsdale
Andrew Lownie
Alicia MacDonald
Shena Mackay
Elizabeth Mann
Cynthia Barlow Marrs
Patrick McCreeth
Kate McFarlan
Eoin McHugh
Elizabeth McKay
Daniel Metcalfe
Ian 'Mitch' Michell
Julia Midwinter

Barbara Milestone
Margo Milne
Emma Mitchell
Sasha Morgan
Georgina Morley
Laura Morris
Anthea Morton-Saner
Kate Mosse & Greg Mosse
Colin Murray
Roger Murray
Dominic Newbould
James Nightingale
Andrew Nurnberg
Carol O'Connell
Kaori O'Connor and Kira Hopkins
Richard Ogle
Jo Ormiston
Paul Pantin and Natasha Kelshall-Pantin
Sarah Patmore
Alison Pearce
Mikaela Pedlow
James Pembroke
Anna Perkins
Lucy Pinney
Nigel Planer
Justin Pollard
Gareth Pottle
Christopher Poulton
Lance and Paula Poynter
Richard Price
Jenny Prior
David Prys-Owen
Rosalind Ramsay
Gail Rebuck
Liza Reeves
David Reynolds
Bobbie Richards
Howard and Hilary Riddle
David Roche
Andrew Rosenheim
Ann Rosenthal
Kate Samano
Heather Schiller
Bill Scott-Kerr
John Seaton
Caroline Sheldon
Hilary Shepherd
Liz Sich
Jack Sidey
Michelle Signore
Brian Arthur Smith
Jason Smith
Colin Smythe
Sally Soames
Donald Spoto
Joel Stagg
Gillian Stern
Amelia Stewart
Will Sulkin
Elspeth Tavaci
Simon Taylor
George Theo

Liz Thomson
Mike Scott Thomson
Jane Thynne
Helen Tiley
Ruth Tinham
Barbara Toner
Jeremy Trevathan
Simon Trewin
Ruth Tudge
Jane Turnbull
Chris Turner
Jessica Velmans
Mark Vent
Hugo Vickers
Henry Vines
Susanna Wadeson
Charles Walker
Selina Walker
Zelie Walker
John Warner
Samantha Webb
Susannah & Adrian Webster
Carole Welch
Judith Welsh
Sarah Westcott
Nick White
Tony and Martha Whittome
Katrina Whone
Nigel Wilcockson
Jenny Wilford
Kate Williams
Mark Williams
Bob Willis
Mary Elisabeth Wingfield
Dar Wolnik
Jane Wood
Gill Woodeson
Doug Young
Vanessa Zainzinger